FEAR CITY

ALSO BY F. PAUL WILSON

Repairman Jack*

The Tomb
Legacies
Conspiracies
All the Rage
Hosts
The Haunted Air
Gateways
Crisscross
Infernal
Harbingers
Bloodline
By the Sword
Ground Zero
Fatal Error
The Dark at the End
Nightworld

The Teen Trilogy*

Jack: Secret Histories
Jack: Secret Circles
Jack: Secret Vengeance

The Early Years Trilogy*

Cold City
Dark City

The Adversary Cycle*

The Keep
The Tomb
The Touch
Reborn
Reprisal
Nightworld

The LaNague Federation

Healer
Wheels Within Wheels
An Enemy of the State
Dydeetown World
The Tery

Other Novels

Black Wind*
Sibs*
The Select
Virgin
Implant
Deep as the Marrow
Mirage
    (with Matthew J. Costello)
Nightkill
    (with Steven Spruill)
Masque
    (with Matthew J. Costello)
Sims
The Fifth Harmonic
Midnight Mass
The Proteus Cure
    (with Tracy L. Carbone)
A Necessary End
    (with Sarah Pinborough)
Definitely Not Kansas
    (with Tom Monteleone)

Short Fiction

Soft and Others
The Barrens and Others*
The Christmas Thingy
Aftershock & Others*
The Peabody-Ozymandias
    Traveling Circus &
    Oddity Emporium*
Quick Fixes—Tales of
    Repairman Jack*
Sex Slaves of the Dragon Tong

Editor

Freak Show
Diagnosis: Terminal
The Hogben Chronicles
    (with Pierce Watters)

Omnibus Editions

The Complete LaNague
Calling Dr. Death
    (3 medical thrillers)

*See "The Secret History of the World" (page 365).

FEAR CITY

A Repairman Jack Novel

THE EARLY YEARS TRILOGY: BOOK THREE

F. PAUL WILSON

TOR®

A TOM DOHERTY ASSOCIATES BOOK • NEW YORK

FEAR CITY

A Tor Book
Published by Tom Doherty Associates, LLC
175 Fifth Avenue
New York, NY 10010

www.tor-forge.com

Tor® is a registered trademark of Tom Doherty Associates, LLC.

The Library of Congress Cataloging-in-Publication Data is available upon request.

ISBN 978-0-7653-3016-1 (hardcover)
ISBN 978-1-4668-5980-7 (e-book)

Tor books may be purchased for educational, business, or promotional use. For information on bulk purchases, please contact Macmillan Corporate and Premium Sales Department at 1-800-221-7945, extension 5442, or write specialmarkets@macmillan.com.

First Edition: November 2014

Printed in the United States of America

0 9 8 7 6 5 4 3 2 1

ACKNOWLEDGMENTS

Thanks to the usual crew for their efforts: my wife, Mary; David Hartwell, Marco Palmieri, and Becky Maines at the publisher; Steven Spruill, Elizabeth Monteleone, Marc Buhmann, Dannielle Romeo; and my agent, Albert Zuckerman.

Once again, *Surviving the Mob: A Street Soldier's Life Inside the Gambino Crime Family* by Dennis N. Griffin and Andrew DiDonato offered valuable insights into Mob life in the 1990s.

Special thanks to Jim Dwyer, David Kocieniewski, Deidre Murphy, and Peg Tyre for writing *Two Seconds Under the World,* an invaluable resource regarding the 1993 World Trade Center bombing.

AUTHOR'S NOTE

Fear City will be the last Repairman Jack novel for a while . . . maybe forever.

After sixteen novels (counting *Nightworld*) in the main sequence plus three juveniles and three prequels, Jack needs a rest. With his return in 1998, he took over my writing career. I don't regret it. We've had a great run and I loved every minute of it. But his tale was never intended as an open-ended series. We had a destination—*Nightworld*—and we reached it. Now I'm going to go back to my genre-hopping ways, and will be plugging new work into the Secret History when appropriate.

I'm not saying I will never write another Repairman Jack novel. If an idea pops up that's perfect for our guy, I won't hesitate to write that book. But the routine of a new Repairman Jack novel every fall is over.

See you again soon, I hope. I've got some surprises for you.

—F. Paul Wilson,
the Jersey Shore

TUESDAY

FEBRUARY 16, 1993

1

"Is this the Shadow?" Jack said, holding up the cellophane envelope. "I mean, *the* Shadow?"

The sixtyish guy behind the counter—lank hair, three-day stubble, ratty brown cardigan—looked annoyed as he brought it close to his smeared glasses and squinted at the label. Jack wondered how he saw anything through them.

"If it says 'genuine glow in the dark Shadow ring,' which it does, then that's what it is."

Attracted by the BACK-DATE MAGAZINES sign, Jack had wandered into this narrow, coffin-sized store off Times Square. The place seemed to specialize in *Life* magazine and had moldy issues piled to the ceiling. Jack had been curious to see if the place stocked any old pulps. It did, but only a few, and those had disconcerting titles like *Ranch Romances* and *Fifteen Love Stories*. None of the *Black Mask* types he was hunting for. But tucked in among the yellowed, flaking issues he'd found the ring.

The white plastic body was shaped like the Shadow on each side—Jack could even make out a .45 Colt semiauto in one hand—but the stone set in the top was bright blue and shaped like Gibraltar.

"But this looks nothing like the Shadow's girasol ring."

The guy stared at him. "Do you even know what a girasol is?"

"Fire opal."

This seemed to take him by surprise. "Okay. Point for you. What are you—eighteen?"

Jack didn't react. He got this all the time. "You're half a dozen short."

"Coulda fooled me. But still a kid. How does a twenty-four-year-old like you know about the Shadow's girasol ring?"

"Read a few old issues."

"That's the pulp Shadow. The character started on radio, sponsored by a company called Blue Coal. That blue plastic 'stone' there is supposed to be a chunk of blue coal."

Jack was thinking it was just about the neatest thing he'd seen in a long time.

"And it glows in the dark too?"

"That's what it says. Never tested it."

"How much?"

"Twenty bucks."

"What?"

"That'll be a bargain next year after the movie comes out."

"What movie?"

"*The Shadow.* Gonna star Alec Baldwin, I hear."

Jack remembered him from *The Hunt for Red October.* Yeah, he had the look for the Lamont Cranston part.

"So if I'm tired of it next year you'll buy it back for more?"

"Can't promise that. Can't even promise I'll be here, what with Disney moving in."

News to Jack.

"Disney? Here?"

"Word is they're negotiating a ninety-nine-year lease on the Amsterdam."

"Donald Duck on the Deuce? No way."

"Everybody's scared shitless because it'll be proof that the Times Square cleanup every mayor since LaGuardia's been talking about is gonna happen, and you know what that means."

Jack pushed aside a vision of Minnie Mouse in hot pants saying, "Hiya, sailor."

"What?"

"Rents through the roof. Guys like me forced out, moving over to Hell's Kitchen or farther downtown or just closing up and walking away."

"Oh, no! Where will people go for their copies of *Ranch Romances*?"

His eyes narrowed behind the grimy lenses. "You a wiseass?"

Jack could see the guy was genuinely worried. He thought about boxing up and moving all those copies of *Life* and regretted the remark.

"Sometimes the mouth runs ahead of the brain."

"People get in trouble that way."

"Tell me about it."

He forked over a Jackson. The guy slipped it into his pocket and didn't ask for sales tax. Fine.

Jack walked out with his treasure and slipped it onto his pinky finger. He ambled east toward Times Square, thinking not of the Shadow but of Disney instead.

What he remembered most about Disney World from the couple of times his folks had taken him there during the seventies was how clean it had been. Could that happen here? Times Square was anything but clean, and 42nd Street even less so. But grime and kitsch and porn and fringe people were part of the ambience. Take that away and replace it with a bunch of high-end chain stores and what did you have? You had a freaking mall. Might as well move back to Jersey.

As he crossed Duffy Square and headed up Seventh Avenue, he realized the writing had been on the wall for a couple of years now, ever since the state started buying up properties along the Deuce, especially the old theaters.

Plus ça change . . . ?

Jack doubted it.

If the magazine guy was right about the Amsterdam, then change was sure as hell coming and, as far as Jack was concerned, not for the better. Well, better if you were a landlord, but no way for a small businessman. Things would not, as the saying went, stay the same. All the quirky little stores and all the quirky people who frequented them and all the quirky people who ran them were going to go the way of the Neanderthals.

His growing dark mood about the end of an era was blown away by the sight of a familiar face trying to hail a cab across the street from the Winter Garden. She was talking on a mobile phone as she waved her arm.

"Cristin?"

She turned and, for an instant, looked not-so-pleasantly surprised. Then she smiled. "Jack! How nice to see you!"

They shared a quick, slightly awkward hug.

He pointed to her phone—one of the new smaller versions. Unlike the older brick-size models with the big antenna, these could fit in a pocket. He noticed NOKIA under the oblong screen.

"Up with the latest technology, I see."

"I looove this thing! It's made my life so easy. No more looking for a pay phone."

He gave her a lopsided grin and cocked his head toward the Winter Garden marquee. "Going to see *Cats?*"

"Not likely."

Their fling thing had lasted two years and during that whole period the only time they'd been to a theater was to see Penn & Teller. Cristin had ended it. She hadn't called it quits, per se, more like weaned them off each other. They used to get together every Sunday—every single Sunday—but last fall she'd started begging off with increasingly lame excuses until Jack got the message.

She may have engineered the actual parting, but Jack had been the reason. They'd gone into the relationship with the understanding that they'd get together one day a week and be friends with benefits, nothing more. Cristin had been very strict about not wanting strings and Jack had been all for it. At least at first. Along the way he became attached and started wanting more. But Cristin wasn't looking for more. She liked things just the way they were and wouldn't bend.

Jack had suffered through the process of attenuation, but after clearing the air at an official breakup lunch between Christmas and New Year's, they'd parted friends.

Seeing Cristin again for the first time in weeks made him realize he was still carrying a torch for her.

"You've let your hair grow," he said.

"A little."

She had a roundish face, dark hair, blue eyes, and a bright smile that always made him want to smile too. She wore her fur-lined raincoat.

"Can I see?"

"What?"

"The *ama-gi.*"

"You still getting off on that?"

"I don't know about getting off . . ."

She rolled her eyes, did a quick turn, and lifted her hair. She had one tattoo and it decorated her nape: a Sumerian symbol known as *ama-gi*.

He caught the briefest glimpse, and then she dropped her hair.

"I was heading for a late lunch . . ." he began.

"Oh, I'd love to, Jack, but I've got to get down to FIT. I have a class."

Years ago she'd dropped out of the Fashion Institute to work full time for an event planning operation called Celebrations. The job kept her hopping all over the city, but she still wanted her degree and took one course a semester to keep herself moving toward it.

"Tomorrow then? Or Thursday?"

He hoped he didn't sound desperate. He didn't *feel* desperate . . . he simply wanted to spend a little time with her.

She gave him a long look. "Just lunch?"

"Two old friends from high school sharing food and small talk."

She smiled. "That sounds great. Dutch, right?"

"Of course."

She'd always insisted on paying her share and, since Jack wasn't exactly flush these days, that was a good thing. Cristin, on the other hand, made excellent money planning events.

But where to eat?

Apparently she already had an idea. "I found a cool little French place on East Sixty-first called Le Pistou."

Jack made a face. "Really? What's choice number two?"

"But you like French."

"I do." He could eat just about anything, even snails. "But I don't know if I could eat at a place called Piss Stew."

"It's vegetable soup."

He held up his hands. "Stop. You're only making it worse."

"You'll never change," she said through a laugh. "Thursday's good. Meet there noonish?"

"Deal."

He hailed her a cab and one pulled over right away.

"But just for lunch," she said as he held the door for her.

"Of course. We broke up, remember?"

"I do. But you don't know why."

That took him by surprise. "I thought it was because I was getting too attached."

"No. I was."

She gave him a quick kiss on the cheek then slipped into the cab. He shook his head as he watched it weave down Seventh.

Cristin, Cristin, Cristin . . .

Despite her paranoia about strings, she seemed happy with where she was in her life. He didn't know anybody else like that. That didn't mean she was going to stay put. He knew she was three years into a five-year plan that involved socking away every extra cent for now and eventually opening her own boutique to sell her original designs.

She was also happy with *who* she was. Jack wondered what that felt like.

He'd read something from Wilde last year and his brain had attached it to Cristin: *Most people are other people. Their thoughts are someone else's opinions, their lives a mimicry, their passions a quotation.* Not because Wilde had been describing Cristin, but because it was so *not* Cristin. He didn't know anyone who thought like Cristin. She danced to her own tune and to hell with what everyone else was playing.

He missed her.

When her cab disappeared into the traffic crush he turned and continued his uptown ramble.

Okay, the week was looking better, even if it involved a French restaurant in the East Sixties. How bad could lunch be? Twenty bucks apiece? Thirty?

Yeah, his resources had dwindled. Perhaps he'd been too generous in his flush days. He didn't regret it, though. He lived a simple life. His two major expenses were rents: on his apartment and on the garage space for Ralph. Other than that, he lived on junk food and beer.

His fix-it business hadn't exactly taken off. He collected a fee now and again, but the jobs were sporadic. Nothing he could count on. So he'd been supplementing his income as a waiter in a hole-in-the-wall West Village trattoria that paid him under the table. Perhaps "paid" was a euphemism—a teeny fraction of minimum wage—but the tips were good. Everybody had heard Dylan's "Positively 4th Street" and all the tourists flocked to West 4th when they visited the Village. Trattoria Villagio waited there to provide drinks and light fare when they took a break from prowling the specialty shops.

He checked his watch. Lots of time to kill before meeting a prospective customer at Julio's. Maybe he'd grab a Whopper and train over to Brooklyn to check on an investment.

2

The frigid February wind off the Hudson cut through Kadir Allawi's fatigue jacket. He stood on the dock by the Central Railroad Terminal with Mahmoud, Kasi, Salameh, and Yousef. Jersey City sprawled behind them, Ellis Island sat off to the right, but their attention was riveted across the river on the twin towers of the World Trade Center.

"You truly believe it is possible?" Kadir said in Arabic.

Yousef nodded. "Properly placed within the base, the right bomb will topple the north tower into the south tower, bringing down both."

Ramzi Yousef, a wiry, bearded Pakistani with piercing black eyes, had learned bomb making in Afghanistan and Pakistan. Just last September al-Qaeda had sent him here to bring jihad to America.

Aimal Kasi, another Pakistani, had been living in northern Virginia since his arrival two years ago. He wore a thick mustache rather than a full beard, and had traveled north this week to help with the bomb. He raised his palms toward heaven: "May Allah make it so."

Kadir sent up a prayer as well. He had long dreamed of the towers' fall, yearned for it, prayed for it.

Mohammed Salameh, a displaced Palestinian like Kadir, said nothing. He did not seem able to pull his gaze from the towers.

"But it will take a big one," Mahmoud said. "And a big one will take money—money we don't have."

Ever the pessimist, Mahmoud Abouhalima towered over Kadir, Yousef, Salameh, and Kasi. He tended to keep his red hair covered but could not hide his red beard.

Yousef only growled in reply.

Kadir could not blame him. Misfortune had dogged their *gamaii* for almost two years now. The money from the Al-Kifah Afghan refugee fund had not been diverted toward jihad as expected. Sheikh Omar had been blamed for the brutal murder of the fund's founder and booed off the stage of the Al-Farooq Mosque in Brooklyn. He had taken up residence here in Jersey City at the Al-Salam Mosque, but he longed to return to Brooklyn.

The FBI seemed everywhere, interfering with the finances of the fronts for jihad that posed as charities. They even blocked a recent money transfer from Yousef's uncle, Khalid Sheikh Mohammed, intended for purchase of the raw materials for the bomb.

"Look at them," Yousef said, nodding toward the towers. "They stand there and mock us."

Mahmoud raised his clenched fists. "And we do not need a fortune, just . . . just . . ."

"Just more than we have," Yousef said. He turned to Kasi. "Didn't you say your father left you money?"

"He did, but I invested it all."

Kadir knew Kasi was part owner of a courier business.

"And you have nothing left?"

He shrugged. "It's growing—I do a lot of the driving myself—but we make barely enough to survive."

And then Kadir had an idea. "I know someone who might help us."

"Who?" Mahmoud said.

"The man from Qatar."

3

A little Dominican girl, black hair, black eyes, and a pink hair band, answered his knock on the rickety side door to the garage. Her face lit at the sight of him and she leaped into his arms.

"Jack!"

"How's it going, Bonita?"

Not exactly statuesque at five feet, but she'd grown a good three inches in the two years or so since he'd saved her from slavery.

"Great! I'm a teenager next week."

He feigned shock. "No! Thirteen already?"

He'd known that, but still found it hard to believe that she'd been not quite eleven when Moose had dragged her onto that Outer Banks sand dune. Jack had followed with a tire iron. Only he and Bonita had returned.

She posed. "Don't I look it?"

She wore a baggy sweatshirt and jeans—necessary apparel in her brother's unheated garage—but even so, Jack could see she was developing.

"You're beautiful." And she was. She lived up to her name. "And I can't believe how good your English is. You couldn't speak a word when we met."

"Better and better."

"Hey, Jack," Rico said, wiping his hands as he approached with a barely noticeable limp. The lanky Dominican wore a concerned expression. "Julio send you?"

"No. Why?"

He shrugged, looking embarrassed now. "I'm a little late this month."

Jack waved him off. "That's between you and Julio. I'm not involved."

Not true—not even close. Jack had wanted to help Rico start a landscaping business but they shared a checkered past and he'd known Rico would never accept a loan from him. So Julio had fronted Jack's money; he collected the payments and passed them on to Jack.

"It's that snow, man," Rico said.

"What snow?"

"That's the problem. We ain't had no snow."

Jack got it. Rico's landscaping work dried up with the coming of cold weather and he depended on plowing parking lots in the winter. But this winter had been pretty dry so far.

"Can't help you there, I'm afraid."

"Just tell Julio when you see him that it's coming soon."

"Sure. But don't worry. He knows you're good for it. And you know Julio by now. He's pretty laid back about the whole thing."

And why not? It wasn't his money. But Jack wasn't worried. Rico was a hard worker with a wide streak of macho honor. Probably starve before he welshed on a debt.

"Yeah, but I feel bad, you know?"

"I know. But anyway, that's not why I'm here. I came to ask your permission to take your sister out for lunch and a movie for her thirteenth birthday."

Bonita squealed with delight. "Yes-yes-yes! Can I go?"

Rico put on a dubious expression. "I don't know . . . what movie we talking about?"

"*Home Alone Two.*"

He'd taken her to *Wayne's World* for her twelfth. The *Home Alone* sequel had come out at the end of last year but was still playing in a couple of second-run theaters around the city. He figured Bonita would like it because of Macaulay Culkin and the Manhattan setting—the subtitle was *Lost in New York,* after all. And as for Jack, he loved the booby traps.

"Can-I-can-I-can-I?"

"I'll have her home in time for dinner."

"Please-please-please?"

"Oh, all right," he said with exaggerated reluctance. "I'll have *bizchoco* ready for you when you come home."

She hugged her brother. "Thank you!"

Rico winked at Jack over the top of her head. "You keep her safe, yes?"

"Scout's honor. I'll pick her up here next week."

4

"Who the fuck?"

Someone was knocking on the door.

Vincent Donato had been sitting at his desk in the office over the Preston Salvage garage working on the papers he'd show his accountant next week. He'd had a good year, better than '91, so the question was how much to declare? The legitimate income paid the guys who worked the yard and did the pickups, but that was about it. Pretty much nothing was left over for Vinny. The under-the-counter business—the money laundering, the chassis recycling from the chop shops, the body disposal service—*that* was where the gravy was, and none of it was ever seen by the tax man. But sometimes he had to pad the legit books to keep them looking kosher.

He'd been having trouble concentrating because of the bundle he'd lost on the Super Bowl. Two weeks ago now but still it rankled. How could the fucking Bills lose three Super Bowls in a row? *Three!* He'd thought for sure this time they'd come out on top and had bet heavy. But no. Un-fucking-believable.

More knocking. He opened his top drawer and gripped the handle of his .45.

"Come in, dammit!"

A guy in dark blue warm-ups with white piping poked his head inside. His hands were empty but that didn't mean he didn't have something hidden in the small of his back.

"Mister Donato?"

"Yeah. Who wants to know?"

"I drive for Mister C. He wants to talk to you."

Tony C? C as in Campisi? *That* Mr. C?

"He usually just calls."

"He's downstairs in the car."

Shit! His crew boss had come here?

"You telling me straight?"

"Absolutely."

Vinny pulled on a Windbreaker but didn't bother zipping it up. No way would it close over his gut. He followed the guy in the warm-up outside and down the open stairway to the parking lot to where Tony's silver Continental waited. The driver opened the door and there, slumped in the far corner of the backseat, sat his capo, Tony "the Cannon" Campisi.

He looked like shit.

Vinny hadn't seen him in a while and had kinda figured he wouldn't be the picture of health—not after getting diagnosed with the Big Casino—but he hadn't expected him to look this bad. His cheeks and eyes were sunken, his yellowish skin looked like it had been painted onto his skull.

"Hey, Vinny, thanks for meeting me here. Those stairs are a little much for me, you know?" His voice sounded like he'd been gargling sand. "Sorry we couldn't do this at Amalia's or someplace nicer."

Vinny did a shocked double blink. Tony saying "thanks" and "sorry" back to back? In all the years he'd been in Tony's crew he couldn't remember hearing either one. Ever. Had the cancer spread from his lungs to his brain?

"Uh, yeah. No problem, Tony. I'da come over if—"

"Nah. Better this way. Siddown." As Vinny eased his bulk into the rear, Tony waved off his driver. "Rocco, why don't you take a walk while we talk."

He said, "Sure, Mister C," and closed the door.

Tony pointed to a small white paper bag on the seat between them.

"I brought those for you."

The grease stains that dotted the bag gave Vinny a pretty good idea what was inside, but he looked anyway. He acted surprised at finding sugar-coated pastries.

He said, "Zeppole?" but was thinking *What the fuck?* Tony the Cannon did not bring gifts.

Okay, something was going on. The whole family had been a mess since Gotti got convicted on a slew of murders and a laundry list of other charges. Sammy the Bull, of all people, had ratted him out and the Chief had wound up sentenced to life with no prayer of parole. He was still trying to run things from inside but that wasn't working out. The "administration" he'd set up with his brother and son and a couple of others was no substitute for one guy calling the shots from the front lines. Lots of infighting and maneuvering and ego wars going on at the top.

"I know you like them, but you ain't ever had any like these. They're from Fratello's in Ozone Park—best bakery anywhere."

Vinny had been trying to cut back but these smelled so damn good . . . he pulled one out and took a bite. Powdered sugar rained on his lap but who cared? They didn't call him Vinny Donuts for nothing.

He offered the bag to Tony who shook his head. "Nah. I'm off my feed."

Vinny tried not to stare as he chewed. "How're you doing, Tony?"

"How's it look like I'm doing? I'm fucking dying."

"But I thought—"

"The chemo? The radiation? Didn't do shit. Burned my skin and made me sick as a fucking dog and that's about it."

"Sorry."

"Don't be sorry. Don't ever be sorry for me. I did this to myself. My doctor warned me, my wife warned me, my brother warned me, but I wouldn't listen. I coulda quit but I didn't *want* to quit. Cancer happened to other people, so why should I quit? Well, y'know what? The day they found that lump in my lung, I fucking quit. Cold turkey. Lotta good it's gonna do me."

Vinny didn't know what to say.

Tony barked a harsh laugh. "You don't know what to say, do you!"

Was he a mind reader now?

"As a matter of fact, no."

Another laugh. "Nobody does! So don't say nothin'. Just sit there and listen to me. We got a problem."

Vinny had been wondering when this would come up.

Tony said, "I can see by your face you know what I'm talking about."

"Tommy."

"Yeah. Tommy. I put him in charge of the loans when I got sick and what happens? The vigorish dries up. What's going on? I can't believe he's holding out on me."

Shit. Not right for Tony to put him on the spot like this.

"Well . . ."

"Hey, look. I don't like asking any more'n you like being asked. I'd handle it myself but I ain't exactly myself lately, if you know what I mean."

"Yeah."

"Tommy keeps telling me there's no vig because nobody's taking out loans. I can't fucking believe it. There ain't no shortage of losers out there, so there can't be no shortage of loans. The reason I'm asking you is I know how you feel about Tommy—sorta the way I feel about Sammy the Nose, y'know? If he's holding out—"

"Maybe he ain't holding out, Tony. Maybe he ain't *going* out. Maybe that's the problem."

Tony frowned. "I don't get it."

"He's got a nice deal with his detailing operation. Maybe too nice."

"Whatta y'mean?"

"I mean he's sold a shitload of policies so all he's gotta do is sit on his ass and collect. He ain't chasing loans. If they come to him, fine, but he ain't on the hunt."

Shylocking had always been one of Tony's main income streams. He had the games and the pony parlor and the fencing, but at ten or twelve percent interest per week, the shy business was like having a printing press for money.

Tony snorted. "His detailing operation. If he's doing so well, how come my beak's dry?"

When you had a side operation, you were supposed to let your crew boss wet his beak. Vinny always sent a piece of his salvage profits to Tony. Tommy was letting that slide, and Vinny knew a couple of reasons why. During the times they were in the same room or same car, the subject of Tony the Cannon would come up more often than not. Tommy would often say that letting Tony dip his beak in his detailing operation was a waste since the guy had "one foot through death's door and the other on a banana peel." But Vinny couldn't tell Tony that. On the other hand, Tommy "Ten Thumbs" Totaro's coke habit was no secret.

"I think most of the extra's going up Tommy's beak."

Tony sighed. "I gotta tell ya, Vinny, that hurts. And to think, I helped him get into it." He gave a slow shake of his head. "No good deed goes unpunished, huh?"

"I guess."

'Specially where Tommy was involved.

"I just got an idea," Tony said.

"Like?"

"What if Tommy's detailing operation runs into some complications?"

And now Vinny got it. This whole dramatic scene—Tony coming to him, meeting in the car here in Canarsie so no one would know they'd talked, the zeppole, acting hurt and offended—was all a lead-in to this. He hadn't "just" got an idea. His idea was behind his trip from Ozone Park.

Vinny played along. "You mean like what if a lot of the cars on the lots Tommy guarantees get mysteriously dinged and scratched?"

"That's exactly what I mean."

"Well, it would put Tommy behind the eight ball, I'd think."

"Right where he should be. Can you and Aldo make it happen?"

Adding a little—or maybe a lot—of misery to Tommy Totaro's life . . . Vinny didn't see a downside to that.

Vinny had to smile. "I think we can arrange something."

"How soon?"

"Tonight?"

Tony grabbed his forearm and squeezed. "That's my boy."

5

"So you think your partner's cheating on you?" Jack said.

"I don't think—I *know* he's cooking the books."

Jack had arrived at Julio's early and seated himself at his table. Even after almost two years, he still couldn't believe he had his own table in an Upper West Side bar. His prospective customer had arrived right on time and Julio had escorted him over. He introduced himself as Jules Willner. Jack usually didn't ask for names but this guy had volunteered. He wore dark slacks and a maroon sweater under a herringbone overcoat. And like the werewolf drinking that piña colada at Trader Vic's, his hair was perfect.

After going through the usual I-was-expecting-someone-older dance, they'd got down to business.

Jack shrugged. "Well, if you know all that, what's left for me to do?"

"I need a little justice."

"Seems like lawyers and accountants can get that for you better than I can."

"No. I don't want anyone looking at the books."

"But—oh."

Willner nodded and waited for Jack to put it together. Pretty obvious: Willner and his partner had been cooking the books for the IRS and now Willner finds out the partner has been cooking them again. Filing suit and bringing in a forensic accountant would mean self-exposure.

"What sort of justice?"

Willner leaned forward. "I have a recurring fantasy. A dream."

Uh-oh.

"And what would that be?"

"I keep dreaming of a fire."

"Really." Jack's heart sank. Not the kind of work he was looking for. "How does that help?"

"We own a warehouse and I keep dreaming of it going up in flames— with my partner in it."

So far he'd avoided mentioning the partner's name. And this dream bullshit was his way of avoiding arrest just in case Jack was an undercover cop.

I never said to kill anyone. I was just relating my dreams.

Riiight.

"Would this warehouse in your dreams just happen to be insured?"

He nodded. "So's my partner. We each have a policy with the company as beneficiary."

A double payday.

"Because you're both so valuable to the company."

He smiled. "At least I am."

Jack wanted to backhand that smile off his face. The guy could be telling the truth, or he could be the one cooking the books and his partner had found out and now the partner had to go. Either way, Jack wanted no part.

He jerked a thumb over his shoulder. "Out."

The smile vanished. "What?"

"Out."

"Hey, listen, I can make it worth your while."

"Out. Don't make me say it again."

The guy got up and stormed out, slamming the door behind him. As the vibrations faded, Julio came over with a pint of Rolling Rock.

"Another one looking for a hit man?"

Jack nodded and sipped. Damn, that tasted good. "Would you believe arson and murder?"

Julio flexed his muscles under his tight black T-shirt. He'd been putting extra effort into his workouts. Maybe he thought it made up for his height—or rather the lack of it.

"Arson and murder . . . man, with all the offers you get, you could clean up in that business."

Jack laughed. "You've got that right."

Amazing how many people wanted someone dead.

"You need a partner?"

"You want in?"

"Nah." Julio shrugged and headed back toward the bar on the other end of the room. "I think I stick with pouring beer."

6

Hadya Allawi kept her *hijab* tight around her head as she passed the Al-Salam Mosque. She walked on the opposite sidewalk to keep her distance from it. She had little choice about her route: John F. Kennedy Boulevard was a main thoroughfare through Jersey City and if she wanted to shop in Journal Square, she had to pass it.

She glanced at the graffiti-scarred doorway in the right corner of the building. She used to climb the steps inside to worship in the mosque on the third floor but had stopped once Sheikh Omar Abdel-Rahman took up residence and began spewing his bile. She could almost feel the hate seeping through the windows overlooking the street. She sent some straight back.

The Qur'an said not to hate, but how could she not hate the blind sheikh for the ways he had twisted her brother into a monster?

She loved her life here in America, even if she could not fully participate, even if some Americans were put off by her Muslim dress. Not that she wore a burka or would even consider it. But her hijab that left only her face exposed and her long sleeves and dark stockings even in summer caused occasional stares. *Why aren't you dressed like us?*

She'd seen orthodox Jewish women with scarf-swathed heads and similar clothing subjected to the same mildly disapproving scrutiny. Strange how two cultures so at odds in world politics were so alike in their lifestyles.

Hadya took a more relaxed view. Weather permitting, American women exposed far more of their skin than Hadya could ever be comfortable with. But on a warm day she might remove her hijab to let the breeze ruffle her hair. Kadir had caught her that way once in Lincoln Park. He hadn't said anything at the time, but shortly afterward he'd assaulted her, tying her in her bed and shaving off her hair, right down to the scalp. Of course she'd *had* to keep her hijab on after that. She still seethed with the humiliation. She'd fled his apartment and moved in with Jala who also worked in Uncle Ferran's bakery.

Her hair had grown back but the terror and humiliation of those moments remained as fresh as if it had happened only yesterday. Even now she had to force her hands to unclench the tight fists they had formed.

More than her style of dress sequestered her from American culture. Although Islam kept her from nightclubs and bars, she wouldn't care to go even if it didn't. But she wished she could feel more a part of the culture and still remain a good Muslim woman. She enjoyed going to the mosque for prayers—as long as it wasn't the Al-Salam with that awful Sheikh Omar—and even enjoyed the fasting of Ramadan because she always lost weight. Staying slim was no easy task when tempted daily by the delicacies of the Ramallah Bakery.

Today the bearded older man she so often saw parked in either an old car or a pickup truck here and there along the boulevard—always in sight of the mosque—was absent. Sometimes if she passed on the same side of the street she would see a Thermos and food and field glasses on the front seat. He was obviously watching the mosque. Although he didn't look it, she hoped he was FBI and looking for evidence against Sheikh Omar. She couldn't very well pray to Allah for something bad to befall an imam, so all she could do was hope that the government found evidence against him for some crime that would allow his arrest. Then perhaps Kadir would have breathing space to come to his senses.

She shook her head. How naively foolish she would be to believe that.

Sheikh Omar had so thoroughly poisoned his mind against America that he would never find his way back to sanity. Because that was how she thought of her brother now: insane.

She didn't want her mad brother to ruin her new life in America.

She glanced again at Al-Salam's door. On occasion—just last week was the most recent—she had seen Kadir standing out front in a cluster of his jihadist friends. Unable to escape Sheikh Omar's gravitational pull, they had followed him here from Brooklyn to resume their orbit around him. She'd noticed some new faces lately and that disturbed her. One of them had moved in with Kadir. Under the blind sheikh's influence, her brother intended to bring jihad to America. She had no doubt that these newcomers were going to help him make that a reality.

She shuddered, and not from the cold wind blowing down the street. The Americans she'd met in her two years here were good people. They knew nothing about Islam. She knew they thought Muslims dressed funny, but she'd experienced no prejudice, no hate. She doubted they ever gave a second thought to Muslims as they went about their workaday lives. But if Kadir and his fanatic friends brought terror here, Americans *would* start thinking about Muslims, and they would not be good thoughts.

After Kadir's assault and moving in with Jala, Hadya had continued studying English, learning enough to work the front counter and deal with the customers. A fair number of them spoke Arabic but the majority were Americans who'd developed a taste for Middle Eastern pastries. She was building a life here, she saw a future here, something she'd had no hope of in Jordan. Kadir was out to ruin all that.

She could not allow it. She had been keeping watch on him in a desultory fashion. She would have to take a more vigorous approach now. Kadir would not steal her future.

7

Jack was still at his table, working on his second beer, when a sixty-something guy with short gray hair that poked every which way stepped through the door and looked around. His straight spine and the way he held himself screamed ex-soldier. Jack knew him: Dane Bertel. He wished for a place to hide but none was to be had, so he waved. Bertel's eyes lit and he headed Jack's way.

"Always know where to find you," he said, smiling as they shook hands. He sat opposite him and pointed to Jack's glass. "What're you drinking?"

"Rock."

"You never change."

"Oh, and you do, I suppose?" As Bertel laughed, Jack said, "Want one?"

"Don't mind if I do, but I'm paying."

Jack signaled to Julio for another pint. "That means you want something."

Bertel put on a hurt expression. "Must you be so cynical?"

"Must you be so you?"

"Couldn't I just be stopping to spend a little time with one of my favorite former employees?"

"You could, but we both know you're not. How's business, by the way?"

"Good. And as long as people keep smoking and certain states keep taxing cigarettes up the wazoo, it'll stay good."

Bertel ran stamp-free cigarettes from North Carolina and sold them to middlemen in places like Detroit and Chicago and Jersey City. After fitting the packs with bogus tax stamps, they wholesaled them to bodegas and delis and newsstands. Everybody along the chain made out—except the local tax men, of course.

After Julio delivered his beer, Bertel said, "How about you?"

"Keeping busy."

"Too busy to help out a friend?"

"We've been down that road and you know the answer."

Jack had driven the Jersey City run for a while. Good money but things got complicated. Despite his diminished income these days, he wasn't the least bit tempted.

"You're welcome back any time, you know that. The door's always open. But that's not the kind of help I'm looking for."

Jack leaned back. "Shoot."

"It's those Mohammedans."

"Aw, man . . ."

Bertel had a bug up his butt about militant Mohammedans—his word for Muslims—especially some blind preacher in Brooklyn. He got all paranoid on the subject of how they were out to blow up America. He'd been going on about it for years, but so far, no bombs, no nothing.

"Hear me out, Jack. I've been keeping an eye on those guys—"

"You're still hanging around that Brooklyn mosque? You might as well become a member."

"They moved to Jersey City. Sheikh Omar got kicked out of Al-Farooq and so now he's at Al-Salam on Kennedy Boulevard. In the meantime, a couple of new players have come on board. One's passport says 'Abdul Basit' but that's bogus."

"See? This is what I mean—how do you *know* that? You've gotta be ex-CIA."

"We've been over and over that. The only 'ex' I am is law-abiding citizen."

"Why don't I believe you?"

"Because you're paranoid."

"*I'm* paranoid?"

"Anyway, I don't know who this new guy really is, but he stinks of terrorist. And guess who he's rooming with?"

"Sacco? No, wait. Vanzetti?"

"Not funny. He's bunking with Kadir Allawi, the guy we followed up from Virginia in that truck—"

"The truck that mysteriously blew up?" Jack said, giving him a look. "We never did get around to discussing that."

Bertel spread his hands. "Nothing to discuss. I don't know a thing about it. But guess who else has been hanging around this Jersey City mosque? A Pakistani named Aimal Kasi."

Jack shrugged. "That's supposed to mean something?"

"I recognized him from when I saw him in the cab of the aforementioned truck in Virginia—before Kadir and your slaver buddy Reggie took it north." He laced his fingers together. "It's all interconnected, all of a piece."

Jack couldn't hide his exasperation. "I *know* they're connected. What I don't know is why I should care."

"You'll care like crazy when things start blowing up."

That again. "You said you needed help. What help?"

"I need an extra set of eyes on the Al-Salam Mosque. I can only spare so much time. I need backup."

Jack needed maybe a nanosecond to think about that.

"Sorry. No can do."

"Why not?"

"Because I have a life and I've no room in it for sitting somewhere on the other side of the Hudson watching a mosque."

"Aren't you from New Jersey?"

"The operative word there is 'from,' and I plan to keep it that way."

"If you won't do it for me, do it for your country."

"I'm not doing it for anyone."

"Christ, Jack, I'll *pay* you."

"You're not hearing me, Dane. My life is in a good place right now. I don't want to mess it up."

Jack figured he was overstating, perhaps, but not much. Yeah, he'd blown it with Cristin and his finances could be better, but his life had been sailing through placid waters for nearly two years straight now. Nothing like the two mass murders he'd witnessed and the one murder he'd committed himself during his first eight months on his own.

Yeah, this was definitely a good place.

"I hope you won't regret it."

"Dane, isn't this a job for the CIA or the FBI or some other acronym? As you said, I'm a guy from Jersey, and you're—well, who knows what you are, but whatever you are, the feds are better equipped to handle this kind of thing. You should be talking to them instead of me."

His eyes bugged. "Don't think I haven't! They won't listen. They're blowing it! They're worried about *assassinations*." He spoke the word like it tasted bad.

"I'd say that's a good thing to worry about."

"Not assassinations of Americans. Foreigners. They hauled in a whole bunch from the Al-Farooq on suspicion of some plot against Boutros-Ghali—"

"And he is . . . ?"

"Secretary General of the United Nations. Sheikh Omar's got it in for him because of his ties to Mubarak who, I'm sure you don't know, is—"

"Head honcho in Egypt. You've talked about him before."

"At least you were listening. Omar hates them both. But the Fibbies should be worried about *bombs* instead of assassinations."

"You're talking about what—blowing up the UN?"

"Why not? Wouldn't that cause a shitload of terror?"

"It would sure improve the view of the East River."

Bertel gave him an angry stare. "Do you have any idea how many lives—?"

"Okay. Bad joke. Poor taste."

"But maybe it won't be the UN. Maybe it'll be the World Trade towers, or the Empire State Building."

"The Empire—now *that* would piss me off. That's where King Kong died."

Bertel was turning red. "This isn't a joking matter, Jack. These assholes want to put their holy war on the map and they're looking to make a statement—the bigger and badder the better. And they don't care how many people they kill along the way. In fact, they want maximum body count."

"But for all you know, the feds may have a guy inside who—"

"They did! But they let him go. A lousy five hundred bucks a week for the inside scoop from one of Omar's bodyguards and they blew it."

"And you know this how?"

"I've got a source."

"From when you used to be in the FBI?"

"Stop it, Jack."

"Okay. And while we're stopping things, let's stop this conversation, shall we? You go ahead and play your undercover games, but I'm for leaving it to the professionals."

Bertel gave him a hard glare as he rose from his seat. "Someday I'll say 'I told you so,' but I won't get one damn lick of pleasure out of being right."

Then he stomped out.

Julio slowed as he circled by. "You on the rag or somethin'? You pissing them off one after another today."

Jack only held up his empty glass. He felt bad for Bertel. The old guy was so invested in his conviction that local Mohammedans were plotting major damage. But from what Jack had seen of them, they appeared to be a bunch of bumblers. He couldn't see them getting their act together for anything major.

8

Ernst Drexler arrived ten minutes late without an apology. Nasser al-Thani would have loved to say something—didn't Drexler always make a remark when he was even a minute late?—but the meeting had been called in haste and so he held his tongue.

As usual, they met in Roman Trejador's current hotel suite. Spanish by birth, he had Latin good looks and appeared perpetually tanned, his dark hair only recently showing a touch of gray at the temples. With no family and no permanent residence, he lived in a series of hotels around Manhattan. Sometimes in a chain, like a Hilton or a Hyatt or a Westin, other times in boutique hotels, but only in those that could provide a luxury suite.

No enduring residence, and no enduring relationships outside the Order. The women in his life were high-end call girls. This was an ongoing cause for concern among certain members of the Order's High Council, but Roman Trejador's defense was that, absent the distractions and demands of a wife and family in a permanent residence, he was able to focus his attention more keenly on the responsibilities of being the chief actuator for the Ancient Septimus Fraternal Order. And since he was the best there was—arguably among the best ever—the High Council let him live as he pleased.

Trejador wore his tacky silk smoking jacket, Drexler wore his perennial. never-mind-the-season three-piece white suit, and Nasser wore a gray *thobe*, floor length with a simple round collar.

Their host said, "At this late hour I assumed we'd all have had our dinner, so I ordered no food." He raised a snifter of amber fluid. "But there's brandy on the bar, Ernst. Nasser already has his water from the fridge."

"It's a cold night," Drexler said, inserting his black, rhinoceros-hide cane into the wrought-iron umbrella holder and rubbing his hands together. "A brandy sounds good."

His words carried a vague Austrian accent. Perhaps a decade younger than Trejador, he had a sharp, aquiline nose and combed his glossy black hair straight back from his widow's peak.

Nasser was the youngest man in the room by a good ten years. The other two were seasoned actuators. Nasser was being groomed for the post. As Drexler splashed some brandy into a snifter, Nasser sipped his spring water. He'd been raised in Qatar, where alcohol was permitted. But despite that and his years at Oxford, he'd never developed a taste for it.

Swirling his own glass, Trejador turned to him. "You said you had important news, my friend. The floor is yours."

Nasser appreciated the "my friend." Over the years he had grown comfortable with Trejador. Not so Drexler. He couldn't imagine anyone being comfortable with Ernst Drexler.

"I didn't think this could wait until our regular meeting. I received a call today from one of our jihadist friends."

"Them again!" Drexler said, dropping onto a nearby love seat. "They want money, I suppose."

"You suppose correctly."

Drexler shook his head. "You called us here for that? Tell those *dummkopfs* to—what's the American expression?—pound salt."

Yes, very hard to be comfortable with Drexler.

"I have a feeling this time is different. I've dealt with Kadir Allawi before. He's highly motivated and fanatically dedicated to jihad."

"As are we," Trejador added with a smile.

Indeed, we are, Nasser thought.

Not for any religious reason, but rather for the chaos it would bring. The Order was all about chaos.

"It appears he has gathered a *gamaii* of equally dedicated zealots and they are ready to make a move."

Trejador said, "A gamaii, I take it, is some sort of cell?"

"Exactly. He told me he did not need a lot of funding, but that the result would make the whole world take notice. 'Shock the world' were his exact words."

"Big talk," Drexler said. "What's the plan?"

"He wouldn't say over the phone. Wants to meet with me tomorrow. I don't see that we have anything to lose."

"Except more money. The Order is already out millions because of these incompetents. I don't see it approving another cent for them."

Trejador said, "It costs us nothing to listen, Ernst. They've been quiet since that truck exploded and sent a dozen or so of their brothers to Allah. Maybe they're ready to move again."

"Let's face it," Nasser added. "Anything they can do to start a holy war in America will be to our advantage. You remember the incident better than I, I am sure, but you may not realize that this year marks the tenth anniversary of the bombing of the Beirut barracks. Nearly two hundred fifty Americans were killed in that single blast, but it caused hardly a ripple over here. Why? Because it was far away, it was over *there*. If something like that happens here—in Manhattan, of all places—the response will not be so blasé. The result will be . . . chaos."

"Yes, it will," Trejador said, nodding. "But it will have to be *big*. As of last month, the Americans have a new president, that Democrat Clinton, blabbing peace-peace-peace. I fear we will find him less aggressive and decisive than his predecessor."

The Americans . . . what a telling phrase, Nasser thought.

The three of them had centered their lives in the U.S. but none of them thought of himself as an American. Nor a member of any other national or ethnic group, for that matter. They existed beyond that. They were members of the Order which superseded all national and ethnic boundaries.

"His predecessor," Drexler said, "though aggressive, was still not decisive enough to strike at Iraq's jugular when he had the chance."

"True. And America will come to regret that, which will be to our eventual advantage. Don't forget, we are playing the long game here. But I fear we will need a spectacular act of terrorism to spur this president to a decisive response. I remember that a single truck bomb brought down the Beirut barracks—flattened them." He turned to Drexler. "Your father had a hand in that."

Drexler nodded. "That he did. Like everyone else in the Order, he was disappointed that it did not draw the overreaction we anticipated from Reagan."

Nasser had never met Drexler's father, but wished he had. The late Ernst Senior had been a legend among actuators. He was said to have played a crucial role in Hitler's ascent within the Nazi party back in the days of the Weimar Republic. Talk about creating chaos! Ernst Sr. was touted by most as the greatest actuator in the history of the Order. Ernst II seemed ever to be trying to separate himself from his father's long shadow.

A good example of that eagerness had occurred a couple of years ago when he had jumped on Reggie's claim to have seen the mysterious "Tony" alive in a cab in Lower Manhattan. Drexler had mounted a search for the supposedly dead man as an avenue toward recouping the High Council's lost millions, but it all had come to naught. Nasser wondered why Drexler couldn't see the supposed sighting as a cynical attempt by Reggie to maintain some level of value to the Order. He still kept the loser around, however, promising that he would prove valuable someday.

Trejador said, "If these jihadists can detonate such a bomb here, in some iconic location, it will spur others of their ilk to try the same. Then the U.S., even with Clinton at its helm, will have to retaliate."

"A spectacular act of terrorism," Nasser said, more to himself than the others. "I'll think on that."

"Do that," Trejador said. "We will do the same. In the meantime, hear what they have to say. And if it's not ambitious enough, spur them to greater heights. What say you, Ernst?"

Drexler fixed Nasser with his icy blue gaze. "Fine. Listen to them, but make no commitment until we've discussed it."

Nasser wanted to fling his water bottle at his smug face. The comment was as demeaning as it was unnecessary. Nasser was acutely aware that he had no decision-making power. He swallowed the bile and forced a smile.

"Of course. Perhaps you could arrange to have one of your operatives drive me. For appearance sake."

9

"You wasn't shittin' us, was you," the kid said as Vinny pulled to a stop in the shadows beside the high chain-link fence.

"No, I wasn't," Vinny told him.

He'd already forgotten his name—a street name, so who cared anyway? Five teenage *melanzanas* in his car, four thirteen-year-olds in the back, and the old man of the troupe—all of fifteen—in the front. Aldo had another five in his car. All runners for Umeme and Chaka Raysor, the kings of the Bed-Stuy crack trade. Not that the brothers limited themselves to rock. They'd push anything that turned a buck. Late last year Vinny and Aldo had come into possession of a truckload of high-end sneakers—mostly Air Jordan VIIIs. Knowing how moulies went bugfuck nuts for overpriced kicks, they hauled them into Bed-Stuy and wholesaled the lot to the Raysor brothers. Since it was Christmastime, everybody made out.

All the dealers used kids as runners, usually on bikes. They passed unnoticed most of the time, and were hard to charge when caught. And they worked cheap. So when Vinny approached the brothers with an offer to rent ten of their kid runners for a couple of hours, no problem—just pay up front. He and Aldo had divided up a list of new and used car dealers who had contracts with Tommy. Aldo had taken Queens, Vinny had Brooklyn.

The kid in front was doing the talking.

"F'reals? You payin' us to bust up cars?"

"That's what I said."

A big grin. "Shit, we do that for free!"

Vinny held out his hand. "Then gimme my money back."

Laughter from the front and back seats. Right. Like that was going to happen.

"Just remember: Don't bust them up too bad. These are used cars here and we don't want the owner feeling they're too banged up to fix. Just a bunch of dings and cracked windshields is all. Now get going. We got a lotta stops to make tonight."

As the other kids piled out of the car and began scrambling up the fence, the older one hung back and said, "Why you hatin' on cars so much?"

Hate cars? Nah. Vinny hated Tommy. And so he was only after cars connected to Tommy.

The car detailing idea had hit Vinny a couple years ago when Tony the Cannon took them on a window-breaking spree to get even with the Genovese family. At that time Tommy had been horning in on Vinny's salvage operation and Vinny had thought it could be of big-time benefit to him to help Tommy find something for himself. Something that perfectly suited a dick like him.

So Vinny went hunting and found a guy with a car-detailing business. The owner of Augie's Auto Detailing & Repairs was in to Tony for big bucks. Arrangements were made and soon Tommy took over as the new proprietor of the business while the previous owner, the aforementioned Augie, was demoted to manager but still ran it. After all, with hands like those, what did Tommy Ten Thumbs know about detailing?

Almost immediately after Tommy's arrival, Augie's clients began to experience huge jumps in vandalism. Vinny and Aldo each lent a personal hand to help make that happen. The damage sent Augie and his crews to work. But soon after they'd fixed everything good as new, it would happen again. And again. This was getting expensive for the dealers. So Tommy, sympathetic soul that he was, stopped by the clients and offered complete coverage for a single annual fee. Consider it an insurance policy: No matter how much damage happened over the course of a year, Augie's Auto Detailing & Repairs would be good for it. Just pay the annual fee and fuhgeddaboudit.

The dealers knew a bargain when they saw one and got in line to pay up. They put the word out to other dealers who weren't Augie's clients but were experiencing their own upsurge in vandalism, and the new guys got on board too.

Miraculously, the vandalism stopped almost as suddenly as it started. But the annual premiums kept rolling in. With almost no detailing to be done, Tommy fired Augie and the work crews. He hired freelancers for the occasional little job now and then, and frittered away whatever revenue from the annual premiums didn't go up his nose.

He visited the otherwise empty Augie's office once or twice a week to check the mail. Sitting pretty, Tommy was.

Well, tonight was the wake-up call. But just to keep things from being too obvious, Vinny and Aldo were going to ferry the kids to a couple of lots unconnected to Tommy. That oughta muddy the waters enough to keep Tommy's coked-up brain from connecting the dots.

Vinny gave the kid a shove toward the door. "A car ran over my puppy when I was a kid and I never got over it. Now move your ass out there! And make sure you're all back here in five minutes."

He watched him go. Those little monkeys could do a shitload of damage in five minutes—and enjoy every second of it.

Tomorrow was one of Tommy's days to visit the office. That was when Vinny's fun would begin.

WEDNESDAY

1

Dane Bertel parked his 1984 junker Plymouth Reliant fifty yards down Kennedy Boulevard from the Masjid Al-Salam. Time for a stint of stakeout. On the seat next to him he had the morning papers, a Thermos of coffee, and his favorite breakfast—fried egg and cheese with Taylor ham on a kaiser roll. It didn't get any better than that. He poured some coffee and slouched into a comfortable position.

The Mohammedans who ran the mosque sure as hell didn't advertise its presence. A block-printed sign in the upper right window of the three-story, flaking brick building was the only clue. A nameless, low-end electronics shop, the China Lee Kitchen takeout, and a toy store took up the commercial spaces at street level. A mailbox/money-order/check-cashing place occupied the second floor; the mosque had the top to itself.

Who'd ever guess that worldwide jihad was being planned in these seedy surroundings?

Quite a comedown for Sheikh Omar—banished from the heart of the action in Brooklyn to this relative backwater. But faithful lunatics like Kadir Allawi and Mahmoud Abouhalima had followed him over. A dozen or so more surely would have trailed along had they not been blown to pieces on Long Island's south shore a couple of years ago. But no shortage of crazy Mohammedans here in Jersey City. Omar had found a fresh audience for his hate-America rants.

Dane had little doubt he'd been noticed. This section of Kennedy Boulevard, just off Journal Square, ran two lanes each way and was busy at all hours, but he'd parked along here too damn often to believe no one had made him. Still, he varied his vehicles and varied his parking spots up and down the street, sometimes near, sometimes far, but always with a view of the doorway, either straight through the windshield or reflected in one of the side-view mirrors. Today he sat on the opposite side with a straight-ahead view.

He wondered what they thought of him. FBI? Dane had spotted Fibbies off and on taking a pass at surveillance, but mostly the Bureau seemed interested in Omar's old digs, the Al-Farooq Mosque in Brooklyn.

Dane stared at the doorway. Yeah, you *wish* I was FBI.

When he was on watch like this, he wore an oversize boonie cap and a ratty beard—one that would never pass even a cursory inspection close up—and alternated this old Plymouth with his pickup truck. Kadir Allawi worked for the Mummy, one of Dane's cigarette customers, and he couldn't risk being recognized.

He was reaching for the Taylor ham-and-egg sandwich when a black Mercedes rolled up and stopped in front.

"Hello . . . what have we here?"

Benzes passed by all the time but Dane couldn't remember ever seeing one stop on this block. The driver was not an Arab, but that was all Dane was sure of. The combination of glare and tinted windows kept the inside hidden. All doors except the driver's opened. From the rear emerged the unholy trinity: Kadir Allawi, Mahmoud Abouhalima, and Allawi's roommate who had so many names Dane couldn't be sure who he was. And from the front passenger seat . . .

"Well, well, well! We meet again."

The trim Arab in the thobe . . . Dane had seen him on the beach that night two years ago. He hadn't known who he was then and still didn't know. He reached under the front seat and pulled out his Nikon with the telephoto lens. He already had plenty of pictures of the others, but this guy . . . who the hell was this guy?

He took a few quick shots—making sure to include the Benz's license plate in one—then leaned forward to study the group.

Though clearly an Arab, the stranger didn't seem part of the jihadist clique. Dane knew body language and this guy kept himself a step back, physically and categorically, from the other three. As if he were better than they. They in turn acted deferential, almost like supplicants.

And then he knew.

"Christ, they're looking for money."

Two years ago the mystery Mohammedan had set up a sting to trap the hijackers who'd made off with the money the jihadists had been planning to use to buy teenage sex slaves. Jack had known about the sting and had involved Dane, and he'd be forever indebted to Jack for that.

Because that was the night Dane had become convinced that another player was operating behind the jihadists. Not controlling them, per se; more like whispering in the ear of whoever back home was giving them orders. He'd sensed it for some time, but that night had crystallized it. And this Arab in the thobe could very well be connected to those unseen players.

The four of them seemed friendly enough, all smiles and nods as the mystery man slipped back inside the car and the other three headed for the door to the mosque. He must have picked them up this morning before Dane arrived. He wondered where they'd gone, what they'd talked about. Up to no good, no doubt, but what exactly were they planning?

He gulped the rest of his coffee and started the engine. Much as he hated leaving the jihadists behind—if they had fresh funding in their pockets, knowing what they did for the rest of the day might prove invaluable—he needed to see where this clown was headed, and maybe get a bead on his identity.

Damn, he wished Jack were on board.

He followed the Benz north on Kennedy, leaving a car between them. It looked like the Benz was headed for the Pulaski when the light turned amber and the jerk in front of him stopped instead of rolling through. Dane pounded the wheel in frustration as he watched the mystery Mohammedan glide away. Never catch him now.

God *damn*, he needed Jack.

2

Tommy Totaro stood over the answering machine and stared at it. The LED indicator read *12*.

"What the fuck?"

He'd walked in this morning on one of his twice-weekly swings by to check the mail and saw the message light on the machine blinking. That happened maybe once every three or four weeks, and even then the messages never totaled more than one.

But a dozen?

He started listening. Every call was from one of his policy holders, and every single one of them, one after the other, said the same damn thing: vandalism. Each of them screaming about twenty, thirty cars with dinged hoods and fenders and cracked windows and when was he gonna get out there and fix them? They couldn't sell cars in that shape. They'd been paying their premiums, now it was time for Augie's Auto Detailing & Repairs to deliver.

Tommy dropped into the desk chair and ran his fingers through his thinning hair.

Shit!

What was he gonna do? He had no crews. He'd let them all go.

As he sat there the phone started ringing. He let the answering machine pick up.

"Hey, Augie's. This is Hal down at Morgan's Used Cars. We had some assholes come through last night and . . ."

He dialed the volume to zero and pounded his fist on the desk. This couldn't be an accident. Somebody had targeted him. But who? The Genoveses? Had they gotten wind of the hurt he'd put on their windows contracts during his little midnight ramble with Tony C a couple years ago? This would be payback in kind.

But no, they'd blame Tony for that. And anyway, that water was too far under the bridge. But he'd been targeted, no question.

He looked up the number of one of the freelancers he used and called him. He didn't like what he heard.

"Hey, no, Tommy. I can't. I'm up to my ears with Queensboro Dodge."

"They got hit too?"

"Yeah, bad."

He didn't hold a policy on them. So it wasn't just him. Maybe he wasn't being targeted. But who . . . ?

"Any word on what's going on?"

"I heard that witnesses saw a buncha black kids—young ones—running through the lot with hammers."

"No kidding. So you can't help me out."

"Wish I could, Tommy. If you'd called sooner, I'd be there, but I gotta take the work when it comes."

"Yeah-yeah. I'll remember that."

He slammed down the phone.

A buncha black kids . . . that didn't sound like a Genovese thing. That sounded like some fucking moulie trying to move in on his business. Well, he'd soon find out he'd picked the wrong fucking guy.

3

Nasser mentally shooed the room service waiter out the door as he watched him make a few final adjustments to the tray of club sandwiches. Finally he slipped out of the suite.

"Really, Nasser," Drexler said, placing half a sandwich on a small plate. "Twice in less that twenty-four hours? That is a bit much."

"This couldn't wait."

"There's always the phone," Trejador said, helping himself to a full sandwich. He wore a light gray turtleneck and charcoal gray slacks.

Nasser couldn't help the brittle laugh that escaped, sounding almost like a bray. He fairly vibrated with excitement. Eating was out of the question. He couldn't even sit, so he paced before them.

"Oh, no! No, phone. You do *not* want to trust this to a mobile or even a landline. Once you hear it, you'll understand why."

Trejador stared at him. "I am, as they say, all ears."

"I picked up three of the jihadists this morning. I was already familiar with Kadir and Mahmoud. The new one's name is Ramzi Yousef, a trained bomb maker."

"Bombs!" Drexler said around a mouthful. "I like this already."

Trejador's eyebrows lifted. "A bomb? A big one, I hope."

"They plan to fill a panel truck with a combination of nitroglycerin and a urea-based explosive."

"Just like the Beirut barracks bomb. Excellent. What's their target? The UN, I presume."

"Better. One of the members of their gamaii is an engineer of sorts. He inspected the parking area under the target and he's sure they can bring the building down. Not only bring it down, but topple it into another skyscraper."

Drexler's eyes widened as he lifted his green bottle of beer. "The Empire State Building?"

"No! Even better. They're going to place the truck bomb in the basement of the north tower of the World Trade Center and position it so that the explosion tilts it off balance and topples it into the south tower, which will then crush the rest of the Trade Center." He laughed as he clapped his hands. "Can you believe the sheer audacity of it?"

He expected his revelation to spark an enthusiasm that mirrored his own. Instead he saw wide-eyed shock. Trejador had frozen with the sandwich poised before his lips, and Drexler's beer had stopped halfway in its ascent to his mouth. Didn't they think it possible?

"What?" he said, halting his pacing. "I know they're crazy, but they believe they can do it, and so do I."

"No!" Trejador and Drexler cried in unison. "No!"

Nasser's dazed brain tried to fathom their reaction. Did they think it would be too expensive?

"Compared to what's been lost on less reliable ventures, the cost of this will be negligible. If the High Council balks, I'll gladly put up my own—"

"No!" Again, in unison.

Nasser felt like a punctured balloon. "I don't understand."

Drexler coughed on his food as Trejador spoke: "The World Trade Center is off-limits!"

What?

"I don't understand. The Twin Towers have surpassed the Empire State Building as *the* Manhattan icon. Bringing them down would electrify the world. Even this Clinton would have to issue a call to war."

Drexler finished a quick swallow of beer and said, "No-no-no! Listen to Roman. The World Trade Center is not to be touched. Not only must you not fund this plan, it is imperative that you steer them *away* from it."

Nasser dropped into a chair. "Someone has to explain this to me. What am I missing?"

A look passed between Trejador and Drexler.

"You cannot be privy to that information yet."

"What?" That stung. "I've been a faithful member of the Order for over a decade now and if I haven't yet shown that I can be trusted—"

"Easy, Nasser. It's not a matter of trust or years. It's a matter of level within the Order."

"One needs a minimum of actuator status to have access to that knowledge," Drexler added.

Trejador nodded. "And you'll be there soon. You're an excellent candidate. But until you earn that status, certain things will be withheld from you. It's simply the way it is."

"Does it make sense for me to operate in the dark? Really, it hardly seems fair to expect me to effectively dissuade them from their plan when I don't know why I'm doing it."

Drexler's expression turned sour. "You don't *need* to know the facts. Even if you did, you certainly wouldn't be able to use them. You'd still have to fabricate a reason to convince them."

"If it were up to me," Trejador said, "I'd tell you—"

"But the protocols were put in place for a reason," Drexler added, "and it's not up to individual members to bypass them."

"You'll learn in time," Trejador said. "And when you do, you'll understand."

"Don't we have to take it up with the High Council?"

Trejador shook his head. "Don't even consider it. In fact, I'd rather the Council remain in the dark about this. If they know, they might take drastic measures."

"Drastic? How drastic?"

Drexler said, "Order us to arrange the extermination of that entire Jersey City— What did you call it?"

"Gamaii."

"Right. Gamaii. Or even more extreme: Wipe out all the worshippers at the mosque during Friday prayers."

"Thus depriving us of useful tools," Trejador said. "So this must stay confined among us three. Therefore it is imperative that you divert this gamaii from their intended course as soon as possible."

"You must," Drexler said. "You *must*." He put down his plate with the remainder of the club sandwich. "I've lost my appetite."

Trejador did the same. "Me too."

Dumbfounded, Nasser could only lean back and stare. What could be so important about the World Trade Center that the Order could not allow it to be damaged? He could not imagine . . .

Wait. When he'd learned that he'd be working with Drexler, he'd asked around the Order about him. No one liked him and seemed much more interested in talking about his father. And a number of members mentioned Ernst Sr.'s only failure: Despite his determined efforts, he failed to block the construction of the World Trade Center. Details filtered through Nasser's haze of confusion . . .

Back in the early sixties, about the time of Nasser's birth in Qatar, the Port Authority wrangled permission to raze thirteen square blocks in lower Manhattan to build the World Trade Center. The Order appointed Ernst Drexler Sr. as the point man and put all its resources of power, money, and influence behind him. Usually nothing could withstand an onslaught of that magnitude, but the PA prevailed. The blocks were razed and a huge hole seventy-five feet deep was dug in their place to serve as the foundation of the center.

The Order had failed, but why had it objected in the first place?

Nasser realized he must push the buzzing questions aside and focus on the moment. He'd learn the truth once he achieved actuator status. After reaching that, all the Order's secrets would open to him. The downside was that, once on that path, he would not be allowed to turn back. Once you cross a certain line in the Order, you are committed for life. You cannot change your mind and leave. And even when you reach the point where you can no longer discharge your duties, no retirement is offered. At least not in the usual sense. Retirement was a cyanide capsule. Each actuator kept one handy at all times to guarantee that no secrets would be revealed under duress. If unused during his career, it became the simultaneous beginning and end of his retirement. The Order did not offer a pension.

Nasser rose and faced the two actuators.

"Divert them from their course, you say. They'll never agree to *not* building a bomb. Nor can I say the World Trade Center is off-limits because they'll want to know why. I can't think of a single plausible reason why they shouldn't want to bring down the skyline's most visible structures."

Drexler gave him a challenging look. "A man worthy of the designation 'actuator' will find one."

And there it was: a thrown gauntlet. *Prove yourself.*

Well, he would do just that. He'd drive over to Jersey City and meet with Kadir immediately. He'd set him and the rest of his gamaii straight . . . somehow.

"If you don't succeed," Drexler added, "I might have to call on Reggie to practice his archery skills on your jihadists."

. . . *your jihadists* . . .

They used to be *our* jihadists, he thought. When did they become *mine*?

4

"Might as well work for fucking UPS," Reggie muttered as he stalked into the big stone building. His gaze was drawn, as usual, to the seal of the Septimus Order carved high into the rear wall of the central hall.

He gave it the finger and continued upstairs to his quarters on the second floor.

His life sucked. He still had this free room from the Order, and he got a weekly cash envelope. In return he was expected to be at their beck and call for all sorts of piddly shit. Mostly deliveries. Like just now: Take a cab to a downtown office, pick up an envelope and cab it uptown. Save the receipts and get reimbursed.

Shit, man, he had more talents than that. He could be useful in so many ways if they'd just give him a shot.

Yeah, he knew he'd lost a lot of credibility with that Tony thing. But goddamn it, he *had* seen him in the back of that cab. Trouble was, he could never find him again. The only explanation was that Tony must have been on his way out of town and never came back.

Reggie went to the closet and pulled out his small, lightweight compound bow and a quiver of arrows. He carried them to the long hallway outside his room. The Order owned this old stone building off Allen Street on the Lower East Side. It had been built to house a bunch of people back in the old days but he was the only one who lived here now.

Last year he'd made a man-sized target—really just an orange, one-piece coverall stuffed with rags—and tacked it to the wall at the far end of the hall. He nocked an arrow. The wheels and cams at either end of the bow did their job as he pulled the string back to his chin and took aim along the shaft. No wind or elevation to take into account, just a straight shot.

He imagined it was Lonnie. Not his real name, Reggie was sure, but that was all he had to go on. The guy had gone all crazy on him when Reggie suggested sinking the truck with the girls in it. Drive it into the harbor and have done with it. No one left to point fingers. Shit, it made perfect sense to ditch the evidence, but Lonnie had sucker punched him, then busted his fucking knees.

He remembered the agony of those knees. The Order had paid for their repair but he still walked with a limp and not a single day went by that they didn't hurt. And on cold damp days like this one they ached through and through from morning on and all through the night.

He loosed the arrow and it struck the jumpsuit in the knee.

Someday, Lonnie. Someday we're gonna meet up again, and then we'll see who walks away. You gotta know I'm looking for you, Lonnie. It's a big city, but I spotted Tony, didn't I. And if you're still here, one day I'll spot you too. I don't forget, and I never forgive.

He put another arrow into the other knee.

Where are you, Lonnie?

5

"Struck out again," Jack said as he arrived at the rear counter of the Isher Sports Shop.

Abe lowered his copy of the *Times* and glanced over the top. "Baseball already?"

"No."

"A woman then?"

"Well, yes and no."

"Yes and no a woman? This is possible? You're not sure? *She's* not sure? A hermaphrodite?"

"My latest prospective customer was an older woman."

"Nu. Your saying 'prospective' and 'was' in that sentence tells me what you meant by 'struck out.' Let me guess: She wanted you to kill her husband."

"No. This one was totally out of left field."

"Another baseball metaphor already."

"Listen: I walk into Julio's and she's already there, waiting at my table. Late fifties, maybe sixty, very well dressed, very much out of place in those surroundings."

"She wants you to torture her husband maybe?"

"She tells me she wants me to right a wrong."

Abe shrugs. "They all want that, don't they. What did her husband do?"

"So I ask her who committed this wrong, fully expecting her to say—as you keep insisting with your interruptions—that it was her husband. But no. She says, 'I did,' and proceeds to tell me how she torpedoed her daughter's wedding years ago because she didn't approve of the guy, and the girl has been miserable ever since."

"So she wants *you* to marry her? How much is she offering to pay?"

Jack ignored him—he was coming to see that sometimes selective deafness was the only way to deal with Abe.

"Her daughter remained single and the man she never married turned out to be an all-right guy whose wife just died. She wanted me to get them back together."

Abe did something then that Jack had never witnessed: He burst out laughing. "Matchmaker Jack! Oh, my brain! A *shray* in my brain! It cries *oy gevalt* at the thought!"

"It's not *that* ridiculous," Jack said, feeling a little miffed despite agreeing with him.

After regaining control, Abe said, "So you turned her down, I hope. A *shadchan* you're not."

"Of course I turned her down. What the hell do I know about playing Cupid? Jeez, why do the wrong people keep showing up on my doorstep? What am I doing wrong?"

"You need better marketing."

"I've got word of mouth and that's it."

"It's not enough. You should take out ads already. I see it now: *Got a problem? Call Repairman Jack.*"

"'Repairman Jack'? Where did you come up with that?"

"Off the top of my head just now. You like?"

"I hate."

He searched for a sign that Abe might be offended but saw no trace.

"What's to hate? It's brilliant, a thing of beauty."

"Sounds like an appliance repairman."

"To you maybe. But remember, I didn't say, 'Got a problem with your toaster?' I said, 'Got a problem?' Keep it vague and open-ended. Let the person fill in the blanks."

Jack's turn for a laugh. A small one. "You're joking, right?"

"Not a *biseleh*. Get a separate phone line, get an answering machine, and put classified ads in the papers."

"Under what? *Business Services?*"

"Under *Personal Services*, of course. The kinds of problems you service tend to be very personal. Trust me, a flood of calls you'll see."

"Mostly about broken toasters, I'll bet."

"Of course. From nutcases you'll hear as well."

"I already do."

"Just because they're nuts doesn't mean they don't have problems—other than being nuts, that is. But amid the flood of responses you may find gold in your pan."

"I doubt it."

"I'm missing something maybe? Your current situation is just the way you like it?"

"No . . ."

"And you've got how many more prospects lined up at the moment?"

"Um, none."

"Oh, well then don't listen to me. You've got everything under control."

"Repairman Jack? Seriously?"

"Excuse me. I should have said Repairman Shmuck."

Okay . . . *now* Abe was annoyed.

"You're really serious about this, aren't you."

"You want my advice, there it is. For free already."

He was serious. Jack thought it was a terrible idea but sensed he might have already bruised his feelings.

"Well . . . I'll . . . I'll have to think about it."

But he knew he wouldn't.

6

A moving car seemed the safest place to discuss terrorism, so Nasser had directed his driver to keep moving through the back streets of Jersey City.

"Is there a problem?" Kadir said in Arabic from the rear, where he sat sandwiched between Mahmoud Abouhalima and the horse-faced newcomer, Ramzi Yousef.

Nasser turned in the front passenger seat and replied in Arabic as he faced them.

"Why do you ask?"

Kadir glanced at the back of the driver's head. "Are you certain he does not speak Arabic?"

Nasser smiled. Brajko Klarić was another of Drexler's Eastern Europeans— a Croat who barely spoke English, let alone Arabic.

"Not a word. Go on."

"There must be a problem. All you had to do was give us the money, but we are going for a ride."

"Yes, there's a problem. My people have rejected the idea of funding a Trade Center bomb."

Three sets of dark eyes widened as one. A wave of protests arose. Mahmoud's voice cut through the babble.

"Your 'people'? We believed this to be *your* money. We believed you were in charge of it!"

Nasser gave a helpless shrug. "We all answer to a higher power. My higher power does not believe the fall of the towers will have the desired impact."

"That is insane!" Yousef said in Pakistani-accented Arabic. "It will shock the world!"

"No argument that it will shock America, but my people do not believe it will have sufficient international impact."

More babble.

"The towers are the symbol of capitalism!" Yousef said. "America embraces capitalism and ignores Allah."

Personally Nasser was rather fond of capitalism. It worshipped markets rather than the local deity. Markets were reliable. Deities not so much.

Kadir raised a fist. "By destroying the symbols of capitalism, we strike a blow for jihad, for Allah himself!"

More babble, through which Nasser said, "But the rest of the capitalist world will remain untouched. Do you want that?"

Wary silence followed.

Nasser added, "Remember, you will get only one chance to shock the world. After the first bomb, security will clamp down like a vise, and placing a second bomb will be next to impossible. So you must think of the first bomb as the *only* bomb. And as such, you must choose the target that will offer the most wide-reaching impact."

He thought he was making a reasonable argument. Personally he agreed that knocking down the towers would be more shocking, but plausible alternatives remained and he had to push them. He only wished he knew why.

"And what would that be?" Mahmoud said in a sour tone.

"The UN." He raised a hand to head off any premature objections. "Think about it. Picture the Secretariat reduced to rubble. At forty stories it's nowhere near the height of the towers, but it dominates the East Side waterfront. In destroying it you bring down more than a mere building, you attack more than one country, you strike a blow at *all* the member nations." He pointed to Kadir. "And those member nations do *not* include Palestine, because the UN doesn't recognize Palestine, does it."

Kadir's lips tightened to a thin, grim line.

Nasser continued. "You will be striking a blow at the international body, controlled by infidels, the same infidels who sanctioned the invasion of Iraq. You will strike at *all* nations, and you will do it in midtown Manhattan, which is spitting in the eye of America at the same time. What more can you ask for?"

He could sense Kadir and Mahmoud wavering, but Yousef was shaking his head.

"No. It must be the towers. My uncle sent me here to make the towers fall and that is what we must do. That is what we *will* do."

"Your uncle? Who is your uncle?"

Kadir looked ready to respond but Yousef jumped ahead of him.

"That is not your concern."

Nasser already knew. After their first meeting this morning he'd made a few quick calls back home and learned Ramzi Yousef was the nephew of Khalid Sheikh Mohammed, a high-up in an unsung jihadist group that called itself al-Qaeda.

"Well, then, let your uncle pay for the bomb."

"He would, but the money can't get through."

"The FBI," Mahmoud said through a snarl.

The Bureau had finally managed to do something useful. The Order had influence there. He'd notify the High Council to instruct the members within the Bureau to put extra effort into blocking money transfers from Khalid Sheikh Mohammed.

Kadir gave him a plaintive look. "That is why we came to you."

Nasser shrugged. "My hands are tied as far as the towers are concerned. But we will gladly fund the destruction of the UN."

Kadir and Mahmoud both looked at Yousef, who resolutely shook his head.

Nasser faced front and spoke to his driver in English. "We'll drop them back at the mosque now."

If they had other options, he was sure they'd already exhausted them before contacting him. He'd let them stew for a while, then renew contact later.

He spent the rest of the trip back to the mosque listening to the jihadists muttering among themselves in the rear.

7

Vinny had been keeping an eye on the salvage yard's parking lot through his office window. He was ninety percent sure Tommy would show up unannounced. And wouldn't you know, just after four P.M., a brand-new, cherry red Z-car roared in from Preston Street and skidded to a halt next to Vinny's Crown Vic.

He watched Tommy remove a cardboard box from the passenger seat and start up the stairs. Vinny stepped out and blocked his way to the landing—and he had the bulk to do it.

"Tommy. What's up?"

Tommy had to stop two steps from the top and look up at Vinny.

"Just dropping off some office supplies."

"Thanks, but I don't need any."

He laughed. "Oh, no. These are mine. I shut the detailing place."

"Yeah? How come? I thought that was going great."

"It was till last night. I think some spook is tryin' to move in on the business. Sent a whole buncha little moulies through all the lots last night, dinging up everything in sight."

"Lot of those places have contracts with you, I take it."

"Yeah." Another laugh. "My phone won't stop ringing. Good luck waiting for an answer. Like I'm really gonna go fix up their dinged cars, right?"

That was the way the racket worked. Collect the premiums during the quiet time, but should the shit hit the fan, close up shop and disappear.

"Yeah, that would break the bank."

"Damn fuck right it would. So I closed up till I can track down this mook. Hey, do we have to stand out here?"

"I was just going out."

"Yeah, well, I'm just coming in."

"Where?"

"Where else? The office. I'm back."

Vinny shook his head, real slow like. "No, you ain't back."

Tommy looked all offended now. "What? We're partners."

Another slow shake. "We was never partners, Tommy. Tony stuck you in here because you had no place to go. Soon as you sniffed a better deal, you lit out like you had a rocket up your ass."

"Hey, if you're pissed at that, I can make it up to you."

Pissed? After orchestrating the whole detailing opportunity, Vinny had done a happy dance when Tommy left.

"Nothing to make up. I didn't even notice you was gone."

"Yeah, well, this is our junkyard and—"

"No, it's mine. And it's staying mine."

"Fuck that. I got an interest here and—"

Vinny started reaching for his wallet. "Tell you what, Tommy. I'll pay you back two bucks for every one you invested here." He stopped his hand halfway there. "Oh, that's right. You didn't put shit into it. You only took out. Come to think of it, you owe *me*."

"You can't do this, Vinny. You can't fuckin'—"

"Go home, Tommy. You left. You ain't coming back. Don't take it personal. We're still in the same crew so we still gotta work together, but not here."

Tommy glared at him, then headed back down the stairs. At the bottom he turned and pointed up at Vinny.

"You ain't heard the last of this. Not by a long shot."

Vinny knew he'd go call Peter or Junior and whine to them, but that wasn't going to work this time. Tommy Ten Thumbs Totaro might be a connected Gambino, but with the Chief sent up for life and being pressured by the other families to let go, the Gottis had their hands full. No time for Tommy's piddly-ass bullshit. And if he went to Tony he'd get a fucking earful.

Vinny watched Tommy burn rubber leaving the lot, then returned to the warmth of his office.

His office.

8

Kadir shivered in the icy wind blowing down Brooklyn's Atlantic Avenue. And yet as cold as it was, it felt positively balmy compared to the reception he and Mahmoud had received in the Al-Farooq Mosque behind them. They were identified with Sheikh Omar, who wasn't welcome there, and consequently neither were they.

They'd found themselves even less welcome in the Al-Kifah office, home of the Afghan Refugee Fund. The fund had suffered a huge fall-off in contributions after the brutal murder of its founder, Mustafa Shalabi. Many in the mosque and the Al-Kifah office blamed Sheikh Omar for that. Being blind, he couldn't have done it himself, but shortly before the murder he had issued a *fatwah* condemning Shalabi.

Kadir and Mahmoud's pleas for money had fallen on deaf ears. They weren't asking for a handout, just a loan. Instead they had been shown the door.

"I can't believe Allah is allowing this to happen!" Kadir said.

Mahmoud nodded as they began walking toward the subway station on Flatbush. "The call to jihad goes unanswered for lack of a few thousand dollars. How pathetic we are."

"There must be *some* way we can get money."

"If we can convince Yousef to turn from the towers to the UN, we can go back to the man from Qatar."

Kadir shook his head. "Yousef is set on the towers. It will take more than a lack of funds to change his mind."

"But with no money, we have no bomb."

"And without Yousef, we have no one trained to make a bomb."

The walked on in silence for a while.

"If only we had credit or something of value," Kadir said, grinding a fist into his palm. "We could go to a bank."

Mahmoud grinned. "I would love that." He changed to a wheedling tone. "'Please, Mister Capitalist Infidel Dog, sir. Will you lend us ten thousand dollars so that we may destroy your unholy system?'"

They both laughed as they reached Flatbush, but on the corner Mahmoud stopped and grabbed Kadir's arm.

"Wait. We don't need a bank. Some of the other cabdrivers who have as little credit as we do have borrowed from private lenders. The interest is very high, though."

Kadir shrugged. "What matter? It's not as if we're going to stay around to pay it back."

Mahmoud laughed again. "True! When I go to work later I'll ask around for a name and a number."

For the first time since this morning, Kadir felt a ray of hope.

9

Nasser ran into Drexler waiting for the elevator in Roman Trejador's hotel. Drexler had called this emergency meeting less than half an hour ago, but Nasser had precipitated it.

As planned, he'd placed an early-evening call to Kadir to prod him into changing the target. The response had shocked him: They'd found another way to get the money.

Nasser had immediately called Trejador but got the hotel's voice mail instead. So he'd contacted Drexler with the news. Drexler got through to Trejador and they set out from their respective apartments for the hotel.

They found Trejador in a robe, mixing a martini.

"Was all this rush really necessary?" he said.

"We need to change their minds," Drexler said.

Two sets of eyes focused on Nasser.

"Well?" Trejador said. "How set are they?"

"Allawi and Abouhalima are not the problem—they just want to blow up some Manhattan real estate, and the bigger the better. It's the newcomer, Ramzi Yousef, who's the problem. He's fixated on the towers."

Trejador shrugged. "So? Make it without him."

Drexler smiled. "We can arrange an accident."

"He's their bomb maker."

"Ah." Trejador sipped his martini. "That's the catch twenty-two, as they say. What can we do to change his mind?"

"Not easy. His uncle is with al-Qaeda and sent him here specifically to bomb the towers."

Trejador began wandering the front room of his suite. "All right, then. We must sweeten the pot."

Nasser shook his head. "I've looked into his eyes and I don't think he can be bought."

"No, I meant sweeten the UN pot—make it an irresistible target. Who do the jihadists hate most in the world?"

"Israel," Drexler said. "It's at the top of every hit list."

"Well, since you can't kill a country, who in Israel would they most like to see dead?"

Drexler shrugged. "The prime minister, I suppose."

"All right, then. What if Prime Minister Yitzhak Rabin sets up a secret meeting in the UN with Boutros-Ghali?"

Nasser found himself nodding. "Sheikh Omar hates the secretary general because he's so cozy with Mubarak."

"But let's sweeten it even further. What American do they hate the most? Whose head would they most like to see on a pike?"

"The last president has got to be up there—he invaded Iraq."

"Bush? That might be a stretch. We're in New York. What New Yorker?"

"That would have to be D'Amato," Drexler said.

Nasser said, "Alfonse D'Amato, the senator? Why?"

"Why wouldn't they? He is perhaps the most vocal supporter Israel has in Congress. A bit of a grandstander about it too. When Iraq began firing Scuds at Israel during the war, D'Amato made a big point of flying over there to demonstrate his solidarity."

Trejador looked at Nasser. "Can you come up with someone better?"

"No. D'Amato is loathed by jihadists."

"Excellent." Trejador clapped his hands. "Rabin, D'Amato, and Boutros-Ghali all meeting at the UN." Another look at Nasser. "Will our pet jihadists be able to refuse?"

Nasser had to smile. "I do not see how."

"Then we need to set a date for this momentous meeting. How long for them to make the bomb, do you think?"

Drexler frowned. "They told al-Thani they're planning a van bomb. Even something that size . . . If they can get the materials quickly, I'd say no more than a week."

"Let's give them a few days more. And let's make it a Friday, since that's a day of prayer for all of the participants. That brings us to . . ." He briefly shut his eyes. "The twenty-sixth. Good. The secret meeting will take place at eleven A.M. on the tenth floor of the UN Secretariat Building on Friday, February twenty-sixth."

"Wait-wait-wait," Nasser said. "I know the Order has reach, but how can we possibly . . . ?" Trejador's smile and Drexler's disdainful look stopped him. "Oh, I see."

He now understood that when Trejador said "secret" meeting, he meant so secret that even Rabin, D'Amato, and Boutros-Ghali wouldn't know about it.

He felt like an idiot.

Drexler said, "Our people in the UN can find some excuse to lure D'Amato over. Boutros-Ghali is already there, of course. The Israelis never advertise their prime minister's whereabouts unless it's a state occasion, so for all anyone will know, Rabin can be anywhere we wish him to be that day."

"Rabin, D'Amato, and Boutros-Ghali," Trejador said. "The Unholy Trinity for our jihadists. If they—"

He turned at the sound of a door opening down the hall and then a young brunette appeared. Nasser knew her—the alluring Danaë.

"I'm leaving now," she said in a soft voice. "I have another appointment."

"Of course," Trejador said. "I'll be in touch."

She smiled. "Of course you will."

She turned her blue gaze on Nasser and held the smile, then winked and turned away.

Nasser's knees felt semi-solid. Danaë . . . one of Trejador's prostitutes. He seemed to hire the same ones over and over. Nasser had been infatuated with Danaë since he'd first seen her a number of years ago. He'd caught glimpses of some of Trejador's other call girls, but none had ever tempted him like Danaë.

He would love to hire her—just for one night—but feared he might be committing some sort of breach by sharing a woman with his superior. As he watched her glide toward the door, he noticed Drexler's livid expression. Danaë removed her coat from the front closet and made her exit.

As soon as the door closed behind her, Drexler turned on Trejador and exploded.

"You had one of your whores here while we were discussing the greatest act of terrorism this city, this country—the *world* has ever seen?"

Trejador appeared unfazed by the outburst. "Well, I *was* expecting to have the evening to myself. You called the meeting rather abruptly, if you recall."

"But this is unconscionable! You have no idea what she might have heard!"

"The door was closed. And besides, Danaë is a pro. She doesn't peek, she doesn't pry, she doesn't *care*."

"She may have heard something without even trying. How can you risk that?"

"I'm not risking anything."

Drexler grabbed his coat and his cane. "I can't stay here any longer." He pointed the silver top of the cane at Nasser. "You come with me. We have matters to discuss."

Nasser glanced at Trejador. Both were his superiors, but the Spaniard had seniority. Trejador gave a go-ahead shrug.

Moments later Nasser found himself in the hotel hallway with a very agitated Drexler.

"Come!" he said, grabbing his arm and tugging him toward the elevators. "I want her followed!"

"Where?"

"Wherever she goes." He jabbed the elevator's DOWN button repeatedly. "I want to learn who she is and who she knows—everything about her!"

"She's just—"

"What? Just a prostitute? You don't know that. She may have a second line of business—like blackmail. Or worse. Did you ever hear of Mata Hari? We can't risk this."

When the doors parted he fairly pushed Nasser into the car ahead of him and stabbed the LOBBY button. The car made an uninterrupted descent, and as the doors opened he propelled Nasser into the lobby.

"Hurry! She's probably waiting for a cab out front. Don't let her get away."

Nasser rushed through the lobby and emerged onto the sidewalk just as a bellman closed a taxi door behind Danaë. Nasser ran to the line of waiting cabs and jumped into the rear of the first.

"You have to wait your turn, mister."

"A hundred dollars if you follow that cab to wherever it's going!"

The taxi lurched into motion and caught up to Danaë's in no time.

THURSDAY

1

"Okay, you two guys listen and listen good," Tony said. "Because here's how it's gonna go."

Vinny had better things to do but Tony the Cannon had called the meeting for eleven this morning and wasn't taking no for an answer. Since Tony, sick though he was, hadn't stepped down as crew boss, Vinny obeyed. He showed up at Tony's appliance store on Liberty Avenue in Ozone Park a couple minutes early. He was surprised to find Tommy already there. Tommy glared. Vinny stared.

"Now I know things ain't good between you two," Tony went on, looking small and frail behind his desk, "but that ain't gonna interfere with business. And speaking of business," he said, focusing his hard dark eyes on Tommy, "you've been fucking off."

Tommy spread his hands. "The business just ain't out there, Tony."

"Bull*shit*! Don't try to gimme that. You just ain't been lookin'. Just this morning I got a call from an old customer about someone who wants a loan. So you know what? You're gonna go meet him at the taxi depot, and you're gonna check him out."

"Sure, Tony."

"Name's Mahmoud or something like that."

"Mahmoud?" Tommy made a face. "We're loaning to ragheads?"

"We're loaning to guys who can pay back. If this guy can pay back, you make the fucking loan."

"Awright. Gotcha."

"And Vinny's going with you."

Shit.

"Ay, Tony—" Vinny began but Tony karate chopped the air.

"You're both gonna spend some time together and iron out this beef you got with each other. But I'm setting some ground rules. First off, Vinny's junkyard stays his and his alone."

"But—"

Another karate chop. "Vinny bought it. He let you in by the goodness of his heart as a favor to me. You left the business on your own. You don't go back unless he wants to take you back." He looked at Vinny. "You want him back?"

"No way."

"Then that's settled. But here's what you will do: You'll help Tommy get the loan business healthy again. *Capisce?*"

Vinny nodded. "*Capisco.*"

So there it was, all settled, all done. Their crew capo had spoken: Tommy was out of Preston Salvage and not coming back. That was the good news. The bad news was he'd be sharing a car with the jerk for the next few weeks.

"Which taxi depot we talking about?" Tommy said through clenched teeth. "Long Island City?"

"Nah. West Fifty-third—*way* west. Guy'll be there noonish."

Tommy said, "What're we charging?"

"Twelve. But if that looks like a deal breaker, Vinny here will mention a special this week: ten."

"And if he pulls some rug-merchant shit and tries to Jew us down?"

Tony stared at him. "Did you just say what I think you just said?"

Tommy looked around. "What?"

Tony sighed. "Never mind. If he don't like ten percent you bust his face for wasting your time."

"You got it," Vinny said. "I'll drive."

No way was he going to try to squeeze into Tommy's Z.

"Damn right you will," Tommy said.

2

If Tony thought putting them together in a car would ease things, he was dead wrong. Usually Vinny hated when Tommy sat in the back, making it look like Vinny was his chauffeur, but this trip he was glad for it. And usually Tommy talked nonstop, but he said maybe six words on the way across town.

The taxi depot turned out to be a long, one-story brick building with a rolling steel door. A few yellow cabs sat in the long lot next to it, the rest presumably out on the street hunting fares. Eleventh Avenue rumbled half a block away.

Turned out they were dealing with two Arabs—a tall one with weird red hair and a short one—who were looking for one loan of ten Gs. As the four of them stood in the cold on the sidewalk in front of the depot, Vinny took an instant dislike to both of them. Something not right about these bozos. They didn't even blink when Tommy said the vig was twelve percent per week. If it was up to Vinny he wouldn't lend them a friggin' dime.

But Tommy had had a couple of snorts on the way over from Ozone Park, so maybe his judgment wasn't the best. And since nothing else was happening for him, he was looking to do business.

"You got jobs?" Tommy said.

Both nodded.

The tall one said, "I drive a cab from here."

"Yeah?" Tommy said. "Let's go in and check that out with the dispatcher."

As they went inside, Vinny looked at the little guy.

"What's your name?"

"Kadir."

"Kadir, eh. What kinda name is that?"

"I am from Palestine."

The other guy had better English. This one's accent was so thick he shouldn't even have bothered trying English.

"What're you gonna do with this money, Kadir?"

His gaze slid away. "We are starting a business."

"Yeah? What kind?"

"Delivery."

Start a delivery business with ten grand? Good luck. Bad lie.

"You got a job, Kadir?"

"Yes."

"What do you do?"

Again the sliding gaze. "I . . . I run a machine. I put labels on things."

This was starting to make sense now. These guys weren't getting into a legit business they could talk about. Nothing wrong with less than legit.

"Where's this job?"

"In Jersey City."

Tommy and the tall redhead returned.

"Okay. He's for real. What about this guy?"

"Does piece work over in Jersey City."

"Yeah? Let's go see your boss."

The little guy suddenly became hyper. "No-no! I cannot! He will not like that!"

Tommy grabbed him by the collar of his coat and dragged him toward Vinny's idling car.

"I said we're going to see your boss."

As Tommy tossed him into the backseat, Vinny looked at the tall one, Mahmoud.

"You too."

For an instant he looked like he might run for it, then shrugged and followed Kadir.

Looks like we're headed for Jersey City, Vinny thought.

3

Jack arrived promptly at noon, just ahead of the lunch rush, and got a table for two near the rear of Le Pistou. Still hated the name, but it seemed like a friendly enough place. He asked about French beers and Kronenbourg 1664 was suggested. It sounded more German than French, and the Germans knew beer, so he ordered.

He checked his watch: ten after. Well, she'd said noon*ish*.

He peeked at the menu and spotted a prix fixe lunch for $19.93. Weird number. Did they price it by the year? Could he have saved a penny by coming here back in December? He checked out the possibilities. It started with choice of garlic sausage in brioche or duck liver paté, followed by a hangar steak with French fries, or a navarin of lamb, or a duck, pork, and sausage cassoulet.

Helluva lunch for under twenty bucks. He could get to like this place.

He finished the beer and still no Cristin. The waiter was acting antsy. Jack spotted a phone in the corner near the restrooms and called her apartment. He left a message on her answering machine. He remembered she had a mobile phone and kicked himself for not getting her number.

He gave the waiter ten bucks for the beer and for blocking his table from paying customers, then went outside to wait. He wandered down to the corner of Lexington and Sixty-first, then back. Still no sign of her.

Had she forgotten? Not like her to forget. She lived a dozen blocks uptown and a little east of here. Easy walk. Why the hell not?

4

"All right," Tommy was saying as he pointed to one raghead and then the other. "I know where you work and I know where you work."

The four of them stood next to the Crown Vic outside the short one's workplace. Vinny now understood why he hadn't wanted them to check it out. Tommy had barged into the office, pushing Kadir ahead of him, and had got confirmation from the older fat raghead inside that Kadir did have a job there. Tommy had then bulled into the garage area and Vinny had followed. They'd both seen the labeling machines and the crates of cigarettes stacked against the wall.

"So how this loan is gonna work," Tommy continued, "is you're both responsible. If one of you dies, the other is still on the hook. I'll show up at the depot back in the city at noon every Thursday and one of you had better be there with an envelope. If you ain't, and I gotta come looking for you, you'll wish you'd never been born."

"Yes, we understand," the short one said. "When can we get our money?"

Damn, he seemed anxious to lay his hands on cash. All the more reason not to give it to him.

"Tommy, you sure?"

That earned Vinny a glare. "You stay outta this. Just unlock the trunk."

Clenching his teeth, Vinny keyed the trunk open and stepped back. He watched Tommy open the briefcase inside and put two rubber-banded stacks of fifty C-notes each into a manila envelope. He handed the envelope to Kadir.

"There you go. Ten Gs." When Kadir started reaching into the envelope, Tommy slapped his hand. "It's all there. You can count it later."

Kadir nodded and folded the envelope over.

Tommy said, "Just so's there's no confusion: You're gonna have one thousand two hundred bucks waiting for me at the taxi depot at noon one week from today. We clear on that?"

Kadir nodded. "Yes. Very clear. We will be there."

"Good." He glanced at Vinny. "Let's go."

With Tommy in back again, Vinny got the Vic moving. He wasn't familiar with Jersey City—the ragheads had guided him in—but he remembered the route.

"'You sure?'" Tommy said from behind. "What the fuck kinda thing is that to say?"

"I don't trust them."

"Neither do I."

"But you hand them ten large of Tony's money?"

"Yeah. 'Cause I know where they work. They try to stiff us, we squeeze the guys they work with till we find them. But yeah, I was on the fence till I saw the operation in that garage."

"The cigarettes."

"Right. The cigarettes. Like a way to print money. I want an excuse to come back here, because if I ain't getting a big piece of that action before spring arrives, I'll be getting it all."

"You're moving in?"

"Damn right. I'll leave the main raghead in charge to keep his lines of distribution, but I'll be calling the shots." He clapped his hands. "This is gonna be sweet."

Sweet indeed, Vinny thought.

The only downside he could see—at least from where he stood—was the Jersey City location. The wrong side of the river. But he wasn't going to say nothing to discourage Tommy. The farther away, the better.

5

For the second time in half an hour, Jack punched the combination into the keypad at the entrance to Cristin's apartment building. He'd seen her enter it enough times to know it by heart. On his first trip he'd buzzed her unit but got no answer, so he'd let himself in and climbed the stairs to the third floor. Knocking on her door got the same response as the buzzer: *nada*.

Worst-case scenario? She'd suffered a heart attack or stroke during the night and was lying unconscious on the floor. No, even worse, she'd found a new boyfriend who'd strangled her when she wouldn't let him stay over—*no one* slept over at Cristin's.

All possible, none likely.

He didn't have a key so he'd cabbed home and back with his lock-picking tools. Back on the third floor, he knocked again on her door, but still no reply.

The hallway was empty and he had the Schlage open in thirty seconds. Calling out her name, he did a quick walk-through. No body on the floor, nothing out of place, the bed made, an empty coffee cup in the sink. All as normal as normal could be.

So why this gnawing unease?

Because Cristin was as efficient and organized as anyone he'd ever met. She had a calendar and a Rolodex embedded in her brain. She made her living planning events and that meant keeping appointments. If something had come up, she would have called Le Pistou. But she hadn't.

So where the hell was she?

He decided he'd be here to ask her when she came home.

He saw copies of *Vogue* and *Cosmopolitan* stacked on an end table. He sat on her sofa and picked one at random. This issue's cover blared *Cosmo's Annual Bedside Astrologer Tells What's in Store for You in 1993*.

Well, how could he resist that?

6

Kadir came out of the Space Station on Mallory Avenue waving the keys at the waiting car. He'd taken some of the freshly borrowed cash and rented a ten-by-ten-foot storage locker here while Mahmoud hurried off to round up Yousef and Salameh.

Salameh's battered green Nova was idling at the curb with him behind the wheel and Mahmoud beside him.

"We have a space," Kadir said. "Now we have to fill it." He slipped into the backseat beside Yousef. "Where to next?"

"We're meeting someone at City Chemical," Yousef said.

"Someone? Who?"

"His name is Nidal Ayyad. I told you about him. He is the engineer who inspected the North Tower for us. But he works for a company called Allied Signal. We will need his contacts there."

Kadir wasn't sure he liked the idea of adding a newcomer to their inner circle. This Ayyad might already know of their desire to topple the towers, but he didn't know when. As far as Kadir was concerned, too many people knew already. Aimal Kasi had gone back to northern Virginia, saying he had to attend to his business, but he swore an oath to look for ways to bring jihad to the American capital on his own.

"How do we know this Ayyad? Can we trust him?"

"He was recommended by my uncle. He is a member of the Muslim Brotherhood and, although he was born in Kuwait, he is a Palestinian, just like you. He has a degree in chemical engineering from an American university. He is devoted to jihad. We will need him to show us the best spot in the basement to place the bomb to topple the tower. He will be very helpful."

Kadir sighed. If this Ayyad was good enough for Khalid Sheikh Mohammed, then he supposed he was good enough for Kadir Allawi.

Salameh put his old Chevy into gear and headed for City Chemical. Kadir had the address—in the area known as the Heights—and they pulled to a stop before a young Arab waiting out front.

Yousef introduced Ayyad around, then spoke in Arabic. "You placed the order?"

Ayyad nodded and handed him a slip of paper. "I need money to pay for it and an address for delivery."

Kadir studied the handwritten sheet over Yousef's shoulder.

$$Urea—1,200\,lbs$$
$$HNO_3—105\;gal$$
$$H_2SO_4—(93\%)—60\;gal$$

He had no idea what it all meant, but it included more than half a ton of urea, whatever that was. Was the storage space going to be big enough?

"How much?" Mahmoud said from the front seat.

"Thirty-six hundred and fifteen dollars."

Kadir blinked. He had paid 772 dollars for the storage locker. No one would rent on a monthly basis so he'd had to pay a year in advance. And now another 3,600 dollars. That meant they'd run through almost half the money in less than an hour after they'd borrowed it. And they still hadn't found a safe place to mix the chemicals. What would that cost?

Mahmoud had the money, and as he began counting, Kadir gave Ayyad the address of the Space Station on Mallory Avenue.

"Locker four-three-four-four," he told him.

Yousef said, "Have you found a mixing space?"

Ayyad nodded. "A converted garage on Pamrapo Avenue. I spoke to the owner. It's available immediately."

Kadir had to ask. "Did he say how much?"

"Five hundred fifty per month and he'll let us rent month to month."

"Good." He smiled with relief. "We won't need more than a month."

"But he also wants a month's security, so we'll have to give him eleven hundred in advance."

Eleven hundred . . . that put them past the halfway point in their funds. Kadir would have to cut his hours at Diab's labeling machines to devote his time to the bomb. He wondered if he still even had a job. Diab had to be furious at him for bringing those criminals to his place. But what choice did Kadir have? He was being manhandled, and if he'd somehow managed to escape and run, he would have ended the day with empty pockets. They'd have no money at all.

If only that greedy Egyptian Diab supported jihad in America, he would understand and make allowances, but he did not. He was making too much money selling his smuggled cigarettes. America was a land of milk and honey for him.

"This place will suit our needs?" Kadir said.

Ayyad nodded. "It has cinder-block walls and is back from the street. It is perfect."

"Yousef said you have a degree from an American university. Which one?"

"Rutgers."

"And yet you risk everything for jihad. May Allah bless you into eternity."

Before Ayyad could reply, Mahmoud handed a roll of hundred-dollar bills through the window. "You can add the last fifteen yourself?"

Ayyad shrugged. "I can. But you should know that when I spoke to them inside they said it's too late for a delivery today. So I'll arrange a time for tomorrow. Is ten A.M. good? I'll tell them one of you will be waiting for the truck then."

"Why not have it delivered straight to the garage?"

Ayyad shook his head. "The owner will cancel the lease if he sees all those chemicals going in. We need to do it piecemeal." He patted the Nova's roof. "You can use this car. How old is it?"

"Nineteen seventy-eight," Salemeh said.

"Let's hope it holds up. Who will be at the storage place to take delivery?"

"We'll all be there," Yousef said.

"Good. Meanwhile I will need another eleven hundred to secure the rental on the Pamrapo place."

Mahmoud counted out another eleven bills and handed them through the open window.

The four of them watched Ayyad walk inside, then they drove away.

It's happening, Kadir thought as his stomach tingled with anticipation. It's really happening.

7

"Damn." Jack slapped a rolled-up *Cosmo* against his thigh. "Where the hell are you?"

Almost midnight and still no sign of Cristin. He'd watched TV—*Top Cop, Cheers, Wings, LA Law,* and made it through *The Tonight Show* monologue with that new guy, Jay Leno, before bailing. He couldn't stand any more waiting.

Okay. She probably had an event tonight, some party or reception for one of her CEO or politician clients, and she had to stay until the end to make sure everything ran smoothly. But midnight? What event ran till midnight?

She's fine . . . she's fine . . .

He kept telling himself that, but it didn't ease the neck-tightening tension. He couldn't put it off any longer. He'd told himself he wouldn't go through her things to see if he could track her down, but the imminence of the midnight hour changed the rules.

He started searching through her drawers. He found a checkbook, he found an electric bill, a water bill, a NYNEX bill and a Nokia bill.

Wait. He'd spotted a Nokia label on her mobile phone. He unfolded the bill and found her number. Great! He grabbed her home phone and punched it in . . . and listened to ring . . . after ring . . . after—finally she answered.

"Cristin?"

But her recorded voice told him she couldn't answer the phone right then but just leave a message and a number and she'd call him right back.

"Shit!"

The corkscrew winding through his neck tightened further.

He saw her checkbook and bank statement. He hadn't gone looking for them, but since they were right here . . .

He flipped through her check register. Nothing unusual there . . . Victoria's Secret and places like that. He unfolded her bank statement.

"Holy shit!"

Her balance was $52,647.38. She couldn't make that much as an event planner, could she? Must have inherited a good piece of it . . . a dead grandmother or something.

He pawed deeper into the drawer and came across a box of business cards. He'd seen these before: bright red with *CELEBRATIONS* across the middle in lemon-yellow script and "Events" below in smaller block print. An 800 number beckoned from the lower left corner.

The company she worked for. Okay . . . call her bosses, wake up their asses and ask them where the hell she was. He punched in the number and a woman came on the line.

"Celebrations. How can I help you?"

They had someone answering the phones at this hour. Cool.

"Hi, I'm looking for one of your party planners, Cristin Ott?"

"Cristinott? Is that one name? How do you spell it?"

"Two names." He spelled it for her.

"No, I'm sorry, we have no one by that name."

This couldn't be right.

"Whoa-whoa-whoa! She's one of your event planners. She's worked for you for years."

"I'm sorry, sir. She's not listed. How did you get this number, if I may ask?"

"It's right here on her card."

"A Celebrations card?"

"Yes—bright red with yellow printing."

"That would be it. But the only name printed on those cards is the company's. Did she write her name on the back?"

Jack knew the reverse would be blank but flipped it over anyway.

"No. But I happen to know her personally—know her well. She works for you people."

"I'm afraid you've been misled, sir. No one by that name works for Celebrations—or let me put it this way: That name is not on my list of Celebrations employees."

Jack clenched his teeth against a swelling knot of anger.

"Have you got a supervisor I could speak to?"

"Sorry, no."

"Where are you located? I need to have a talk with someone in charge there."

"I'm the only one here and I've told you all I know."

"I just need your address."

"Sir, this is an answering service."

Jack bit his upper lip. Should have guessed that. He took a breath, gathered himself.

"Okay, fine. Just tell me where Celebrations has its office and I'll check directly with them."

"I don't have that information available. And even if I did, I'm sure it would be against our rules to give it out."

Jack pulled the receiver from his ear but stopped himself from smashing it against the wall.

Not my phone.

Try another tack.

"Please. She's missing and I'm worried ab—"

"I'm sorry, sir. I can't help you and I have other calls. Good night."

The line went dead.

With deliberate slowness and exaggerated gentleness, Jack replaced the receiver on its cradle as the woman's words came back to him.

I'm afraid you've been misled, sir. No one by that name works for Celebrations . . .

What the hell?

FRIDAY

1

"You stayed there all night?" Abe said around a huge bite of a bialy.

"Till the dawn's early light."

Jack knew better than to show up twice in a row without an offering of consumables, so he'd brought Abe half a dozen bialys, still hot from the oven of a kosher bakery down the street. He nibbled at his own, not really hungry.

"And she never showed?"

"I stayed up calling every hospital in the five boroughs and asking to be connected to Cristin Ott's room. When I struck out on that I'd ask the operator to switch me to the emergency room. Then I'd tell the emergency room that my sister, Cristin Ott, had been taken away in an ambulance but I didn't know where to. Was she there? And between hospitals I'd call her cellular."

"Maybe she slept over at a friend's."

"That's what I'm hoping. But she'd still answer her cell phone, don't you think?"

"Maybe she turned it off."

"I wouldn't be doing any of this if she'd only called Le Pistou to cancel our lunch—"

"Oy. You'd eat at a place called 'Le Pistou'? Where is it? Next to Le Chazzerai?"

"Abe, I'm worried. This isn't like her."

"Sorry. I see that you are. But what do you know of her already? Sure, you saw her every Sunday for two years, but now the place where she said she worked has never heard of her."

"That's what I don't get. That's what scares me."

"She was a party planner, you say?"

"She preferred 'event planner.'"

"Whatever. Never in those years did she invite you to one of her events?"

"No."

"Not even to sneak you in?"

"No."

"And you never wondered why?"

"To tell you the truth: no. Probably because I never *wanted* her to sneak me in. I'm not a party person, and the last place I want to be is stuck in a room with a bunch of people I don't know, especially if they're corporate types, or account execs, or deputy mayors, or state assemblymen. She organized private parties, not open to the public. Sneaking me in—even if I wanted in—would jeopardize her job, and that was something I did *not* want to do."

"So maybe she just had second thoughts. She didn't want to start up with you again."

"Maybe. But I know her, Abe. She's an up-front type. She would have called."

"Then you need to find this Celebrations place."

"Don't think I haven't tried. I went to the library and scoured all the phone books—went out as far as Suffolk County. No dice."

Abe's expression turned dubious. "In all five boroughs and Nassau and Suffolk there's no place called Celebrations?"

"Oh, sure. About a dozen. But they sell party hats and helium balloons. And they don't have eight hundred numbers."

"So give me this eight hundred number."

"No use calling. It's just an answering service. I called back three times last night and got, as you like to say, bupkis." A thought hit him. "Maybe I should try again this morning. Probably hit a different shift and might get a more cooperative operator."

"You shouldn't count on it, so don't do it. Like I said, give me this eight hundred number and I'll find out the address."

"Of Celebrations?"

"No, the answering service. Then you can go there and work your magic."

"If I could do magic I could find Cristin. But you can do that—find the address?"

Abe gave one of his shrugs. "In my business I shouldn't want to know who's calling? And who I'm calling back?"

"Yeah, I guess you would."

"Of course I would. I have a guy who can back-check numbers. Not out of the goodness of his heart does he do this, so you'll have to pay."

"Whatever he wants."

"Good. I'll have it for you later. Be somewhere I can call you."

"If I'm not home I'll be at Julio's."

Abe had both numbers.

He'd call Cristin's place when he got home, and keep calling till he'd heard from Abe. And then he'd have a heart-to-heart with someone at Celebrations' answering service.

2

Kadir was waiting by the Space Station's front gate with Yousef and Salameh when a City Chemical truck arrived.

"Got a delivery for unit forty-three-forty-four."

"That is us," Kadir said, and punched in the code that would unlock the gate.

They directed the truck to the center building and spent the next hour watching him unload the chemicals and store them in locker 4344 on the second floor. The driver asked them a number of times what they were going to do with all this stuff. Each time Kadir put him off by saying, "Manufacturing."

And that was true, in a way: They were manufacturing the downfall of the driver's country.

When everything was off-loaded and the driver gone, they found a dolly and brought containers of urea and nitric acid down to Salameh's Nova and filled the trunk. After locking the unit, they drove over to JFK Boulevard and took it south into the Greenville section of Jersey City—so far south they were almost in Bayonne. There, following Ayyad's directions, they found Pamrapo Avenue.

Pamrapo was only a couple of blocks long but they missed the address on the first pass. The converted garage was not visible from the street. The driveway was little more than two ruts through winter-blighted weeds curving around the rusting remains of junked cars.

Ayyad must have heard them coming because he stepped out the porchless front door as they arrived. He didn't offer to help them as they unloaded the chemicals.

Kadir and Salameh struggled with the heavy container of urea, maneuvering it through the door and into the unfurnished front room within. Yousef waited inside.

"This is where we will do most of the mixing," he said in Arabic. He pointed to the ceiling. "And by the way, we have an American neighbor upstairs—lives there with his dog. This is a thick-walled building, so it is unlikely he can hear anything, but just to be safe, we say nothing in English while we are here."

Kadir nodded as he looked around the empty room. "You said we'll be mixing here. In what?"

"That is your next assignment. We'll need metal drums—the fifty-five-gallon size are easy to find and will work best."

"I know where we can get some," Salameh said.

"Good. Bring three. Oh, and pick up as many old newspapers as you can find."

"Newspapers?" Salameh said. "Why?"

"I'll explain later. Now get moving. The sooner you get them, the sooner we begin."

Kadir tugged on Salameh's arm. "Let's go. We're wasting time."

He couldn't wait to get started.

3

Abe had phoned and said the 800 number went to an answering service company located on Ninth Avenue in Hell's Kitchen. When Jack arrived at the address he found himself peering through the window of an XXX peep-show and porn shop.

Crap. What was going on?

He backed up and took a look at the converted five-story tenement. A sign in the second-floor window said ANSWER MANAGEMENT in red block letters.

Okay. Got it.

The narrow door to the right of the store had been painted and repainted so many times that the trim had lost all its detail. A short row of black buttons was inset to the right. He pressed the one labeled *ANSWER MANAGEMENT* and waited to be buzzed in. Instead a woman's tinny voice screeched from the speaker.

"Who is it?"

He should have anticipated this. When you worked above a porn shop, you didn't simply buzz in everyone who rang. He used the name on his ID.

"My name's Jeff Cusic. I'm here to apply for a job."

"We're not hiring."

"Is it because I'm a guy?"

"No, because we're not hiring."

"Do you have any males answering your phones?"

"None of your business."

"Well, if you don't, that's sexual discrimination. Look, I'm not trying to cause trouble. Just let me fill out an application for when you do hire."

"Or what?"

"Or I pay a visit to the city Commission on Human Rights and file a complaint."

The speaker went silent for a while and Jack wondered if maybe she'd hung up, but then her voice returned.

"Stand back and let me see what you look like."

"What does that—?"

"If you look like trouble, you're not getting in."

He stepped back from the door and spread his arms as he looked up. He couldn't see anyone in the window.

"Okay?"

The door buzzed. He leaped to it and pushed his way inside. The woman who met him at the top of the stairs had a face only Anne Ramsey's mother could love.

"Are you for real?" she said.

He held up his hands, showing his empty palms. "I come in peace. I just want to fill out an application."

"Why bother me?"

"I'm trying all the answering services. My day job doesn't pay enough, so I need a night job."

"What's your day job?"

"I move furniture. I need something off my feet at night."

Her expression looked even sourer as she shook her head. "You mean a job you can sleep through."

"Just let me apply."

With a sigh she motioned him into her small office. "We don't have a form. I'll give you an index card and you can leave your name and number."

"Fair enough."

As he was filling it out with his phony name and a made-up number, he checked out the three-drawer filing cabinet against the wall. The top drawer was labeled *A-J.* Clients?

When he finished the card he said, "Can I peek at the working conditions?"

With an exasperated look she walked to a door at the other end of the office. Jack caught a glimpse of a number of women sitting in little booths talking into headsets before he stepped to the filing cabinet and pulled open the top drawer.

"Hey!" the woman said. "What do you think you're doing?"

As she came toward him Jack found the C's and flipped through the folders. The third was labeled *Celebrations.* He pulled it open as the boss lady arrived and tried to close the drawer on his hands.

"Get away from there!"

He backed away, but not before spotting the billing address, and a name: Rebecca J. Olesen.

"Just curious."

Her face was red with fury as she reached for her phone. "I'm calling the police!"

"No need," he said, hurrying for the door.

He hit the stairs running and burst out onto Ninth Avenue where he quick-walked down toward 42nd Street. He headed east, stopping along the way to buy a large, padded manila envelope. When he reached Grand Central Station, he turned downtown for three blocks to East 39th.

Murray Hill. A high-rent neighborhood and home to a host of foreign diplomats connected to the UN. The number in the folder turned out to be an old brownstone renovated into office space.

He took the two steps down to the entrance. A world of difference from Ninth Avenue. The door was thick, unsmudged glass. As he'd suspected when he'd seen the address, a security camera was mounted on the ceiling and pointed right at him. He checked the call buttons, set in polished brass. The third one down was labeled *CELEBRATIONS*. He pressed it.

Eventually a woman's voice said, *"Yes?"*

"Package for Celebrations," he said, sounding bored.

Whoever she was she probably had a monitor that let her see who was at the door. She must have been satisfied with his appearance because she buzzed him in.

As he entered the vestibule, a woman stepped through a door at the end of the hall and approached him. She had ash-blond hair, wore a business pant-suit, and looked to be in her late forties. Jack found her fairly attractive for a woman twice his age. She held out her hand as she neared.

"Celebrations?" he said.

She nodded. "Do you need me to sign?"

"No," he said as he handed her the unsealed, unaddressed envelope. "I need you to tell me if you've heard from Cristin Ott."

"Who?" Did she flinch at the name? He couldn't be sure.

"Cristin. Ott." He pronounced the name carefully. "She didn't come home last night."

"I'm sorry. I've never heard of her."

The concern in her eyes said otherwise. But concern for whom? Herself or Cristin?

"I'm pretty sure you have, Rebecca Olesen."

"I don't know how you know my name but I'm very sure I have not heard of hers."

"She says—has said for years—that she works for Celebrations. Is there someone higher up the chain I can speak to?"

"I'm it, I'm afraid. *I'm* Celebrations. And I don't know your Cristin Ott." She pulled a cellular phone from her jacket pocket. "And if you don't leave right now I'm going to call the police."

The same threat, twice in an hour. For an instant Jack considered grabbing the phone and threatening to flatten her nose with it if she didn't tell him. Because she knew—even if she didn't know Cristin personally, she knew the name.

Instead, he said, "You won't help me find her? I've got a bad feeling about her."

There. A flinch. No question about it. "I wish I could help you, I really do, but I simply don't know her. Now please leave."

Jack decided this was neither the time nor place to press the issue. He'd watch her, and when the time was right . . .

Without a word he turned and walked away.

4

Mir Aimal Kasi followed Dolley Madison Boulevard on his way back from a delivery in Arlington. He had no idea who Dolley Madison was, and it wasn't the fastest route back to Reston where his courier service was based, but it took him past a certain driveway in a section of McLean called Langley. He passed whenever he could. The trees along the road hid the headquarters of the hated CIA, the eyes and ears of the Great Satan where the ruination of Islam was plotted.

The road was nearly empty now, but in a few hours the plotters would stream out onto the highway, heading for their homes. And every weekday morning the eastbound cars backed up at the traffic light that controlled their left turn into the headquarters.

He could strike a blow for Islam then.

He imagined lobbing hand grenades between the twin rows of waiting cars as he drove by, shrapnel piercing gas tanks and igniting them, secondary detonations causing more explosions. And amid the fiery thunder the screaming cries of infidels as they burned alive.

A pleasant fantasy.

But where could he get hand grenades? He had the whole weekend to seek some out.

5

"Good," said Yousef as he positioned the three fifty-five-gallon drums around the front room. "These are perfect."

Kadir wished he'd help them carry the second load of urea and nitric acid in from the car, but he seemed to think he was above that. Ayyad had gone back to his job.

When the car was empty, and Kadir and Salameh were gathered in the room, Yousef said, "We have enough here now to get started with the first batch. You two will mix nitric acid into the urea crystals until it forms a gel. When that happens I'll show you how to add strips of newspaper to thicken it into a paste."

"What will you be doing?" Kadir said.

"I will be mixing the nitroglycerin in the kitchen. That's a more delicate job."

Kadir had heard of nitroglycerin but knew little of it beyond that it had to be handled with care.

"Isn't that dangerous?"

"Very. That's why I'll be in a different room where it won't be jostled. We'll store it in the freezer for safekeeping."

Kadir still didn't like it. He pointed to the barrels of urea and bottles of nitric acid lining the floor against the wall. They'd only scratched the surface of what was stored back at the Space Station locker.

"Do we need two explosives? We'll have over half a ton of the urea mix."

Yousef's voice took on a lecturing tone. "I have made this kind of bomb before. It will consist of four explosions." He held up a finger. "The first will be blasting caps set off by standard fuses." Another finger came up. "The blasting caps will set off containers of my nitroglycerin." A third finger rose. "The nitroglycerin will set off your urea nitrate paste, which will do the bulk of the damage." The fourth finger jutted up. "The nitrate will then rupture the hydrogen tanks."

"Hydrogen?" Salameh said.

"We use it all the time back home," Yousef said. "It creates an extra explosion and a huge fireball."

"But we have no hydrogen."

Yousef smiled. "We will when the time comes."

He ducked back into the kitchen and returned with two sets of swimming goggles and an oblong cardboard box. From that he withdrew small paper surgical masks to cover their mouths and noses.

"You are going to need these."

Kadir took a mask and a set of goggles. "Why?"

"Fumes," Yousef said. "The fumes are not pleasant. And be careful with the nitric acid," he added. "It is highly concentrated and if it splashes on you it will make a hole through your clothes and burn your skin."

Kadir was no longer so eager to start the process.

6

Rebecca Olesen stepped out of the brownstone and onto East 39th Street at a little past eight. Jack had thought she'd never leave—had started to fear he'd missed her during one of his infrequent food and bathroom breaks. He'd spent most of the time freezing his butt off at a NYNEX kiosk on the corner of Lexington, pouring coins into the phone as he repeatedly called Cristin's home and cellular phones.

He'd even called New Jersey information for her parents' number in Tabernacle. He told her mother that he was a friend from FIT who was trying to get in touch with her about an assignment. Nope. Cristin wasn't there. Hadn't heard from her since Monday but that wasn't unusual since she rarely called in more than once a week.

And all the while, no sign of Rebecca Olesen. He was beginning to wonder if she lived in her office when she finally appeared.

She turned and began walking away from him toward Park Avenue. Event planners worked late, he guessed as he followed in the dark. Not many pedestrians at this hour in this kind of cold, so he hung back, staying on the downtown side of the street while she held to the uptown.

He didn't have a plan yet, at least not beyond learning all he could about this woman. He knew where she worked. Now he'd learn where she lived. With those two established, he could track her movements and start looking for ways to pry into her life. While she was at work he could find a way into her home; and while she was home he'd find a way into her office. Somewhere in those two places he'd find her bank statements and phone bills and what he wanted most of all: her address book. Wouldn't it be something to check under "O" and find, *Ott, Cristin?*

But that would only confirm what he already sensed in his gut: Rebecca Olesen knew Cristin. Maybe she didn't know where she was, but she knew her name. Which led to a big ugly question: If she knew of Cristin, why the hell wouldn't she admit it? Why lie?

Unless she was involved in something illegal.

Jack stopped walking.

Crap. That hadn't occurred to him.

He started moving again.

He couldn't see it. Cristin was kinky as all hell in bed, but otherwise pretty much a straight shooter. Never once had he seen her light up a joint or snort a line. In their two years of Sundays she'd never appeared high on anything, never even mentioned drugs. Nothing stronger than tequila—she did love her Cuervo Gold.

But that didn't mean people wouldn't bring drugs to one of her parties. He was pretty sure a bigwig party being busted for drugs would have made the news, though.

He saw Rebecca Olesen turn uptown on Park. He hurried to the corner to see if she grabbed a cab. But no, she kept walking . . .

. . . straight into Grand Central Terminal.

Aw, hell. She was a commuter. Now things were going to get dicey. Because Jack had never commuted anywhere.

He followed her through the faded glory of the historic station, thinking this place could do with a good scrubbing as he wove his way through the panhandlers to the Metro North lines.

Jack didn't know where the trains went, how many lines they ran, didn't even know how the ticketing worked.

Well, he was going to have to learn, and learn fast.

SATURDAY

1

"You followed her all the way into Westchester County," Abe said, "and all you got was a license plate number?"

"You sound like a T-shirt slogan."

Jack had bird-dogged Rebecca Olesen onto a Metro North train on the Harlem Line where he bought a ticket to the last stop from the conductor. Turned out he didn't need all that distance—she got off at Pleasantville. Jack had followed her down to the parking lot, only to be left standing after she got into a Lexus SUV and took off. No taxis were waiting around the station to help him follow her, so he memorized her plate number and found a phone booth on the platform. No Olesen, Rebecca or otherwise, was listed in the county phone book. Silently cursing fate and anything else he could think of, he'd boarded the next train back to the city.

Jack added, "But at least it's something. You can find out who it's registered to, right?"

Abe shook his head as he smeared cream cheese on the bottom half of a poppy seed bagel. The tiny black seeds rained on the morning's *Post*, spread open on the counter. Jack had splurged on lox and bagels this morning as thanks for tracking the answering service number and in anticipation of tracking the license plate.

"In the DMV I've got no connection. Maybe Ernie you should try."

That was a thought. Ernie specialized in fake driver licenses. He had to have contacts in the DMV.

"Good. Of course with the way my luck's been running on this, the car will turn out to be leased to Celebrations under her office address."

"Sounds like a good prediction."

Abe began to smear cream cheese on the top half, causing a virtual monsoon of poppy seeds. As Jack watched them bounce across the paper he saw the front-page headline.

"What's this?"

Abe pushed it toward him with his knife hand. "A newspaper. You should read one sometime."

"No . . . really. What's this about?"

He pointed to the front page image—the outline of the upper half of a female body. Printed within it were the words:

WHO

IS

THE

DITMARS

DAHLIA?

Abe began laying slices of lox on the bottom half of his bagel.

"Where have you been hiding? It's all anyone's talking about."

Jack had had little sleep Thursday night and had been running around all yesterday. After getting back from Grand Central, he'd conked out without bothering to turn on the TV. He'd arisen with Ms. Olesen's license plate number running through his brain and had headed for Abe's.

"Well, then, I guess we should be talking about it too. Since I've been a little preoccupied of late, how's about you give me a quick rundown?"

"Quick is all I can give because they know nothing: The body of a young woman was found floating in the East River last night. No hands, face burned by acid. They're calling her 'the Ditmars Dahlia.'"

"Ditmars . . ." Jack said. "That's a street in Astoria, right?"

Abe nodded. "Actually, the whole upper corner of Astoria is known as Ditmars. They pulled her out of Bowery Bay, which is right off Ditmars. Thus the name."

"Okay, I get the Ditmars, but why the 'Dahlia'?"

Abe put the top on his bagel-and-lox sandwich and took a huge bite. After a convulsive swallow, he said, "Someone on the paper wants to boost circulation with a 'Black Dahlia' reference. You've heard of the Black Dahlia murder, haven't you?"

"I think I saw a book with that title—"

"Book, shmook. It was a real-life murder in Los Angeles, but she was mutilated even worse—cut in half at the waist, her face and body slashed. Since this girl is going to be hard to identify, the paper is taking advantage."

"Swell." Jack shook his head and opened the paper to the story.

"You're not having?" Abe said, waving his bagel.

"In a minute."

The guy who found her had been walking his dog along the shore and the *Post* had caught up with him.

"She was facedown and naked and at first I thought it was, like, one of those window mannequins. I mean, because she had no hands, you know? And then I notice the stumps and I know that ain't no mannequin."

The guy had run to the nearest house and had them call the police.

"I didn't know about her face until the cops pulled her out and put her on a stretcher. All burned and eaten away, even the eyes. She was stabbed all over her front—all these little holes in her."

Jack straightened up from the paper. "Okay, I've officially lost my appetite."

Abe was nodding and chewing. His appetite seemed unaffected. But then, nothing affected Abe's appetite.

"Gruesome," he said around another huge bite. "Obviously someone doesn't want her identified."

Jack was about to close it when one final quote froze him.

"But the weirdest thing was the cut I noticed when I first found her: a nice neat rectangle of skin sliced from the back of her neck."

"Oh, no." Jack leaned on the counter for support as all his blood seemed to drain away. "Oh-no-no-no-no!"

"What?"

"Th-this thing about the skin cut from the back of her neck. Cristin had a tattoo back there. Her *ama-gi*."

"What this ama-gi already?"

"A Sumerian symbol. Very distinctive. A sure giveaway it was her."

Abe put down his bagel, his expression stricken. "You don't think it's your missing girl, do you?"

"I don't want her to be—you've no idea how I don't want that. But what else can I think? Christ, Abe, I've *got* to see that body."

"Really?"

"I mean, I don't *want* to see it—Christ, no—but I *need* to. I need to know if it's Cristin and I can't wait days till the cops figure it out—if they ever figure it out."

"But her face is gone. How will you know if it's—"

"I'll know. If I can just get in the same room as that body I'll know. Gotta be a way . . ."

His gut crawled at the prospect but he had to see her.

Abe pulled a Rolodex out from under the counter. "I know a guy . . ."

2

Hadya stepped out of the Ramallah Bakery for a breath of fresh air—*cold* fresh air. As her English improved, her uncle Ferran had begun letting her work the counter now and again. With Ramadan beginning in just a few days, the counter was busy so she'd been working there since the shop opened. The heat from the ovens in back and the press of customers in front made for a stifling atmosphere.

Ramadan . . . a month of daily fasting, no food or drink from sunrise to sunset. Hadya enjoyed the self-discipline it required, though sometimes she felt weak and light-headed toward the end of the day. The bakery was especially busy because of it.

Uncle Ferran would be angry if she took too long a break, but she needed a moment to herself. As she stood watching the traffic, she saw a familiar face in the passenger seat of a passing car. Her brother Kadir in a battered green car, in animated conversation with the driver as they headed down Kennedy Boulevard. She wondered where they were going. Coming from visiting their hate-filled leader in the Al-Salam Mosque, perhaps?

All his talk years ago about bringing jihad to America and so far nothing. Good. She hoped things could remain that way. But she did not trust him. And who was his new friend?

She returned to the crowded bakery, wondering what they had been discussing so intently.

3

The East Side had no subways to speak of, at least none east of Lexington, so Jack took a cab down to Bellevue Hospital at First Avenue and East 30th Street. The hospital housed the city morgue. The Ditmars Dahlia was in the city morgue.

Abe had called his "guy" in the morgue. While they were waiting for a call back, Jack had phoned Ernie and given him Rebecca Olesen's plate number. Ernie was happy to do it for a reasonable fee but said it would take him a while. Jack left him his apartment number and told him to leave the address on the answering machine.

Abe's "guy" was named Ron Clarkson and for another reasonable fee—larger than Ernie's—he'd agreed to meet Jack at noon and arrange a look at the Ditmars Dahlia.

Clarkson turned out to be a thin guy with long light hair and a matching goatee. He was waiting, as promised, by the bank of phones in the hospital lobby, dressed in scrubs and smoking a cigarette.

"You Abe's friend?"

Jack nodded. "How do we do this?"

"Follow me."

He led Jack to the elevator bank and tapped down. They stepped into an empty car and Clarkson hit the bottom button.

"Got something for me?" he said.

Jack pulled an envelope from his jacket and handed it over. He felt he should say something but his mind was blank except for the fervent hope that he'd just wasted his money because this wasn't Cristin. He *prayed* he was wasting that money.

"Since Abe sent you," Clarkson said as he tucked the envelope into the pocket of his scrubs, "I'm assuming that you ain't no perv who gets off looking at naked dead women."

That didn't deserve an answer so Jack just gave him a look.

"Okay. I'm just warning you, this one's a little rough on the eyes. She may have been a looker once, but she's been messed up. Especially her face. And she was in the water awhile—not long enough to do any real damage, but it does cause changes."

Jack's already churning stomach gave a slight lurch.

"Why are you telling me all this?"

"Because you can't go all pussy on me and blow lunch or start screaming and crying or pass out or any of that shit. It happens all the time with people who come here to identify a corpse, but that's okay because they're supposed to be here. You, on the other hand, ain't. The cops are holding back things about her so—"

"Why?"

"Front page murder like this brings all the kooks out of their little cracks and crevices. I mean they're like cockroaches, man. Five'll get you ten homicide's had a couple dozen confessions already. Keeping stuff secret helps the cops weed out the cranks with just a question or two. So *no one* is supposed to see her unless they might be family, and they'll be heavily screened before they're allowed down here."

"I guess I should feel privileged." Jack hoped Clarkson had an ear for sarcasm.

"Damn right you should. So you gotta stay calm and quiet or my ass is grass and so is yours."

"Got it," he said with more confidence than he felt. This was all new to him.

The elevator doors opened on the basement level.

"Welcome to the city morgue."

They stepped out into a fluorescent-lit hallway. Clarkson led him to a doorway marked MEN and pushed it open.

"It gets quiet here at lunch hour but we've still got to make you look like you belong. Locker seventy-seven has a set of scrubs in it. Change into them real quick-like and I'll meet you inside in about two minutes."

Jack found the locker and was dressed in the scrubs when Clarkson returned. He led them out another door to a gurney-lined hallway. Some were empty, some were occupied by black plastic body bags. Then through a set of double swinging doors to a small room with a battered metal desk littered with papers and clipboards, a half-filled Styrofoam coffee cup, and the *Daily News* opened to the sports pages.

Another set of double doors admitted them to a chilled, white-tiled room lined with drawers stacked three high. Jack noticed a drain in the center of the concrete floor.

"Okay, no dillydallying," Clarkson said, leading the way. "We don't have a whole lot of time. She's in row twelve, middle drawer."

He stopped before a row, grabbed the handle on the middle drawer and pulled. Wheels squeaked as the drawer rolled out, revealing another black body bag. The head bulge was near the front of the drawer.

"Ready?" Clarkson said as he grasped the zipper pull.

Speech was impossible with his tongue stuck to the top of his mouth, so Jack simply nodded.

"Just remember what I said about being cool."

Jack clenched his fists, digging his fingernails into his palms as the zipper slid down. Clarkson pushed back the sides, revealing what was left of a woman's face.

Jack found his voice but could barely hear himself. "Christ!"

Her eyes, her nose, and most of her facial skin, including her lips, had been burned and disfigured with acid, leaving her unrecognizable. But her hair . . . her matted hair was Cristin's color, and her ears were like Cristin's, but Jack couldn't be sure. Why hadn't he paid more attention to her ears?

"More," he croaked. "Zip it down."

Clarkson complied, revealing a stitched-up Y incision running from her collarbone, above her breasts, joining at the sternum, and running straight down to her pelvis. Her skin seemed to be punctured everywhere. Especially her knees. He took only a quick glance at her ragged wrist stumps.

"The ME posted her first thing this morning," Clarkson said.

Even distorted by death and water immersion and multiple punctures,

Jack knew those breasts. He knew that black patch of neatly trimmed pubic hair. He felt a sob building in his chest, working its way to his throat.

"Turn her over," he managed to say around it.

"You okay?"

Jack made a frantic turning motion with his hand.

Clarkson said, "You're gonna have to help me."

Jack didn't want to touch her. He wanted to remember what she felt like when warm and alive. Not like this. But he forced himself.

Her flesh was hard and cold as they gently rolled her onto her side. Jack lifted the back of her hair to reveal the rectangle of raw flesh where the skin had been removed.

No question . . . exactly the size of her ama-gi.

Finally the sob escaped. Just one.

"Be cool. Be cool."

Jack could only nod.

How could this lifeless lump be Cristin, the woman he'd pleasured and who'd pleasured him every Sunday for two years? Cristin with the easy smile, the giggly laugh, the potty mouth.

"I'm guessing she had a pretty distinctive tattoo there because whoever did this took facial recognition and fingerprints off the table as far as identifying her, and so they took that as well. The other guy wanted to see her neck too."

Jack's head snapped up. "Wait. You brought another guy here? What other guy?"

"Oh, I didn't bring him. He came officially. Some foreigner, I think. Said one of his secretaries was missing, was worried this might be her. After looking he said he'd never seen her before, but he was lying."

"How do you know?"

"Because he asked for a look at the back of her neck too. I caught his reaction when he saw that missing skin. He knew her. Just like you know her."

"What kind of foreigner?"

"He was from the British embassy or something, I think. Sounded a little like that first James Bond guy."

"Sean Connery?"

"That's the one. Same accent, only more so."

"A Scot?"

"If you say so. Called me 'laddie.'"

Jack looked down at Cristin again. None of those stab wounds on her back.

"Seen enough?" Clarkson said.

Jack was about to say yes when he noticed something on her right buttock. It looked like letters had been scratched into the skin there.

"What's this?"

"The ME says it was done with a fingernail. He thinks she scratched it there while she was being tortured. But he can't say for sure since we don't have her fingers."

Jack leaned closer. The letters were difficult to identify in her pale, dead flesh, but he could swear they formed the word *DAMATO*.

"Does that say . . . ?"

"Yeah. Same as the senator, only without the little thingamajig."

"Apostrophe."

"Yeah. The cops were very interested in that."

Senator Alfonse D'Amato was in the papers enough so that even Jack, despite his aversion to political news, knew who he was. Especially after the all-night filibuster he'd conducted last fall. Earned lots of ink with that.

"They can't really think . . ."

"The ME says she worked hard to scratch that into her skin. Must mean something. Help me flip her back. We've been here too long already."

Jack helped return her to her original position and was again taken by the number of wounds on her front side. Bile rose as he realized she must have suffered the tortures of the damned before she died.

"What . . . what did they use on her?"

"That's one of the things the cops are holding back. The ME thinks the killer tied her to a post somewhere and tortured her by using her for target practice. Those cuts are from arrows."

Arrows? Jack flashed back to a house on the Outer Banks where a couple of guys threatened to kill Tony if Jack didn't drive a truck north for them. One of them brought out a bow and arrows and was readying to put a shaft through Tony's heart when Jack agreed.

Reggie . . .

Everything went dark for a few seconds. When his vision cleared he took one last look at that ruined face, then zipped the bag closed to the top.

"How . . ." His throat felt thick. "How did she finally die?"

"Arrow through the heart."

A quick end after what had probably seemed an eternity of agony.

Why would anyone torture and kill Cristin like that? Had someone made a pass and she turned him down? What? What? *What?*

Reggie . . . if indeed it *was* Reggie . . . why? He was a sociopath and a killer—he'd been ready to sink a truck full of little girls in the water off Staten Island—but was he this sick? He was connected to the Arab slave brokers. Was this connected to them?

"What kind of sick fuck does this?"

Sliding the drawer closed with a bang, Clarkson said, "The ME thinks it was some sort of interrogation because the only part of her body left completely undamaged was her mouth. That says whoever did this wanted her able to talk."

"The acid?"

"Done postmortem. Same with the hand amputations."

Thank God for small favors.

"Whoever it was must have learned what he wanted then."

What could Cristin know that would lead someone to do this to her?

"I guess so. Just what he did to her knees alone would have been enough to make anyone talk."

Jack had noticed how they'd seemed especially chewed up.

"What did he do?"

"Looked like he kept shooting arrows into them, on either side of the patella, twisting them around, then ripping them out and shooting again."

Jack shuddered as he tried to imagine what it would feel like to have just one arrow in his knee joint.

"Come on," Clarkson said, heading toward the doors. "People will be getting back from lunch soon. You've gotta be gone."

"What about . . . rape?" Jack said as he followed.

"You really want to know?"

"No, but I need to."

"Front and back, if you know what I mean."

Jack knew.

The darkness was expanding again.

Clarkson waited for him in the locker room while he changed back into his own clothes. In a daze, Jack followed him to the elevators and soon he was back in the Bellevue lobby. He walked outside and headed up First Avenue. At the first phone booth he found he dropped a few coins and convinced the operator to connect him to the Astoria precinct. He didn't know the number.

"I know the name of the Ditmars Dahlia," he said when they put him through to homicide. "She's Cristin Ott. O-t-t. She's from Tabernacle, New Jersey."

Then he hung up. He didn't want Cristin in that drawer any longer than she had to be. He'd never met her parents but they deserved to know she was dead. They didn't deserve the details. He hoped someone spared them those.

Cold, numb, he flagged a taxi and took it back uptown. Half-formed questions swirled through his head as the cab cruised up First Avenue, passing the UN along the way. Celebrations . . . Rebecca Olesen . . . a guy with a Sean Connery accent . . . arrows . . .

Reggie? How on Earth could he connect to Cristin? But if by some stretch it had been Reggie, then Arabs too? What could the Arabs possibly have against poor Cristin? What could they think she knew?

Finally his apartment. Home. No message from Ernie on the machine. He took a beer from the fridge and brought it to the round oak table he'd refinished when he first moved in. He didn't open the bottle. Instead he sat and sobbed.

4

Hadya was walking home from the bakery along Virginia Avenue when she spotted the old green car again. She was standing on the corner of Mallory—she lived three houses in on the other side—when it passed. Again, Kadir was in the front passenger seat next to the same stranger. But this time they were headed south on Mallory and Kadir wasn't talking. He kept looking over his shoulder, almost as if he was worried about being followed.

Then she noticed the large canisters in the backseat. Was he looking at them? Why would he be concerned about them?

Unless they contained something dangerous.

Oh, no. Oh, Kadir, please don't be planning something crazy.

She began to hurry along the sidewalk, trying to keep the car in sight, to see where it was going. It didn't turn off but remained on Mallory until it was lost from sight.

Hadya balled her fists in frustration. If only she could follow. But she didn't have a car—didn't even know anyone who had one except Uncle Ferran, and he'd never lend it to her. She didn't have a driver's license.

But she *would* find a way to follow her brother. And if she discovered that he was cooking up terror, she would find a way to stop him.

5

Jack had taken a shower—he'd felt a need to wash off the morgue—and was about to head out to Julio's when the phone rang. He grabbed it before the answering machine could pick up.

"Ernie?"

"Yeah," said the nasal voice. "Hey, how'd you know it was me?"

"Lucky guess."

Truth was, nobody ever called him. Except maybe Cristin back when—oh, jeez, Cristin. Cristin would never call anybody again.

"It took some doing, but I tracked that plate for you."

"W-what?"

"Something wrong with the connection? You're voice sounds funny."

He cleared his throat. "Sorry. What've you got?"

"It's registered to Celebrations."

"Shit."

"What's wrong?"

"I was afraid of that. An East Thirty-ninth Street address?"

"You got it. What were you looking for instead?"

"Someplace in Westchester."

"Sorry. Manhattan only. I didn't know you was into that sorta thing."

"What sorta thing?"

"Call girls."

Jack nearly dropped the receiver. "What? Did I hear you right? Did you just say call girls?"

"Told you it was a bad connection. Yeah. Escorts, whatever. High-end stuff."

Jack eased himself into the nearest chair. Cristin . . . a call girl?

"No way."

"You sound surprised."

"I'm . . . I'm shocked."

"You didn't know?"

"How am I supposed to know something like that?"

"Well, I know you know Abe, and from our transactions I figure you've got at least one foot in the Life."

Jack guessed Ernie was naturally oblique about his business, and it took a second to translate. By "transactions" he obviously meant Jack's purchase of phony IDs, and by "the Life" he meant the wrong side of the law.

"And so you're saying people in the Life tend to know other people in the Life?"

"Or have transactions with them."

"You've had transactions with Celebrations?"

"I've had referrals."

"So this 'escort' thing isn't just rumor."

"Nope. Word is Becky treats her girls right, that's why she has the best."

Rebecca Olesen . . . somehow Jack didn't see her as a Becky, but . . .

"Thanks, Ernie. I'll stop by with something tomorrow."

"Any time, Jack. Any time."

Jack hung up and sat there, unable to move from the chair.

Cristin . . . a prostitute? How had he missed that? How could he be so clueless?

He straightened in the chair. Had Abe known?

6

"This is where you must park the truck," Nidal Ayyad said.

He had driven Kadir across the Hudson in his Ford Taurus and taken him to the World Trade Center. He entered the basement parking garage of Tower One—the north tower—and wound his way down to the B2 level where he found a space and nosed into it.

"Why here?" Kadir said, looking at the blank concrete wall facing them.

"I have reviewed diagrams and they show that this is the southeast corner of the north tower, where it is closest to the south tower." He pointed through the windshield. "When the explosion blows out this wall and the girders behind it, the tower will tilt toward the weakened point. All it takes is the slightest tilt, no more than a few degrees, to exert enormous leverage on the already damaged beams. They will crumple further, increasing the tilt. Each tower is more than a quarter of a mile high. With a damaged base, the tilt will pass the point of no return at somewhere between three and five degrees. And then the tower can do nothing else but fall. And because the damage occurred at this spot, it will fall to the southeast, directly into its sister tower, bringing her down too."

Kadir suppressed the giggle that bubbled into his throat as he pictured the event: one colossal domino tipping, toppling into another, the two going down in a stupendous, roaring blast of smoke and flame and flying debris. A deafening, mind-numbing disaster.

He had dreamed of this for years. Now it would come true.

"You are sure of this?"

Ayyad had a degree in engineering—but in chemical engineering. How well did he know structural engineering?

"With Allah's guidance, it will happen. We are fashioning a very powerful bomb. The concrete floor of each level of the garage is eleven inches thick. The bomb will blow out levels above and below, but most of its force will be directed against that wall. This tower will fall, I am sure of it. The only thing I cannot predict with the utmost surety is whether it will make enough of a direct hit on the south tower to bring that down too. A little variation this way, a little variation that way in angle of fall and it may only damage it."

Even so. To bring down one tower and damage the other . . . Kadir could be satisfied with that.

Ayyad put the car into reverse.

"Remember this spot. Anywhere near the center of this wall. If there's no empty spot, park behind the cars. If anybody notices and complains, no matter. There will not be enough time for anyone to move it."

Kadir doubted he could forget if he tried.

7

Abe's eyebrows rose almost to where his hairline would have been had it not receded to the top of his head. "I should know about call girls and escorts?"

"I'm not sure if that's a yes or a no."

"That's a no, a *nein*, a *nyet*."

"And you never heard of Celebrations before I mentioned it?"

"No, nein, nyet. Why do you think I would keep it from you?"

"To spare my feelings?"

"Spare, shmare. If you didn't know already, you were going to find out sooner or later. For me, sooner is better. I would have told you."

Jack had no choice but to believe him because Abe had never steered him wrong.

"Why didn't I see it?"

"You were too close maybe?"

"Maybe. But you were right when you questioned why she'd never invited me to one of her 'events.' Now I have the answer: There weren't any. Why didn't I suspect?"

He remembered the day he'd followed her from FIT to her apartment, and hung outside all day until he watched her get into a limo with a well-heeled, middle-aged couple. *A couple.*

Abe said, "Maybe love really is blind."

"Wasn't love."

"What was it then?"

"Like. Very heavy like." He pounded a fist on the counter. "Now I see why she kept our lives so separate—easier to maintain the lies."

"So now to someone else she's lying."

The words struck Jack like a low blow. A lump swelled in his throat.

"Aw, Abe. She won't be lying to anyone. Ever."

Abe stared at him for a long moment. "The Ditmars Dahlia?"

Jack could only nod.

Abe came around the counter and put a hand on Jack's shoulder. "I'm so sorry. That must have been terrible for you."

It took everything Jack had to keep from losing it and bawling like a baby. Anger saved him. Anger at himself. He'd returned from the morgue a ball of grief around a core of rage. But the rage had no target until he'd heard the truth about Celebrations. It leaped at Cristin for lying to him, because he found anger easier. He'd always been more comfortable with anger than grief.

And that anger had numbed the pain of her death . . . but for only so long.

"You would have loved her, Abe," he said when his throat unlocked. "So full of life, enjoying every moment and yet planning for the future. I want to find whoever did this, Abe."

"I will help you."

"And after I find them I want to take a long time killing them."

"That I will leave to you."

8

Jack sat alone at his table in Julio's and sipped a Rock.

Lou and Barney had offered to buy him a beer when he walked in but he'd taken a rain check. If Julio's were *The Muppet Show*, those two would be Statler and Waldorf, and he wasn't in the mood for them. Or anyone, for that matter.

Julio had never met Cristin and so Jack hadn't told him that she was the Ditmars Dahlia. The news hadn't broken yet. Most likely the cops were verifying the tip and bringing in the Otts to take a look at the remains. Poor people. Bad enough to lose a daughter, but to lose her like that, to know what she suffered before she died . . .

"Mind if I join you?"

Jack looked up. Bertel. Just the man he didn't need right now. But he sat down before Jack could answer.

"This isn't a good time, Dane."

"Not a good time for me, either."

Jack wanted to punch him. The guy had no idea.

Bertel slapped the table. "Damn Mohammedans. They're up to no good. I know it just as sure as I know you're sitting there across from me. They're up to something and I can't keep a close enough eye on them to find out and still run my business. Sometimes I have to be down south to oversee things."

"And you want me to spell you. We've been through this."

Last time Bertel was here he'd tried to enlist Jack by saying the guy who'd driven the decoy truck with Reggie was involved.

"Yeah, we have, and I know you don't want to get involved, Jack. I know you don't want to risk exposure. But this is your home, and a man defends his home."

"I just rent here."

"You *live* here, dammit. That makes it your home. There's an old movie called *Ride the High Country* that's—"

"Peckinpah."

"You know it?"

"Sure."

"Well, it's got a line in it about entering your house justified."

"Joel McCrea—'All I want to do is enter my house justified.'"

"Jesus, how many times have you seen that goddamn movie?"

"A few."

Truth was Jack had lost count.

"You understand what that means—the 'justified' part?"

"I can guess."

"It means acting with honor, doing the right thing. It means spending your day in such a way that at the end of it you can go home—enter your house—with your head high, without guilt or regret. Well, this city is your house, and if you can't find it in yourself to defend it when it's threatened, then you can't enter your house justified—you can't walk these streets justified."

Jack stared at him a moment, then, "Speech over?"

"Yeah, I guess so." Bertel leaned back. He looked tired and old, but not defeated. More like disgusted—with Jack, with the whole world.

"What'd they do, freeze you a couple hundred years ago and then thaw you out?"

"You're saying I'm old-fashioned?"

"Old-fashioned? Old-fashioned barely touches it. You're Paleolithic, you're Triassic, completely out of sync with the modern world. A walking, talking anachronism."

"Well, then, so be it. I am what I am. Fuck you all."

Arrows . . . Cristin . . . Reggie . . . Arabs . . . sex slaves . . .

Shit.

The silence lengthened between them until Jack shrugged. "Okay."

"*Okay?* Okay, what?"

"Okay, where is this place and when do we start?"

9

Tommy Ten Thumbs Totaro hung up his phone and leaned back. It had been a short conversation with Aldo. So short that his pre-call hit still burned his nostrils and the back of his throat a bit.

Something had been bugging him. Not just how a bunch of rampaging moulies had fucked up his detailing gig, but the timing of it. Everything goes to hell and practically the next day Tony's got him on the carpet for slacking on the loans. That had a bad smell to it.

What Tony didn't know was that Tommy hadn't been slacking on loans—just Tony's loans. Tommy had been investing his profits in his own shylock game. Tommy had been scared that was what the meeting was about.

But this other thing . . . he'd called around and found that at least a dozen lots had been hit in Brooklyn and Queens that night. A bunch of kids couldn't get around like that unless they had cars, or unless someone was driving them.

So maybe some Harlem type was trying to move in, but so far Tommy hadn't heard a thing about it. And that got him to thinking: What if someone was trying to get him out of the detailing business so he'd pay more attention to someone else's loan business?

Only two guys Tony would go to: Vinny and Aldo. Tommy couldn't talk to Vinny about it, but Aldo . . .

Aldo had said he didn't know nothin' about it, and hadn't heard anything about it except what Tommy had told him.

He didn't know if Aldo was involved or not, but he knew he was lying about how much he knew.

This whole thing stank to hell of Vinny Donuts. He had connections with the dealers in Bed-Stuy, especially after he'd delivered that bunch of Air Jordans back in December.

Time to get out on the streets and do a little research. He couldn't let this slide. If Vinny and Tony were behind this, it required a response—a *big* response.

10

Jack located Rebecca Olesen's Lexus SUV in the Pleasantville train station parking lot, then found a spot for his Corvair with a clear view of it, and waited. Not many cars in the lot on a Saturday night, so he had plenty of parking choices.

As he watched and waited, he thought about Cristin, and about Bertel too. The guy had been confused but delighted by Jack's agreeing to join The Great Mohammedan Watch. Jack didn't tell him why.

The truth was that he had no leads on who killed Cristin, and he had a feeling the police didn't either—besides the *DAMATO* scratched into her skin. He couldn't very well hunt down and brace a U.S. senator. He'd leave that to the cops. For Jack, the arrow wounds pointed to Reggie only because he was the only one Jack knew who was into archery. With the gazillion people owning bows and arrows, the chance that it was Reggie was less than slim. But Jack had no place else to go.

Except to Rebecca Olesen.

Which was why he'd turned down Bertel's offer to treat him to a steak at Ben Benson's and taken the gamble to come here instead. If Celebrations was an escort service, then he assumed Saturday night would be busy, keeping Rebecca in the office until late. And what do you know, the Lexus sat here waiting for her.

All right, how to play this? Jump in and carjack her? No. Too many ways that could go wrong. Best to follow her home, learn where she lived, and ad-lib from there.

A train pulled in from the south, stopped, then moved on. Rebecca Olesen and three males entered the parking lot and fanned out, each to a different car. Jack watched her approach her Lexus, looking like a typical middle-aged, middle-class hausfrau. No way would anyone guess she ran a call girl service. Meet the new Mayflower Madame.

He followed her on a twisty-turny path into a *Leave It to Beaver* middle-class neighborhood where she pulled into the driveway of a white, two-story colonial. The garage door was sliding up as Jack cruised past.

He parked Ralph near a hedgerow between two houses a couple of lots down. A black van was parked across the street, so he guessed they didn't have an ordinance against street parking. He pulled his Glock from the holster under the front seat and stuck it in his jacket pocket. He had no intention of pulling the trigger but it might come in handy for intimidation. He hopped out, eased the Corvair's door shut, and trotted back to her yard. Good thing the weather was staying cold. Not likely anyone was going to be out for a stroll.

He made directly for the side of the house, ready to turn and bolt if any motion-sensitive floodlights came on. But the yard remained dark. Praying she had no dog, he began peeking in the lit windows, looking for kids, a husband, a live-in maid.

The first window looked in on a dark room. Light from the hall limned a desk, a computer, a printer—some kind of home office. He pushed up on the window but it wouldn't budge. Locked.

The next were paired and looked in on a large kitchen where he spotted her opening a bottle of white wine. That was encouraging. If a husband or boyfriend was about, wouldn't he be doing that for her? He saw the keypad for an alarm system on the door to the garage. The indicator light glowed green. Looked like she'd turned it off upon coming in but hadn't turned it back on.

Keeping to the deep shadows at the very rear of the backyard, he moved around to the garage side of the house, then crept to the shrubbery in front. A peek revealed the living room, lit but empty.

He returned to the side of the garage to decide his next move. He needed a way in, but how? Knock on the door? She'd know him from their meeting yesterday. No way she'd open for him. Probably go straight to the phone to call the cops. Had to be sneaky about this.

Not expecting any results, he pushed up on the garage window. It moved. No way. He pushed harder and it slid up. Talk about luck. But he supposed if any window was going to be left unlocked, it would be in the garage. Who checked their garage windows?

He levered himself up and slid inside. He closed it behind him and crouched beside the Lexus where he listened to the ticking of its cooling engine for a few seconds while he eyed the glowing edges of the door into the house. His palms were sweating despite the cold. This was a big step. An armed home invasion was nothing to take lightly. If things went south he could be sent away for a long, long time.

But he had to know about Cristin, and that required a one-on-one with the lady of this house.

He pulled the Glock and checked the doorknob. It turned. He took a deep breath and charged through a dark utility room into the kitchen where he waved the pistol in Rebecca Olesen's face and shouted at the top of his lungs.

"DO NOT MOVE, DO NOT SCREAM, DO NOT DO ANYTHING UNLESS I TELL YOU TO!"

She screamed and dropped her wineglass. It shattered on the floor.

"I said QUIET!" He lowered his voice. "I'm not here to hurt you. I'm here for answers. But I *will* hurt you if you try holding back on me."

"Y-you were at the office yesterday, with that fake delivery."

"Right."

"You were looking for someone I'd never heard of."

"You've never heard of Cristin Ott?"

"No! I swear!"

Jack wished he'd brought the Ruger. Then he could make that nice ratcheting sound as he cocked the hammer. Since that wasn't an option with a Glock, he lowered the barrel and put a slug into the floor. She jumped and screamed.

"Okay! I know her, I know her, I know her!"

"That's better. She worked for you, right?"

She nodded.

"Did you kill her?"

Her eyes bulged. "What? Nobody killed Cristin, especially me! Why would I do that? I love Cristin. Everybody loves Cristin!"

Jack noted her use of the present tense.

"Somebody didn't."

"Wh-what do you mean?"

Might as well lay it on her.

"You've heard of the Ditmars Dahlia?"

"What? Of course—" Her jaw dropped. "Oh, no. Oh, NO!"

And then her eyes rolled up and she crumbled. Jack wasn't able to catch her in time. Lucky for her—and Jack as well—she didn't land on the broken wineglass when she hit the floor. The last thing he needed was to have to call in the EMTs.

He put the Glock away—he didn't think he'd need it—and squatted beside her, wondering what to do. She wasn't faking this. She was really out.

Fortunately she didn't stay out long. Her eyes fluttered open and she tried to get up.

"Please tell me you're lying," she whispered as Jack helped her to her feet.

"I wish I were."

He guided her to the living room, where she collapsed in a sobbing heap on the couch, moaning an endless stream of, "No-no-no . . ."

Jack sat in a chair across from her and watched. She wasn't acting. She hadn't known, hadn't even suspected. Finally she pulled herself together and looked at him with teary eyes.

"If you'd told me this yesterday we could have avoided all this drama."

"I didn't know yesterday. Only found out today."

He'd found out so much today.

"How?"

"I got a look at her body."

"But—?"

"I know a guy who knows a guy. Look, I'm asking the questions—"

"I'll tell you everything I know, but I need to understand some things first. How do you know her?"

Christ, she wouldn't stop.

"From high school."

"It's more than that. You wouldn't sneak into the morgue and then burst in here with a gun just because you happened to know her in high school. Were you her lover?"

Jeez.

"For a while, yes."

A faint smile. "Only on Sundays, right?"

That jolted him.

"How did you—?"

"Because she refused to work Sundays. Not for religious reasons but be-cause of that old movie."

"Oh, hell. *Never on Sunday.*"

He'd heard of it but had never seen it. Another clue he'd missed.

"Right. You are a very lucky man to be chosen by her."

Yeah, he was. Or had been. But . . .

"I just wish she'd told me . . ."

"About her profession? How would that have sat with you?"

Jack didn't want to get into any of that.

"Never mind me. Who would do that to Cristin?"

The tears welled up again. "I don't know . . . I can't imagine."

"Had to be one of her johns."

"We call them 'clients' and we screen them and—"

"Is Senator D'Amato one of your 'clients'?"

He saw a reflexive retreat in her expression, as if she was ready to say that was confidential, but after an instant's hesitation she shook her head.

"No. Never. Why do you ask?"

If the police were pursuing that sub rosa, he didn't want to queer it.

"I can't say. Anybody famous on her list?"

"Some. No one you'd see in *People*, but their names pop up in the papers now and again."

"I want to see that list."

Again that instant of retreat, then a curt nod. "I'll print it out."

She rose and Jack followed her across the living room to the little office he'd peeked in on earlier.

"I'd figured you'd fight me on this."

She whirled, her face snarling with fury, and jabbed a finger at him as she spoke through her teeth.

"I want this animal found. And if you find him I want you to bring him to me. I want you to leave him with me. Loss of his hands and acid in his face will be the least of his worries!"

You don't know about the arrows, he thought. You don't want to know.

"You can have what's left of him after I'm through."

She grinned then. A scary grimace, utterly devoid of humor. "Good."

She sat down before the computer and lit up the screen.

"You keep it on computer? What happened to the little black book?"

"I have one of those too."

She typed a string of asterisks into a password box, did some typing, and soon the name *Danaë* appeared at the top of the page over a list of names in alphabetical order.

"Danaë? We're looking for Cristin."

"Danaë was her working name."

She hit a couple more keys and the printer began to whir. Less than a minute later she handed him three typed sheets. The first name was Edward Burkes. The second was Roman Trejador. Jack noticed a fair number of lines with both a male and a female name.

"Couples?"

"Danaë was our couples specialist. She was bi, you know."

He nodded. "She told me."

She'd told him that during college she'd even made it with Jack's old high school girlfriend.

"Some of the more open married couples like to invite in a third to spice up their relationship. Danaë was happy to oblige—for an extra fee, of course."

"Oh, Christ. Couples . . . I never guessed."

"What do you mean?"

"I spotted her one day and, on a lark, I followed her around. I saw her get into a limo with a middle-aged couple and figured, there she goes, planning another event."

"It's a great cover. Danaë built up quite a couples following."

"Let's call her Cristin."

"We try to stick to working names at the office, so it's automatic. But yes, sure."

He wanted to punch himself.

"Never on Sunday . . . only on Sunday . . . never available weeknights . . . event planning . . . why didn't I see it?"

"Don't be too hard on yourself. Looking from the outside, it might seem obvious. But from the inside, this was a girl you knew from high school. Escort simply wasn't on your radar."

"You've got that right. Any Arabs on this list?"

"No. We have a few Arab clients but they're not Cristin's."

"Who was the last guy to . . . ?" Words failed for a second. "Employ her?"

She didn't have to look at the list. "Wednesday night. Roman Trejador, one of her regulars."

Number two on the list.

"Could he—?"

She shook her head. "No. He's been her client for years. Calls for her almost weekly. She likes him. Good tipper. Besides, she called me when she got home to let me know she was in."

"Really? Do they all do that?"

"Many of my girls do. They know I care and that I worry."

How weird. A maternal madam.

"So someone grabbed her between calling you Wednesday night and noon on Thursday."

"Noon? How do you—?"

"We were scheduled for lunch and she never showed, never called. That wasn't like her."

"I know. I was worried sick about her when she didn't answer her phone yesterday. I was trying to confirm a date for her that night. The client called later to say she never showed."

He glanced at the top name on the list. "That would be this Edward Burkes."

"Another regular." She sobbed. "Poor Cristin. I can't imagine anyone doing that to her."

"And no Arabs?"

"That's the second time you've asked that. Why? Do you know something?"

"I wish I did."

She rose and slipped past him. "I need that wine."

Jack knew exactly how she felt.

She ignored the broken glass and spilled wine and removed two more glasses from a cabinet.

"You want some?"

"Got any beer?"

"Afraid not."

"Then wine is fine."

Not really. He wasn't a wine fan but any port in a storm. And this was one major shit storm.

But how weird was this scene? A little while ago he'd been shouting and pointing a gun in her face. Now she was pouring him wine. Surreal.

"How did Cristin get involved with you?" he said.

"Referral. A lot of my girls do modeling too, and they often meet FIT students. She and Cristin wound up in a threesome and my girl was impressed by her enthusiasm. She suggested Cristin give us a call. She came in for an interview, said she'd try it, and was an instant success."

She handed Jack a glass. He took a sip. Kind of puckering but it didn't totally suck.

"What qualifies as 'success' in your, um, industry?"

"Callbacks. One date with Danaë—as she'd decided to call herself— and they all wanted another. Well, almost all."

That surprised Jack.

"Who wouldn't?"

She shrugged. "Cristin was uninhibited but not kinky. No B-and-D, no S-and-M, no rough stuff, no anal, no bareback. If you were into that, then Danaë was not your gal."

Jack found himself nodding. Even with him, Cristin had always insisted on a condom.

She was staring at him. "How did you become involved with her?"

"We bumped into each other a couple of years ago. She'd been my girlfriend's best friend back in high school. We had dinner, then went back to her place. After a tequila or two she said, 'Now let's fuck.'"

Rebecca laughed. "That sounds like her." She sipped. "I take it you broke up?"

Jack nodded. "A few months back."

"Why?"

"She was afraid I was getting too attached."

"Were you?"

"Probably. Hard not to."

Rebecca's face scrinched up and tears began to slide down her cheeks.

"I know," she said through a sob.

And then it all became clear.

"You and Cristin?"

Another sob and a nod. "For a very short time."

Jack sipped in silence, at a loss for words.

When she pulled herself together with a deep shudder, Jack said, "I hate to ask you this, but could Cristin have known something she shouldn't have known?"

"What do you mean?"

"According to the medical examiner, she wasn't tortured just for fun—it was an interrogation."

"Oh, God. I don't know. She never mentioned anything to me. What could she know?"

"Maybe someone said something he shouldn't have during sex. I don't see her as the blackmailing type but—"

"No! Never!"

"Okay, then. But think on it. What could she have known that someone would torture her for?" Jack couldn't get the *DAMATO* image out of his mind. "If you come up with something—anything—write it down. I'll call you every day to check."

He gulped his wine.

"Gotta go." He folded the list and shoved it into his back pocket. "I'll leave by the front. You should lock your garage window."

She frowned. "Really? I don't recall ever *un*locking it."

"That's how I got in."

"Are you going to tell the police who the Dahlia is?"

"Already have."

Her eyes widened. "When?"

"Around noon. I don't think it's hit the news yet."

"The police will be tracing her every move. I've got some housecleaning to do."

"Your computer?"

"Paper records too. It's a cold night. Good time for a fire."

He left her, exited through the front door, and cut across the lawn. He'd just reached the hedgerow where Ralph waited when two dark forms darted from the shadows and grabbed him by the arms.

"Hey!"

After the initial shock wore off, he struggled and kicked at the two silent men but could not free his arms.

"Bugger! He's just a kid," one of them said with a British accent.

"Well, we're taking him anyway."

They were strong as hell and, despite his struggles, easily dragged him to the black van parked across the street. The side door opened and he was pushed inside and pinned to the floor while his wallet and his Glock were removed from his pockets. After his wrists and ankles were bound with plastic zip ties, he was hauled to a sitting position. A shadowy figure swiveled in a chair to face him.

"Who the bloody hell are you?"

He had a deep voice that sounded a little like Sean Connery. Only more so.

11

Exhausted, Kadir stumbled into his apartment with Yousef close behind. Yousef fell onto the couch where he slept and Kadir dropped into a chair. His skin burned where it had been exposed to the fumes of the nitric acid. His eyes too, despite the goggles he'd worn all day. His clothes were spotted with holes from where the acid had splashed and eaten through, occasionally burning his skin. Tomorrow would be more of the same. But all he wanted right now was a shower and—

The phone rang. Kadir looked at Yousef, hoping he'd get up and answer it. But Yousef didn't budge. He knew it wasn't for him. The hour was too late for his jihadist contacts in Hamburg or the Middle East to be calling.

Who would be calling me? Kadir thought as he pushed himself from the chair and stumbled across the small front room.

"Hello?" he said in English.

"*Kadir?*"

"Yes. Who—?"

"*At last I find you,*" the voice said in Arabic. "*This is your friend from Qatar and I have been calling all day.*"

The man from Qatar. Why was he calling?

"I have been busy."

"*Yes, and you have no answering machine, so I've been calling and calling.*"

"Why?"

"*A matter of mutual concern. I have information that I think you and your imam will find extremely interesting.*"

"I am listening."

"Not on the phone. It is known only to a select few and cannot spread further."

Did he suspect that the apartment's phone was tapped? Possible. The FBI was everywhere.

"I am very busy—"

"You will want to make time for this. I have startling information and an offer of assistance. Shall we meet, say, outside your mosque tomorrow morning? And be sure to bring your friend Yousef. He will want to hear this too."

"Yes, but early. As I said—"

"You are very busy. I appreciate that. But you will be glad you made time for this. Eight o'clock then?"

"Yes. Eight."

Kadir hung up, wondering what could be so interesting.

. . . startling information and an offer of assistance . . .

He had to admit he was intrigued.

12

"What do I call you, laddie?" the man said as the van lurched into motion.

A tensor lamp attached to the wall clicked on and beamed light over his shoulder. He was on the heavy side, with short brown hair and a trimmed beard; most of his face remained in shadow. Jack's wallet lay open in his hands.

"Jeff Cusic? That's you?"

Only on paper.

Jack's first thought was that he'd fallen into the hands of Cristin's torturers, but he was too confused to be afraid. Besides, he didn't sense any menace in these three. The two big guys up front had been very casual about grabbing him. They radiated professionalism—soldiers or mercenaries of some kind, he guessed. And the guy in the chair, the boss man, seemed relaxed, used to being in control. What the hell had he stumbled into?

Jack said, "How about telling me what this is all about."

The boss held up Jack's pistol. "Look, it's a wee Glock. What'd you do, leave it out in the rain?" He checked the breech, then dropped it on the carpeted floor. "That's not a pistol." He reached into his coat and removed a big 1911 .45. "*This* is a pistol."

Jack couldn't resist. "Okay, so you've seen *Crocodile Dundee*. Good for you."

One of the guys up front snickered.

The boss said, "You're in no position to be haverin'. You just committed an armed home invasion."

True enough, but Jack doubted Rebecca Olesen would be pressing charges. And since the best defense was a good offense . . .

"So you say. But you've just kidnapped me. One's a local crime, the other's federal." Counterjab done, now the haymaker. "And how'd you manage to get into the morgue this morning?"

He saw the man stiffen, then laugh. "That's the way we're gonna play it, eh?" He stared at Jack. "So you were Danaë's bidie-in."

"What? First off, there was no Danaë. Danaë was a fiction. There's only Cristin."

"I knew her only as Danaë," he said in a somber tone. "I'm honored to know her real name."

"One of her clients."

A nod. "I was very fond of her."

"So was I. And what the hell's a bidie-in?"

"Boyfriend, bedmate." He shook his head. "You're just a wean. I thought she'd go for someone more experienced."

"'Wayne' being . . . ?"

"A child. How old are you, lad?"

"Twenty-four."

"Rob, Gerald," he said to the guys up front. "He look twenty-four to you?"

"Not a chance," said the driver.

"Twenty, tops," said the shotgun.

The story of his life since he'd come to the city.

The boss said, "You're a gutsy one, I'll give you that. But you have something I want."

"What would that be?"

"The list the lady gave you."

The list? How could he know about—? And then it all came into focus.

"I don't know anything about a list, but let me guess how you spent your day. You saw the comment in the paper about the skin missing from the Dit-mars Dahlia's neck and had the same horrible suspicion I did."

He nodded. "Especially when she didn't show up Thursday night. Not like her slaggin' me off. When I called Celebrations, they had no explanation. They offered to send a replacement but . . ." He shrugged. "No one could replace Danaë—sorry, Cristin."

He'd said *sorry*. That was something. And he'd also said he was sched-uled for Thursday night. Pleased to meet you, Edward Burkes.

Jack remembered what Ron had said about the guy with an accent being from some embassy.

"So you used your embassy connections—"

"Wait-wait-wait! Did you say 'embassy connections'?"

Jack's mind bounced over the possibilities. The guy was a Scot, but Scot-land didn't have an embassy because it was part of . . .

"Yeah. The UK."

Wash from a passing streetlight showed a craggy face, smiling as he nod-ded. "Close, close. What else?"

"You turned her over and saw that the place where her tattoo had been was missing. You knew it was Cristin. You used more embassy–NYPD con-nections to learn that Rebecca Olesen ran Celebrations and lived up here. So while she was in the city today, you or one of your guys came up here and bugged her house."

The guy in the passenger seat clapped three times. "Young Sherlock Holmes."

"You broke in through the garage window," Jack added, remembering Re-becca's remark about never opening it. He was on a roll and wanted to maintain momentum. "By the way, I appreciate your leaving it unlocked on your way out. Made things a lot easier for me."

"It wasn't neglect," Burkes said. "Easy enough to pop open those things with the right tool, damnably hard to relock them from the outside."

"So then the three of you sat out here and waited to see if she'd give any-thing away."

"Well, there you're wrong. Rob and Gerald were in the city. When she showed up here I set them to work bugging the Celebrations office."

"I guess I wasn't in your plans."

"Not at all. I thought you were some perv peeper or someone going to rob the place. I was sure you were going to bollocks up everything. When I heard your gun go off, I was afraid you'd shot her. Then I heard her talking again."

"Put a hole in her kitchen floor."

"That was when I told these two to get up here. I thought we might have to go in and grab you. Fortunately you came to us."

"Yeah, fortunately."

Jack shook his head in disgust. He hadn't dreamed anyone would be laying for him near Ralph.

"I keep thinking about her missing tattoo," Burkes muttered. "Probably working its way through the gut of some East River fish."

"So you remembered it?"

"Can't forget it. Used to study it as we did it doggie style. She liked doggie style."

Jack wanted to block his ears but his hands were tied.

"Hey, back off of that, huh?"

"Sorry, lad." Burkes sounded like he meant it. "Forgot your relationship was different." He sighed. "I'm never sure where I'm gonna be year to year, so I tend to hire my women. After a couple of times with Cristin it wasn't like a transaction. It was like a friend." His tone turned wistful. "Y'heard what I said—about how *she* liked it? That was how it was. You start out hiring a woman to pleasure *you*, but with Cristin you end up looking for the best ways to pleasure *her*."

"Can we change the subject?"

Instead of replying, Burkes picked up Jack's Glock, popped the magazine, then ejected the chambered round, catching it in midair. As the round and the mag disappeared into a pocket, Jack leaned forward.

"So where do we go from here, Mister Burkes?"

Burkes damn near dropped the Glock and the driver said, "Bugger! He *is* Sherlock!"

"I doubt it," Burkes said. "Gerald, cut him loose."

The guy in the passenger seat turned with a long dagger in his hand. Jack twisted to present his wrists. A second later they were free. His ankles followed. As he assumed a cross-legged position, Burkes thrust out his hand, palm up.

"The list."

"What list?"

He snapped his fingers. "Come now. No talking out yer fanny flaps. You'll get it back, but if we're going to find this guy—"

"'We'?"

"Yes. As you've guessed, I'm not a U.S. citizen. I occupy a sensitive position."

"With the UK Embassy."

"Afraid not. That's in D.C. Nor with the consulate on Third Avenue."

"Then what—?"

"Since you already know my name, you can easily find out the rest: I'm Chief of Security at the UK Mission to the UN. Unfortunately diplomatic immunity does not come with the job, so I must be circumspect in my extracurricular activities. But as a result of my position, I have access to intelligence and data far beyond your reach."

Pretty damn impressive, if true.

"You, on the other hand," Burkes went on, "*are* a citizen and seem to have street smarts despite your lack of compunction about blindly barging into a situation. Our methods and resources complement each other rather nicely, I think. We share a common goal. If we work together we can achieve that goal."

Jack was sure of the answer but had to ask. "Which is?"

They'd stopped at a traffic light. The red wash lit Burkes's features, giving his hard expression and harder eyes a demonic glow.

"Find the cunt who did this and make him pay."

All Jack knew about this guy was what he'd said about himself, and that could all be fiction. But if he was who he said he was, his "resources" could come in handy.

Jack thrust out his hand. "You're on."

As they shook, Burkes said, "Now let's see that list. The name of our quarry is very likely on it. Or, if not, it has the name of the one who ordered it."

Jack pulled it from his back pocket and handed it over. Burkes unfolded the sheets and held them under the tensor. He smirked.

"Look who's first on the list." The sarcasm thickened. "Brilliant piece of ratiocination, Sherlock."

"Hey, you guys brought him up, not me." Jack reached over and tapped the pages. "D'Amato's not on the list. Rebecca said—"

"—he wasn't a client. I was listening."

"Oh, right. Slipped my mind." He found the idea of someone eavesdropping on him like that unsettling. "You believe her?"

"I do. She seemed genuinely upset. As for the good senator, he was down in D.C. at a fund-raiser Wednesday night, after which he was dropped off at his home down there. He spent Thursday in his office or out for lunch and dinner. Da—Cristin's body was found late Friday night. He never got within two hundred miles of her."

"And you know this how?"

"I have contacts in the NYPD—lots of them—and they checked it out as soon as they heard about those scratches."

Jack leaned back. "Okay, let's assume that's all true: Then why would she scratch that name into her skin?"

"You do know it was a torture-interrogation, right?"

"So I was told."

"Right, then. What if, because of her profession, whoever did this *thought* she knew something damaging about D'Amato."

"And tried to torture it out of her?"

The horror of that . . . a murderous psychopath demanding an answer you don't know.

"Exactly."

"But that would mean they'd somehow linked her to D'Amato—and supposedly there is no link."

Burkes sighed. "I know. I'm grabbing at straws. What was all your talk about Arabs back there?"

"Another straw, I'm afraid."

"Well, let's hear it."

"This guy I have the misfortune to have met—named Reggie—is completely capable of torture and murder and was ready to use his bow and arrow to kill someone else I knew."

"'Knew'? As in past tense?"

"Murdered."

"Reggie is not an Arab name."

"No kidding."

"Then what—?"

"In copspeak he'd be a 'known associate.' He's done dirty work for some Arabs."

Burkes stroked his beard. "That *is* a straw—a slim one. How would you characterize your relationship with this Reggie?"

"He'll probably try to kill me next time he sees me."

"Interesting. What if he was trying to get to you through her?"

The question sent a jolt of alarm and dismay through Jack, but he immediately dismissed it.

"If he was torturing her about me, why would she scratch *DAMATO* into her skin?"

Burkes shrugged. "As I said, just grasping at straws." He snapped his fingers. "Wait-wait-wait. Senator D'Amato is very unpopular with a certain breed of Arab."

"The jihadist kind?" Bertel's Mohammedans came to mind. "Because that's the kind Reggie's been connected to."

"Could they have been torturing Cristin to find something on D'Amato?"

"As good a theory as any. Know any you can ask?"

"Good luck that. But I'll see what I can scrounge up from my saner Mideast counterparts."

"Why would they want to help?"

"Many see the jihadists as a threat to the regime they serve. We tend to cooperate on security matters because what threatens one mission can easily threaten others."

"You might want to see if they know anything about a big-time U.S. hater named Sheikh Omar in a Jersey City mosque."

"Got that?" Burkes said toward the front.

"Got it," said Gerald.

"Also, I know this guy who's got a hard-on for Omar and his crazy Mohammedans, as he calls them."

"Really? What's his name?"

"I doubt you'd know him."

"You never know what I'll know, laddie."

Jack pondered that a bit. Paranoid Bertel probably wouldn't want his name mentioned, but what was the harm? How would this Scot have ever heard of him?

"Name's Dane Bertel."

Jack saw Gerald, the passenger, take a quick look back, then face forward again. That was it. Nothing dramatic. Just a quick glance at his boss. Why? To make eye contact? To see how the boss was going to react?

As for the boss, Burkes was stroking his jaw again.

"Dane Bertel . . . no, you're right. Never heard of him. How old is he?"

He *had* heard of him. How the hell . . . ?

"You know him."

Burkes smiled. "Dane Bertel? I think I'd remember a name like that." He leaned toward the front. "Take the lad back to his car." He looked at Jack. "We'll trade contact info on the way. Let's keep each other up to speed on this. Be nice to find this bawbag before the coppers. See if he can take what he dished out."

Fine, Jack thought, but you're lying about Bertel.

Why the hell was he lying? Why didn't he want to admit he knew him?

Burkes tossed him his wallet. "There you go, Jeff."

If Jack was going to be dealing with this guy, he didn't want to keep answering to the wrong name.

"People call me Jack."

"Jack for Jeff. That's an odd one."

"Lots of odd stuff around."

"No argument there."

Burkes returned his "wee Glock" along with its magazine. When they dropped him off in front of Rebecca's house, Jack noticed smoke streaming from her chimney.

SUNDAY

1

"Thank you for meeting me," Nasser said in Arabic to the men in the backseat as the car got rolling.

Sunday morning traffic was virtually nonexistent in Jersey City at this hour. He'd arrived promptly at eight to find the three of them waiting.

Kadir had brought Yousef along, but even better, the redheaded Mahmoud had joined them. One more to put pressure on Yousef to change his target. The three of them carried a pungent, acrid odor.

Kadir spoke first with a wary glance at the driver. Nasser was glad about their caution in front of strangers. He'd already assured them on previous occasions that Klarić spoke no Arabic.

"I await your 'startling information.'"

"Through my contacts in the UN—"

"I knew it!" Yousef said. "I knew it as soon as Kadir told me. You're wasting your breath. We will not change the target!"

"Hear him out," Mahmoud said.

Yousef folded his arms across his chest and glared at Nasser.

"Speak," Kadir said.

"Very well. Through my contacts in the UN I have learned that Israeli Prime Minister Rabin is flying to New York at the end of the week for a secret meeting with UN Secretary Boutros-Ghali."

The news evoked the anticipated response: wide-eyed shock. Even Yousef's jaw dropped a little.

"Are you sure?" Mahmoud said. "Are you absolutely *sure*?"

Nasser nodded. "I have confirmation from a second source, one outside the UN."

"Who?" Yousef said.

"Someone who works in Senator Alfonse D'Amato's New York office."

"That swine!" Yousef said, baring his teeth. "Why should he know?"

"For a very good reason. As you know, he's a great friend to Israel—went there during the war to mock Saddam's Scud missiles. He is going to be at the meeting."

The car fell silent—so silent it might have been a coffin on wheels.

Finally Kadir spoke in a hushed tone. "All three of them? In the same room?"

"When?" Yousef said.

"The meeting is set for Friday morning at eleven A.M."

The horse-faced man's eyes narrowed. "This seems too good to be true. And very convenient for the man who prefers to see the UN harmed rather than the Trade Towers."

Nasser had expected this and gave an elaborate shrug. "As Kadir and Mahmoud can tell you, I have always been a friend to jihad. I always will be."

"I have friends at home who can confirm whether or not the Zionist has left the country."

"I hope you won't mention anything about this meeting over an international phone line."

Yousef sneered. "I am not an idiot. I will simply be curious about his whereabouts on Friday."

"I am sure you will find that he is scheduled for an appearance or two in Israel that day, but wait and see: They will be canceled at the last minute due to 'pressing matters of state.' In reality he will be arriving at JFK on an El Al flight early Friday morning and leaving again on Friday afternoon."

An Israeli member of the Order had already phoned an anonymous tip to Shin Bet that someone might make an attempt on Rabin's life during the first Friday of Ramadan. Security would clamp down tight and disinformation about the PM's schedule for that day would be rampant. Anyone asking about Rabin's whereabouts would find themselves the object of intense scrutiny, perhaps even interrogation, which would only bolster Nasser's story.

"Rabin, Boutros-Ghali, D'Amato," Mahmoud said. It sounded like a litany.

"Yes," Nasser said. "Think about it: When will the three of them be together in the same room again? And only a few miles from where we sit?"

How could they resist? And they mustn't resist. Yousef had to give in and
change course because the Trade Towers were not to be touched. Nasser was
sure he could be even more convincing if he knew the reason for their pres-
ervation, but he still did not rate that level of confidence.

All eyes were on Yousef now.

"My uncle Khalid—" he began.

"Fuck your uncle!" Mahmoud said. "He sits in faraway comfort while we
poison our lungs and burn our skin. He doesn't even send us money. He no
longer has a say in what we do."

Yousef's mad little eyes bored into Nasser's. "But if he is lying . . ."

Kadir said, "He has never lied to us before. And even if he *is* wrong, even
if Rabin changes his plans and is not there, we will have blown up the UN for
the cause of jihad. If Rabin *is* there, then all the world will reel in shock and
will tremble before Allah. We cannot lose!"

Nasser saw Yousef wavering before the potent argument and decided to
sweeten the pot.

"Here is something else to consider: To assure maximum destruction, you
will need two bombs."

"Two?" Kadir said. "But we have enough only for one."

"I will contribute whatever you need for the second bomb."

"Why two?" Mahmoud said.

"Unlike the Trade Center, you will not be able to get inside the UN Plaza
unless you have diplomatic plates. You will only be able to get close to it—
curbside at best—unless you are willing to be a martyr and run the gates."

"I would do that for Allah," Yousef said.

Let's hope you do, Nasser thought.

"So would I," Kadir added, his eyes alight with religious zeal.

"Even so, only one truck would be able to get through the front gate. But
the rear is vulnerable."

"Of course!" Mahmoud said with a sudden grin. "The FDR! The south-
bound lanes run right under the UN!"

Nasser had fully expected the cabdriver to know that.

"Exactly. The explosions wouldn't have to be perfectly timed. In fact, staggering them might even be better. Detonation within a minute of each other

will be perfect. No sooner will the survivors realize that they're under attack than they'll be rocked by another massive blast. Imagine the terror, the panic as they wonder when the *third* will go off."

"But there won't be a third," Kadir said.

Nasser grinned. "You and I will know that, but they won't."

At the sight of three nodding heads in the rear, Nasser pulled a thick envelope from the inner pocket of his jacket and held it up: bait, a worm wriggling on a hook.

"This envelope is empty now, because I did not know what you would decide. But I am willing to fill it with ten thousand dollars to further the cause of maximum terror. Enough for a second bomb and a second truck to level the UN."

Kadir slapped his thighs. "That is what we must do."

"But—" Yousef began.

Kadir's voice rose. "Rabin! Boutros-Ghali! The Jew-loving senator! They are known the world over as enemies of Islam and jihad. We cannot pass them up for buildings full of faceless workers!"

"Our names will be carved in the Halls of Heaven," Mahmoud said.

Kadir turned to Nasser. "When can we have the money?"

"Can you build the second bomb in time?"

"We will work day and night!"

"Then I can have it for you first thing tomorrow morning. Same time, same place?"

"Yes. We will be there."

Nasser tapped Klarić on the shoulder and spoke in English. "Back to the mosque."

His work here was done. All that was left was to deliver the money.

2

Jack spotted Bertel and his goofy fake beard in an old Plymouth on Kennedy Boulevard. No empty parking spaces in sight—lots of folks sleeping late, he guessed—so he turned a corner and hunted down a side street. He was driving Bertel's pickup. The old guy had forbidden him from bringing the Corvair, saying it was too eye-catching. Jack couldn't argue. Ralph was proving impractical. He needed to be less impulsive with his purchases in the future, at least with something like a car.

He found a spot and walked back up to Kennedy. He knocked on the passenger window of the Plymouth and Bertel unlocked the door for him.

"That's one crummy beard," Jack said as he eased into the seat.

Bertel kept his eyes straight ahead as he spoke. "It gets the job done."

"Any excitement?"

"Nothing. Just got here a few minutes ago. Could've used you last Wednesday, though."

"Yeah?"

"I was here in time to see our dear jihadists get back from a ride in a long black Mercedes."

"They suddenly inherit a fortune?"

"Wasn't their car. Some white guy driving it. But the Mohammedan in charge was someone I'd seen before."

"Who?"

"Don't know his name. I call him the mystery Mohammedan. But remember a couple years ago—two years almost to the day, in fact—when we were trailing Kadir and your friend Reggie in that truck?"

Why did he always have to precede "Reggie" with "your friend"? Jack wasn't going to correct him this time.

"Yeah."

"Well, if you remember, after we parted ways, I continued following that truck. Guess who Kadir and your friend Reggie met up with at the end of the road."

"Your mystery Mohammedan."

"Bingo—along with Mahmoud the Red."

Jack's memory was starting to make connections. "Where exactly was this end of the road?"

"I believe it's called Sore Thumb Beach."

"Isn't that where a truck filled with a dozen or so Muslims blew up that night?"

His eyes stayed fixed through the windshield. "I believe you're right."

"And you just happened to be there."

Finally he looked at Jack. "No need for that suspicious tone. A mere correlation, and correlation is not the same as cause and effect. You have to remember, these jihadists play with explosives. They were there to ambush your friends. No telling what sort of ordnance they brought along. Some of that stuff can be temperamental—downright cranky at times."

Jack had long suspected that Bertel was behind that explosion. Now to hear him admit he was there . . . well, that was enough to convince Jack that, at least in this case, correlation coincided with cause.

"But let us return to the matter at hand," Bertel said. "The mystery Mohammedan from the beach met again with the jihadists and—"

Another correlation struck like a blow.

"Holy crap! Did you say Wednesday?"

"Early morning."

"You didn't happen to see Reggie with them, did you?"

Bertel shook his head. "Nope. Nowhere in sight. Why?"

The mystery Arab seen with Reggie two years ago meets with jihadists the day before Cristin is abducted and tortured with Reggie's weapon of choice. Connection?

"Nothing."

"Bullshit. For a second there you looked like someone had just kicked you in the balls."

"No, really. Just had a crazy thought."

"Thoughts are good. Let's hope you have another one real soon."

"Very funny." Jack shook off the unease—no way at the moment to follow it up—and changed the subject. "Ran into a fellow I think you know. Edward Burkes?"

Bertel frowned. "Burkes? Don't think so."

Jack watched closely for a spark of recognition but couldn't find one.

"A Scotsman. With the UK Mission to the UN."

He shook his head. "Doesn't ring any sort of bell. I don't—" He straightened in his seat and gripped the steering wheel. "Well, speak of the devil . . ."

A long black Mercedes was pulling to a stop before the mosque.

"Is that the same car?"

"Sure as hell looks like it. I *know* that's the same driver."

Jack peered through the windshield as the rear doors opened. Kadir, Mahmoud, and a third Arab got out.

"Who's the new guy?"

"He's calling himself Ramzi Yousef." He handed Jack a pair a field glasses. "Take a look."

Jack focused on the twitchy guy, got a good look at his long face. He lowered the glasses.

"He's got Manson eyes."

"What?"

"Ever see those pictures of Charles Manson after he was caught? This guy's got the same eyes."

And then a fourth Arab stepped out of the front passenger door—tall, trim, wearing a skullcap and a fitted gray robe that buttoned to the throat.

"There he is," Bertel said. "The mystery Mohammedan." He laughed. "Do you have some sort of psychic link to these Mohammedans?"

"What?"

"Did you draw them here? I mean, it's like I'm getting a second chance. The exact same thing happened last Wednesday: The jihadists got out and the car took off. I had to choose which to follow. I chose the car but lost it in traffic and came up empty-handed all around. If you'd been here, you could have followed the jihadists and maybe we'd have learned something."

Jack already had his door open. "Dibs on the mystery Arab."

"Okay. But why?"

"Because any friend of Reggie's is a friend of mine."

He hurried back around the corner to the pickup. He didn't know for sure whether Reggie was linked to Cristin, but Bertel said Reggie was linked to the mystery guy, and that was enough for Jack at the moment.

Because he didn't have a single goddamn other thing to go on.

3

Nasser and the Mercedes glided away from the curb, leaving the three jihadists clustered in a knot on the sidewalk. He hoped they kept their word. No worry about them pocketing the extra money he'd promised. He had no doubt they would build two bombs, but he didn't know if they might decide at the last minute to place both in the Trade Towers.

His driver, Brajko Klarić, said, "They are—what is word? Unagreeable?"

"Disagreeable." Nasser had moved to the rear seat. "And they are indeed that." He lowered the window to freshen the air. "What a stench."

"They are building bombs?"

The question startled Nasser. Had he been listening? "You speak Egyptian?"

The driver laughed. "No. I know smell."

"You've made bombs?"

"In my spare time back home I blow up Serbs."

"I see."

Drexler had a cadre of East European and Baltic operatives he used, preferring them to Americans and Western Europeans. This Croat was proving more interesting than his predecessor, Kristof Szeto, who had been Drexler's favored driver and operative for years.

"By the way, what happened to Szeto?"

"He goes home to get mother."

"Is she ill?"

"No. Order brings her to city to work."

"To New York?"

Women weren't allowed in the Order. Why—?

"She is to be housekeeper for special person on Fifth Avenue."

"Ah."

Now he understood. The Order owned a penthouse on Fifth Avenue over-looking Central Park. The One was going to be staying there. His staff would be connected to the Order, of course.

He noticed a Nikon with a telephoto lens sitting on the front seat.

"What have you been photographing?"

"Remember man who follow us from mosque last week?"

"Vaguely."

Nasser remembered Klarić saying they were being followed, but he'd managed to lose the tail before they'd left Jersey City.

"He is there this morning in same car. I think he is watching mosque."

Nasser didn't like that. The bomb-building jihadists weren't the brightest he'd dealt with. Had they given themselves away?

"Could be FBI."

"Is what I am thinking. I take pictures while you are outside talking to the disagreeable ones."

"Good thinking. We'll pass them around when they're developed."

"He have visitor today."

"In his car?"

"Yes. I take picture of him when he get out just before we leave."

Nasser turned in the seat and peered through the rear window. "Is he following us?"

"I do not know for sure. I did not see him drive up. He will be in un-known car. Is hard to tell, but I will watch."

Nasser settled back. "You do that."

He noticed an unusual fob hanging from the keys in the ignition—rectangular parchment with a strange symbol:

"What does that mean?" Nasser said, pointing.

Klarić shrugged. "I do not know. Is tattoo. I take it from whore."

Nasser's stomach lurched. "Whore? Not Danaë—"

"We learn is not real name. Is—"

"Don't tell me. I don't want to know."

"I take from back of neck. We do not want her known, so I take and cure with salt." He flicked it with his finger. "Is nice, no?"

Nasser could not answer. He leaned back and fought his rising gorge.

Last Wednesday, after Danaë had walked through their meeting at Trejador's suite, he'd followed her to an apartment house in the East Seventies. He'd reported the address to Drexler, who then told him that Trejador had decided that it was too risky to let her go. Drexler gave him two names suggested by Trejador. Nasser was to instruct them to take the girl and find out what she'd heard about Rabin and D'Amato; if she knew something, find out who, if anyone, she'd told and go after them as well.

The two names were Reggie—American white trash Nasser had dealt with before—and Brajko Klarić, the fellow sitting behind the wheel. Nasser would have much preferred to hire Danaë and gently inquire as to what she knew during the course of an intense sexual encounter. But orders were orders, especially when they came from Trejador.

Reggie and Klarić eventually reported back that she knew nothing and that her body would never be found. Or if by some chance found, never identified.

"And even if she is found and identified," Klarić said, "who care? She is only whore. She is nobody."

She was someone to me, Nasser thought.

Someone he'd wanted to bed.

"I tell you what we did. Is very interesting man, that Reggie. First he—"

"Stop. I don't have time for this now. I have other things to think about."

He didn't want any details, especially the taking of such a grisly trophy. What sort of person even thinks of that, let alone does it? Really, the things he had to do and the people he had to deal with in the course of trying to change the world . . .

He'd managed to block the whole episode from his consciousness, but that grisly key fob brought it all back.

He didn't say another word until the Croat pulled to a stop on Second Avenue outside his building.

"Get that film to a one-hour developer and have the photos dropped off at my apartment. I want to waste no time identifying these two men."

As he strode toward his building's entrance, the giant headline of the *New York Post*, on prominent display at the corner newsstand, caught his eye.

DD
ID'd!

DD? That had to mean the so-called Ditmars Dahlia that had so dominated the news recently. He hadn't been interested but the story proved inescapable. Now that she'd been identified, perhaps they'd move on to something else.

A yearbook photo of a pretty brunette occupied the lower right corner. Nasser walked over for a closer look and almost tumbled over when he recognized Danaë. Only this said her name was Cristin Ott.

Reggie and Klarić had said her body would never be found! And if found, never identified. Yet here she was for all to see.

Cristin Ott . . . a beautiful young woman tortured and mutilated . . . all upon his order. And for what? For something she'd never overheard in the first place.

His gorge rose again and this time he could not hold it down.

4

Jack had pulled to the curb by a fire hydrant when the Mercedes stopped near the corner of Second and East 51st.

Following had been easy. Assuming they'd be heading for Manhattan he'd hung far back. When a light went wrong for him, he waited it out and then hustled toward the Holland Tunnel. Eventually he caught up to them and trailed them into the city and here to Turtle Bay.

Mystery Arab exited the car across the street and Jack expected him to enter the apartment building there. But first he wandered over to the newsstand

and stared at the papers. Then, instead of buying anything, he lurched to the curb and vomited.

Some bad hummus for breakfast, maybe?

Here was a chance to play Good Samaritan and find out who he was. He left the truck illegally parked and tried to cross the street, but a surge of traffic held him up. The guy had recovered and was moving toward the front door of the building by the time Jack trotted across.

Okay. Next best thing: follow him inside.

But again he was too late. Jack was hurrying toward the entrance as Mystery Arab tapped in the entry code, but the man slipped inside and let the door close behind him before Jack could scoot through.

He resisted kicking the glass door and peered through it instead. Across the vestibule, the elevator sat open and waiting. He ducked back as Mystery Arab stepped inside. No sense in being seen if it wasn't necessary. He counted to five, then returned to the door. He watched the red LED display above the call button count up from *L* to *9*. After *9*, it began counting down again.

Probably not a risky guess to assume that Mystery Arab lived on the ninth floor. Jack checked the call buttons to the right of the door. Only one Arab name on nine: *N. al-Thani.*

Had to be him. Mystery Arab now had a name. Jack was pretty sure it hadn't been on the list Rebecca had given him, but he'd had time for only a quick scan.

He spotted a pay phone near the corner newsstand. He dropped a quarter and called the number Burkes had given him.

Watch it be a wrong number, he thought. But a familiar voice answered.

"Burkes."

"It's Jack from last night. Got that list handy?"

A heartbeat's hesitation, then, *"Right here."*

"Is the name al-Thani on it?" He spelled it.

"That's Arab, and there's no Arabs on the list."

"Just checking. When do I get it back?"

"I've already run off a Xerox. Where are you?"

"Turtle Bay."

"Brilliant. Right in the neighborhood. Got a car?"

"Got a pickup."

"Swing by One Dag Hammarskjold Plaza—Second Avenue between Forty-sixth and Forty-seventh—and I'll have Rob out front with the copy."

"Got it. Be right there."

As he headed back to the truck, he wondered how Bertel was doing on his end. Too bad he didn't have a cellular phone so they could check in whenever they needed. Maybe he should think about joining the 1990s.

5

When Kadir returned from calling Salameh on the phone inside the mosque, he found Mahmoud and Yousef in a heated discussion. They stood in front of the Chinese takeout storefront—closed at this hour—gesticulating wildly as they argued in Arabic.

"I still think I should call my uncle," Yousef was saying. "He went to much trouble and expense to bring me here. Ajaj is still paying the price."

This was true. Last September, Yousef's uncle, Khalid Sheikh Mohammed, had sent Ahmad Ajaj through JFK immigration at the same time as Yousef with a deliberately sloppy passport forgery. The resultant commotion allowed Yousef's passport—also forged, but a much better job—to pass muster. Ajaj was still in jail.

"Call your uncle," Mahmoud said, "but no matter what he says, the plan is changed." He jabbed a finger into Yousef's bony chest. "And if you don't help us, you will be a traitor to jihad. And if I tell Sheikh Omar, you will soon hear of a fatwah telling everyone of your treachery."

Yousef stiffened. Everyone knew that people named in Sheikh Omar's fatwahs did not have long for this world. President Anwar Sadat was a prime example. And Kadir knew Yousef was well aware that Omar had been plotting a double assassination against his fellow Egyptians, Mubarak and Boutros-Ghali. The UN bombing fit beautifully into the imam's plans. One could almost see the hand of Allah Himself in this.

"Why tell your uncle anything?" Kadir said. "The fewer who know of our plans, the better."

"I agree," Mahmoud said.

Yousef was silent for a moment. "I will have to think on this."

"Don't think too long," Kadir said. "We take the Qatari's money tomorrow. And if we don't have our"—a quick glance around—"preparations completed, we will have to let the opportunity of a lifetime slip past."

A *toot* drew their attention: Salameh's car was pulling to the curb.

"Where to from here?" Salameh said as they climbed in.

"The storage space," Mahmoud said. "We might as well bring more supplies back to the garage while we are out."

"We'll have only the trunk," Kadir said.

He wasn't about to drive with a container of nitric acid on his lap.

"We'll fill it with whatever we can and make another trip later. We've got to speed this up if we're to have two bombs by Friday."

"Two?" Salameh said.

"We'll explain along the way," Kadir told him.

Salameh hit the gas and they roared onto Kennedy Boulevard.

6

As Dane watched the jihadists standing on the sidewalk, he wondered if Jack was having better luck following the mystery Arab than he'd had last week. It looked like these three were arguing. About what? Then an old Chevy Nova pulled up and they all piled in. Dane started his Plymouth and had it moving by the time they took off.

He hadn't identified the guy behind the wheel yet, but he would. Only a matter of time. Whoever he was he drove like a drunk, weaving back and forth and drifting over his lane lines.

The Nova led him on a meandering path down Kennedy to Communipaw Avenue, then onto Mallory where they turned into the driveway of a storage locker place called the Space Station. The driver hopped out and punched in a code. As the gate slid back, they drove in and pulled around to the back. Even if Dane had the code, following them in would be pushing his luck way past its tensile strength. So he cruised past, turned around, and found a spot with a good view of the place.

From what he'd seen, the facility consisted of a huge, two-story U-shaped building lined with roll-up doors; the base of the U looped around the back end of its lot. A single long, straight building—also two stories—ran up the valley of the U, leaving wide driveways on each side.

Twenty minutes later they pulled out and headed back the way they had come. Dane followed, wondering what the hell they'd done in there—drop-off or pickup? He didn't know if it was his imagination, but the back of the Nova seemed to be riding a bit lower.

He tried to stay as close as he could without being obvious, allowing only one car between his and theirs as they made their way back to Kennedy. But then the light ahead turned amber. The Nova sped up while the car ahead of him stopped. Again! Dane wanted to get out and throttle the driver. Instead he sat and watched the Nova sail away. This was getting to be a habit.

A tracker . . . he needed to attach a tracking transceiver to that damn car. Trouble was, he didn't know where they parked it. And if he knew where they parked it, he probably wouldn't need a tracker.

Besides, the only tracker he had was taped to a brick of C4.

7

"For some strange reason," Drexler said, staring at the photo, "I feel I've seen this one before."

After Klarić dropped off the photos, Nasser had called Drexler to set up a meeting where he and Trejador could have a look at them. Normally he would have called Trejador directly but he didn't want to speak to the man who had ordered Danaë's death. Not yet. He was afraid he might betray his warring emotions.

More than anything in his life, Nasser wanted the High Council to appoint him an actuator. As an actuator, he often would be called on to put all his personal feelings and priorities aside and act in the best interests of the Order. Nasser understood that. He was ready to assume that responsibility.

But he didn't know if he could have ordered the torture and murder of Danaë. Yes, she was a prostitute, a call girl, a whore. She sold her body to pleasure men. A nobody, as Klarić had called her. But she was a beautiful nobody who'd shared Trejador's bed. Many times. To dispose of her like so much trash . . . Nasser didn't know if he had that in him.

But no one could know that. If Trejador or Drexler suspected that he might put his emotions before the Order, they would not recommend him for actuator. If the subject of Danaë arose, Nasser might have trouble hiding his emotions. Not from Drexler. No worry about a man who didn't seem to have any emotions except anger, and even that was icy on the rare occasions he let it show. He was too self-absorbed to notice anything as subtle as conflicted emotions. But Trejador . . . Roman Trejador was another story. He would see through whatever façade Nasser erected.

And so he was relieved when Drexler had called back to say that Trejador had other business that required his personal supervision for the next few days and could not attend. So the two of them would meet at Drexler's place.

"Who?" Nasser said.

Drexler turned the photo around. "The young one."

Nasser had studied the photos on the way over. The older bearded man in the driver's seat had been photographed through the windshield, and so his face was somewhat indistinct. But Klarić had caught the younger one as he'd exited the car and his features were sharp and clear.

"Your driver thinks they might be FBI."

Drexler's smile was tolerant. "Yes. So Klarić told me. He showed initiative in bringing his camera. Do you see why I choose the operatives I do? An American never would have thought of that."

"Yes. He's quite innovative."

Nasser wondered if an American operative would have thought to slice off Danaë's tattoo, cure the skin like animal hide, and use it as a key fob.

"Not innovative enough, I fear. Did you see the papers?"

Nasser fought to keep the wave of revulsion from showing on his face. He chose his words carefully.

"You mean about the . . . whore?"

"Yes. Didn't they assure us that she'd never be identified?"

"They did."

"It's that Reggie, I'll bet. Burning her face and cutting off her hands were good ideas, but throwing her in the river? They had to know she'd wash up somewhere. Simply burying her would have been better."

Nasser wanted to scream, *Simply leaving her alone would have been best! Because she knew nothing!*

Instead he said, "Why do you keep that Reggie around anyway? He's not in the Order."

"That is *exactly* why I keep him around. It costs the Order nothing to house him and a meager stipend keeps him fed and clothed. The important thing is he'll do anything I tell him and has no direct connection to us."

"I don't trust him."

Drexler laughed. "Do you think I do? Do you remember that story he cooked up a couple of years ago about seeing the supposedly dead Tony in a taxi?"

Nasser nodded. Reggie had gone on and on about how tracking down this miraculously alive Tony fellow—who was listed by the North Carolina police as a murder victim—would lead them to the hijacked millions. Nasser and Drexler had wasted a lot of time and effort toward that end with no results.

"I think he was afraid of becoming disposable and thought he had to come up with something to justify his continued existence."

"I do trust Klarić, however," Drexler said. "But as much as I appreciate his enthusiasm, his opinion as to these observers' identity is quite another matter."

"How so?"

He tapped the photo. "Unless the FBI has changed its hiring practices, this . . . *boy* is far too young to be any sort of agent, especially a field agent." He reversed it to stare again. "And yet I am almost certain I've seen him before. I just don't know where."

"What about the older one?"

Drexler picked up the photo that gave the clearest view of the driver's face. "He, on the other hand, looks rather old to be a field agent. But if he is an agent, he must be working on his own time."

"Why do you say that?"

"When Klarić voiced his opinion, I was naturally alarmed. So I called one of our brothers in the Bureau to have him check out the FBI's interest in that mosque. He called back just before you arrived to say the Bureau had been very interested in the mosque's imam, Sheikh Omar. But after numerous false leads and dead ends, they dropped surveillance in mid-January."

"Then who are these two?"

"Considering their age difference, they could almost be father and son. Perhaps they have something personal against the mosque."

Nasser considered that. "Possible. But then why would the older one follow me, as he did last Wednesday?"

"That concerns me. If his interest is our jihadists—are you *sure* they have agreed to change their target?"

This was the third time since Nasser's arrival that Drexler had asked for confirmation.

Nasser spread his hands. "Who can be sure of anything when dealing with fanatics? Right now Kadir and Mahmoud appear to have overruled Ramzi Yousef. I will reconfirm that when I drop off the money tomorrow. But Yousef's uncle is with al-Qaeda, and for some reason al-Qaeda finds the World Trade Towers especially attractive."

"They *must* leave the towers alone."

Again, Nasser wanted to know why but knew asking was futile.

"I'll stay in close touch with them up until Friday. But you had a thought on my being followed?"

"Yes. If the watchers' interest is in the jihadists, the older one could have seen you pick up and drop them off and decided that made you a person of interest as well."

"If he's interested in Kadir and his cohort, for whatever reason, he may well stumble onto their bomb-making activities."

"Exactly my concern. Let's have Reggie and Klarić pick them up and find out what they know."

"After they botched their last assignment?"

"I wouldn't say they botched it. They learned from the whore what we needed to know—that our secret is safe—and now we no longer have to concern ourselves with her."

Nasser kept his voice even. "I'll get right on it."

"But we'll work it differently this time. I want to be there when they question the young one. I want to know why he looks familiar."

"Very well." A new aspect of the situation occurred to him. "What if the watchers already know of the bomb plans and are waiting to gather hard evidence?"

Drexler shrugged. "What of it? Then we'll know."

"So will Klarić and Reggie."

"I hadn't thought of that. If that happens, Klarić and Reggie will become immediately expendable. I'll arrange for the contingency. Meanwhile, I'll have Klarić drive you down to Reggie's quarters and you can brief them both at the same time."

In the same room with the two men who had tortured and murdered Danaë . . . the day was getting worse and worse.

8

The knock on his door startled Reggie. The old building was mostly deserted. When he opened it and saw Klarić and al-Thani, he knew what it had to be about.

"Now wait a minute," he said, backing up. "I can explain about the girl."

Al-Thani gave him a disgusted look. "Did I mention anything about the girl?"

"Well, I saw the papers and—"

"Shut up and listen," al-Thani said. "This is about something entirely other."

Well that was good news at least. Bad enough she'd washed up, but at least at first no one had known who she was—except him and Klarić, and they weren't about to talk. As long as the Order stayed in the dark along with everybody else, all would be cool. Then he'd seen the headlines this morning and damn near shit his pants. He wouldn't have been surprised to get kicked out on the street.

Reggie leaned on the wall next to his room's only window.

"What's up?"

Klarić was holding what looked like photographs. Al-Thani pointed to them and said, "Show him."

Reggie took the stack—maybe half a dozen or so—and started shuffling through them. He blinked in shock, then straightened off the wall when he came to the third.

"Holy shit! It's Lonnie!"

"You know one of them?" al-Thani said.

Reggie showed him. "Yeah. This one. It's the guy I drove up with the truckloads of girls."

Al-Thani gave him a *yeah-right* look. "Oh, is this like seeing the dead Tony?"

"I wasn't shitting you about that and I'm not shitting you about this. This guy is the fucker who broke my knees! Where'd you find him?"

Klarić said, "I take picture of him in this morning."

"Where?"

"In front of a mosque in which we have an interest," al-Thani said. "It appears this young man and the other have an interest there as well."

"The place in Brooklyn where I picked up your little buddy Kadir a while back?"

"No. This is in Jersey City. You may be interested to know it is now Kadir's mosque, so you may see some familiar faces."

Reggie wasn't the least bit interested to know. And as far as he was concerned, the fewer Arab faces he saw, the better. Including al-Thani's.

"What's the deal? He's following Kadir?"

"We do not know, but we intend to find out. We wish to know exactly what they know about Kadir and his associates."

"You mean you want us to find out, like with the girl?"

Something flickered across the Arab's face. Distaste? Disgust? Hey, he was the guy who ordered the hit. He'd known she wasn't going to survive the night.

"Do whatever is necessary. Find out everything they know about the mosque and the people who frequent it, especially Kadir and his friends."

What was so important about Kadir? Reggie had spent a whole day driving up and down the interstates with that little raghead and he was nothing. A major camel-humping loser.

"Okay. And after they spill, then what?"

"Then I never want to see them again. Never. Do you know what 'never' means?"

"Yeah, yeah. I gotcha. We'll be more careful this time."

"See that you are. But the procedure will be different with the one you call Lonnie. Mister Drexler wishes to be present for his interrogation."

"Fine. But it won't be pretty."

"Mister Drexler has a strong stomach."

"Good. We'll grab Lonnie first. I can't wait to get my hands on him. I'm gonna get real creative on his ass. We'll let you know when we have him."

"When do you expect that to be?"

Reggie looked at Klarić. "You know where this mosque is, right?"

The Croat nodded.

Al-Thani said, "He's been there numerous times."

"Great. We'll use that van y'all have—makes it easier to transport someone who doesn't want to be transported. We'll stake him out in Jersey City first thing tomorrow and wait for a good time to grab him. We'll take him to that same loft where we worked on the girl and Mister Drexler can meet us there."

"Very good," the Arab said. "But don't start without him. I know you have a personal issue with this Lonnie, but you will be wise to wait for Mister Drexler."

"You got it. Can I ask why Mister Drexler is so interested in this guy?"

"I do not see why not. You can ask him yourself when you capture this Lonnie. And he will tell you if he so desires."

"You might want to be there too," Reggie said.

Al-Thani's eyebrows lifted. "What makes you think so?"

"Remember that hijacking a couple years ago when all your Arab buddies got massacred and three million of your money went missing along with two truckloads of girls?"

"Such a thing is not easy to forget."

"Well, you just may be finding out where those girls and that money went. Because I got a feeling this Lonnie knows. Maybe not everything, but he knows *something*, and by the time I'm through with him, he'll be blubbering every single fucking thing he knows, just like that whore."

Again, that weird look as the Arab gestured to Klarić. "After you drive me home you can return here and the two of you can make your plans."

After they were gone, Reggie went to the closet and pulled out his bow and quiver.

Strange how things happened in circles. Back in 1990, Lonnie and Tony wandered into the Outer Banks house and Lonnie wound up driving a truckload of kids for delivery to some Arabs. The deal goes sour, he and Lonnie fight, Lonnie breaks his knees and pretty much disappears. Couple of years later, Lonnie's back and the Arabs want good old Reggie to deal with him.

Sweet.

Oh, yeah, he'd deal with Lonnie. He'd find out everything the Order wanted to know, and then he'd learn other stuff. Like Lonnie's real name. And after that he'd learn the names of his folks and his brothers and his sisters and his girlfriend. And one by one, Reggie would make them all pay just for knowing the guy who'd called himself Lonnie.

He took aim at the stuffed jumpsuit and hit it in the right shoulder—just where he'd been aiming. Not a kill shot—a maim shot. The kill shot came last—after many, many other maim shots.

Like with the whore. Damn shame to mess up a sweet piece of ass like her, but orders were orders. Al-Thani had told him Drexler had handpicked him and Klarić, so that meant he'd better deliver. But that hadn't prevented the two of them from having a little fun with her first, poking her every which way with their own personal arrows before Reggie took out the bow and got down to the serious business.

He'd set his mind to go at it like a test of his archery skills. Where to put an arrow to cause the most pain, and how many of those arrows could he put into her without killing her.

He aimed again and hit the dummy's left knee.

What goes around comes around, Lonnie, my boy. And now it's coming for you.

MONDAY

1

"The old one," Klarić said, "he is parked along this street in morning and he watch. There he is now."

They sat on rain-swept Kennedy Boulevard in a Dodge Caravan that had all the side and rear windows painted over on the inside. Reggie wasn't used to getting up this early. Despite the coffees he'd downed on the way, he was still bleary eyed as he squinted at where the Croat was pointing.

"Hit the wipers. I can't see shit."

The wipers cleared the rain from the windshield, revealing a dented mid-eighties Plymouth Reliant with the bearded guy sitting behind the wheel.

"Where's the young one?" Reggie said. "Where's Lonnie?"

He didn't care about this guy. The old fart could wait. Lonnie was their target today. Lonnie was the one he wanted. Fantasies of subjecting Lonnie to the tortures of the damned had filled his dreams last night.

"I do not know. Maybe he doesn't come."

Oh, he'd better, Reggie thought. He goddamn fuck-well better.

Klarić reached into the pocket of his overcoat. "I did not get chance to show you this." He pulled out a key ring and grinned as he held it up. "Look what I made."

Reggie saw keys and a one-by-two-inch rectangle of what looked like heavy beige paper. Then it flipped around and immediately he recognized the tattoo.

"You saved it? You were supposed to burn that along with the hands."

"No-no. Is too good to waste. Nice souvenir, no?"

Reggie wanted it—wanted it *real* bad.

"What's it worth to you?"

"Is not for sale. I keep."

"I'll give you a hundred bucks for it."

He didn't have a hundred, but he wanted to see what it would take to make Klarić part with it.

Klarić shook his head. "No-no. Much more than that before I even *think* to sell."

"How about—?"

A Ford pickup passed them and then slowed by the Plymouth.

"Whoa," Reggie said. "What have we here?"

The old guy leaned out the window to say something, then pointed north. The pickup pulled to the curb a couple of spaces ahead and who stepped out but the man of the hour: Lonnie himself, carrying a cup of coffee as he hurried through the downpour to the Plymouth.

A sudden burst of rage narrowed Reggie's vision to a tunnel with Lonnie framed at the end. Of its own accord, his hand fumbled for the passenger door handle. Klarić reached over from behind the wheel and grabbed his arm.

"What you are doing?"

Reggie realized he'd been ready to step out and go after him right here and now. He leaned back in the seat.

"I want him, Klarić. I want him real bad."

"Cannot do here. Cannot be seen."

"I got that. I got that."

He watched Lonnie, moving all casual and loose-limbed as you please, hop into the passenger side of the Plymouth.

Enjoy your life while you can, fucker. You ain't got much of it left.

2

"Happy Presidents' Day," Jack said as he slammed the door behind him.

Bertel looked confused. "What?"

Jack couldn't resist a little ribbing as he shook off the icy rainwater. Rotten weather for a stakeout.

"It's Presidents' Day. I expected the inside here to be done up in red, white, and blue bunting."

Bertel did not appear amused as he sipped from his Thermos. "Forgot to look at my calendar today."

"But how could you miss it, what with all the car dealer ads and—?"

"Can it. Did you manage to tail the mystery Mohammedan?"

Okay, time to get serious, Jack guessed.

"Yep. To an apartment house in Turtle Bay. He went to the ninth floor. And on the ninth floor lives someone named 'N. al-Thani.'"

Bertel gave him an appraising look. "Nice work."

"Know anybody by that name?"

"Nope. But it's the same name as the ruling family of Qatar."

"How do you know stuff like that? How does *anyone* know stuff like that?"

Despite all of Bertel's protestations to the contrary, Jack remained convinced he had some intelligence background. CIA, FBI, NSA, whatever. He was also convinced that Burkes and his guys had recognized Bertel's name—maybe they didn't know him personally, but they knew *of* him.

"It's in the papers," Bertel said.

"Not in the comics and sports sections."

"So you're a big sports fan?"

The change of subject wasn't lost on Jack but he went with it.

"I'm a fan of sports *scores*. The games themselves bore me. But let's get back to this N. al-Thani. You're telling me he's like royalty?"

"Probably not. Maybe distantly related. A prince of the line of the royal family of Qatar wouldn't be caught dead with the likes we're watching. Be like rolling in mud for him."

Royal family . . . that started wheels turning.

"Let's piece this together," Jack said, thinking out loud. "Reggie was involved in selling little girls to some Arabs. The three million in cash intended for the sale was hijacked. Where did the three million come from?"

"Could've come from anywhere."

"Right. But a few months later you see Reggie and this al-Thani—"

"Along with a couple of our jihadists."

"Right. You see them on a beach where they've set up an ambush for the guys who hijacked the money. What does that tell you?"

"Obviously you're thinking it came from al-Thani."

"Well, yeah. Aren't you?"

"Not so sure."

"Why not? You yourself said the al-Thanis run Qatar. I don't know a damn thing about Qatar but I figure any royal family of an Arab country has got to be up to their ears in oil money. I mean, they're rich, right?"

"As Croesus."

"So there's a good chance our al-Thani was funding them, and the ambush was an attempt to get his money back."

"It makes sense but it may be a leap to assume he was funding them with his own money."

"You've gotta figure some of the royal al-Thani wealth bled out to the relatives."

"Enough to make them comfortable, yes. But comfortable enough to take a three-million-dollar flyer on a shipment of sex slaves? I don't think so. I suspect someone or something else is backing him."

Uh-oh. Here we go.

"The 'Something Bigger' you mentioned once?"

Bertel smiled. "You remember?"

They'd had this conversation while tailing Reggie and Kadir up route 95 a couple of years ago. Jack had never forgotten it because it had wormed under his skin.

"I'm distracted sometimes," Jack said, "but I'm a long way from senile. Since then have you found any proof of 'Something Bigger'?"

He shook his head. "Nothing concrete, but I'm more convinced than ever that I'm right."

Jack had to ask: "When you say 'some*thing*,' you don't mean some evil supernatural force or anything like that, right?"

Bertel gave him a scathing look. "I mean an organization made up of some*ones*."

"Like the Illuminati? Or the Masons? Or the Knights Templar? Or the Trilateral Commission? Or the Bilderberg Group?"

"You seem to know them all."

Jack was fond of conspiracy theories, but more for their entertainment value than their real-life relevance.

"Those are just the tip of the iceberg."

"I'm sure. But the organization I'm talking about is so pervasive that it has influential members in all those groups. And so subtle that no one suspects it."

"Nothing can be that influential and remain secret."

"It can if it hides in plain sight."

Jack sighed. "To tell the truth, I don't see the point in worrying about 'Something Bigger' until we know a little more about this al-Thani guy. All we've got right now is a name."

"True. But I know what my gut tells me."

"I'm more interested in what your eyes tell you. You've been watching Kadir and his friends for a couple of years now and no second coming of this guy al-Thani till last week?"

Bertel nodded. "Right. And what's gone on since then—or what *hasn't* gone on, I should say—has me a little worried."

"Like what?"

"Well, it's nothing definite, but for the past week or so, ever since al-Thani reappeared, the jihadists haven't been hanging around the mosque like they used to."

"Didn't they used to be at a Brooklyn mosque before they moved here? Maybe they've found yet another—"

"No, they're still in town—we saw them just yesterday. But ever since they moved here, the Al-Salam has been their social center of sorts. They were in and out of there every day. Now they show up to go for a ride with this al-Thani character and then head off somewhere else."

"You think he financed a new project?"

"I can't think of anything else."

"Another slave shipment?"

Bertel shrugged. "No idea. That's why we're here: to watch, to follow, to find out." He gestured toward Jack with his Thermos. "You know the two who hijacked the money. What did they say would have happened to the girls had they not crashed the party?"

Jack ran through his conversations with the Mikulski brothers and distilled them to a bottom line.

"They said preteen girls like that go for two hundred thou to two fifty apiece at auction."

"And there were how many?"

"Twenty-eight." His gut tightened as he remembered a conversation between two of the slavers. "Supposed to be thirty but two didn't survive the trip."

The slavers had referred to the loss as "spoilage."

Bertel was nodding. "That means the three million would have more than doubled after the auction. Assuming al-Thani or his backer"—a glance at Jack here—"put up the initial three, he would have had his principal back with interest by the next day, leaving the jihadists with a fortune to spend on terror."

"Instead they wound up *out* three million plus a bunch of dead buddies. And no girls."

"Right. And things went from bad to worse for them after that, ending with their fearless leader being kicked out of the Al-Farooq Mosque and banished to Jersey City."

"So you think they've been marking time since then?"

"Or waiting to gather the right personnel."

"For what?"

"What else? Bombs."

"Oh, hell."

"I wish I could find out more about this Ramzi Yousef character."

"The one with the Manson eyes?"

"Right. He's got a bunch of different names—goes by 'Rashed' on the street—which is a sure indicator that he's a bad actor. He may be the bomb guy they've been waiting for."

"Oh, yeah. I could see him as a bomb maker."

"Well, shortly after Yousef arrives, al-Thani reappears. Could be they hit him up for money to buy the ingredients."

Jack caught the drift and didn't like where it carried him.

"And they're not hanging around the mosque these days because they're mixing those ingredients."

"Exactly. Jersey City has a large Mohammedan population, so it's not as if we can go door to door looking for a bomb factory."

Not that Jack could ever see himself doing that anyway.

Bertel straightened in his seat and put on the windshield wipers. "There's a familiar car."

Up ahead and across the street, an old Chevy Nova pulled to a stop before the three-story building that housed the mosque. He didn't recognize the Arab who got out of the driver's seat, but he'd seen the other three before: Kadir, the redheaded Mahmoud, and Manson-eyed Yousef.

"Hail, hail, the gang's all here. Who's the driver?"

"Don't know. Saw him yesterday."

They clustered in a knot out of the rain under the toy store awning next to the entrance to the building. By the way they looked up and down the street they seemed to be waiting for someone. Jack let his gaze wander up to the check-cashing/notary-public signs on the second floor, and then to the crude Al Salam sign in a third-floor window. He remembered how the second-floor Al-Farooq Mosque—which at least announced its presence with a neon sign at street level—shared space in a commercial building in Brooklyn.

"I thought mosques were supposed to have golden domes and high towers."

"You mean minarets," Bertel said. "That's in the Middle East. Lots of Mohammedans here in Jersey City, and over in Brooklyn as well, but nothing like the numbers back in Araby. And so they don't have the kind of money it takes to build one of those. These mosques here are like the storefront Bible-thumping churches you see on the far West Side and down along the Bowery. Really, what's a church but a place to pray and study your holy book? The rest is just window dressing. Like those big ostentatious cathedrals of the Middle Ages."

"I guess so. It's just that sharing space with all those low-end businesses doesn't seem very . . . I don't know . . . holy."

Bertel looked at him. "What do you know about holy?"

Jack had to smile. "Not a goddamn thing."

"Starting tomorrow morning, things will get holier around here."

"Meaning?"

"Ramadan begins with sunrise."

"You say that like I'm supposed to know what you're talking about."

"It's the Mohammedan holy month where you don't eat or drink or have sex from sunrise to sunset."

"How do you *know* that?"

"I read."

"What? You study Islam?"

"Know thy enemy."

"You read Machiavelli too?"

"That was Sun Tzu."

"Whatever." Jack gestured to the mosque. "They're all enemies?"

Bertel shook his head. "Most of them are decent, hardworking folks who just want to earn their daily bread and raise their families, and maybe see a better future, which will never come because their religion mires them in the past. But that's not my business. Everyone chooses their own path. The enemies are the psycho-sickos like Sheikh Omar and his minions who think it's their divine mission to make all the world bow to Allah. They hide behind the skirts of their religion and kill noncombatants."

"You think they'll be fasting too?"

"Most certainly."

"A whole month?"

"Twenty-nine or thirty days, depending on the moon."

"That can only make them crankier than they already are."

"I wouldn't be surprised if they're thinking their holy month of Ramadan is the best time to strike a blow for jihad."

Jack was still trying to get his head around this whole fasting thing. Self-imposed hunger and thirst . . . for what? What kind of supposedly benevolent god finds it appealing for his followers to do that?

"Not even water?"

"Not during the daylight hours. And no beer either. Ever."

Unimaginable. He'd never understand why people do those things to themselves.

"I'd be so out of there."

"You might try it sometime. For the self-discipline."

"It's like Lent on steroids."

"You were raised Catholic?"

"Nah. My parents weren't into religion—weren't against it, weren't for it . . . it just never came up. But I had friends who were Catholics. They'd give up chocolate for—what's Lent run? Forty days? Anyway, a bunch of the other kids would cluster around them with packs of M&Ms and chomp away and smack their lips. But at least they could eat and drink other stuff."

"This time of year daylight runs from about six thirty to five thirty— eleven hours. Not a big deal to go without food or water for eleven measly hours. Although by the end of Ramadan daylight will have stretched to twelve hours. Still no big deal."

"Yeah? Ever try it?"

Bertel kept his gaze focused on the mosque building. "I've gone *days* without food or water."

"Really? Why?"

"Circumstances out of my control."

"Care to elaborate?"

"Nope."

He wished he knew more about Dane Bertel—where he'd been, why he'd been there, who he'd been working for at the time. Jack bet he had some amazing stories to tell.

He laughed. "Well, if I was Muslim, I'd be hitting Mickey D's at six A.M. sharp to pound down a whole tray of Egg McMuffins before sunrise."

And then the Mercedes pulled up.

Bertel lifted his field glasses and adjusted the focus.

"Same car, different driver."

Jack watched Kadir step up to the car and bend to speak to someone in the rear seat. After a brief exchange, a manila envelope was handed out. Kadir stepped back as the Mercedes waited for a big enough break in the traffic, then made a U-turn and zoomed away. He turned to his friends and held up the envelope like a prize. The other three grinned and gave him congratulatory pats on the back.

Bertel lowered the glasses and said, "Payday. You want to follow the Mercedes? Ninety-nine to one it's your N. al-Thani, but let's be sure."

"On my way. What about you?"

"I'm going to have another go at our jihadists and see if I can find out what they're up to."

"Right." Jack hopped out but leaned back in before slamming the door. "Talk to you later—much later."

"Why much later?"

"Got a date for lunch and a movie."

Bertel's expression turned sour. "This is important, Jack."

"So's this."

He trotted ahead to the pickup, got it running, and tore off after the Mercedes. Yeah, that had been al-Thani. No one else it could be. He knew they'd be heading to the Holland, just like last time. He'd catch them, no sweat.

3

"There he goes," Reggie said.

Klarić nodded as he put the car in gear and got rolling. "I see."

"Looks like he's following al-Thani."

"What is plan? Do we wish to stop him from learning who is al-Thani?"

Reggie thought about that a second. "For all we know, he's already followed him home."

Klarić shook his head. "I do not think so. I have been driving him and I have been on lookout for follower. I would have seen."

Reggie didn't want to argue with him. Nobody was perfect.

"Either way, it doesn't matter. He ain't surviving the day."

"Ah yes. I see. You are right." He smiled. "It does not matter."

Reggie thought Klarić was following Lonnie way too close.

"It *will* matter if he spots us on his tail."

"He will not spot. Easiest man to follow is one who is following someone else. His eyes always straight ahead. He is never looking behind."

"And you know this how?"

"I follow many people many times. Besides, we only think he follows al-Thani. What if he is not? If I am not close, I can lose."

Reggie hadn't considered that. Good thought, although he'd be damned
if he'd say so.

Since being assigned to snatch and interrogate the whore, he and Klarić
had been jockeying back and forth for a pecking order between them. Reggie's bow and how he had been able to use it on her had put him in charge
then.

She'd told them at the start she hadn't heard anyone say a word about
Senator D'Amato, and was blubbering the same at the end before he put a
shaft through her heart. The hours of torture—okay, and a good bit of tying
her over a table and diddling her as well—hadn't accomplished anything.
Well, maybe they had. At least they'd ended up sure she hadn't heard anything.

He'd never tortured anyone before and had wound up liking it. Really
got into it. He'd never heard of torturing anyone by making them an archery
target, but doubted he could be the first. The trick was not to hit a vital organ
until you learned what you were after. That meant sticking to the legs, hips,
shoulders, arms. Especially the knees. They'd gagged her, so she didn't make
much noise when he put the first arrow into one of her knees, right into the
joint space, but her eyes had damn near bugged clear out of her head.

Yeah, the bow and arrow had made him *numero uno* then, but his own
bad knees made him only a so-so driver, which gave Klarić a leg up today, so
to speak.

"Mister al-Thani's driver goes to Lincoln Tunnel," Klarić said as they
rolled along. "I prefer Holland."

"Whatever." Reggie was dreaming of the near future. "As long as we catch
him."

Eventually they followed Lonnie's pickup into the Lincoln Tunnel.

"Where do we take him?" Klarić said.

Reggie laughed. "Well, not in here, that's for sure. He's got to stop sometime. When he does, we'll grab him and toss him in the back."

Just like with the whore. They'd watched her apartment building. When
she came out they double-parked ahead of her and pretended to be unloading
the van. When she came abreast, ox-sized Klarić had lifted her off her feet
and hurled her into the rear of the van where Reggie had waited. The door
slammed, Reggie stuck a knife against her throat, and she was all theirs.

Lonnie wouldn't be so easy, but between Klarić's strength and Reggie's
lead-filled sap, the result would be the same.

And just like the whore, they'd take him to the Order's run-down loft in the Meatpacking District. But this time there'd be no diddling—unless Klarić was so inclined. They'd call Drexler, and when the man in white arrived, they'd go to work on Lonnie. What a shame if Drexler's suit got splattered with red.

Lonnie, Lonnie, Lonnie . . . can't wait to see your face when you see mine . . . can't wait to get reacquainted . . . can't wait to learn your real name . . . can't wait to watch your eyes bulge like the whore's. Can't wait, can't wait, can't wait.

4

"Okay," Dane muttered. "You've got your money. What are you going to do with it?"

Shortly after al-Thani left, Kadir had entered the doorway to the building, presumably to go up to the mosque. Why? To tell Sheikh Omar? Make a call? Both?

He came back a few minutes later and the four of them hung around under the awning of the Chinese takeout until a blue late-model Ford Taurus rolled up. Kadir got in and the Ford started moving north again. Dane checked out the driver as it passed but had never seen him before. That made two new Mohammedans into the mix in two days. He was going to need a scorecard soon to keep them all straight.

The Nova, with the other new one driving, Abouhalima in front and Yousef in the rear, made a U-turn and headed south.

"Shit!"

Why the hell had he sent Jack after al-Thani? Well, he couldn't have predicted this.

All right—which way to go?

Kadir had the money. Follow the money. He was facing south on Kennedy so he had to wait to make his own U and follow the Taurus. A few more seconds behind and he would have missed seeing it turn right on Newark

Avenue. He followed as it made a left on Summit Avenue. As they bore up the incline, it looked like they were heading for the Heights. What did the Jersey City Heights hold for a couple of crazy jihadists?

He stayed a few cars back but that proved a mistake when traffic was halted to allow a super-long tractor trailer to back into a driveway. When the road cleared, the Taurus was gone.

Cursing a blue streak, Dane raced around the Heights for a good twenty minutes without spotting them. Finally he gave up and headed back the way he had come. He parked near the base of Summit and waited, figuring if they'd gone up this way, they'd come back down this way.

Or so he hoped.

5

Aimal Kasi drove along Dolley Madison Boulevard on his way to pick up a package in Georgetown and deliver it to an office in Tyson's Corners. As he neared the entrance to CIA Headquarters in Langley, he slowed to inspect the double row of cars stopped at the traffic light, waiting to make the left turn into the complex.

Despite his best efforts over the weekend, he had been unable to purchase any hand grenades. A Kashmiri friend in Reston knew of a Saudi who had a number of assault rifles and might be willing to sell one. Aimal had met him in a public park on Sunday where they came to terms. A Type 56 assault rifle—the imitation AK-47 made by the Chinese—now rested in his trunk, equipped with a full magazine. All he needed was a chance to use it.

But how to put it to best use? How to do the most damage to the Great Satan in his blow for jihad? He thought of racing into the entrance and charging toward the headquarters, but certainly roadblocks and armed guards lined the path. He might be killed before he fired a single shot.

No, he had to find a better way.

Trusting in Allah to enlighten him, he drove on.

6

Soon after Reggie and Klarić exited the Lincoln Tunnel into midtown, it became clear that Lonnie was going to be following al-Thani all the way home. As the Mercedes fought the crosstown traffic, the pickup hung back. That told Reggie that Lonnie already knew where al-Thani was going. Klarić stayed a few cars behind Lonnie.

As al-Thani's driver—maybe Klarić knew the guy but Reggie didn't—dropped the Arab off at his place on Second Avenue, Lonnie didn't stop or even slow to watch. Instead he turned downtown.

"This could be interesting," Reggie said.

They followed him down to the East Thirties where he took the ramp to the Midtown Tunnel.

"Looks like he's heading for Queens."

They followed him through the tunnel and onto 495.

"Long Island?" Reggie said. "Let's hope so. Less crowded out there."

But no, he turned south on the BQE.

"Brooklyn. Damn."

They needed an opportunity to roust Lonnie into the van with a minimum of fuss and, ideally, no witnesses. Or at least none who'd care enough to drop a dime.

Lonnie got onto Broadway in Williamsburg and followed that to Myrtle Avenue in Bushwick.

"Where the hell is he going?"

"You know this city good?" Klarić said.

Reggie nodded. "Been here a few years now. Don't have a car but I've bused and subwayed all over."

Not much else to do. Living in the Order's building and waiting for them to give him something to pick up or deliver had offered him virtually unlimited free time. Unfortunately he'd had extremely limited funds. But if he planned his transfers right, he could ride all day, all over the five boroughs, on a single subway token. He'd done just that, many times. He'd taken the M train out here on numerous occasions. Most of the subway lines in the outer boroughs weren't *sub* at all—they ran on elevated tracks. Reggie preferred those because they gave him something to look at besides a tunnel wall. Right now Lonnie was leading them along the tracks that ran above Myrtle Avenue.

Finally he pulled in before a small garage flanked by abandoned buildings under the tracks near Palmetto and St. Nicholas. Its corrugated overhead door was down. Klarić slowed a little as they cruised by.

"This might be good," Reggie said as he watched Lonnie enter through the smaller door to the side. "Depending on who and what's inside, this could be *real* good."

Klarić's head was swiveling like a radar dish. "I do not know. Maybe we should wait for night."

"Night? Who knows where he's gonna be by night? Listen. It's still early in the morning and it's Presidents' Day—"

"What is this Presidents' Day?"

"A holiday. The kids are off school. Most of them are sleeping in. And the ones that ain't—man, it's not only fucking freezing out there, it's pouring, so if they ain't watching 'toons, they're playing Mario Brothers or Mortal Kombat."

"I don't like," Klarić said. "Too much light."

"The amount of light don't matter—the amount of people matter, and there ain't hardly any around. Let me out here, then hang a U and come back while I take a peek inside."

As Klarić pulled over, Reggie grabbed his short bow and quiver from behind the seat.

Klarić pulled a pistol from a shoulder holster and held it up. "Why you so old-fashioned? This is better."

"I'm better with this. I might kill him with that." He showed him the tip of the two-blade broadhead he used. "Besides, this hurts more."

He'd told al-Thani that he needed a long coat and Klarić had arrived with a lined raincoat this morning. He hooked the quiver to his belt and slipped the bow under the flap of the coat.

Doing his best to look like he belonged there, he strolled most of the way to the door Lonnie had entered, then slowed and sidled the last few feet. The door had no windows and was even more beat-up than the rest of the building. Its warped wood made it hang crooked on its hinges, leaving a gap between the edge and the frame. Reggie peeked through . . .

. . . and there he was: Lonnie.

Reggie contained the eruption of rage. Had to keep calm, check out the scene. Anyone else around? No, just the little spic chick he was talking to. She looked fourteen, tops. What was he—?

That dirty motherfucker! She was the right color and the right age now to be one of the kids they'd trucked up to Staten Island. Had he kept one for himself?

Reggie's hand shook as he pulled the bow from under his coat and grabbed an arrow. Plenty of space in the gap to place one in his shoulder—his right shoulder, because that would make that arm useless but leave all the rest of his body to have fun with when they dragged him back to the West Side.

He nocked the arrow onto the string . . .

7

"First stop will be FAO Schwartz where we can—"

"Can we go on the big piano?" Bonita said, her dark eyes flashing. "The one on the floor?"

Jack laughed as he helped wrap a scarf around her neck. Damn, her English was better every time he saw her.

"You don't know how to play piano," said Rico from where he was adjusting the hydraulics on the plow attachment to his truck.

The forecast predicted snow for Friday so Jack guessed he was getting ready.

"Doesn't matter," Jack called back. Then to Bonita, "Have you been watching *Big* again?"

"I love *Big*!"

"So do I. But is he right—you can't play piano?"

"No."

"Neither can I, except for 'Chopsticks.' I'll show you how when we get there—if they still have the keyboard and if they'll let us."

"They did in the movie."

"Yeah, well, that was a movie. We'll be in real life."

Bonita had never been in FAO and neither had he. What for? He was the only kid he knew, and he preferred toys from the time when his father was a kid.

"And then we go to the movie?"

"No, then we go to lunch. I think you'll like Mickey Mantle's. It's just down the street from FAO. Your brother's gonna be so jealous 'cause I hear they have great burgers. After our bellies are fit to bust, we go see *Home Alone Two*. I—oops, your shoe is untied."

As he dropped into a crouch to fix it, he heard a *thik!* and a soft grunt from Bonita. He looked up and she was falling backward with an arrow shaft protruding from her chest.

It took a heartbeat or two to process the impossible sight playing out right in front of him. Bonita's expression showed more shock and surprise than pain as she continued to stumble-fall backward. He heard Rico scream her name but he wasn't rushing toward her. Instead he was charging to Jack's right, his face a mask of rage. Jack's first instinct was to grab for Bonita but another more primitive part made him seek out the origin of the arrow.

Arrow . . .

That could mean only one thing . . . only one person.

As he spun he saw a pale skinny guy with a red mullet standing inside the door that was still swinging open.

Reggie.

He was nocking another arrow and his narrow little eyes were on Jack. But those eyes shifted right and he couldn't help but know he wasn't going to get a second shot at Jack with Rico so close. So he swiveled and loosed it at Rico. It pierced his throat, the point erupting from the back of his neck. Rico stumbled and dropped to his knees, clawing at his throat as blood gushed from his mouth.

Jack was already moving. He'd left his Glock under the front seat of the pickup and didn't have time to go for the Semmerling in his ankle holster, so he grabbed a small wooden bench and raised it as he charged Reggie. He peered over the top edge as he held it before him like a shield. He saw Reggie nock another arrow—damn, he was fast—and aim it straight at the bench. Jack didn't believe for a second that Reggie thought he could put it through the two-inch board, so he watched his eyes, and when they flicked down, he lowered the bench and it caught the arrow loosed at his legs.

And then he was on Reggie, ramming him back against the door just as someone else started to come through. The door slammed against the newcomer. Jack had time to notice he was big and had a semiauto in his hand before slamming the bench against Reggie again, knocking him down. The bow fell from his grasp as his arrows scattered across the floor.

The big guy pushed through then but tripped over the fallen Reggie. The new guy's arm was closest so Jack slammed the bench down hard against it. A bone crunched in his elbow and the gun dropped. Jack swung the bench again, this time against the guy's head.

Reggie was up and moving—toward the door rather than Jack. Jack grabbed for him, caught a piece of his coat but couldn't hold him. He threw the bench at him, hitting his upper back. It staggered him but didn't knock him off his feet. He banged against the door frame, bounced off, and stumbled outside.

"Oh, no! Not this time!"

The new guy lay prone, reaching for his gun with his good arm. Jack jumped on him, landing knees first full force on his back. He heard ribs shatter as the air rushed out in an agonized *whoosh*. Grabbing the bow and picking up an arrow as he rose, Jack took off after Reggie. He wanted to go to Bonita and Rico, but if he didn't stop Reggie now, no telling what further harm he'd do. He might be going for an Uzi or the like.

As he came through the door he saw the mullet-haired bastard climbing into a Caravan. Jack reached it just as the door slammed shut and locked. He stood in the rain smashing his hands against the window. Just inches away on the other side of the glass, Reggie grinned as he gave him the finger.

But the grin disappeared when he reached for the ignition. His expression became frantic as he began looking around the front seats.

Jack could think of only one reason for that: no key. And he had a pretty good idea where that key might be.

He dashed back inside and found the big guy grunting in agony as he inched along the floor on his belly toward his fallen semiautomatic. Jack kicked it away, then jumped on his back again. More ribs cracked. Jack pawed through his pockets, finding a wallet, some cash, some keys—

A door slammed outside.

The Caravan? Reggie making a run for it?

Grabbing the bow and arrow again, he dashed back outside. Sure enough, Reggie was hurrying away through the rain as best he could on the knees Jack had once broken. Jack knew nothing about bows, but it seemed pretty cut and dried. He nocked an arrow with a nasty-looking head, pulled it back to his chin, aimed it at Reggie's back, and let fly.

Missed. By at least a dozen feet.

He was going to have to do this the hard way.

Still holding the bow, he gave chase at full speed. Reggie glanced over his shoulder and cried out when he saw how fast Jack was gaining. He tried to increase his pace but his knees wouldn't allow it. When Jack was close enough, he reached out to grab his collar, then had a better idea. Instead, he swung the end of the bow over Reggie's head and yanked back, catching him by the throat.

With a choking cry, Reggie's feet flew out from under him and he landed hard on his back. As he lay there stunned, with the wind knocked out of him, Jack used the bow to begin dragging him by the neck back toward the garage. By the time they reached the door he was kicking and clawing at the floor and the jamb, trying to regain his feet, but a series of yanking twists of the bow kept him on the ground until he was inside.

Jack dragged him through his spilled arrows.

"You're into arrows, Reggie?" he said as he knelt beside him and grabbed one from the floor. "How about we put one into you?"

He rolled him over and rammed it into his throat. The wicked barbed head plunged into the flesh left of center. Reggie levered up, eyes bulging. He looked like he was howling in pain but only a hoarse rush of air came out his wide-open mouth. He kicked and twisted as he made that strange sound.

Jack checked the new guy, who looked like he was having trouble breathing. Punctured lung maybe?

Satisfied that neither would be doing much more damage for a few minutes, Jack rushed over to where Bonita lay flat on her back, her arms flung wide, her sweater soaked red, her eyes open and glazed, fixed on the ceiling.

"No! No-no-no-no!"

He wanted to press on her chest. He didn't know CPR but even if he did, how do you resuscitate someone with an arrow in her heart? He'd seen the barbed heads on Reggie's arrows and knew he couldn't pull this one out without shredding her insides. He checked for a pulse, for breathing—nothing on both counts. He blew into her mouth and saw dark blood bubble up around the arrow shaft. He tried pressing on her chest but it only pushed more blood out around the shaft.

He heard a gagging cough—Rico.

Jack reached him in time to see him breathe his last. Reggie's arrow had pierced his neck so Jack pumped on his chest but it succeeded only in making crimson bubbles in the blood filling his mouth.

Jack felt himself losing it. He tried to keep a grip but the dark genie had escaped his bottle and was exulting in its freedom.

Jack stalked over to Reggie and began kicking him. He'd worn sneakers today so he wasn't doing near the damage he wanted. Cristin dead, Rico dead, Bonita dead, all because of this piece of human garbage. All Jack's fault.

"I let you live!"

The Mikulskis had warned him.

"They told me to kill you!" He kept kicking. "But I couldn't do it!"

One of the brothers' words echoed back . . .

These subhumans are like boomerangs. They somehow find their way back to you.

And Reggie had done just that. If Jack had dumped him in the channel as they'd wanted, or if he'd used the tire iron on Reggie's head instead of his knees, three people very dear to him would still be alive.

. . . the subhumans . . . once they're gone, you don't have to give them another thought. And believe me, they're not worth a thought after they're gone.

More kicking . . .

"I can't believe I let you *live!*"

Panting, he stopped and stood over the rasping, retching Reggie.

Time to rectify that mistake. And never, ever would he make it again.

As he reached for the arrow in Reggie's throat, to drive its ugly head deeper into his neck, he heard a groan. The big guy was trying to turn over.

Jack took a step toward him. "And who the fuck are you, by the way?"

Big Guy had arrived too late to hurt Bonita and Rico, but had he anything to do with Cristin? His wallet lay on the floor beside him. Jack checked it and found a driver's license under the name Brajko Klarić. Probably real. Who'd make up a name like that?

He tossed it onto the keys and was turning back to Reggie when something caught his eye. A key fob . . . the familiar symbol on it stopped him cold. He picked it up for a closer look. No . . . couldn't be . . .

He slumped as he stared at it.

"Oh, no . . . oh, no . . ."

He was holding a piece of Cristin . . . made into a key fob.

Jack retched.

Here it was . . . the final proof that those were Reggie's arrow wounds in Cristin. And this guy, this Brajko Klarić was there too . . . had cut off Cristin's tattoo, cut off her hands . . . probably raped her too.

Brajko Klarić groaned as he flopped onto his back. His eyes showed no fear, only hate for Jack.

"You will die," he rasped.

"Will I?"

Jack looked around for something, anything that would hurt him, maim him, damage him like he'd damaged Cristin.

Arrows . . . yes, the arrows.

Still on his knees, he grabbed one and rammed it into Brajko Klarić's left eye. His scream was music.

"Was that how Cristin screamed?"

Jack found another. Brajko Klarić's right eye was squeezed shut. No problem. Jack shoved the arrowhead through the lid and into the eye beneath.

Another scream—a long undulating openmouthed wail.

"Shut up!"

Jack grabbed a third shaft and plunged the point into his mouth, lodging the two-bladed head deep in the tissues at the back of his throat.

Brajko Klarić bucked and kicked and spasmed and choked and gagged as blood filled his mouth. He had both hands on the shaft, trying to pull it out, but those big barbed blades were staying right where they were.

Jack rose and stepped back and watched him die.

It took a while.

Not nearly long enough.

When it was done, he turned back to Reggie. The subhuman lay on his back with blood pooling under his head—not a lot, nothing life threatening. By some miracle the arrowhead had missed the big arteries.

Too bad.

Jack hunted around until he found Rico's machete. He checked the edge—nicely honed. This would do.

He waved it before Reggie's fear-filled eyes.

Reggie couldn't seem to make any sounds except harsh, breathy rasps, but his mouth was working as if he was trying to say something. Finally . . .

"No!"

The arrow must have cut something speech related in his throat. His voice had no volume, no tone. More like air hissing out of a cut hose.

"For the moment we'll put aside the atrocities you committed here. Let's focus on the girl you raped, tortured, dismembered, and splashed with acid. Remember her? The one they called the Ditmars Dahlia?"

"Just a whore," he said in his steam-hiss voice. "A nobody."

"Not to me. She had a name: Cristin. And she was a friend . . . a very dear friend."

And now the fear turned to horror. Weak as he was, with an arrow shaft jutting from his throat, Reggie tried to scrabble away on his back.

"Don't leave. I'm just getting started. How about I do to you what you did to her? You cut off her hands. Let's start there. After that, I'll find some acid for your face. I'm sure Rico has something around that will do the job."

Jack wasn't sure of anything right now. He was out of control and he knew it. But every time he tried to get a grip he'd see Bonita or Rico lying dead with Reggie's shafts protruding from them, and then the dark would retake the helm.

Reggie's cry was more leaking steam.

"You want to say something? Don't bother. Nothing you can say will change what's going to happen here."

He raised his hand and Jack swung the machete at it. Looking to lop it off at the wrist. At the last second he angled the blade upward so it would miss.

What am I doing?

If he cut off Reggie's hand he might not be able to stop the bleeding.

Reggie would die. And as much as a dead Reggie was all Jack wanted in the world right now, this wasn't the time.

Not yet . . . not yet . . .

Because Reggie had had no beef with Cristin. He and the other guy had been put up to it. But by whom?

Cristin hadn't scratched *DAMATO* into her skin for nothing. She must have known she was a goner. Jack groaned at the thought of the terror, the helplessness, the hopelessness she must have felt toward the end. She'd wanted to leave a message that would help find her killers.

Well, Jack had found them. Or rather they'd found Jack. But who had sicced them on her?

Arabs . . . had to be Arabs. Reggie was linked to them, D'Amato was linked to them too, though in a negative way.

Jack would never know the answer if he killed Reggie now—*now* being the operative word.

He realized he had no idea what to do next. He was standing in a garage in Bushwick with three corpses and a speechless man that he needed to interrogate. Except he didn't know how to interrogate anyone. One wrong move and he could kill Reggie.

Not yet . . . not yet . . .

He couldn't afford to flub this. He had one source, one opportunity to answer the big question. This was too important to trust to his own inexperienced hands.

Call someone. Simple enough: When you're out of your depth, get advice. Well, he was sure as shit out of his depth. But who to call? Bertel? Yeah, he had a feeling Dane Bertel would know what to do, but he was out tailing his Mohammedans around Jersey City and Jack wouldn't be able to reach him until tonight. And would Bertel be all that interested? This might have some link to the jihadists, or just as easily might not. Bertel had no personal stake in this.

But Jack knew someone who did. Someone who carried a phone with him everywhere. Someone he was quite sure knew all the fine points of interrogating a person who might not want to talk.

He looked around. Rico had to have a phone here somewhere. . . .

8

Exactly ten minutes after Dane had parked—thirty minutes after he'd lost them—the Taurus with Kadir and the new Mohammedan passed by on its way back down from the Heights. He didn't see anyone new in the car, or anything visible in the rear seat.

He followed, expecting them to turn on Newark, retracing the way they'd come here, but instead they stayed on Summit all the way to Montgomery. Right on that and back to Kennedy. Kennedy south to Communipaw . . .

"Okay, I know where you're headed."

He eased back and let them get farther ahead. They'd be turning onto Mallory and heading for that storage area, the Space Station.

Sure enough, the Taurus turned in there. Question was: Where were the rest of them?

Twenty minutes later the Taurus reemerged with Ramzi Yousef in the rear. A chance then that Abouhalima and the other unknown Mohammedan were still there, but far from definite. His best bet was to chase the Taurus. But as he put his Plymouth in gear, he saw the Chevy Nova easing up the Space Station driveway from the rear. It parked maybe twenty feet from the sliding gate. Redheaded Abouhalima stepped out from the passenger seat and trotted through the rain to the gate. He stared along Mallory Avenue, not in the direction the Taurus had gone but the way it had come, then trotted back.

They were expecting someone.

Something . . . a feeling that pieces were poised to fall into place made Dane take his car out of gear and wait a little more.

9

"Jesus cunting Christ!" Burkes said as he surveyed the carnage. "It's like William Tell meets Sweeney Todd!"

"Hey, watch it," Jack said. "That little girl was very dear to me."

He looked at Jack and must have seen the truth of that in his face, because he held up his hand, palm out, and said, "Easy, lad. I meant no disrespect to your fallen."

After his call to Burkes—telling him the address and obliquely conveying that he'd encountered two people who'd been involved with their mutual friend—Jack had found a couple of dropcloths to cover Bonita and Rico. But the way the arrows stuck up under the cloths disturbed him, so he'd cut off the shafts just above the skin. Not an easy task because they were made of some kind of composite over an aluminum core. Took a hacksaw to get the job done.

He'd left Brajko Klarić where he'd fallen.

Jack had cooled by the time Burkes arrived with his two bodyguards or whatever they were, all three wrapped in hooded rain parkas. Without a word they'd fanned out through the garage, taking it all in.

Burkes pointed to Rico's draped form. "Another friend?"

Jack nodded.

Burkes wandered over to where Brajko Klarić sprawled with the three arrow shafts jutting toward the ceiling from the eyes and mouth of his blood-coated face.

"And this, I take it, was not a friend." He showed Jack a tight, grim smile. "Had a wee bit of a temper tantrum, did we?"

"Yeah. A wee. His license says his name is Brajko Klarić."

"Sounds Croatian. Anything else?"

Jack handed him the semiautomatic. "He was carrying this."

Burkes turned it over in his hands. "Piece of crap Tokarev. Goes with the name. And what's his part in our drama?"

Jack hadn't mentioned the fob when he'd called. He pulled out Klarić's keys and handed them over.

"I found this in his pocket."

Burkes gave him a questioning look as he took the keys. He turned the fob over. He dropped the Tokarev as he stared. Then he looked up at Jack, his lips working but making no sound.

Jack nodded. "Yeah, I know."

The unspeakable was . . . unspeakable.

Burkes averted his eyes as he handed back the keys. "Here. It's giving me the boak."

He took a couple of deep breaths, then kicked Klarić's body so hard it came off the ground.

"Cunt!"

A few more deep breaths, then he approached Reggie. Rico had had plenty of duct tape around, so Jack had virtually mummied his torso into a chair. He looked pale and weak and sweaty and frightened and miserable. Perfect.

"And who's this minger?"

"He's the Reggie I told you about—owner of the bow and the arrows. He's the guy who used Cristin as a target."

More deep breaths, then, "I'll get no closer. We need him in one piece." He turned to Jack. "So there were two of them?"

"At least. Maybe more. We need to find out."

"Aye. That we do." He gestured around at the carnage. "How'd you manage all this? How'd it all come about?"

Jack hadn't wanted to risk telling him on the phone so he gave him a quick rundown.

"But how'd they know you'd be here?"

Jack had been thinking about that. "They had to have followed me from Jersey City."

"Why on earth would they want to follow you?"

"The archer here and I have a history. But I think here's where the Arab connection comes in."

"That again."

"Listen: I was watching the Jersey City mosque with that fellow I mentioned."

Burkes frowned. "Bertel, was it?"

He'd heard the name only once but could call it up right away. Yeah, right, he'd never heard of him.

"Right. We saw that al-Thani guy I asked you about pull up, hand over what we assumed was a wad of cash, and take off. I followed him. They must have followed me from there."

"And you didn't notice?"

"I was following al-Thani. Never dreamed anyone would be following me."

He felt like a jerk. If only he'd been on guard, Bonita and Rico might still be alive.

"What's done is done. The important thing is we've got this one. Rob and Gerald will find out who else was with him during Cristin's torture, and who put him up to it."

"We need to find out everything he knows. And I mean, *everything*."

Burkes took his arm and led him away. "There's no 'we' when it comes to this type of interrogation."

"Bullshit!" Jack yanked his arm free. "You wouldn't have anyone to interrogate at all if it wasn't for me."

"I know that, laddie. And I appreciate how you feel. I know how I feel, and you were much, much closer to her. But what's about to happen isn't for you."

"You can't—"

"Can you just trust me on this? Much as you hate that lump of scum and want him hurt and want him dead, you're only twenty-four—"

"What's that got to do—?"

"You're young. There's deeds you can't undo, sights you can't unsee, sounds you can't unhear. There's a line, laddie, and it changes you if you cross it. And once you cross it, there's nae going back."

Jack looked into his eyes and knew Burkes had crossed that line—a number of times.

"Isn't that my decision?"

"Eventually, yes. Some day you may cross that line and wind up doing and seeing and hearing those things, but it won't be on my watch."

Jack backed up a step and set his feet. "If you think you're gonna kick me out—"

Burkes was shaking his head. "Not me." He pointed to Rob and Gerald. "Those lads are SAS. I don't know if that means anything to you, but they're two of the toughest sons of bitches you'll never want to meet. If I tell them to get you out of here, you'll be out of here. But I don't want it to come to that. Take some avuncular advice and go sit in your car till we signal you to come back in. You can be privy to all the intelligence we reap from this little cunt, you just can't witness the means we'll have to use to harvest it."

Jack looked at Rob and Gerald, who were hovering around Reggie, then at Burkes's determined face. He was outmanned.

"Shit. Okay."

"There's a good lad—"

"And stop calling me 'lad.'"

Without looking at Burkes or the SAS men, he walked out of the garage and headed for the pickup.

10

Every time Dane thought he'd made a mistake by waiting here, Abouhalima would get out of the Nova and look up the street, and Dane would decide to wait a little longer. Might be important to know who they expected.

The rain tapered off but still no sign of anyone entering or leaving the Space Station. And then, finally, a panel truck with CITY CHEMICAL emblazoned on its flanks turned in and stopped at the gate. Abouhalima ran out and punched in the code. The gate opened and the truck followed the Nova. Both disappeared around the back.

City Chemical? He'd never heard of it, but the word *chemical* set off all sorts of alarms. Was that where they'd gone when he lost them? What in blazes . . . ?

The more Dane thought about it, the less he liked it.

11

Jack had barely settled into the cab of the pickup when he saw Rob waving to him from the garage.

Already?

Burkes met him inside the door.

"Looks like all our interpersonal drama of a few moments ago was for nothing. Gerald didn't do anything but ask him who hired him to kill the girl and we couldn't shut him up."

"He can talk now?"

"Well, not so's you can hear him or understand him very well. We had him write it down."

"Well, don't keep me in suspense. Who?"

"The guy you were following today: Nasser al-Thani."

Jack went cold. He'd been within a dozen feet of the man yesterday.

"I know where he lives."

"Good. That's a start."

"What else he say?"

"Al-Thani instructed them—and they were the only two involved—to find out if she'd overheard anything about Senator D'Amato."

"That's it?"

"Well, that and then kill her."

Jack swayed. The dark was coming again. He pushed it back.

"Where was she supposed to have heard this?"

"He says he doesn't know."

"Why was it of interest to al-Thani?"

"He says he doesn't know."

"You believe him?"

"Yes. He's scum. He's got no loyalty. Gave up al-Thani immediately. I don't think he was told any more than he needed to know. Really, would you tell an insect like that any more than you absolutely had to?"

"No way."

"Exactly. We have a place where we can hold him. We'll keep him until we have al-Thani in hand."

"Why?"

"In case we need clarification on anything." He patted Jack's shoulder. "Looks like you were right about the Arab connection."

"You think they're planning to assassinate D'Amato?"

"Why not? It's the way they deal with people they disagree with. Believe me, after too many run-ins with Provisionals and INLA nutters, I know their type. Violence is both a means and an end."

"But there's no Arab connection to Cristin."

"There is. There has to be. We simply don't know it . . . yet. Once we have al-Thani, we'll have our answers. Then we'll move up the line and Reggie will become immediately expendable. But first we've got to clean up here."

Jack pointed to Brajko Klarić. "What do we do with him?"

"He's the least of our problems. Rob and Gerald know a fire pit up in Ulster County where he will be reduced to ashes. And just to make your police crazy, I'll have them cut off his hands."

Jack nodded toward the two SAS men who were hovering over Reggie. "What's their connection to you? They work for you or the embassy?"

"Mission. The embassy's something altogether different. Officially they work for the mission but we go back a long ways, all the way to the Grand Hotel bombing in Brighton."

Jack had no idea what he was talking about, but nodded like he did.

"They're loyal to the crown first, but we're also loyal to each other. They know this is important to me and so they'll do what's necessary." He pointed to Bonita's and Rico's sheet-covered forms. "But what do we do about the child and your friend?"

Jack felt his throat tighten. Bonita . . . a couple of years ago Reggie had wanted to drown her and the other girls so they couldn't testify against anyone. Jack had helped save her then, only to lead Reggie right back to her today.

What kind of world allowed that to happen? Who was in charge?

Obviously no one.

Jack's brain was numb. "We can't leave them to rot here."

"No family?"

Jack shook his head. "Their father's dead and their stepmother . . . well, she sold Bonita to some slavers."

Burkes winced. "Where are they from?"

"Dominican Republic."

"I know people at the DR mission. What we'll do is this: We'll wipe this place down and move the Croat out for burning. Then we'll phone the police about this place. The coroner will cart the girl and her brother away and I'll see to it that the DR folks claim them."

"I'll pay for their burials."

"You can't be in any way connected. But I can see to it the funds get where they're needed."

Jack nodded. He was suddenly exhausted. He wanted this day over.

"Let's get to work."

12

The City Chemical truck didn't exit until three quarters of an hour later, turning back the way it came. The Nova did not reappear, so Dane made a snap decision to follow the truck. He didn't know if it was headed for another delivery or back to base. Either way, he needed to know what it had just delivered to the Mohammedans.

Chemicals and jihadists were usually a lethal mix.

Sure enough, the truck led him straight back to the Heights. He followed it to a one-story building in a small industrial park. A *CITY CHEMICAL* sign out front said it had come home. He watched it pull around to the fenced-off parking lot in the rear. Throwing all caution to the wind, Dane entered the driveway and eased around the side. When he reached the rear lot, the driver had already gone inside.

"I see no good reason to lock the empty trucks back here in the private lot," he muttered. "Let's hope you agree."

He parked his Plymouth so that the delivery van was between him and the building, then got out and peeked through the passenger-side window. A clipboard lay on the front seat. He tugged on the door handle. It opened.

"Yes."

He grabbed the clipboard. The top sheet had the Mallory Avenue address. Ice formed in his gut as he scanned the list: half a ton of urea . . . nitric acid . . . sulfuric acid . . .

Christ, they were building a bomb. A big one.

He ripped the sheet off the board, jumped back into his car, and roared out of the lot.

His watching and waiting were over. They were making their move. It would take them days to mix all that, so he still had time.

Time to come in from the cold.

Time to head home.

13

Nasser recognized Drexler's voice. He'd been expecting the call.

"Any word from those two?"

Always cautious. No names would be mentioned, no details about what was expected from the unnamed.

"Nothing."

"Isn't that odd?"

Nasser had spent quite a few hours now thinking the same thing. His unease had grown through the afternoon.

"A bit. I told the Croat to call in every two hours or so."

"When did they begin surveillance?"

"Early this morning."

"It's now midafternoon and you've heard nothing?"

"Nothing."

"Perhaps we should have given them a mobile phone."

And have its calls traced to me? Nasser thought. No, thank you.

"Their vantage point is near"—he bit off mentioning Journal Square—"a central commercial district with easy access to public telephones."

"What are your thoughts then?"

My thoughts? That something has gone terribly wrong.

"Best-case scenario? They may have got themselves involved in a prolonged pursuit that doesn't allow them to stop for a call."

"My man would find a way to call in. He's very good that way. A prolonged pursuit would make it even more likely that he would do so, if only for backup."

"I agree. But he's paired with your other man, who I've never considered reliable."

"What's your worst-case scenario?"

He didn't feel free to say that the FBI could have somehow connected them with the jihadists and arrested them, although he couldn't see how that was possible.

"Let's just say that they might have run into something they couldn't handle."

"Exactly what I am thinking. Be out front in twenty minutes and I'll pick you up. We'll go have a look for ourselves."

Trapped in a car with Ernst Drexler—not the way Nasser wanted to spend the rest of the afternoon, but unquestionably something was wrong. They needed to look into this themselves.

14

Their driver guided Drexler's Mercedes on a slow course along the blocks of Kennedy Boulevard north and then south of the Al-Salam Mosque while Nasser and Drexler stared out their respective windows in the rear. The photos Klarić had taken lay between them on the seat.

"Nothing on this side," Nasser said as they entered Journal Square and the mosque's building receded from sight.

Drexler pounded a fist on his thigh. "Same here." He leaned forward. "Turn around and make another pass."

As the driver began the circuit of a block to get back on Kennedy going the opposite direction, Nasser watched Drexler stare at the photo of the younger watcher, the one Reggie had called Lonnie.

"What is it?"

Drexler shook his head. "I've seen him before, I just don't know when or where. He could be living in my building for all I know."

Nasser laughed. "Not a pleasant thought."

"No. Especially considering the fate of the last two men I sent after him. Remember?"

Nasser nodded. "Indeed I do."

A major embarrassment for Drexler. A couple of years go he'd sent two of his East European operatives to intercept this Lonnie while he drove a truck full of contraband cigarettes up from North Carolina. Both had wound up dead. The police report had said their car appeared to have rolled after being side-swiped. One operative had been thrown free of the car, the other had died of a broken neck behind the wheel.

Accident? So it had seemed. But both men dead—and one while seat-belted in the driver's seat. That seemed odd. Especially since the coroner had not been able to come up with a satisfactory answer as to how the driver had managed to break his neck.

Whatever the cause, the mysterious Lonnie had never been heard from again until yesterday morning.

"I hope we will not experience a repeat of that."

"Do you really think that is possible?"

Drexler gave him a sidelong look. "Anything is possible." He gestured toward the window. "We're about to make another pass. Watch carefully."

Nasser scanned the cars but saw no sign of Reggie or Klarić, including the van they were using. No sign of their prey either.

He eyed the building that housed the mosque on its third floor. He knew Reggie and Klarić weren't in there. Were the jihadists? Praying for guidance? Or were they somewhere else in Jersey City, mixing death? Tomorrow began Ramadan. Was bomb mixing permitted in the holy month? He doubted the Qur'an addressed that. He'd been forced to study it as a boy but he'd long forgotten anything it contained.

Islam meant *submit,* and he had—but to the Order.

"*Verdammt!*" Drexler muttered. "Klarić is gone, Reggie is gone, the old man and the young one are gone. Where? And why hasn't anyone called?"

Nasser considered those rhetorical questions so he did not answer directly.

"It could be worse."

"Really?"

"We could have passed their empty, bullet-riddled van. It's not here so obviously they've driven it somewhere."

Drexler's upper lip curled into a snarl. "You don't even know if they arrived here."

Nasser had to admit he hadn't thought of that. "No, I do not."

"And if they *did* drive off from here, it could have been into a trap."

"I do not see Klarić as the type to easily walk into a trap."

"No, you are correct there," Drexler said. "He is experienced and well blooded. But the facts are: no Klarić, no Reggie, no van, no call. I have a bad feeling about this."

So did Nasser.

"Perhaps we should call Roman and—"

"No!" Drexler all but jumped at him. "He is occupied with something else. He told us that. He will not want to be troubled with this."

Nasser wondered if Roman Trejador was mourning the loss of his favorite courtesan. That must have been a tough decision to make. And all for naught. The girl had known nothing.

Such a waste.

But Nasser wondered at Drexler's quick negative response. Almost too quick. Almost too negative. Nasser thought he understood: Drexler had been embarrassed before by the loss of two operatives. He no doubt wanted to give Klarić and Reggie time to resurface.

But would they?

After all this time without contact, Nasser had a feeling deep in his gut that he'd seen the last of both of them.

And maybe that was not such a terrible thing. Anything that lowered Ernst Drexler's standing in the eyes of the High Council could only be good for Nasser al-Thani.

What was that German word? *Schadenfreude*? Yes . . .

Schadenfreude.

15

"SAS?" Abe said. "For days you don't call, you don't write, now suddenly you're here wanting to know about Brits?"

Jack had arrived at the Isher Sports Shop just as Abe was closing up. With the front door locked, they'd convened at the rear counter.

"I ran into a couple of them today—"

"SAS? And you're still in one piece? That's good."

"They're that tough?"

"The SAS stands for Special Air Service. Started out as a paratrooper unit in World War Two, now they're the Brit equivalent of US Delta Force and SEALs and the like. Their wrong side you don't want to see. How does one run into SAS men in the city? Who does that? Only you."

"They're attached to the UK mission to the UN."

"Well, that makes everything perfectly clear." He made a gimme-gimme motion with his hands. "Tell."

"Long story."

"Time I've got."

Jack laid it all out for him, from the second Westchester trip to parting ways with Burkes and company this afternoon—Burkes and Rob taking Reggie to some safe house in Jersey, Gerald carting Klarić's body upstate for hand lopping and burning while Jack drove here.

"So that's why I haven't seen you," Abe said. "You've been busy like a bee. But the little girl and her brother . . . you left them there?"

Jack closed his eyes. It still hurt.

"What choice did I have? I called nine-one-one from the first phone I found. Think about it: a double homicide and both the perps carted off. That garage was no place to be when the cops arrived."

"I'm sorry for you, Jack. First that girl Cristin, now these two. Such *tsuris* in your life these days."

"I feel like a Jonah. Who's next?"

A brief silence, then Abe said, "Maybe it isn't such a terrible thing, your not coming around so often like you used to."

Jack stared at him, then burst out laughing. Either that or burst into tears.

"I hate you, man, I really do," he said when he was able.

"Me? Who lives only to serve?" He rubbed his stippled jaw. "But back to these SAS men . . . they wear uniforms?"

"No. Civvies."

"Probably special projects team."

"Meaning?"

"Antiterrorist wing. And this Burkes fellow . . . if he mentioned the Brighton hotel bombing, he's probably SIS."

"Like Gerald and Rob? I don't think so."

"You're not listening. I said S-*I*-S. M-I-Six."

Jack hated sounding ignorant again, but . . . "Okay, either way, you've got me. What's that?"

"Secret Intelligence Service. Or Military Intelligence, Section Six. The British CIA."

"You're just a font of wisdom."

He shrugged. "Know thine customer."

"Wait . . . you don't mean . . . ?"

Another shrug. "Sometimes they need a weapon that's not government issue."

"And they come to you?"

"You can think of somebody better?"

Jack had to admit he could not.

16

Jack found a message on his answering machine. Though Dane didn't identify himself, Jack recognized the voice immediately.

"Jack . . . I did a little bird-dogging today and came across something big . . . much too big for the two of us to handle. I'm going to disappear for a day or two, then I'll be returning with help. Hang on to the pickup but stay away from Jersey City till I get back. I don't want you upsetting the apple cart."

Jack replayed the message just to be sure he'd heard right. Yeah, he had.

. . . big . . . much too big for the two of us to handle . . .

What the hell did that mean?

Staying away from Jersey City was easy enough because he had other plans for tomorrow. He was to drive over to Turtle Bay and rendezvous with Burkes's van near al-Thani's apartment building. From there they'd follow him until they had an opportunity to nab him.

Once that was accomplished, they'd take him to the same safe house where they were keeping Reggie.

N. al-Thani had ordered the torture murder of Cristin Ott. Jack could not wait to get his hands on him.

TUESDAY

1

Since this was the first day of Ramadan, Hadya had intended to awaken early to make sure she had a substantial *suhoor* to prepare her for the day's fast. But she'd slept through the alarm. This was one of her roommate's days to work the ovens at the bakery, so Jala was long gone. Hadya worked the counter today so she wasn't expected until shortly before the Ramallah bakery opened its doors.

So now she had time only to wolf down slices of peanut-buttered toast in the last minutes before sunrise. Certainly no shortage of bread in the apartment with both her and Jala working for her uncle Ferran. The bakery's day-old bread that didn't sell went home with his employees. He would have sold two-day-old bread if he could, but since he used no preservatives, by then it was good only for toast.

Ramadan . . . after sunrise, no food or water allowed until sunset. No smoking either—no sacrifice there since she'd never been even tempted. And no sex. She smiled sourly. No problem there either. In the two years since her arrival she'd met a few young men—Muslim and non-Muslim—who'd shown an interest, but none had struck sparks with her. And she wanted—*needed* sparks. At least here in America she could wait for those sparks. If she'd stayed in Jordan with her family, her parents would have been trying to arrange a marriage for her.

She was so thankful she'd taken the big step of leaving for America. First off, she had a job here. In Jordan jobs were virtually impossible to find due to the crush of refugees. And second, she'd escaped all that family pressure to get married and have children. Children were a blessing from Allah, true,

but Jordan did not need more children now, especially children of Palestinian refugees. Here the marriage decision was left entirely to her.

But she cared not about marriage now. She cared about what her brother
was plotting.

That was why yesterday had been so frustrating. She had off one day a
week—Monday—and had planned to devote it all to tracking Kadir up and
down Mallory Avenue to find out what he and his sinister companions were up
to. Whatever they were planning could not be good for America and therefore
not good for her.

But the freezing rain had hampered her. She'd posted herself on the street
where she'd last seen him but the weather had driven her inside before she
sighted him.

Today was clear and dry, but very cold. She bundled up and headed out
just as the sun was rising. She strode along Virginia Avenue at a brisk pace,
stopping at Mallory. She saw no sign of him or the battered car that ferried
him about. As she continued down Virginia she nearly stumbled with surprise as she saw the familiar green car whiz past from behind on its way toward Kennedy.

Her fists knotted in frustration. All those hours spent cold and wet and
shivering yesterday when she had all the time in the world to follow—and
she'd seen nothing. Now, on her way to work, she sees it. And yes, Kadir occupied his usual place in the passenger seat.

Why these repeated trips? What were they doing and where? She would
find it if it was the last thing she did.

2

Nasser yawned as he exited the Lincoln Tunnel and turned south toward Jersey City. He had slept poorly. He kept expecting the phone to ring and hear
Klarić's voice on the other end, telling him they had Lonnie tied up in the loft
and offering a reasonable explanation for their lack of communication.

But no call came. And in the hour before dawn he made a call of his own to Kadir and arranged to meet with him in front of the mosque.

He used his own car—a discreet Volvo sedan—this morning. He wanted to try to resolve this problem on his own, to be able to report back to Drexler and ultimately to Trejador that the two missing men were accounted for and everything was under control. That would be the ideal outcome. If he failed to turn up anything new, better not to let on that he had even tried.

As he had done yesterday with Drexler, he cruised the blocks north and south of the mosque looking for the two watchers. And just like yesterday, he found no sign of them.

He parked in front of the mosque and waited for the green Chevy Nova. Instead, a Ford Econoline van with HERTZ emblazoned on its sides pulled up beside him. The passenger window rolled down to reveal Kadir's face.

Nasser lowered his own window. "We must speak," he said in Arabic.

Kadir frowned. "We could have spoken on the phone. We have much work to do if we are to be ready by Friday."

"I understand that, but this is not a matter to be trusted to the phone lines nor to be called out between idling cars. I will be brief." He pointed to the passenger seat. "Join me."

Kadir jumped out and hurried around the front of the car. When he'd slammed the door and settled himself in the seat, he said, "Well?"

"You remember the red-haired American you drove with back and forth to Virginia?"

His face darkened. "Reggie. I remember him—the pig who did nothing but insult me the whole trip. I was a different person then. If he spoke to me that way today I would slit his throat."

Nasser didn't know if Kadir would really carry through with the threat, but no mistaking the anger and hatred behind the words.

"I take it then that you didn't see him around here yesterday?"

"Around here? No. I would have spit on him if I had."

"And how about the man who was my driver the last few times we met?"

He shook his head. "No. Why do you ask?"

"They are missing."

"Well, you are well rid of that red-haired one. Is this why you called? You could have asked me this over the phone." He reached for the door handle. "You have made me waste precious time."

"We fear the FBI might have them."

Kadir froze, then released the handle. "The FBI? Why do you say that?"

"Someone has been watching the mosque. Reggie and Klarić were to find out who they were. We did not think they were FBI, but now that our two men have disappeared, we have begun to wonder."

Kadir twisted in his seat, looking up and down the block. "Where are they?"

"They've disappeared as well. You can understand my concern: Were they simply watching the mosque, or were they watching you?"

Concern replaced hostility in Kadir's expression. "We have not been followed."

"You're sure?"

"Absolutely." But his eyes said otherwise.

"Be extra watchful," Nasser said. "Especially at this crucial juncture. Speaking of which, you were able to procure sufficient supplies for a second bomb?"

He nodded. "We ordered immediately and they were delivered that very day."

"And how is the manufacturing going?"

"It is slow but we are making progress. We have mixed enough for the first and we have started on the second." He gestured past Nasser to the truck. "Each will fill an entire van. We will need two of those. We rented this one now to be sure we would have it ready. Another will be available Thursday."

"Friday is the day, then?"

Kadir's eyes lit. "Yousef will leave his van by the front of the UN. I will park mine on the highway that runs beneath the building. On Friday morning we will turn the world on its head."

Nasser smiled. "May Allah guide you until then."

At least this end was going as planned.

He let Kadir get back to his work and made one more circuit of this section of Kennedy Boulevard, but still no sign of Lonnie or the older man.

Reggie and Klarić disappeared just as those two stopped watching the mosque, he thought. There had to be a connection.

The Holland Tunnel was just a little way east of here, so he decided to take that back to the city. It would put him farther downtown than the Lincoln, but it was closer.

As he passed through Hoboken along the way, a pickup truck made a reckless swerve around him. Nasser figured this was someone in a hurry, but once he got in front of him he barely did the speed limit. Nasser was tempted to give him a blast of horn but thought better of it. This was not a very congenial-looking neighborhood.

As they were passing through an area of boarded-up factories, the pickup stopped midblock. Nasser had to slam on his brakes to avoid plowing into him. *Now* he hit the horn.

A burly-looking man jumped out and hurried toward him. He carried some sort of expandable metal wand in his hand. This didn't look good. Nasser locked his doors and began turning the wheel so he could pull out and away. But just then a black van with tinted windows pulled up.

Everything happened very quickly then. The man from the pickup smashed Nasser's window as the side door of the van slid open and released another bruiser. A hand reached through the window, unlocked the door, and pulled it open. The second man carried a dagger that cut through Nasser's seat belt like tissue paper. With frightening efficiency he was pulled from the Volvo and hurled into the van. Nasser resisted but he was outweighed and overpowered. The two men pinned him to the van floor by kneeling on his back as they expertly bound his wrists and ankles with plastic ties. One of the men exited and slammed the door closed. Immediately the van began moving.

All within fifteen seconds at most.

Had he fallen victim to some sort of paramilitary organization?

"Who are you?" Nasser said, hiding his fear. "What is the meaning of this?"

He realized he sounded contemptibly trite, but those were the words that sprang to his lips.

"Mister Nasser al-Thani, I presume," said a Scottish-accented voice from somewhere behind him. "We have some questions for you."

Still on his belly, Nasser couldn't see who had spoken.

"I'm happy to answer questions. You didn't have to abduct me."

"Well, we want *straight* answers."

"What about?"

"A young woman. Known originally as Cristin Ott. Then later as simply Danaë, and later still as the Ditmars Dahlia."

Nasser's saliva evaporated. How had they connected him with Danaë? Oh, wait. Klarić and Reggie were gone, and now this. Obvious. Klarić would never break. But Reggie . . . Reggie would spill his guts. But how much had he known?

Stall . . .

"I've read about her, of course. But I know only what was in the papers."

A fist slammed into his right kidney.

"Wrong answer."

The pain left him breathless and unable to speak.

When he managed to regain his voice, he said, "Why are you asking me? And why are you interested? The papers said she was a call girl, a nobody."

Another blow, this time to the left kidney.

"She was a *some*body," said another voice from another direction. "Very much a somebody."

Nasser lifted his head to see. The driver had spoken. He turned and glanced over his shoulder at Nasser and the look on his face was enough to freeze the blood. Good thing he was driving or he might be tearing at Nasser's face right now.

And then Nasser realized he'd seen that face before. In a photograph.

Lonnie.

3

Jack ground his teeth in rage. This al-Thani was the second slimeball to call Cristin a nobody. Where did they get off? They were the nobodies, and they'd soon see how little they were worth.

Jack had expected to return to the city but Burkes instead directed him to the turnpike via Tonnelle Avenue. They traveled north to route 17 and took that farther north into the wooded hills of Bergen County. At the end of a winding, sloping driveway in Mahwah they came to a long, low ranch house in the woods.

"Whose place is this?" he said as he pulled the van to a halt beside a black sedan parked by the front door. Rob parked Bertel's pickup a few feet away.

"Ours," Burkes said.

"As in the UK mission's?"

He nodded. "A little woodsy getaway for the diplomats. None of whom are here now."

"This where you took Reggie?"

"He's cuffed up inside."

Rob and Gerald carried the bound but still struggling al-Thani out of the van. Burkes walked ahead and unlocked the front door while Jack brought up the rear. They trooped inside where al-Thani was dropped on a couch.

"I'll check on the other one," Rob said.

Jack followed him to a rear bedroom where Reggie lay cuffed to a bed. He didn't look so hot—pale, sweaty, with the arrow protruding full length from his throat.

Some of the glaze burned off his eyes when he saw Jack.

"Fuck you!" he rasped, still unable to speak above a harsh whisper.

"Well," Jack said, "just let *me* say, 'Thank *you*' for your help in tracking down your pal al-Thani. He's in the next room. Want to say hello?"

Reggie said no more, simply closed his eyes.

Rob checked his manacles to make sure they were secure, then led Jack back out to the main room.

"You're leaving the arrow in his throat?" he said when he saw Burkes.

"Don't have much choice. We'd have to wriggle the head to get it out and who knows what that would do? Might sever one of his carotid arteries. If that happens he'd be dead in less than a minute and not a damn thing we could do to save him. Same risks from trying to saw off the shaft to shorten it."

"So he's sort of a human weather vane."

Burkes smiled. "You could say that."

"You really worried about him dying?"

"For the nonce." He gestured to al-Thani. "As I told you, once this tosser opens up, Reggie becomes redundant."

Burkes opened a door that revealed stairs going down.

"All right. Let's get started."

He held the door for his two men and their captive but stepped in front of Jack as he tried to follow.

"Here's where you go for a drive, Jack."

"What? Again? Forget about it."

He blocked Jack's way as he tried to pass. "We've had this discussion already."

"Yeah, and it was for nothing. You didn't have to do anything to Reggie to make him fold like wet cardboard, so—"

Burkes shook his head. "This one will be different. I can tell already he's going to be a tough break."

"He called Cristin a nobody."

"Be that as it may, we've got a nice windowless room down there. I'll be asking the questions while Rob and Gerald—who've been trained in advanced interrogation techniques—get down to the rough stuff."

"I'm staying."

Burkes sighed. "You're going. Take the pickup."

"Shit, Burkes. That's the guy who ordered the other scumbags to torture and kill Cristin!"

"So Reggie says. We'll find out. And we'll also find out if someone higher up ordered her death. I don't think it ends with al-Thani. And we'll find out *why*. We'll find out why D'Amato was so important and—"

Jack heard his voice rising. "I don't give a shit about D'Amato! I want this bastard's ass!"

"Don't make me call the lads."

After his conversation with Abe last night, Jack knew he needed to respect the physical prowess of anyone who'd gone through SAS training. He'd read what SEALs went through, and if theirs was anything like that, he knew that if they wanted him out the door, he'd be out the door no matter how he resisted.

"This sucks," he said, although a secret part of him was glad that he wasn't being given a choice.

"That's what you think now. Someday you'll thank me."

Would he? Maybe. Despite the rage boiling within him, and as much as these fuckers deserved to die in agony, he wasn't sure how much he could inflict. He'd have to be cool and methodical to do it right. He didn't think he could be cool and methodical about something like that.

"Yeah, right."

"Buck up, lad. We'll have him broken in time for a leisurely lunch."

4

Kadir had borrowed Salameh's car for an hour or so to drive into the city. This was a reconnaissance mission. Last night he and Ayyad had pored over maps of Manhattan's Midtown East and the UN Plaza. Ayyad had decided that the most effective place for an explosion in the FDR underpass would be five hundred feet from the end—the spot closest to the base of the towering Secretariat building.

Kadir entered through the Lincoln Tunnel and crossed to the East Side where he entered the FDR Drive. The expressway had few off-ramps and seemingly fewer on-ramps. The closest entrance uptown from the UN complex was at East 63rd Street.

Traffic was moving well as he drove under the Queensboro Bridge, then into the Sutton Place underpass. As he emerged from that, he saw the glass-sided domino of the Secretariat Building looming less than half a mile ahead, almost edge on.

He had been practicing measuring five hundred feet by eye, and so he kept careful watch on the ledged inner wall of the UN underpass. He could see daylight ahead and slowed as he marked the spot in his mind.

Here he would have to stop the van and immediately light the fuses. Then he would put on his emergency flashers, get out, and open the front hood to make it look like he was having engine trouble. As soon as that was done he would climb onto the ledge and run the five hundred feet to the end of the underpass where he would duck around the corner. Once there he would be protected from the direct force of the blast, but he wouldn't stop moving.

The explosion would demolish everything in the underpass, expending most of its force upward and outward. The underpass would collapse and, with Allah's help, the blast would undermine the Secretariat Building, tumbling it into the East River. That was why Kadir would keep running—rounding the big playground and moving up 41st Street—because no one had any idea how much debris would be in the air and where it would land. By that time Yousef's bomb in the front of the UN would have detonated and Kadir could walk up First Avenue and pretend to be just another shell-shocked survivor as he gloried in the destruction and chaos he had helped create.

He came out into the sunlight again and took the first off-ramp. He made his way to First Avenue and headed back uptown. As he passed the UN, he noticed yellow-vested policemen waving the traffic on, keeping it moving, not allowing any vehicles except buses to stop.

Alarm jolted through him. How would Yousef be able to position his van and light the fuses if he wasn't allowed to stop?

Unless they found a way to bring the traffic to a halt.

He continued uptown and made another trip through the UN underpass.

Yes, ten minutes seemed like plenty of time to clear the blast area—*if* everything went as planned. A slip or a trip resulting in a sprained ankle or knee could slow him considerably.

He sighed. Well, if the blast caught him, he would find a martyr's reward waiting for him in the next life.

But before all that, he needed a way to stop traffic on First Avenue.

As he headed back to Jersey City, an idea began to form.

5

After ending her shift at three, Hadya had posted herself at the intersection of Virginia Avenue and Kennedy Boulevard, waiting for Kadir to pass. But two hours on watch yielded no sign of him or the green car. She was sure if she quit now that the car would pass as soon as she turned her back. Not only was she weak from hunger and thirst after her day-long fast, but her fingers and toes were numb with cold.

She needed food and water. Jala had been home for hours now and would have a plate of dates ready to start *iftar*, the fast-breaking meal, at 5:40, right after sunset. Her mouth watered at the thought.

But instead of heading back toward the tiny apartment they called home, she walked north toward the Al-Salam Mosque. Perhaps she would see Kadir there.

Instead she spotted a familiar pickup truck parked at a corner just off Kennedy but with a view of the mosque. However, instead of the bearded older man she'd seen before, a clean-shaven young man now sat behind the wheel. As she watched, he exited the truck and walked to the pay phone a few steps away. After a brief conversation that seemed more like an argument, he hung up—none too gently—and stalked back to the truck.

She hesitated, then overcame her customary inhibitions. Taking a deep breath, she strode toward the passenger door.

6

We'll have him broken in time for a leisurely lunch . . .

Bull*shit.*

Not wanting to waste his period of banishment from the Mahwah house, Jack had decided to devote the time to pursuing the Arab connection to Cristin. He couldn't imagine what it might be, but since he was already in north Jersey, and since Bertel was no longer on the job, he assigned himself the task of watching the mosque.

He'd anticipated a brief stakeout, so he'd parked near some phones, allowing hassle-free call-ins. But each call had been the same: Sorry, no, they hadn't broken him yet.

Jack's watch had been equally fruitless. Lots of Muslims going in and out the doorway next to the toy store. Bertel had mentioned that today started their holy month of Ramadan and so Jack guessed that was why. He'd learned nothing and had been zoned out—eyes in a half-dazed stare at the mosque but mind somewhere else—

A *knock-knock* on the passenger-side window jolted him to full alertness.

His hand was automatically reaching for the Glock under the seat when he saw the young woman with some scarflike thing around her head—similar to all the Muslim women he'd watched entering and leaving the mosque. What he could see of her face was kind of pretty. With her wary dark eyes she looked harmless enough, so he rolled down the passenger window.

She spoke as soon as the upper edge cleared her lips.

"You are government? Police?" she said in heavily accented English.

He hadn't been prepared for that level of directness.

"Not even close."

"Why you are watching the mosque?"

"I'm not."

"Where is the old man who once drive this truck?"

So much for the clandestine part of Bertel's surveillance.

"I don't know what you're talking about."

"You are watching my brother?"

"Lady, I don't know you, I don't know your brother, and I'm not watching anyone."

"His name is Kadir Allawi. I want you to arrest him."

Holy crap. He knew that son of a bitch. And here was his sister looking to get him arrested. Talk about surreal.

He forced a laugh. "Like I told you, I'm not police. Have you called the cops?"

"I have called FBI."

"No kidding? What did they say?"

"They say they are 'aware' of Sheikh Omar and that is all."

Sounded like a brush-off. Bertel had said the Bureau was no longer watching the mosque. Maybe they didn't want any reminders.

"Not much help. But just out of curiosity, why would you want your own brother arrested?"

"He is planning something bad."

"How bad?"

"Very bad."

Jack stiffened. Just what Bertel had been saying. Maybe his rants about those clowns bringing jihad to America weren't so far out after all.

He noticed her shivering.

"Do you want to tell me about it?"

"If you are not police, you cannot help."

"I might know some people who can." He leaned over and unlocked the door. "Come in out of the cold," he said as he cleared off the passenger seat.

She shook her head. She looked scared. "No. I cannot."

"Don't be afraid. I've no wish to harm you." He gestured at the traffic on Kennedy Boulevard. "Besides, there's too many people around for me to try."

A gust of cold wind ruffled her scarf and she seemed to waver. He pulled the keys from the ignition, placed them in the ashtray in the center of the dashboard, and pushed it closed.

"Look. Now I can't drive away with you either. You have nothing to fear."

Setting her lips in a tight line, she pulled the door open and stepped up to the passenger seat. She slammed the door behind her and immediately rolled up the window. He noticed a paper bag labeled "Ramallah Bakery" in her lap.

"So . . . what is your brother planning?"

"I do not know," she said, rubbing her hands together.

He pointed to the ashtray. "If you let me start the engine, I can put on the heater."

She shook her head. "No. That is all right. I fear Kadir will hurt people."

That didn't sound good.

"Hurt how?"

She shook her head and he could sense her frustration. "I do not know. I see him driving up and down the boulevard—"

"In a Chevy Nova?"

A shrug. "I do not know cars. It is old and green."

"I know it."

A sharp look. "Then you *have* been watching him."

"I've seen that car pull up in front of the mosque quite a few times with different men inside."

"Yes . . . his friends." That last word was laced with acid.

Jack decided to take the plunge and see how much she knew.

"Are they interested in jihad?"

Her light brown skin paled as she looked at him in shock. "How do you know of jihad?"

He shrugged. "I know nothing for sure. I've been told by the older man you saw in this truck that the preacher in there"—he pointed to the mosque building—"hates America and that he has followers who feel the same way."

"He is called an 'imam.' Yes, he hates America, but I have listened to him and I know that he also hates many Muslims who do not agree with him. He says he speaks for Allah and my brother believes him, but Allah does not hate."

Jack remembered something Bertel had told him.

"But doesn't Allah reward those who die for jihad?"

The girl looked away. "It is . . . what is English word for not simple?"

"Complicated?"

"I do not know this word."

"Yeah, well, religion is always complicated. But all that aside, I haven't seen—" He stopped himself from saying *your brother*. He wasn't supposed to know Kadir. "—that car all day."

"I wish to know where he goes, but I have no car." She looked at Jack. "If you see him, will you please follow him and find out?"

That might not be a bad idea.

"Time permitting, I'll try. And if I do find out what he's up to, how do I tell you?"

She hesitated, then seemed to notice the bag in her hand. She held it up and showed him the label.

"I work here."

He shrugged. "Okay. I'll do what I can. That's all I can promise."

She smiled for the first time. A nice smile. "Thank you."

Without another word she got out and walked off. Jack watched her for a moment, then retrieved the keys and started up the truck. He considered calling in again, then thought, screw it. He'd head back to the Mahwah house and they'd have to deal with him.

7

Tommy piloted his Z through the Stuy. He cruised around Marcy Park, looking for a likely suspect.

He'd got to thinking about the moulies who busted up the cars he covered. And he'd kept on thinking about them. Why would they do that? It hadn't been just Tommy's lots, but like nine out of ten was his. That didn't sit right.

So he'd had a little talk with himself: Let's just say, for the sake of argument, that somebody put them up to it. Who gained from that?

Tony the Cannon Campisi.

Okay. So if Tony wants Tommy out of the detailing business, he dings up all the cars Tommy covers. But he's too sick to do that himself. And if someone else is gonna do it, it's gotta be on the down-low. Gotta be a trusted guy in his crew who don't have no love for Tommy Totaro. Who would that be?

Vinny Donuts.

But fat Vinny ain't about to go running around car lots with a ball-peen hammer. He's gonna find someone to do it for him. Someone with no connection to family business. Someone who can talk about it all they want but nobody that matters will hear. Who would that be?

Moulie kids.

But what does Vinny know about moulies? Well, there was that deal a couple months ago where he off-loaded a truck full of Air Jordans to the Raysor brothers. The Raysors use kids to take orders and deliver product. If the price is right, they might be favorably disposed to letting Vinny take a bunch of their runners for a joyride.

Like this skinny kid with the cockeyed cap under the hoodie and the saggy pants and the shades up ahead, lounging on the corner right here.

Tommy slowed, then stopped, but left the car in drive. He lowered the passenger window as the kid sidled up. Smooth cheeks and good teeth—couldn't have been more than fourteen, maybe younger.

"What up?"

"Thirsty."

"For what?"

"Coca-Cola."

"Yeah? What you like? Powder, cake, rock? You look like powder to me."

"You got a good eye. How much will an ounce hurt?"

"Three C's."

"Whoa!"

Tommy was used to wholesale prices from his friends in the family. Was that what the suckers were paying on the street?

"Primo product, man. Gotta pay for quality, know'm sayin'?"

Okay, here was where it was gonna get dicey.

"For that price it better be fuckin-ay pure as new snow."

He pulled three Franklins from his pocket. As he extended them across the passenger seat, his free hand found the window button. When the kid reached in for the cash, Tommy dropped the bills, grabbed his wrist, and hit the button. The window slid up, trapping his arm.

Tommy let the kid thrash and scream and fill the air with motherfuckers. When he paused for breath, Tommy said, "Where were you last Tuesday night?"

More rage and screams about it being none of his fucking business.

Tommy repeated the question with the same result.

"Okay."

He took his foot off the brake and the car started to roll. Now the kid's rage turned to fear.

"Hey, what you doin', muthafucka?"

"You're a runner, right? Let's see how fast you can run."

After being dragged for a block, where the fear turned to agony, the kid told him that his boss had rented him out to some fat greaseball type who took him and his buddies around in a big black Crown Vic to a bunch of car lots where they dinged everything in sight.

Tommy roared away, leaving him lying in the street.

Vinny . . . Vinny and Tony—and maybe Aldo too—had fucked up his business.

Time for payback. *Big-time* payback.

8

Bertel hung up the phone and wandered to his hotel window. The Tyson's Corner Marriott didn't offer much in the way of a view, but he could appreciate the last orange rays of the setting sun lighting the tops of the downtown office buildings.

He'd placed his calls and made his contacts. Tomorrow he'd return to HQ with the City Chemical bill of lading in hand. They'd have their usual skepti-

cism on display, but the bill would force them into action. They couldn't ig-
nore the list. They'd know the end product of proper mixing of those ingredients,
and the damage that more than half a ton of said end product could do. They'd
have to place the storage facility under watch, track the conspirators to their
bomb factory, and shut them down.

And then they'd have to admit that Dane Bertel had been right all along.

Perhaps if he'd been more politic. But that simply wasn't his nature. Still,
his decades as a field agent in the Middle East should have lent him some
credibility.

Once the shah had been kicked out of Iran, Dane had warned that the
U.S. embassy in Teheran would be next on the revolutionaries' list. Sure enough,
he witnessed the so-called "student riot" back in 1979 and, because of his
preparedness, managed to ferry a few Americans to safety before they could
be taken hostage. After that he saw Mohammedan fundamentalism spread
like wildfire through the region, and he knew that wasn't going to be good for
the U.S.

The only bright spot had been the commie takeover in Afghanistan and
the civil war it started. The Russians moved in and became the focal point
for all the Mohammedan crazies. It could have stayed that way. If Carter and
Reagan and that damn Congressman Wilson had kept their meddling hands
off, the crazies would be calling Russia "the Great Satan" instead of "the Lesser
Satan."

Dane had warned that once the Lesser Satan withdrew from Afghanistan—
and it had been clear in the mid-eighties, with the Company supplying Stinger
missiles to the Mujahedeen, that their occupation was unsustainable—the
hatred would refocus on the Great Satan. But his warnings fell on deaf ears.

Well, they'd have to listen now.

He turned away from the window and reached for the blazer he'd brought
along. Never a bad idea to look professional. He'd go down to Shula's for a
rare steak and a bottle of decent red wine, then early to bed. He intended to
be ready for battle first thing in the morning.

9

Jack had expected resistance to his arrival at the Mahwah house but Gerald admitted him without comment.

"Where's Burkes?" Jack said.

Gerald nodded toward the cellar door. "Downstairs."

Again no resistance as he started for the cellar.

In the long, windowless room below he found Burkes and Rob standing near a bloodied, hooded figure slumped in a chair bolted to the floor. Al-Thani's hands were manacled behind him and he was either asleep or unconscious.

Burkes looked surprised to see Jack. "I thought you were going to call in first."

"I got tired of calling in and getting the same message." He gestured toward al-Thani. "Success?"

He shook his head. "No. Nothing."

With rage exploding, Jack started toward the chair. "Give me five minutes—"

Rob pulled him back. "He's been schooled in resistance."

"Really? You can do that?"

Burkes nodded. "Aye. Usually employed by intelligence agencies."

"You think he's—?"

"I don't know what the fuck he is 'cause he's not talking."

"At least not to us," Rob added. "And we're running out of time."

That puzzled Jack. "Are we on a schedule?"

Burkes said, "In a way, yes. The clock started running when we nabbed the Croat and Reggie. Once they don't report in, people up the line get concerned. When someone higher up the food chain like al-Thani here falls off the radar, they start getting nervous. Might even start thinking about packing for a vacation."

"Which means we have to call in a pro," Gerald said.

Jack frowned at him. "I thought you guys were the pros."

Burkes shook his head again. "Not like the one we're calling in."

Gerald's expression was grim. "*Nobody's* like that one."

"Someone at the mission?"

"No. An independent contractor."

How do you build up a client base as a freelance torturer? he wondered. Not like the Inquisition was still on.

"She's going to be expensive," Gerald said.

Burkes sighed. "I know. I think I can finagle her fee through the mission's security slush fund."

Wait—

"*She? Her?*"

"Yeah. Goes by the name of *La Chirurgienne*."

Over Burke's shoulder Jack saw al-Thani's hooded head snap up.

10

"I know you didn't want to be bothered," Ernst Drexler said when Trejador answered the phone.

"*This had better be important.*"

"You said not unless it was too important to wait, and this fits that criteria."

"*Whatever it is can wait until you answer one question: Danaë . . . was that you?*"

Ernst had been expecting the question. The only surprise was that it had taken this long.

"Of course. It was something that needed to be done and so I did it."

"*Without consulting me?*"

Ernst had no fear of Trejador here. He knew he'd be on firm ground if the matter ever came before the High Council.

"I considered your judgment in that area severely compromised, so I acted independently."

"*Where do you get off appraising my judgment?*"

"Would you have gone along with what needed to be done?"

"*I always do what needs to be done. Just as I would have in this case. But you were led by a false premise that preemptive action was required when, in fact, nothing needed to be done.*"

"There was no other course after you allowed a fourth party to become privy to plans that had to remain exclusive to us three."

"*She wasn't privy to anything.*"

"You could not know that. And neither could I. So I took action. As a result, we have no worries on that score. We can be certain that all knowledge of the matter is limited to the three of us."

"*You had no right.*"

"I had *every* right. More than a right. I had a *duty* to settle the matter in the best interests of the Order."

"*You will regret this, Ernst.*"

"Listen to yourself, Roman. Your emotional reaction only confirms your compromised judgment on the matter. I had no emotions either way to cloud my decision."

"*Never a worry about emotions from you.*"

"Exactly. Which is just the way it should be for an effective actuator. And as for regretting anything, I doubt that. I believe I would have more regretted *not* doing it. If you're hinting at bringing this to the Council, I welcome it."

Ernst could have added, *You know how they feel about your whores,* but felt it gratuitous. Trejador was well aware of the High Council's long-standing disapproval. Let him fill in the blanks.

When Trejador didn't reply, Ernst went on. "Can we move on to the reason for my call—something that really matters? Lonnie has reappeared."

A pause, then, "*Lonnie? That kid who drove those girls who were hijacked? Why this obsession with him? You lost two men trying to track him down before.*"

Ernst's next words were going to be very difficult to say, but he had no choice.

"We may have lost two more. Possibly three—the third being Nasser al-Thani."

A pause, then, *"You have my attention."*

He told of Lonnie being recognized in the photos of two men watching the jihadists' mosque, how Reggie and Klarić had been sent to interrogate him, and had not returned.

"And now tonight comes word that Nasser's car has been found abandoned on a Jersey City street with a smashed window. And no sign of Nasser himself."

"It would seem this Lonnie is connected to a larger entity than you thought."

"I have always suspected he was connected to the hijackers."

"Again you've made a potentially disruptive move without consulting me."

"You said you were not to be contacted. Here we have a man who has already caused us untold trouble observed ostensibly spying on the Jersey City mosque. So we had to ask ourselves: What if the object of his surveillance was not the mosque itself but our jihadists?"

"But the first two men you sent after him back in ninety came back dead. Didn't it occur to you to try a different approach this time? And Reggie of all people. Really."

His tone dripped scorn. He was trying to reverse the tables by calling Ernst's judgment into question now. Ernst would not allow it.

"Reggie identified him from the photo. He knew Lonnie. His presence was necessary."

"The fact that you haven't heard from them in two days tells me they'll turn up like the first two. This Lonnie is proving to be quite an interesting young man. Everyone sent after him ends up dead."

Was that a trace of admiration in Trejador's voice?

"We don't know that yet. I—"

"Reggie is no loss, but how did Nasser get involved? He's the one that concerns me."

"And I as well. Nasser gave them the assignment and—"

"Ah! If Reggie is a captive, I'm sure he told Lonnie and whoever is with him everything they wanted to know. The first question would have been: Who sent you? Which put them on the trail of Nasser. That is the same question they will be putting to Nasser. Sounds to me as if you'll be next on their list."

He sensed a savage glee in Trejador's tone.

"Nasser will not break. He has been taught the Entungfer technique."

"Let's hope for your sake he learned it well."

All actuators and those aspiring to the post learned an ancient technique of walling off the pain centers of the brain, making them immune to torture. Al-Thani would say nothing.

"Any suggestions?"

"A little late to be asking me for advice, don't you think?"

"Let us not be petty when the interests of the Order are involved."

"No pettiness, Ernst. Had I been consulted, I would have advised an entirely different approach. But since I wasn't, and since yours has gone seriously off course, I believe I'll leave it to you to straighten it out."

He hung up.

As Ernst replaced his own phone in its cradle, he idly wondered if now might not be a good time for a trip back home to Austria.

WEDNESDAY

1

Forest Hills . . . funny how events always seemed to run in circles.

Jack remembered these streets well. He'd cut a lot of lawns, weeded a lot of gardens, planted a lot of shrubs out here when he was working for Giovanni Pastorelli and Two Paisanos Landscaping. Rico had been in that crew as well. Rico wasn't dead twenty-four hours yet and here was Jack driving Burkes's van through the streets where they'd both worked. Burkes sat in back with al-Thani. Gerald had stayed in Mahwah to babysit the failing Reggie, so Jack had inherited the driving chores.

"This is it," Rob announced from the passenger seat.

Jack pulled to the curb before a two-story brick colonial that looked pretty much like every other house on the block. A little sign out front read:

DR. ADÈLE MOREAU
APPOINTMENT ONLY

Dr. Moreau? Really?

Had to be a joke. Didn't it?

Burkes exited by the side of the van and walked up to the front door. A tall, thin woman with odd-colored hair answered his knock; she carried a little dog in her arms. She pointed to the garage, then closed the door.

Could she be the torturer known as La Chirurgienne?

The white garage door began to rise and Burkes motioned Jack to back into the driveway. By the time Jack had done so, Burkes was waiting with a wheelchair he'd found inside. They loaded al-Thani—dressed in an over-sized hoodie to hide his gag and manacles—into the chair and Rob wheeled him into the garage. Inside they rolled him up a short ramp into the house.

The woman was waiting. Jack put her in her forties. She had a brittle look—painfully thin arms, a tight face, and big orange hair done up like Jackie Onassis but looking brittle as well, like it would crumble into splinters if squeezed. She still held her dog—a Yorkie—and it yipped at them.

"Hush, Charlot," she said with a pronounced French accent. "This way, gentlemen." Her *this* sounded like *zis*.

They all followed her down the hall to a brightly lit, windowless, white-tiled room. A bizarre steel contraption, all gleaming chrome plate and leather straps, occupied the center of the space. In a corner he noticed a wicker basket with a plaid cushion. A doggie bed?

"Welcome to my workshop. First thing, you must remove that awful shirt from our guest."

Rob pulled off the hoodie, revealing al-Thani's battered face and bloodied thobe.

"You have been crude with him," she said in a disapproving tone. "You know I do not like to receive damaged goods."

Burkes gave her a little bow. "We didn't realize at the time that your skills would be necessary. Your fee has been deposited."

"Yes, I know. I checked with my bank." She fluttered a hand at al-Thani. "Well, strap him in and we shall get started."

Jack had no idea which way was up or down with that contraption, so he stood back and watched. Al-Thani's struggles were weak. Jack looked for the rage he'd felt toward the man since Reggie had fingered him, but it seemed to have dissipated overnight. Nasser al-Thani was now a pathetic creature who was about to undergo, by all accounts from Burkes and his SAS men, the tortures of the damned.

Which he richly deserved. But Jack wasn't into pain right now. He was into answers: *Who, what, where, when, why?* Reggie had already supplied the *what* and *where*. As far as *who* went, they had three, al-Thani being the latest, but certainly not the last. Jack wanted every *who* to pay, but before they paid, more than anything, he wanted to know *why*. Why had a sweet, harmless creature like Cristin been singled out for torture and murder?

When Burkes and Rob stepped away from the contraption, al-Thani was suspended within the chrome frame. Leather supports ran across his chest, his pelvis, and his knees, both front and back.

"What *is* this thing?"

La Chirurgienne glanced at Burkes. "I *thought* he was new."

"The lad's new at everything."

"Ah. Well, then." She pressed a button on a steel shelf against the wall. "*Voilà.*"

The frame began to rotate along its long axis. Within seconds al-Thani was facing the floor.

"You see? No need for lifting and turning. All parts of him are accessible."

"I have a list of questions we wish answered," Burkes said.

She thrust out her hand. "Give."

"Do you want me to stay and write down his answers?"

"I work alone. And I record everything. There's a waiting room outside. Go there and . . . wait."

"Want us to strip him before we go?" Rob said.

"Not necessary." She pressed another button to rotate al-Thani faceup again. "I find proximity to a naked human, how shall we say, distasteful. I can cut away to expose whatever area I wish to explore."

Explore . . . Jack shuddered at the way she said that.

2

Dane Bertel idled in the two lanes of cars waiting for the left-turn signal that would allow them to turn off Dolley Madison Boulevard into CIA headquarters. The light took forever and never failed to back up the traffic this time of morning. A lot of people worked in there and the Company had never been into staggering shifts.

Which was another reason why Dane was glad he'd been a field agent instead of an analyst. Sure, analyst was safer, but analysts had to wait in this backup every morning. He knew it would drive him crazy.

He dried his sweaty palms on his suit pants. He admitted to being a little tense. Hadn't been back in a while. He'd left under a cloud, and he'd be viewed through that cloud until he could blow it away with the City Chemical bill.

He saw a brown Datsun station wagon coming the other way brake for no good reason as it passed him, then speed up again. Drivers around here were terrible.

He concentrated on the red light way ahead. It should be changing soon. He hoped he made the turn this cycle and didn't have to wait through another.

3

The return route from an early delivery near Fort Marcy Park brought Aimal Kasi west along Dolley Madison Boulevard. As usual at this time, he passed the two lanes of eastbound cars headed for the CIA entrance. As he did every morning, he wondered if this would be the day he would strike that blow for jihad.

He'd had no contact with Kadir and Mahmoud and the others. But as much as he yearned to know if they'd made any progress on the bomb, he knew he could not risk asking them over the phone.

Traveling in this direction, he could see the faces of the drivers. He stared at the idling rows of spies behind their wheels, wondering if he would ever recognize one of them on the street. And then he almost slammed on the brakes, but stopped himself in time.

He'd recognized one of those faces.

On a night almost exactly two years ago, he had been waiting in a rented truck near a Hertz lot in Alexandria. He'd received a call from New York telling him to hand the truck over to Kadir and an American for a mission that would bring riches to jihad.

An older American with gray hair had knocked on the truck window asking for directions to the Pentagon. Aimal had been concerned that he seemed more interested in the interior of the truck cab than the directions Aimal offered. And then, after Kadir and his American companion had left in the truck, Aimal had seen the gray-haired man racing after them. He had been driving a pickup then. This man was in an old sedan, but Aimal recognized that face. After he'd learned that the rental truck had been blown up while full of brother soldiers of God, he'd vowed never to forget it.

The man with that face sat in a car near the end of the line.

Here was the sign he had been waiting for. Here was Allah pointing the way.

The eastbound and westbound lanes were separated by a flat grassy median no more than twenty feet wide. Aimal swerved across it and parked at the end of the left-turn line. He quickly pulled the assault rifle from under the blanket behind the front seat, worked the slide, and then hurried up the line of cars.

Along the way he decided that it didn't matter who was in that car—the same man or someone who simply looked like him. Allah had given him a sign: Time to declare war on the spies.

When Aimal reached the car, the driver looked up at him. Yes! The same man!

"Allāhu Akbar!"

Aimal fired three shots at his shocked face, shattering the window and blowing his head apart. Then he walked back down the line, firing randomly into other cars as he passed. He killed or wounded at least five more before he reached his car. Tossing the rifle into the rear, he roared back across the median and sped away.

"Allāhu Akbar!"

4

"I must say, I am impressed," the woman said in her French-accented English.

Nasser opened his eyes and squinted into the overhead surgical lamp. It wasn't aimed at his face, but close enough. He couldn't ask what impressed her because he was gagged.

The woman, La Chirurgienne, never shut up. Was it because she lived alone with only a rat-size dog to talk to day in and day out? Or was keeping a running commentary on what she was doing a part of her technique? Simply another tool: ramble on and on in her French accent until her victims pleaded for death.

"I am quite precise in my approach to interrogation. I abhor brutality—the fists, the truncheons, the waterboarding. And the mutilation of genitalia—*dégoûtant!* So crude. So unnecessary. Brutality is ultimately counterproductive. Knock a man unconscious—concuss and contuse and confuse his brain and then expect coherent answers? Break his jaw and expect him to talk? Absurd. The work of sadists, or worse—idiot sadists."

He heard a buzz nearby and felt a pain in his right arm, but it seemed far away. More like the memory of pain.

"I am not a sadist. I am a trained physician. I started out as a surgeon—thus my appellation, La Chirurgienne—but I switched to anesthesiology. And in the course of relieving and blocking pain, I became interested in pain itself. So no, I am not a sadist. I am not even an interrogator. Not really. I prefer to think of myself as a researcher—a nociresearcher, to be exact—and these interrogations allow me wonderful opportunities for pain research."

That's your vital lie, Nasser thought. Self-delusion is a wonderful thing.

Another buzz, another faraway pain.

"You are quite fascinating, Monsieur al-Thani. I have exposed your right brachial nerve and have been sending jolts of current through it. You should be screaming and flopping around like a beached trout—or at least attempting to."

What an awful image.

"Which leads me to believe you have been taught a central blocking technique. And very effectively, I might add. Now who would teach you something like that, hmmm? The question is rhetorical, as I know you are gagged. This room is soundproofed but I find the sound of screaming offensive, and it disturbs Charlot. So, even though you are not screaming now, you might begin to. So we shall leave the gag in place, *n'est pas?*"

He closed his eyes again. Through the Order he had learned the ancient art of Entungfer, handed down from the First Age. It wasn't for everyone. Some minds could only partially grasp it, others not at all. Nasser had taken to it like the proverbial duck to water. He'd been delighted to become an Entungfer adept because it qualified him for the position of actuator within the Order. At this moment, however, he had other reasons to rejoice for his adept status.

"Pain, you see, does not happen in the peripheral tissues. It happens in the center of perception: the brain. The pain fibers—we call them nocireceptors—record the damage to the somatic tissues and report it to the brain. But if the brain doesn't receive that message, due to, say, a local anesthetic nerve block or a severed spinal cord, no pain is perceived. Without the brain, pain does not exist. The tissue damage is just the same, but . . . no pain.

"Now what you are doing, and doing extremely well, is controlling your pain pathways through the brain. Animals do that when threatened. When a mouse sees a cat, its nervous system anticipates tissue damage that will cause pain. Pain can be incapacitating, and that would lead to even more tissue damage, so mice and other fauna have developed the ability to put a temporary damper on the perception of pain. It's not a conscious thing in them, but in you it is. But it doesn't come naturally. It has to be taught. And during our time together, you will tell me where you learned this. Not for your captors' sake, but for my own."

I'll die first, Nasser thought.

He had no doubt that this was his last day—or at best, next-to-last day alive. He had accepted that. But he wished to determine *how* he would die. And he wished to die in silence.

Suddenly he began to rotate.

"You have somehow learned to activate the periaqueductal gray area in

your midbrain. You are doing more than secreting endorphins to keep the
pain at bay, you are directly interfering with pain-pulse transmission. A
nociresearcher's dream. But let's have a look at your spinal cord, shall we?"

The frame stopped rotating and he found himself staring at the gleaming white tile of the floor. He felt a tug on the back of his thobe, heard it tear,
then—

"*Ça alors!* What have we here? You are scarred. No, I take that back.
You have been branded."

Nasser knew she was looking at the Order's sigil on his back. Question
was: Would she recognize it?

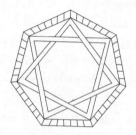

"You belong to the Septimus Order."

First question answered. Now for the second: Will it matter?

"This is a complication. I have done some work for your Order."

Nasser had heard La Chirurgienne mentioned between Trejador and Drexler as some sort of interrogator of last resort, but never any details.

"This presents a bit of a, how you say, an *énigme*. I believe conundrum is
the English word. The Septimus Order is very secretive. Your captors have
led me to understand that you are to die after they obtain the information you
are withholding. If the authorities find you and identify your brand, it will
embarrass the Order. If the Order recognizes evidence of my handiwork on
your remains, its High Council will be unhappy with me. Not because I have
participated in your demise, dear man—they understand that I am a free-
lancer and not beholden to anyone. And besides, I am never the one to administer the coup de grâce. No, they will be incensed by the fact that I allowed
the Order to be embarrassed by your death."

He wished he weren't gagged. He'd tell her to let him sneak out and all
would be forgotten.

"But I believe I know a way to please all parties." She patted his back.
"Except you, of course."

He gasped with the sudden stab of pain at the rear of his left shoulder. He'd relaxed his Entungfer block while she'd prattled on. He set it up again and the pain faded. What was she doing?

As if reading his mind, she said, "The simplest thing is to remove the brand. Then if your body is found, you will not be connected to your precious Order and I won't have to answer pointed questions as to why I allowed the organization to be embarrassed."

He imagined from the far-off burning pain that she'd cut a circle in his skin and was fileting it off.

"Now. How to dispose of it?"

A grim thought slithered though his brain: You could always salt cure it and make it into a key fob.

"I know. I'll just cut it into strips and . . . Charlot! Here, dear boy. A little treat for you."

The rapid clatter of tiny claws on the tile and then her Yorkie skittered into view.

Oh, no. She wasn't . . .

"Ready? Catch."

The tiny dog leaped and caught a bloody strip of flesh in midair.

"Chew carefully, *mon cherie*. Human skin is tougher than you would expect."

She was feeding his branded skin to her dog.

5

After the shooting, Aimal Kasi had raced east on Dolley Madison Boulevard to Fort Marcy Park. He waited with his assault rifle across his lap, ready for the police to appear. He would not be taken captive, and he would not die without a fight.

But after waiting for an hour and a half, and seeing no sign of police or any suspicious-looking cars, he started up the Datsun and headed out. He did not take Dolley Madison, however. The George Washington Memorial Parkway ran right by the park so he took that to the Beltway, then took the Dulles toll road to Reston.

He drove past his apartment complex twice but saw no police activity, and no one watching. He rushed inside with the rifle and hid it under the living room couch. Then he grabbed whatever cash he had, a change of clothes, and fled back to his car.

He had just killed or wounded six CIA employees. Why weren't the authorities swarming all over him?

6

Jack was scanning through a year-old issue of *Sports Illustrated* as he half watched the flickering TV in the waiting room. Just like any other doctor's office, La Chirurgienne's waiting room had old paneling, industrial-grade carpeting, poor lighting, an ancient TV, and older magazines.

The cable TV news channels were all amped up about the morning's shootings outside CIA headquarters in Virginia—two dead and three wounded. The killer was still on the loose but described as an Arab male of about thirty. The names of the dead and wounded were being withheld until families were notified.

If Bertel were here, Jack knew what he'd be saying: *And now it begins.* Maybe . . . maybe . . .

Jack put down the magazine as La Chirurgienne sauntered into the waiting room, pulling off a pair of bloody surgical gloves as she entered. Her dog trotted behind, chewing on something.

"No results yet, I am afraid."

Burkes looked perplexed. "Really? Why not?"

"He has learned blocking techniques I have never encountered before. Fear not, I can get around them. It is simply going to take a little longer."

"How much longer?"

"Not much. Right now I am to have lunch. I suggest you do too. The Tower Diner on Queens Boulevard is very close and very good."

Burkes's voice dropped to a grumble. "I thought we'd have our answers by now. We don't want people further up the line to take off for parts unknown."

"I understand. Not much longer now. Go. Eat. You will have your answers. I have never failed." As they turned to go, she said, "*Un moment, s'il vous plaît*. I found this under his skin."

She fished a small gelatin capsule from a pocket and handed it to Burkes.

"Under his skin? What is it?"

"Be careful. I believe it is a hydrogen cyanide solution."

Jack leaned in for a better look. "Really?"

"I noticed a small lump on the inner surface of his left upper arm and cut it out."

"A suicide pill?" Jack said.

She gave him a tolerant smile. "Not to be swallowed. Merely ruptured under the skin. The poison leaks into the bloodstream and inhibits cytochrome c-oxidase."

"I knew that," Rob said with a grin.

Dr. Moreau gave him an icy stare. "It prevents cells from using oxygen. Therefore the heart and central nervous system, which use the most oxygen, are the first to die. When inhaled as a gas, or directly entered into the bloodstream—as this capsule would do—death is almost immediate."

"Bloody hell," Burkes muttered. "Who *is* this guy?"

Dr. Moreau looked like she had more to say, but instead she turned and walked away.

Burkes pocketed the capsule, then turned to Jack and Rob. "Well? Hungry?"

Rob put on a French accent, obviously trying to sound like Dr. Moreau but coming out more like Inspector Clouseau. "Ah theenk zee Tow*aire* Dine-*aire* on Queens Boule*vaird* sounds gewd."

Jack laughed. "Fine with me." He could always eat.

As they trooped out to the van, Jack thought about Kadir's sister—he'd never got her name—and how he'd promised to follow her brother today. The way things had gone this morning, that was going to be an unkept promise.

Whatever her name, she was on her own today.

7

Since Ramadan left her unable to eat lunch on her lunch break, Hadya walked up Kennedy and passed the mosque going north and south. She saw no sign of the pickup truck. The young man or the old man might be using a different car, but she saw no one like them in any of the parked vehicles.

Had they given up on the mosque or was the young one following Kadir as he had promised?

She hurried the two miles to Mallory Avenue. Along the way she traded her hijab for a blue-and-red plaid scarf. She felt she'd draw less attention that way, especially when she leaned forward like an old woman. From a distance, in her long, baggy cloth coat, she could easily be taken for someone in her sixties.

She positioned herself at the Virginia Avenue intersection. Maybe the green car—the young man had called it a Chevy Nova—would pass. She watched for it up and down Mallory and almost missed it to her south as it pulled out of Claremont Avenue onto Mallory and came her way. She hurried after it but didn't have to go far because it soon turned into a storage facility called the Space Station.

Taking a chance, Hadya hurried back to Claremont and walked along until she reached West Side Avenue. She found a shadowed corner at the base of the rail terminal that shielded her from the cold wind, and waited. She didn't have much time to spare, but she had a feeling they wouldn't be long at the storage place.

Sure enough, no more than twenty minutes later the Chevy reappeared, heading her way on Claremont. It then made a right onto West Side Avenue and roared south. She didn't bother chasing it. She was going to be late returning to work as it was.

What she needed was a map. Maybe her uncle Ferran had one at the bakery.

8

After spending an hour or better alone and facedown in the rack, Nasser heard La Chirurgienne and her dog return.

"Here you go, Charlot. Have some more."

And then he was rotating again. He ended faceup, squinting into the surgical lamp again.

"So," she said. "You have presented me with a challenge. This does not cause anger or resentment in me. More like admiration, if you will. Because I am one who loves the challenge. I will confess that sometimes these interrogations get boring, at least for me. Mine rarely last more than twenty minutes. I spent most of the morning on you with no result. That, monsieur, is a challenge. You have energized me. I am feeling very much alive today."

Nasser wasn't sure he liked the sound of this. No, he was quite sure he didn't like it. He noticed her hanging a bag of clear fluid from a pole beside the frame. He liked that even less.

"Like anyone else, I am left-brained and right-brained. The left side of my brain is my nociresearcher side, all science. My right brain sees the infliction of pain as an art form—how to maximize pain while minimizing tissue damage. To that end I have been developing certain neurotropic infusions."

She punched the end of a length of clear plastic tubing into a receptacle in the base of the bag.

"I doubt you understand the neurophysiology of your blocking technique. It is probably something you were simply taught to do through intense coaching."

She was right about that. He had no idea how the Entungfer technique worked.

"I shall explain what we scientists know: Certain lobes of your brain—the frontal and temporal lobes, plus an area call the amygdala—connect via a circuit to the brain stem that moderates the pain perception. The circuit, however, is bidirectional. That means it can be manipulated not only to reduce pain—as you are doing—but it can be reversed to enhance it."

He felt a faraway prick in his arm. He couldn't move his head to look, yet he was pretty sure she was starting an intravenous infusion. But of what?

Again, she seemed to read his mind.

"Merely a saline drip, in case you are wondering."

She fussed at the counter to his right, then returned to view holding a syringe filled with amber fluid.

"This is my own concoction. If it works, it will block your blocking technique and allow you to perceive the full brunt of the pain I am inflicting. If it does not, I have others I can try. You, dear man, are a perfect test subject."

She jabbed the syringe's needle into an injection port in the tubing, then emptied the barrel into the flow. Nasser watched with dread as the amber fluid crept toward his arm. Unable to watch it any longer, he closed his eyes and waited.

Slowly he became aware of a growing agony in his right arm.

"I do believe you are feeling something, monsieur. The exposed portion of your brachial plexus must be quite painful. Excruciating, really. Even without stimulation."

He clenched his teeth against the pain and worked his Entungfer techniques harder to block it, but they no longer seemed effective.

"You have broken out in a sweat. Let us test this further by applying a little current to the plexus."

He heard a faint buzz and it felt as if someone had ripped off his arm.

Nasser al-Thani screamed into his gag.

And behind that sound, muffled in the room but clear and loud in his ears, he heard La Chirurgienne say, "I do believe it is time to turn on the tape recorder."

9

La Chirurgienne returned to the waiting room a little after three holding a sheet of paper.

"Here are your questions, with his answers."

Jack shot to his feet. At last! "Who did it?"

Her penciled eyebrows lifted. *"Pardon?"*

"Who ordered her killed?"

She consulted the sheet. "Someone named Roman Trejador."

"He's on the list!" Jack said. "One of her regulars. Why?"

She frowned. "That is a bit confusing. This Roman Trejador was concerned that she had overheard a plan to blow up the United Nations."

Burkes was on his feet now. "Are y'daft? Blowing up the UN?"

"These are not my words, monsieur."

"Well, then, is *he* daft? Have you done something to the minger's brain?"

She lost a smidgen of her icy reserve. "Well, I did have to try an experimental infusion to break through his defenses. It worked, but he is somewhat confused . . . tends to ramble in his speech."

"Wait-wait-wait!" Jack was trying to wrap his brain around this. "This Trejador guy thought Cristin knew about a bomb plot and so he had her tortured and killed?"

Dr. Moreau nodded. "According to your captive, Trejador—who is his superior in this plot—had hired this young woman for the evening and had her in his suite while they were laying their plans."

"Why on God's earth do they want to blow up the UN?"

"I didn't ask that. I mean, you didn't have it on your list and really"— she shrugged—"doesn't everybody want to blow up the UN?"

"Bloody hell not!"

"Anyway, it is not them actually doing it. They are funding a group of fundamentalist Muslims who want to blow up Prime Minister Rabin—"

"Rabin?" Burkes said. "As in Israel?"

"I do not know of another Prime Minister Rabin. Do you?"

"All right. When is this supposed to happen?"

"During his visit on Friday."

"Friday? Which Friday?"

She shrugged. "The day after tomorrow, apparently. Isn't this exciting?"

"It's bollocks is what it is! If Rabin was visiting, I'll bloody hell know about it!"

Another shrug, accompanied this time by pursed lips. "I am but relating to you what he told me."

"It's still bollocks!"

"Hold on," Jack said. "I was talking to the sister of a crazy Moham"—he'd almost let a little Bertel slip through there—"Muslim who thinks he's up to something big—something serious."

"But blowing up the *UN*?"

"Why not?" Jack turned to Dr. Moreau. "Did he mention a Senator D'Amato?"

She consulted her notes. "*Oui.* He will be there with Prime Minister Rabin."

"There you go," Jack said. "Two guys on the top of any jihadist hit list—probably even ahead of Bush. And they'll both be in one spot right here in the city. How can the crazies resist?"

"But I'd have *heard*," Burkes said, reddening.

"Maybe it's a secret trip."

"We have excellent relations with Mossad. Even with a secret trip, they might not have offered details, but they'd have asked us to be on extra alert for anything regarding Israeli interests. Did al-Thani say why he's coming?"

"To meet with the Secretary General."

Burkes grunted. "Boutros-Ghali? Well, he's another who's no favorite of the radicals, now, is he?"

Jack said, "Sounds like a big bomb in the right place would give them a triple play."

"This is all damn bloody strange," Burkes said. "I'm going to have to do some asking around."

"Oh, jeez," Jack said, remembering his answering machine.

"Now what?"

"That Bertel fellow I told you about—the one you say you don't know."

"I still say I don't. But what about him?"

"I've been helping him watch a mosque—the one where we tracked al-Thani yesterday. He left me a message Monday night about coming across something big—too big for us to handle. He said he was going to disappear for a day or two, then return with help."

"Help from where?"

"He didn't say. But that 'something big' could be a bomb. He may have found proof."

"This is too crazy." Burkes turned to Dr. Moreau. "We need to speak to him straight off."

"I'm afraid he's temporarily . . . incapacitated."

"What the hell does that mean?"

"The ordeal of the interrogation, the infusion . . . he will be unconscious for a while. But I taped it all. You can listen for yourself."

"Let's do that," Burkes said. "Let's bloody well do that. And while we're listening, good doctor, I have a candidate for your *IV* procedure."

"You mean someone other than Monsieur al-Thani?"

"Yes. Al-Thani will get his soon enough. I'm calling my man at our safe house. He'll bring your new candidate."

Jack wasn't following the rest, but knew that "candidate" had to be Reggie.

"*Bon*," she said. "But you do understand this will require an extra fee."

Burkes stepped closer and jabbed a finger at her. "No, it won't. This is less than satisfactory. You've messed up the brain of a subject we brought to you. That wasn't part of the job description. You will make up for that deficiency by performing *IV* on a second captive—*gratis*."

She blinked in surprise, obviously unused to people getting in her face like Burkes. But she didn't look terribly put off by the idea.

"And there will be no mention of . . ."

"Al-Thani becoming 'incapacitated' under your guidance? No."

"Very well." She smiled and walked away. "I shall await his arrival."

"'IV'?" Jack said. "Like a needle? Like death from lethal injection? Reggie deserves more than—"

"With La Chirurgienne, 'IV' means *Infernum Viventes*."

"Still no help."

"It's Latin." Burkes's grin was not a pretty thing. "It means 'Living Hell.'"

10

"You're probably wondering why I called you two here today," Tony C said from behind his desk.

Vinny thought he'd heard that line before—a movie, maybe? Anyway, yeah, he was wondering why he was standing here with Tommy in the back office of Tony's appliance store when he had business to attend to. But when your capo called, you came.

"Vinny," he went on, "I know your junkyard's going real good, but I want your help on something."

"Sure, Tony."

"For the past week, Tommy here's been doing a great job putting my money back to work." He looked at Tommy. "How much we got out now?"

Tommy said, "Just over forty Gs."

His voice sounded funny—low and mean, like he wanted to be here less than Vinny.

"That's pretty damn good," Tony said, nodding. "Pretty damn good. And none of them too big." He stopped nodding. "Except one."

Tommy glared at him. "Hey, if you're talking about the towel-heads—"

"I *am* talking about the towel-heads. Ten grand?"

Yeah, Vinny hadn't liked that one either. Coupla shifty-looking mooks. Up to him, they wouldn't have got a freakin' dime.

Tommy wasn't budging. "You're the one sent me to them."

"Yeah, but I didn't tell you to lay ten grand on them."

"Then maybe you shoulda fucking told me that before you sent me out!"

Tony gave him a look, like, *You kiddin' me?*

Vinny knew what he meant. Tommy had a chip the size of Staten Island on his shoulder. Where'd that come from?

Tommy took a breath. "Don't worry your ass about it, Tony. Like I told you last week, I laid it off on both of them. So that's like really only five grand apiece. I know they both got jobs—I checked myself—and I know where they both work."

"I know what you told me, but we ain't collected any vig yet."

"Not due till tomorrow."

Tony banged a bony fist on his desk. "What? You think I'm senile or something? I fucking well know that! And I want *you* to know that I am concerned about the first vig payment. If we get that without any excuses or bullshit, it'll be a sign they ain't total-ass deadbeats and I'll feel better. If you gotta go chasing 'em, it's on your ass."

"Hey, now—"

Tony karate-chopped the air. "No excuses."

Much as he liked to see Tommy squirm, Vinny couldn't call this fair. Tony had pushed to get his money out there working for him, and so Tommy had done just that, but now Tony was hedging his bets.

Vinny, though, wasn't about to say squat. This was between those two.

"But I ain't without consideration," Tony added. "To make sure you get maximum results, I'm sending Vinny along as backup."

Vinny was about to protest but Tommy beat him to it.

"I don't need no—"

Another karate chop. "He's goin'. Check him out. The would-be deadbeats take one look at Vinny and start reaching for their wallets." He turned to Vinny. "I ain't expecting somethin' for nothin'. You'll get somethin' for your trouble."

Vinny forced himself to say, "It's okay," and leave it at that.

No amount of beak dipping could compensate for a day spent driving Tommy around.

Tony tapped his desktop. "Right here, this time tomorrow: all the vig on my forty Gs. Got it?"

Vinny saw Tommy reach into his jacket like he was going for his gun. He couldn't be serious. But his eyes had an insane glint that made him look capable of anything. His hand paused, and then he scratched his chest and brought it out.

Whoa. For a minute there . . .

He turned his thoughts toward tomorrow. Who knew? Maybe they'd get lucky. Maybe everybody'd have their vig ready and he'd be done with Tommy in a couple hours.

Somehow Vinny didn't see that happening. Like looking out at a calm ocean on a clear sunny morning and knowing, just *knowing* you'd be better off staying on shore that day.

11

"See?" said the woman with her French accent. "It is out."

The bloody barbed tip of the arrow floated into Reggie's field of vision. His head was fixed, allowing him to follow it with his eyes only, but he recognized it as one of his own. She'd injected his neck with some hellishly painful stuff that was like torture going in, then she'd gone to work on the arrow.

"I used local anesthesia," she went on, "because I did not want you moving while I was extracting the tip. One jerk at the wrong time and *poof!* you are gone. But that is the last anesthesia for you."

"But I'm okay?" he said in a steam-leak voice that wasn't his, was barely a voice at all.

She laughed. "Well, no, you are not 'okay.' It severed your left recurrent laryngeal nerve, which is why you have so little voice. And you were very dehydrated. But I am fixing that now."

Once they'd tied him to this metal . . . whatever it was, she'd hooked up an IV and started pumping him full of "sugar water," as she called it. Had to admit he was feeling better. And fucking-ay good to know that arrow was out.

But the big question remained: Why? It had looked like they were going to let him just fade away with that arrow in his neck. Now they'd had a surgeon remove it. What was going on?

Suddenly the table or rack began to tilt to his left. It kept on tilting but he didn't roll off because of the straps binding him. It stopped when he was facing the floor. He felt the fabric of his shirt tear across his upper back.

"Let us see if you are branded. Ah, bon. You are not. Charlot has had enough snacks for today."

What the fuck—?

"We shall proceed. Allow me to explain what will follow. I do not know what you did to so anger your captors, but it must have been something terrible, for they have requested that you undergo the Infernum Viventes procedure. Well, to be precise, it is not *a* procedure. Rather a *suite* of procedures."

"What are you talking about?"

"I am so glad the arrow cut that nerve. I don't have to worry about you screaming."

Scream? Oh, no! What was she saying?

"Here is what will happen. You have five senses—sight, sound, smell, taste, touch. The IV procedures completely eliminate sight, sound, and taste, and ninety percent of touch. It leaves you with only your olfactory sense. Why leave smell? you ask. You will find out."

Reggie's scream wasn't a scream at all.

"Now," she said. "The first to go is touch. To accomplish that, I am about to sever your spinal cord at the fourth-cervical level. Why that particular level, you ask? American medical students use a little rhyme to help them remember the functions of the nerves springing from the spinal cord in the neck. Part of it is, 'Three, four, and five keep the diaphragm alive.' If I cut above the C-four level—and by C-four I do not mean the explosive—you will require a respirator, which I do not have, and you will die within minutes. So I leave you with C-four and up so that you can still work your diaphragm and breathe. You will also be able to turn your head and perhaps shrug your shoulders. But that is it. You will lose all sensation and movement from there down. Not a finger, not a toe will you ever feel or move again."

"No. Please no."

"But we do not stop there. C-four quadriplegics can often use an electric wheelchair with chin or sip-and-puff controls. But what good is a wheelchair when you are blind? That is correct: In the second procedure I shall remove your eyeballs—enucleation, we call it—and cauterize the stumps of your optic nerves. Then I shall destroy your middle ear and damage your cochlea with cautery to leave you not only permanently deaf but with a persistent case of vertigo. Then I shall sever your other laryngeal nerve and cut out your vocal cords. Lastly, I shall remove your tongue to deprive you not only of taste, but any chance at speech as well. All without anesthesia, I am afraid."

Reggie tried to scream again.

"But as I told you, I will leave you with your sense of smell. That is so you can smell food you will never taste. And there is another reason I leave you your sense of smell, but I will not tell you because you will learn it on your own before very long."

Reggie began to sob. This could *not* really be happening. They were just trying to scare him. They couldn't be this bent out of shape about a whore, a fucking nobody!

He screamed as something cut into the back of his neck. Soon after he felt as if his entire body had been set on fire from the neck down. The fire died as quickly as it came, leaving . . . nothing.

12

Kadir heard a heavy knocking on the door. He stopped mixing his latest batch of urea pellets and nitric acid and went to see who it might be. A peek through the side window showed Ayyad standing outside. He removed his goggles and mask and opened the door.

"Who's with you?" Ayyad said in Arabic.

"Ramzi."

"Come outside. I can't go home smelling like that."

He had been recently married—a match arranged by his parents and hers—but he did not share his efforts for jihad with his bride.

Kadir grabbed his coat and motioned to Ramzi to follow him. They gathered in the lengthening shadows outside the door.

"Are we on schedule?" Ayyad said.

Kadir nodded. "We will have everything mixed by tomorrow. What of the hydrogen?"

"That is proving to be a problem."

"I thought you could get it through your company," Yousef said.

"It is not as easy as I thought. The suppliers I have approached will sell it to me but only with a purchase order from my company's stockroom. That is proving difficult to acquire."

Yousef began waving his arms as he walked in a circle. "We told you from the beginning that we would be needing it. And we need it tomorrow at the latest! After that it will be too late."

Ayyad gave him a stony look. "Do you think you are telling me something I do not already know?"

"I don't know what you know. Kadir, Salameh, and I do all the hard work while you go to your office and drive around in your car. And when it comes time to produce the final ingredient, you show up with empty hands."

"And just what—?" Ayyad began.

"Please, please," Kadir said, raising his hands between them. "Let's be calm. We are all tired, hungry, and thirsty."

He was seeing that Ramadan, even though a holy month, was a less than ideal time to fashion a bomb.

"I have one more place to try," Ayyad said, "but I wanted to make sure we had enough of the nitrate mix."

"Even now we have enough," Yousef said, then added pointedly, "*if* we get the hydrogen."

"You will have it," Ayyad said, then turned and walked toward his car.

Kadir prayed he was right.

May Allah guide you.

13

Al-Thani wasn't quite the guy they'd brought here. Physically he didn't look too much different. His right shoulder and upper chest were bandaged, as was his left upper back, but otherwise pretty much the same. His eyes, though alert, said he'd been through some kind of hell. He seemed to understand the questions, but his answers were garbled.

"He appears to be suffering from a form of expressive dysphasia," Dr. Moreau said as she entered the room.

"And what the bloody hell does that mean?" Burkes said.

"It means what he wants to say does not come out the way he means it to.

It can happen after a stroke in a certain area of the brain. It is not exactly what is called 'word salad,' but it is almost as useless."

"It's permanent?"

She shrugged. "I do not know. We have entered *terra incognita* here."

They'd listened to the doctor's tape of her interrogation but gleaned little more than what she'd had in her notes. Jack had noticed al-Thani's answers becoming less and less focused through the tape . . . could almost hear whatever drug he'd been given decaying his speech.

So they'd gone to the source . . . with zero gain. They gleaned strange snippets of little use, like:

Why bomb the UN?

Towers off-limits.

What towers? The Trade Towers?

Towering towers.

Why are they off-limits?

Because Roman said so.

Why?

Wouldn't tell me. Nobody would tell me. Just that they mustn't be damaged. So we diverted them.

"Could he be faking it?" Jack said.

She smiled as she shook her head. "He is broken."

"And what about the other guest we brought you?"

"The one with the bad hair? He is in hell. Come and see."

They all trooped into her procedure room to look. Jack stopped at the door as a wave of queasiness swept over him. Reggie was still strapped faceup into the frame as they'd left him, but there the resemblance ended. A bandage encircled his head, covering his eyes and his ears. A curved suction hose like dentists use ran from his mouth to a receptacle. Blood oozed through the tube.

"What happened to his mouth?" Jack said.

He could still see bloody teeth. Had she done a *Marathon Man* number on him with a drill?

Dr. Moreau showed him a stainless steel basin containing two eyeballs and . . . was that his tongue?

"What . . . what . . . ?" was all Jack could manage against his rising gorge.

But he settled it back down by picturing Cristin's body in the morgue. Then added Bonita and Rico.

"Are you saving those?" he finally said.

She smiled. "Do you want them?"

"Jeez, no."

"Neither do I. But human remains require careful disposal. They are evidence. I will build a fire tonight and let it reduce the eyes to ash. The tongue will go in the oven."

Jack fought a Hannibal Lecter vibe. "You're not going to . . ."

"Let good roasted tongue go to waste? *Absolument pas!* Charlot loves roasted tongue. And by tomorrow, thanks to him, the evidence will be *merde.*"

Yeah, if anyone deserved IV as well as having a Yorkshire terrier dine on his tongue, Reggie was the guy.

"What . . . ?" He was almost afraid to ask. "What else did you remove?"

"Four of his five senses," the doctor said. "He is in very near complete sensory deprivation except for pain. At the moment he is in agony from the neck up. But that will pass. Leaving him with one sense—smell—and one sensation: vertigo. His inner ear damage and lack of visual input will prevent him from telling up from down. He will exist in a state of constant spinning. As far as his brain is concerned, he has no body and is merely a head whirling in a black void."

Living hell indeed.

"Forever?"

"For as long as he lives."

Jack had wished him dead before. Now he wished him a long, long life.

14

As soon as her shift ended, Hadya gambled by taking a Kennedy Boulevard bus south to a point just past its intersection with Danforth Avenue.

It turned out her uncle did have a Jersey City map—indispensable for a business that made deliveries—and she'd used it to trace possible routes the Chevy might take after she'd last seen it heading south on West Side Avenue. The map showed that particular street ending at Danforth. And Danforth crossed Kennedy. Something in her gut told her the Chevy would take Danforth to Kennedy and turn south.

After getting off at the Columbia Park stop, she again traded her hijab for the plaid scarf and adopted her old lady posture as she waited by the thick trunk of a barren tree. She spent an hour in the chill wind and lengthening shadows before the Chevy surprised her by passing along Kennedy on its way north. She recognized her brother in the passenger seat. Watching it make a left onto Danforth, she knew where it was going—but where had it come from?

At least her hunch had been right: The Chevy had traveled from the Space Station to Kennedy. She began walking south, but slowly. She didn't want the Chevy to return and disappear unseen onto a side street behind her. On the other hand, her brother and his driver could have come from Bayonne and soon be headed back that way, leaving her in the lurch again.

The streets here were lined with garages and muffler shops between multi-family homes. She pretended to look in the shop windows or watch the repairs going on in their open bays, but all the while she was eyeing the street.

Finally the Chevy reappeared, rolling south. She picked up her pace, determined to keep it in sight as long as she could. Because she knew, just knew that with her luck it was heading into Bayonne.

But no . . . its left blinker signal began to flash. It turned onto a side street four blocks ahead. She shook off the old lady guise and rushed along. The street sign said Pamrapo Avenue but when she looked she saw no sign of the Chevy. Was it parked beside or behind one of the houses here? Or garaged?

Did she dare to wander the street looking? No, she decided. She did not. At least not while she knew they were here. But if she could see them leave, see what driveway they pulled out of, she could sneak in for a closer look.

She'd have to warn Uncle Ferran she'd be late for work tomorrow.

15

"Kill me! Please, just kill me!"

At least that was what Reggie was trying to say. He knew his lips were moving but had no clue as to what he sounded like, or if he sounded at all. Or if anyone was nearby to hear him.

They'd moved him, he knew that. He could feel cool air on his face, but that was all he could feel. He guessed he was sitting up because nothing was pressing against the back of his head. He wished they'd laid him flat on his back because then maybe he'd choke to death on his own puke.

He knew he'd hurled. Couldn't taste it, but the acid—the only thing he had in his stomach anyway—burned like a blowtorch where his tongue had been cut out.

The spinning was the worst—spinning in endless blackness. He didn't know up from down and that made him puke some more.

He wanted to cry but he had no eyes, wanted to scream but had no voice, wanted to—

What was that stink? He sniffed again and realized what that French bitch doctor had been talking about before she'd started cutting on him.

And there is another reason I leave you your sense of smell, but I will not tell you because you will learn it on your own before very long . . .

He'd just shit himself.

16

"That was quick," Burkes said, turning off his phone as Jack entered the waiting room.

As soon as dark had fallen, Jack, Rob, and Gerald had bundled up Reggie and taken him away in the van.

"We didn't go far," Jack said. "Left him sitting at a bus stop near the entrance to Saint John's Cemetery."

"Good. Now he's someone else's problem."

Jack wasn't sure how he felt about that.

"What's eating you?" Burkes said. "Not happy with the way things played out?"

"Does it show that much?"

"Seems you've got a ways to go in learning the art of the poker face, lad. You're sitting there not feeling any closure, am I right?"

"Jeez, am I that transparent?"

"You would have preferred to put a bullet in his face, right?"

Jack nodded. "Right. Very right."

"You'll feel different after a while. That bullet would be a gift to him now. He'll never harm another soul, and he'll spend the rest of his days wishing he was dead—wishing for that bullet. And the last thing you want to do is grant that minger his last wish, am I right?"

"Right again."

"Instead, he's been properly paid for everything he did to Cristin and for everyone else he's left hurt or dead in the slime trail of his life. And he'll go on paying and paying. IV is the gift that keeps on giving."

"Yeah, I guess so, but . . ." He shrugged. "Maybe it's because this Trejador guy is still on the loose."

"We'll deal with him tomorrow."

"Aren't you afraid that leaving Reggie where he can be found will spook him?"

"Reggie won't be identified. Part of the IV treatment is scarring the fingertips to preclude that. He'll be tagged a John Doe."

"Yeah, okay. But if we put al-Thani on a bench somewhere he'll be tagged an Abdul Doe and Trejador will figure it out as soon as he hears."

Burkes smiled. "That's why we're going to wait until just before dawn to drop him. We have Trejador's address—"

"Yeah, what's with this hotel suite business?"

"You heard al-Thani's tape: That's the way he lives. But trust me, that will make it easy for us."

Jack would have to take his word for it. Before consigning Reggie to hell, they'd asked him what he knew about Roman Trejador. He'd been anxious to please but couldn't help—he'd heard his name, knew he was al-Thani's boss, but had never laid eyes on the man.

"I want to take him down," Jack said.

"La Chirurgienne will do that."

"I mean bring him in."

Burkes stared at him awhile. "Think you can handle that?"

"I know I can."

He shook his head. "Maybe that's true, but it's too risky. I'll let you go in with Gerald and Rob and—"

"I *need* this, Burkes. Trejador gave the order. And just like Klarić and Reggie and al-Thani, he thought Cristin was just a whore, a nobody who just might have heard something." Jack felt the heat growing. "She was so dispensable, so fucking disposable, with no value to anyone, that he felt perfectly free to wave his hand to his minions and order her taken out and tortured and killed. I just want to see his face when he looks down the barrel and I tell him why I'm there. That it's not because of his plot against the UN and Rabin and D'Amato and Tin Pan Alley or whatever his name is. That I'm in his face because of what he did to a nobody."

"I appreciate your feelings, laddie, but—"

"What you appreciate doesn't matter. You *owe* me this."

His eyebrows rose. "Oh? And how do you figure that?"

"I brought you Reggie, someone you never would have found in a million years. He gave up the Arab. You might or might not have ever found al-Thani, but that wasn't a problem because I already knew where he lived. Your ties to Cristin were hiring her now and again. Mine? I knew her since she was fourteen and we spent two years as lovers—or bidies, as you say. If you don't think that earns me some personal face time with this human dung pile before your guys take over, then fuck you. I'll go myself, right now."

"Easy, lad, easy. Let's not get our knickers in a twist." He chewed his upper lip, then gave a slow nod. "Right then. You make a good case. You can face him, but I'll have Rob and Gerald outside in the hall to help you move him downstairs and ferry him here for some quality time with La Chirurgienne."

"What if that leads to someone further up the line?"

"After what we heard from al-Thani, I don't think it will. Trejador suspected she'd overheard something in his suite. That was where this whole bloody mess started. But if it should lead higher, whoever's up there will be our next stop after Trejador gets his own dose of IV."

"Fair enough."

"Now, something else . . ." Burkes looked uncomfortable.

"What?"

"I've been calling around on that Rabin visit—"

"And?"

"Nothing yet, but I learned something else." Again, that uncomfortable look.

"*What?*"

"Dane Bertel is dead."

The news hit Jack like a bucket of cold water.

"Aw, no. How?"

"That shooting in Virginia? Outside the CIA? He was one of the victims."

Jack shook his head. "No, wait. Can't be. Before we left to take Reggie for his ride, CNN put up the faces of the two dead guys."

"Yeah, I know." He sighed. "But three were killed. Bertel was the third."

Jack didn't get it.

"Then why—?"

"He was deep cover in the Middle East most of his career. Showing his face could compromise people in the field now."

A wave of sadness tightened his throat. Bertel . . . gone . . . gunned down while he sat in his car. Lousy way for anyone to go, especially a good man, a decent man. Jack wanted to stalk around the waiting room and break a few things. No, break *everything.*

He'd always remember that first day they met, when Dane intervened with some guy who was beating up on a woman in a park. The two were obviously a couple and had been sitting together drinking. Dane had refused to get involved when the fight started, saying it was a no-win situation. But the guy was getting pretty rough. After flattening him Dane had explained his change of mind in a way that said everything about the man:

There are certain things I will not abide in my sight.

Jack would never forget those words.

He looked at Burkes. "But you told me you didn't know him."

Burkes shrugged. "Not a lie. I *didn't* know him—we'd never met—but I knew *of* him. I figured if you didn't know who he was, maybe he hadn't told you for a reason. I didn't want to interfere. I don't know how much you know, but he was a legend."

"I had no idea. A legend no one's ever heard of?"

"Well, a legend in the intelligence community, and that sort of notoriety usually remains in the community."

"He was CIA?"

Burkes nodded. "He was let go after becoming too strident about radical Islam's threat to the U.S. They knew—we all knew—but you can't go shouting it in the halls. Your intelligence agencies seem to think they've got a handle on the jihadists and want to keep things quiet. Apparently he mended enough bridges to wrangle an appointment with one of the higher-ups this morning, saying he had 'proof' that their handle was nowhere near as firm as they think."

"That phone message I mentioned!"

"Right. I think we have to take this bomb story seriously."

"This Arab who killed him—do you think he was sent because whoever's behind this bomb found out Bertel was on to him?"

Burkes shrugged. "Could be. The timing makes it bloody damn suspicious, doesn't it? The killer could have shot the others as cover. The CIA investigators and no doubt FBI investigators as well won't know till they catch this bastard and question him."

"Yeah. *They'll* know, but *we'll* probably never know."

"Not necessarily. Al-Thani says he and Trejador have been funding the UN bomb. I'm going to add a few new questions to the list I'll want this

Trejador cunt to answer—like all about the bomb and if he had any connection to Dane Bertel's death."

Jack was remembering Bertel's rambling suspicions about another player in the jihadist drama, another agenda at work, a hidden string puller. It had sounded paranoid as all hell then, but now that he'd been murdered in cold blood, not so much.

"Good. And after that, ask him who he and al-Thani work for."

Burkes frowned. "What do you mean? Like al-Qaeda or Islamic Jihad or the Muslim Brotherhood?"

"Maybe. Maybe something else. Maybe a player no one's heard of yet."

"Sounds a little far-fetched. No harm in asking, though. But I'm not going to wait till then to spread the word that we've got a credible bomb threat against the UN."

"Fine. But if this Rabin guy isn't arriving till Friday, we can pretty much rest assured they won't be setting off any bombs before then. That leaves us all tomorrow to work on Trejador. Nothing's going to get in the way of that, right?"

Burkes's expression turned even grimmer. "You can count on that, laddie."

"But let's do it early. I have plans for later."

"What could be more important?"

"Cristin's funeral."

17

Aimal Kasi sat on the edge of the bed in his Days Inn room, munching a Big Mac as he watched his room's TV. The CNN newscaster told of the manhunt for the crazed Arab killer who had murdered two CIA employees and wounded three others.

He stopped chewing. That made five. Aimal knew he had shot six. Why were they saying only five?

He experienced a shock when they showed pictures of the two dead men and neither was the first man he'd shot. Aimal had not the slightest doubt he'd killed him—the bullets had caved in his face and blown off the back of his head. The inside of the car had been splattered with blood and brain. He could not have survived.

Why were they hiding it?

And then the newscaster gave a description of the killer's car and the license plate number—both wrong!

Weeping, he fell on his knees and gave thanks to Allah for shielding him, for blessing the blow he had struck for jihad.

18

Roman Trejador stood transfixed before the lead story on the eleven o'clock news.

"*. . . a man described by a police officer as 'horrendously mutilated' was found seated at a Queens bus stop a short while ago. The policeman, Sergeant Thomas Carruthers, would not elaborate, deferring details to the doctors who will be treating the man at Forest Hills Hospital where he was taken. He did say that 'the details are not for broadcast TV.'*

"*Unlike the mutilated so-called Ditmars Dahlia who was found last week, this victim is still alive. Witnesses report that—also unlike the Ditmars Dahlia—he still has both his hands, although his fingerprints appear to have been burned off. Another witness—and we don't know how reliable this is—said that his eyes had been removed. He is described as a Caucasian male in his forties. If anyone has any information—*"

Roman hit the mute button on the remote.

. . . a Caucasian male in his forties . . .

That could fit either Klarić or Reggie. No mention of build or hair color. If red hair had been mentioned, or a strange, seven-pointed scar, he would have known.

The talk of mutilations disturbed him, especially the eyes. He knew that a female interrogator known as La Chirurgienne did something like that with a package of mutilations that left her victim alive but completely cut off from the world. If the news story had mentioned removal of the tongue and severing the spinal cord as well, he'd be sure. Still, Klarić and Reggie had mutilated Danaë, then disappeared, and now . . . was this payback?

He shook his head. Klarić and Reggie had been sent after Lonnie—not his real name, Roman was well aware—and Lonnie had no connection to Danaë.

Even if he had, Roman couldn't see anyone going to that sort of trouble, let alone the expense of hiring La Chirurgienne, because of a dead call girl, even one as charming and talented as Danaë.

He wouldn't be surprised over the next day or two if questioning revealed that this blinded man was some hapless, low-level drug runner who had been caught trying to double-cross his boss and mutilated as a warning to others.

Mutilated . . . He remembered the soul-numbing jolt of learning the identity of the Ditmars Dahlia. Like most other New Yorkers, he'd been simultaneously shocked, repulsed, and fascinated when the first stories appeared in the papers. Signs of torture, face mutilated by acid, hands cut off . . . some unfortunate young woman had encountered a psychopath, either by being snatched off the street or risking a dangerous liaison. Whoever her killer was, he'd had his sick way with her, then tried to keep her from being identified.

Roman had never dreamed she was Danaë.

When he'd heard on the radio that she had been identified as Cristin Ott, he still didn't connect her to the young woman who had so often been his sensuous, skilled, and enthusiastic bedmate. How could he? He knew her only as Danaë.

But that night, as he'd sipped his first martini, the evening news had shown the photo from her student ID at FIT. He'd stared with gaping jaw as the glass slipped from his fingers and smashed on the floor. The girl on the screen, Cristin Ott, the Ditmars Dahlia, was both not quite Danaë and yet every bit Danaë.

He'd called the day before to engage her for that very night, but had been told she was not available. He hadn't given it a second thought. He'd never dreamed . . .

The instant he'd seen her picture and realized that Danaë and the Ditmars Dahlia were the same, he'd known who had killed her. Or rather, he hadn't known then that Klarić and Reggie had done the deed itself, but he'd known who had given the order.

After he'd finished vomiting, he'd sobbed like a child. He'd not been unaware that over the nearly two and a half years of their relationship—a business relationship in that money changed hands at every encounter, and yet not without a certain mutual affection—he'd become attached to this delightful woman for hire who was young enough to be his daughter. But just how deeply attached he had never imagined until he realized he would never see her again, and the horror of how her life had ended.

Early on he had tested her, leaving diamond cuff links or wads of cash around to tempt her—or so he thought. Nothing had ever gone missing. That didn't necessarily prove that she had no larceny in her heart, but it did prove she was smart and not impulsive.

In fact, she began turning the tables on him. One time he'd left his fifteen-thousand-dollar Rolex near the suite's front door where she could easily pocket it on her way out. After she'd left, he'd gone to check and, to his dismay, found it missing. Disappointed and—he admitted it—a little hurt, he had gone to pour himself the last of the wine they'd been drinking in bed and found a note under the bottle.

I put your watch on your dresser.
Don't leave it in the foyer.
Someone might steal it.

He'd laughed almost to tears. She'd seen right through him all along.

Later she'd explained it in both personal and business terms. First off, she wasn't the stealing type. She'd been raised with a strong sense of mine and not-mine. Second, between her percentage of Celebrations' high fee and the generous tip Roman always gave her, she was extremely well paid for her time with him. When she measured the short-term gain of giving in to the temptation of grabbing what he'd left lying around against the long-term loss resulting from his never calling her again, the short-term gain came up, well, short.

So, on the night he'd seen her picture on the news, after he'd regained control over his emotions, he gave serious consideration to going over to Ernst Drexler's apartment and beating him to death with his father's silver-headed, rhino hide–sheathed cane.

Fortunately good sense won out and he canceled that idea. But he knew that if he and Drexler wound up in the same room during the next few days, he would do exactly that. He'd had to avoid the man at all cost. Therefore he put out the word that he was going to be away on the Order's business and unavailable for meetings, even for phone calls. No communication except in the case of a dire emergency.

Then the phone call last night . . . a dire emergency indeed. A potential catastrophe.

Yet despite that, Roman had wanted to reach through the phone and throttle Drexler. Somehow—and he still wasn't sure how—he'd managed to stay outwardly calm and conduct a rational conversation.

The passing of Reggie—Roman had to assume he and Klarić were dead or so severely damaged by torture as to be as good as dead—was no loss. Klarić was another matter. He'd saved Roman's life once. What bothered him most was the resurfacing of Lonnie. Not the resurfacing itself, but the fact that he was watching the mosque frequented by the Order's pet jihadists. Why? Lonnie was a nonentity, a mule, a kid driving smuggled cigarettes who'd got caught up in a situation he had no control over. What interest could he have in that mosque?

Obviously there was more to him than met the eye, because people who tried to apprehend him wound up dead.

And now Nasser al-Thani missing. Nasser had sent Klarić and Reggie after Lonnie. Was Lonnie working his way back up the line? If so, he'd next come after the one who had given Nasser his marching orders: Ernst Drexler. *If* Lonnie could break al-Thani. That would not be easy. In fact, Roman was confident it lay beyond Lonnie's abilities. Reggie? No problem. Nasser? He'd die first.

So, unfortunately, Ernst Drexler was safe for the moment.

As for Roman, he wasn't worried. Should Lonnie ever confront him, he had a trump card to play.

THURSDAY

1

"Dane Bertel is dead?" Abe said.

Jack had laid the news on him as Abe was unwrapping one of the sausage egg McMuffins he'd brought along.

It had already been a busy morning. Before dawn, he and Rob and Gerald left al-Thani, now a permanent rag doll after the IV treatment, sitting on a bench in Madison Square Park, wearing big dark glasses and looking up at the Flatiron Building. He wondered how long it would take for someone to realize something was a little off with this guy. All they had to do was remove the sunglasses and see the empty eye sockets to know something was very off.

He'd gone home from there to shower and change, then stopped by Abe's to tell him about Dane. After all, Abe had put them together so that Jack could learn to shoot the first pistol he'd sold him.

Abe rested both hands on the counter and leaned over his untouched breakfast, shaking his head.

"Yeah," Jack said. "Cold-blooded murder as he sat in his car."

Jack gave him the details about his being an unnamed victim of the still-unknown Arab killer.

"A murder happens on the CIA's doorstep and they can't find the killer? This is how conspiracy theories are born."

That jolted Jack. "You're saying he was set up?"

"I'm saying nothing already. But you're telling me this shmuck killed an ex-CIA man in front of a line of cars filled with CIA personnel and nobody can find him. How is that possible? I don't have an answer, but people I know would say they haven't found him because they don't *want* to find him."

Jack had to smile. "I can almost hear Bertel saying that himself."

Abe finally took a great-white bite of his McMuffin. Jack had known it would not go untouched for long. He doubted any news, no matter how tragic, could kill Abe's appetite.

After swallowing, Abe shook his head. "A mensch we've lost."

"Did you know he was ex-CIA?"

Abe's head shot up. "He was? News to me. Ex-military, I thought. Korea, maybe."

Jack bit into his own McMuffin. He loved these things.

"How well did you know him?"

A shrug. "Heart-to-hearts we never had. But in some men you can detect the mensch without many words. A man may hide a lot of himself, but the mensch always manages to peek through."

Jack glanced at his watch. He still had a little time. "I've got to head over to the Lexington Hotel soon."

"Is that why the jacket?"

He was wearing the blue blazer and khaki slacks he'd bought at Brooks Brothers two years ago.

"Yeah. Gotta look like I fit in."

"What for?"

"I'm off to meet up with a guy who's anything but a mensch."

"Oh?"

"Name's Roman Trejador. He ordered Cristin's torture-murder."

Another circle closing: Jack had bought the outfit for his first date with Cristin. It seemed right to wear it now.

Abe's eyebrows rose. "You're not doing anything reckless, I hope."

"Those two SAS guys I mentioned are going to help spirit him away for a date with a woman known as La Chirurgienne."

The eyebrows rose higher. "I've heard of her. And from what I've heard, I would not like to be on the receiving end of her talents. But if he's the one who gave the order, why do you need La Chirurgienne?"

"To make sure the chain of command ends with him. And also to check out a bomb plot."

As Abe attacked his second McMuffin, Jack gave him a quick rundown of what they'd learned from al-Thani.

Abe shook his head as he stared at him. "In town not three years and already you've run into smuggling, mass murder, Dominican gangs, human trafficking, torture, and international terrorism. How does this happen?"

Jack began unwrapping his second McMuffin. "Just lucky, I guess."

"After all this *tummel*, how are you going to go back to being Repairman Jack?"

"I was *never* Repairman Jack. That's *your* thing."

"No, it's *your* thing." He pulled a sheet of paper from under the counter and pushed it across. "Here: for the personals pages."

Jack stared, dumbfounded.

> *When all else fails . . .*
> *When nothing else works . . .*
> *REPAIRMAN JACK*

Abe said, "I can see you're speechless with wonder and admiration. I was quite taken myself when I realized what I'd created. Like poetry it reads."

Jack burst out laughing. "You're kidding, right?"

"I should be kidding about your career? Your future? This is what you need to bring people with troubles to your door—or at least to your table in that bar. Just add whatever phone number you want and you're all set."

"How about I add yours?"

"What do I know from fixing problems? I have your number. I'll—"

"Don't even think about it, Abe."

Abe took the sheet and began folding it. "This will be my gift to you."

Jack couldn't tell if he was kidding or not. "Abe . . ."

"For a year I'll run it. Let's see . . . the *Village Voice*, the *Daily News*, the *Post, Newsday, New York* magazine . . ."

"If I didn't have to run . . ." He began rewrapping his untasted second McMuffin. "I'd—"

"Run? You're going to take that and run? You shouldn't run and eat. Bad for your digestion."

Jack had to smile. "Always thinking of me."

"I look out for people. It's an affliction. The city over I'm known as 'Caring Abe,' a man who lives only for others."

Jack pushed the McMuffin across the counter.

"Okay, watch this for me. If I'm not back in two minutes, eat it."

"*Eat* it? But this will be my third. I should consume three of these sausage-egg-cheese concoctions?"

"I'm sure you can handle it," Jack said as he headed for the door.

Abe loosed an exploited sigh. "Only because I care. Only because I live for others."

2

Aimal Kasi shifted nervously from foot to foot as he waited on line to board the Lufthansa flight to Frankfurt. He kept expecting a platoon of airport security guards to arrive and carry him off, but no one took any notice of him. Life at Baltimore-Washington International Airport was business as usual. Just another work day.

He showed his boarding pass and was passed through without a second glance. As he hurried down the ramp, he again gave praise to Allah for shielding him. At Frankfurt he would transfer to a Pakistan Airlines flight to Quetta, his home town.

Aimal would return with a message for his Muslim brothers: America was ripe for jihad. Americans were vulnerable. With Allah watching over you, you could kill them and walk away with no one stopping you.

Allāhu Akbar!

3

With the plaid wool scarf around her head, her shapeless coat, and sunglasses, Hadya knew she cut an eccentric figure in the dawn light. Thinking she'd need her energy, today's suhoor had been more substantial than usual, augmenting the aging bread with two eggs she had hard-boiled and peeled last night. Sunrise had come at 6:37 this morning so she had eaten early and bused here to the corner of Pamrapo Avenue and Kennedy Boulevard.

She expected Kadir and his friend with the Chevy Nova to appear soon because Ramadan would force them to rise early to eat. And sure enough, shortly before seven o'clock she saw the Chevy approaching. She turned away as it neared and watched from the corner of her eye as it turned onto Pamrapo. Halfway down the block it turned into a drive.

She frowned. There didn't seem to be a house there. Keeping her eyes on the spot where the car disappeared, she waited for the light, then crossed Kennedy's four lanes of traffic. She walked a few hundred feet down Pamrapo until she could see the driveway. It appeared to be a vacant lot. But it couldn't be. There had to be a house back there.

Fearful of approaching any closer, she returned to the bus stop to wait for them to leave. If necessary she would call in sick to the bakery. Today she *would* learn what Kadir was up to.

4

Even though the four of them had one of the Lexington Hotel's elevator cars to themselves, Burkes kept his voice just above a whisper.

"I can't find anyone who's heard even a rumor of Rabin visiting."

Rob and Gerald wore suits and ties, Jack his blazer, Burkes wore a nylon jogging suit. They shared the car with a huge rolling suitcase.

"That means it's top-top secret?" Jack said.

Burkes snorted. "That means La Chirurgienne's pain-enhancing potion fried some of the Arab's circuits. I made some very, very discreet inquiries and the responses I got were pure shock. Looked at me like I was jaked."

"That doesn't mean the bomb's not real. It could be why Bertel was killed."

"I'm aware of that, lad, and I've put out word that I've heard something. I've not rung a full alarm—I need to maintain some credibility if nothing happens—but I've let it be known that there's a rumor floating 'round that some Middle Easterners with a grudge against Boutros-Ghali might take explosive action in the very near future."

"'Explosive action'?"

Burkes shrugged. "They got the message: extra patrols around the perimeter of the UN complex starting today. But we worry about that later. Right now . . ."

"Yeah." Jack straightened his blazer. "Now."

"You sure you can handle this?"

"Very."

Which was a lie. He'd been holding the tension at bay, but now it all came flooding through. In the next few minutes he was going to invade a hotel room in midtown Manhattan, confront and subdue at gunpoint the man who'd ordered Cristin's death, and then, with the help of Rob and Gerald, spirit him away.

Am I crazy?

Yeah, probably. But this needed doing and he wanted—no, *needed* to be the one to do it.

"Do we know anything more about this guy other than he was one of Cristin's regulars?"

Burkes shook his head. "Not much. Did a quick background on him last night. The good thing about him is his name. Not too many Roman Trejadors about, so he was easy to find. The bad thing is there wasn't much to find. He was born in Spain forty-nine years ago but is now a naturalized American citizen. He has no permanent address. He works for an offshore holding company and likes to live in hotel suites. We don't know what he does for the company. We don't even know what the company does. We do know he draws a generous six-figure salary and pays his taxes—although if he's audited, he might have trouble justifying his hotel bills as business expenses."

Jack was impressed. "Pretty good for a 'quick' background check."

"You think so? Actually, it's pretty thin. But not as thin as what we could dig up on you."

Jack's stomach clenched. "You backgrounded *me?*"

"You're surprised? You think we'd bloody well allow you to tag along with us without checking you out?"

"Tag along with *you?* You're tagging along with *me!*"

Gerald laughed. "I love this kid."

Jack was more than fed up with the "laddie" and "kid" shit by now, but this wasn't the time or place to address it. He had another matter front and center—a question he was almost afraid to ask.

"What did you find?"

"Next to nothing," Burkes said. "Trejador's got a lot of blank spaces in his life, but yours is one big fecking void. It's like God created you from nothing and set you down here. If you were older, I'd say you were a field agent for some intelligence agency, but even they create false histories for their people. You don't have *any* history, true *or* false."

That was a relief.

"Can we keep it that way?"

Burkes shook his head. "I don't like mysteries. They keep me awake at night."

Jack wished him a lifetime of insomnia as the elevator *ding*ed for the twenty-sixth floor.

Burkes said, "Weapon ready?"

"Yep."

They couldn't supply a suppressor for his Glock so they'd given him a suppressed SIG-Sauer. They told him it was a P226 chambered for S&W .40 caliber. Jack took their word for it. It presently rested in the small of his back, hidden by the blazer.

"Just remember: Use it as a last resort, but if you've got to use it, go for the kill shot and get out. Either he leaves with us or he leaves in a body bag. No loose ends."

"Got it."

To Rob: "Syringe loaded?"

"All the way."

The plan was simple: Jack would get the drop on Trejador, then let Gerald and Rob into the room. They'd shoot him up with some super sedative they had and cart him off in the suitcase.

"I still don't like him going in alone," Gerald said. "No offense, Jack, but it's asking for trouble."

"Maybe it is," Burkes said, "maybe it isn't. But I gave him my word, so let's make it work."

"It'll work," Jack said.

Jack slipped on a pair of driving gloves as the elevator stopped on the twenty-sixth floor. Rob took hold of the suitcase handle and the three of them stepped out into an empty hallway.

"Meet you downstairs," Burkes said as the doors slid closed between them.

Rob and Gerald had already reconnoitered the floor and led Jack straight to a room door—number 2612. Gerald had what looked like a credit card wired to a black box about the size of a walkie-talkie. He stuck it into the slot of the door's electronic lock. Lights blinked on the box, then stayed lit. Gerald removed the card and a green light lit on the lock.

Taking a breath, Jack slowly depressed the lever and drew the SIG as he entered. He stepped into a large sitting room where a dark-haired man of about fifty sat at a table. He wore some sort of ugly silk smoking jacket as he read the *Times* and munched on a piece of toast.

The door slammed behind Jack.

The man looked up.

Jack nearly dropped the pistol when he recognized him.

"Jesus Christ—Tony?"

5

At last. After an hour and a half in the numbing cold, Hadya saw the Chevy pull out of a driveway and roar toward her. Again she averted her face but took careful note of who was in the car. Kadir and the same unknown friend again.

As soon as they had turned onto Kennedy to head north—back to that Space Station place again, she was sure—Hadya was dashing across the street. She hurried down Pamrapo to the place where she'd seen the car turn. And it did indeed look like a vacant lot, complete with rotting abandoned cars. But a path—two ruts, really—curved through it. After looking back up the street to make sure the Chevy wasn't making a sudden, unexpected return, she followed the ruts. They ended at a ramshackle two-story building.

A dog barked from somewhere inside. She saw a white face appear at a second-floor window, then turn away. She'd been seen. She hadn't wanted anyone to see her. What if the man said something to Kadir?

Nothing she could do about that. But at least she could be sure now that Kadir and his friends were using the ground floor.

Praying to Allah that no one was inside, she crept up to the front door—no porch, no storm door, just a door in the wall. Before trying that, she decided it might be safer to take a peek through one of the windows. But that proved useless. She dared not wipe away the outside grime—that would leave a sure sign that someone had been here. Lights glowed within, but even if she wiped the glass clean, she'd gain no information; the inner surface seemed coated with a glaze of some sort.

She tried the door handle. It turned but the door would not open. It rattled a little on its hinges but refused to budge inward. The reason was right in front of her: a shiny new dead bolt.

She leaned against the door to see if she could catch a glimpse of the interior, but snapped her head back as a sharp chemical odor wafting between the door and the jamb stung her nostrils and made her eyes water.

What were they making in there? Poison gas?

She looked around for something she could use to pry a wider space when she heard a car engine behind her. Without pausing to look, she dashed around the far edge of the building and crouched with her back against the side wall, panting not from exertion, but from fear. She had already suffered the force of Kadir's wrath for simply baring her head in public. What would he do if he caught her spying on him?

She heard doors open and slam, voices muttering. She recognized the language as Arabic but could catch only an occasional word. She couldn't be sure but thought she recognized Kadir's voice.

What was she going to do? What if one of them came around the side of the building for some reason? She had to move.

Frantic, she looked around. The building backed up to a wall of trees and bushes. She could make out some sort of paved area, maybe a parking lot, through the naked branches. If she could slip through there . . .

As she began moving toward the rear, she heard a metallic clang from out front, almost bell-like. And then another. What *were* they doing?

Cursing her curiosity, she inched toward the front edge of the wall. More clangs. Taking a deep breath, she chanced a quick peek around the edge and instantly pulled back.

Metal cylinders . . . they were carrying red metal cylinders from a car— not the Chevy—into the building. She'd seen part of a word on one.

HYDRO . . .

She knew enough English to work the bakery counter and for simple conversation, but this word was beyond her vocabulary.

As she hurried toward the brush at the rear of the building, she vowed to look it up as soon as possible.

6

Lonnie . . . Roman shot to his feet and gaped at him.

He'd hoped that if Lonnie appeared, the shock of recognition would provide an opening. But Roman himself had been too shocked by his sudden arrival to act. Already he could see him tightening his grip on the pistol.

"Lonnie! How did you—?"

The intruder tried to speak but failed on his first attempt. Then he found his voice.

"You're supposed to be dead!"

Roman forced a smile that he was sure looked a little sickly. "The report of my death was an exaggeration."

"Tony . . . Tony Zahler," he said. "Is Tony Zahler really Roman Trejador, or is Roman Trejador really Tony Zahler? Or are both names phony?"

"As phony as 'Lonnie Beuchner'?"

"No fucking games, Tony. Who *are* you?"

Roman leaned to get a look past him. Nothing but an empty foyer. He'd come alone. A rank amateur move. Which meant this was still salvageable.

"Call me Roman."

"All right. Who the fuck are you, Roman?"

"Lonnie . . . should I go on calling you 'Lonnie'?"

He hesitated, then shrugged. "You can call me Jack."

The shrug spoke volumes. It said knowing his name didn't matter because he didn't think Roman Trejador had long to live.

Get him talking. I'm the pro, he's the amateur. Draw him in, draw him closer, then take that pistol away.

"Well, Jack, I'm sorry you thought I was dead. After the incident on the Outer Banks and the massacre on Staten Island, you can understand why I couldn't resurface as Tony."

Good thing he'd had Klarić watching the Outer Banks place. The Croat had killed the Guatemalan slaver who had been assigned to kill Roman, and Roman had left Tony's ID on him.

Jack's lips pulled into a tight line, barely moving. "I mourned you, and then look what you did."

That caught him off guard. "What did I do?"

"You had Cristin killed!"

The sudden ferocity in his young, usually bland face made Roman retreat a step. Maybe he wouldn't survive the day—maybe not the next minute.

"Wait-wait! Cristin who?"

"You knew her as Danaë."

Was that what this was about?

"I assure you I did not have her killed. The last thing in the world I would do was hurt Danaë. You must believe that."

"Why must I?"

"Because it's true!"

"Really? That's not what your minion said."

"My minion?"

"The Arab—al-Thani."

"You broke Nasser?"

He nodded. "He said the order came from you."

Why on Earth would Nasser think—?

Oh, now he saw it. Nasser would hesitate, maybe even seek confirmation if he thought the order came from Drexler. But if Drexler told him that Roman Trejador himself had ordered the death of his favorite call girl, Nasser would see to it right away.

"He's wrong. He may have been told that, but someone else gave the order without my knowledge."

"How convenient. And who would that be?"

"I can't say."

"Oh, but you *will* say. And you'll keep on saying and saying and saying until we shut you up."

As much as Roman would have loved to give this seething young man Ernst Drexler's name, he would not. One member of the Order did not give up another, no matter how much of a snake that other member might be.

But Nasser had . . .

"You say you broke Nasser. How?"

He smiled. "We took him to the Isle of Doctor Moreau."

La Chirurgienne? For a call girl? He shuddered at the prospect. If the infamous Adèle Moreau broke al-Thani, she might well break him.

"I swear I had nothing to do with that! I would never—"

"Everything leads back to you."

"Nothing can lead back to me because—!"

"You sent Reggie and Klarić after me and—"

"I did nothing of the sort!"

"Well, then you had al-Thani do it. I won't even ask why. You'll explain later. Reggie killed two people dear to me before I took him out. And that would have been that, with no connection to you or al-Thani, except I found this on his buddy Klarić."

He removed something from his blazer pocket and tossed it across the room. Roman caught it, stared at it, trying to fathom what . . .

And then he knew.

"Oh, no. He didn't!"

His stomach lurched and his knees weakened. He had to sit. He dropped back into his chair and hurled the grisly thing across the room.

Jack was looking at him with a puzzled expression. "Bravo. If I didn't know better, I'd almost believe you really cared."

"I did. I'd never hurt Danaë. But you . . . what's she to you?"

"We went to high school together. We reconnected here in the city and became close . . . very close."

"Then you should know that anyone who had been with her could never hurt her."

"Apparently you could. You—"

The phone rang. To Roman's surprise, Jack reached for it, saying, "This could be interesting." He raised the receiver. "Mister Trejador's suite. Who may I say is calling?" A surprised look, then, "Oh, hi. Yeah. Everything's cool. We're just having a nice chat." Listening, then, "Okay. Right. Sure. Just give me another minute." He hung up and looked at Roman. "My friends are getting impatient."

So . . . he hadn't come alone. Should have figured that. No one sent after this young man ever returned. He wouldn't be so foolish as to come alone.

"Friends?"

"Yeah, they have all sorts of issues they think are more important than Cristin—like this bombing of the UN you're planning."

Roman hid his shock. Obviously they'd completely broken al-Thani.

"I have no idea what you're talking about."

"Yeah, you do. And you'll tell us. Doctor Moreau found a way to make an end-run around al-Thani's blocking techniques. She'll work the same magic on you. But I've got a couple of niggling questions for you that they won't care about."

"And what would they be?"

Keep him talking, keep him talking . . .

"Why were you working for Dane Bertel?"

"Just a hobby."

Bertel was a pipeline to the Jersey City Arabs and via them to the radicals in the Al-Kifah Center in Brooklyn who wanted to bring jihad to America. Before the Order could help them do just that, they had to be identified. In his guise as Tony, Roman had helped set up the shipment of little girls without tipping either of his identities.

Jack's face hardened. "Did you have anything to do with Bertel's murder?"

Roman didn't have to fake shock. "He's *dead*?"

Jack sighed. "This is useless. But let's try one more: That time back in 1990 when you dressed up as an Orthodox Jew and went down to the Marriott where that Rabbi Kahane got shot—"

"I told you that wasn't me."

"Yeah, it was. What was the deal there?"

"Again, it wasn't me."

But it was. He'd known of the plot to kill Kahane and had gone along to make sure the rabbi didn't survive in the event that Sayyid Nosair missed. Fortunately, the Arab's aim was true and all Roman had to do was pretend to be another shocked follower. *Un*fortunately, the assassination didn't spark the Israeli-Arab conflagration the Order had hoped for.

"All right," Jack said, keeping the pistol trained on him as he backed toward the door. "Time to wrap this up."

Roman had to act now: Get that pistol or die in the attempt. Because he

would *not* allow himself to be subjected to the tender mercies of La Chirurgienne.

He leaped from his chair and charged. He expected to see surprise on
Jack's face, but instead saw a smile.

"Thanks," Jack said.

He lowered the pistol and fired.

In the space of a single second Roman saw the muzzle flash, heard a report, and felt his left thigh explode with the agony of a shattered femur. As he
went down he saw Jack open the door. Two beefy men rushed into the room
with drawn pistols identical to Jack's, one dragging a suitcase.

Through a fog of pain he heard one say with a British accent, "You
wounded him? You were supposed to—"

"He's got too many questions to answer," Jack said. "We can always kill
him. Can we get him downstairs like this?"

"We might," said the other. "Just got to stop that bleeding so it doesn't
seep through."

That was all Roman needed to hear. He reached under his left upper arm,
found the capsule, and squeezed.

A blaze of even worse agony spread up his arm and into his chest. He felt
his body begin to shake . . .

7

"Hey!" Gerald said. "What's he doing?"

Rob said, "Looks like some sort of fit!"

Jack had been picking up the key fob. He turned to see Trejador, eyes
rolled back, flopping around like a beached fish and foaming at the mouth.

"Shit! I'll bet he had one of those cyanide capsules tucked away."

"You mean like the doc found on the Arab?"

Jack nodded. "Gotta be."

Jack couldn't think of anything to do, so they had no choice but to stand by and watch him die. It took less than a minute.

"God *damn* it!" Jack said. "He knows so much—Cristin, the bomb, the Arabs, Bertel, everything!"

He'd never imagined kicking a dead man, but he had to restrain himself from doing that now. Maybe he should be kicking himself. He'd known about al-Thani's implanted capsule. He should have guessed Trejador would have one too. But what he could have done about that he had no idea.

Who *were* these guys?

"Let's get out of here," Gerald said. "I heard that shot in the hall. Not loud, but I heard it."

"Why'd you shoot him at all?" Rob said as they moved toward the door.

"He was charging me. I think he'd decided he couldn't allow La Chirurgienne to get her hands on him, so he was going to get my gun or die trying."

"I don't suppose you took any pleasure in wounding him."

"Not hardly."

Jack had wanted to keep shooting him until he'd emptied the magazine.

The elevator cab was empty and stayed empty for a few floors, giving Rob time to turn on his walkie-talkie and say one word.

"Abort."

A young couple with a suitcase about as big as Gerald's joined them on the twenty-first floor.

Jack smiled at them, then pointed to their bag and said, "That looks big enough for somebody to stow away in."

The woman giggled. "So does yours."

"I know. We have a kidnap victim in ours."

Her smile vanished.

Jack bounced his suitcase up and down, obviously empty.

"Just kidding."

Unfortunately.

8

Although he hated the stinging fumes enveloping him, Kadir smiled behind his mask as he mixed the last of the urea pellets with the last of the nitric acid. Soon this mind-numbing labor would be done and the bomb would be ready.

But that wasn't the only reason he was smiling. He was thinking of that criminal who had loaned him the money for the first bomb. He envisioned him showing up at Mahmoud's taxi depot expecting an interest payment of one thousand two hundred dollars. He would wait. And he would wait some more. And then he would go back to wherever he came from with empty pockets.

He also smiled at the thought of how they had solved the problem of stopping in front of the UN. The plan was simplicity itself. All it required was a stolen minivan and a number of smoke bombs. Salameh had been assigned to the task.

Then Kadir's gaze fell on the six cylinders of compressed hydrogen resting on the floor. The Space Station had refused to allow him to store the cylinders there, so this was the only other place they had. He found their presence unsettling.

Backing away from the drum, Kadir lifted his mask and pointed to them. "Is that really safe?" he said to Yousef.

"Is what safe?" Yousef said.

"Keeping those here with these explosives."

"They are a lot safer than that urea nitrate you're mixing, and urea nitrate is pretty safe."

Last May, on the anniversary of the Hindenburg explosion, the TV news had played a film of the hydrogen-filled zeppelin bursting into flame. He couldn't get it out of his mind. Burned alive . . .

"But hydrogen—"

"It is safe, Kadir," Yousef said, his impatience showing. "I know more about this than you, and I am telling you it is *safe*."

"Well, if it is so *safe*, why wouldn't the Space Station let us keep it there?"

"Because they are ignorant, like you."

Kadir ignored the barb. "And if it is so *safe*, why then are we adding it to the bomb?"

Yousef rolled his eyes. "How many times do I have to explain? When the nitroglycerin sets off the urea nitrate, the nitrate explosion will rupture the tanks—*then* they will explode. Not before."

"I just don't like looking at them."

Yousef's grin looked demented. "We can always move them into the back room with the nitroglycerin—"

"No-no! Here is better."

Yousef stepped closer and put a hand on his shoulder. "Brother, if all this urea nitrate explodes, or the nitroglycerin explodes, the presence of compressed hydrogen will not matter. We will be martyrs in Heaven with our houris before the canisters explode."

If Yousef thought that would comfort him, he was wrong. Kadir's expression must have reflected his horror, for Yousef burst out laughing.

One more day, Kadir thought. One more day and we will be heroes and I will never have to see Ramzi Yousef again.

9

"Park this tank," Tommy barked from the backseat as they eased toward the end of West 53rd. "Things are going good. Those two fucking ragheads better not try to rain on my parade."

He'd hardly said a word all morning. Fine with Vinny. Seemed royally pissed at something. Like he was gonna explode any minute.

Vinny parked his Crown Vic by a fire hydrant across the street from the taxi depot where they'd first met with the Arabs.

Much as he hated to agree with Tommy on anything, collections today had gone pretty smooth so far. Course, they'd been mostly Tommy C's old accounts, paying their vig on time as usual. Now came the first of Tommy's new loans: ten Gs at twelve points a week to the two ragheads. The vig was due at noon. That meant the car would be twelve hundred bucks heavier in a few minutes.

If the ragheads paid up.

Tommy was unfolding a sheet of paper. "Okay. I got their names right here: Kadir Allawi and Mahmoud Abou . . . Abou . . . Abouhalima. Jesus fucking Christ! You're in America, get fucking American names, will ya? Anyway, these two mooks are due here in . . ." He looked at his watch. "No, they should be here now. It's noon. They're supposed to be waiting outside with the money. Where the fuck are they?"

"It's cold," Vinny said. "Maybe they're waiting inside."

"Oh, and they expect me to come in and get them?"

Vinny shrugged. "I dunno. I ain't no mind reader."

"Well, I ain't goin' to them. They gotta come to me."

"Fine," Vinny said, and turned off the engine.

"Ay, whatta you doin'?"

"Could be a long wait, Tommy. I ain't wasting all my gas."

"Fuck!" He slammed the back of the front seat. "Go in and send them out here."

Here we go, Vinny thought. Giving orders again. Hadn't Tommy figured out yet that things was different now?

"Lemme see now," Vinny said. "My memory ain't so good, so maybe you can help me out here. Who did Tony send out to make the collections? I don't recall it being me."

"You're supposed to back me up, Vinny."

"Which puts me behind you, not in front of you. They give you any trouble, I'll be on 'em. But backup don't mean gofer."

Silence from the backseat, then, "Shit!"

Tommy lurched out of the rear door and slammed it behind him. Vinny smiled as he watched him stalk across the street, his suit jacket flapping in the wind. Tommy yanked open the door and stepped into the depot office.

Five minutes later he was back outside, and his expression as he approached the car said things hadn't gone well inside.

"Motherfucker!" he shouted as he dropped into the rear seat.

He repeated the word half a dozen times, each accompanied by a punch against the seat.

"I take it they ain't there," Vinny said.

"Neither one of them! Neither one!"

Vinny could've said, *I told you so,* but what good would it do with this asshole? He'd just deny it. Those two Arabs looked like deadbeats from the get-go, but Tommy always thought he had all the answers.

"What about the tall one, the guy with the red hair? He still driving for them?"

"Yeah, but the dispatcher says the fucker called out sick yesterday and today too, and he don't think he'll be in tomorrow either. Some kinda flu."

"Well, it *is* flu season."

"Bullshit!"

"You don't buy that?"

"Fuck no."

"This dispatcher have an address for him?"

"Yeah. Back in Brooklyn."

"So maybe we go over and, like, administer to the sick. If you know what I mean."

"Don't want to go back to fuckin' Brooklyn. Least not yet."

"What about the little one? What's his name—Kadir?"

"Guy doesn't know him. But hey—we can hop over to Jersey City and maybe find him on the job."

"And if we don't?"

"I'll have a little talk with his boss. Get his address. Besides, I want to take another look at that cigarette operation anyway."

Vinny knew they were heading for a dead end, but he started up the Vic anyway.

"Let's go."

10

Jack had planned to drive down to Tabernacle while La Chirurgienne was having her way with Roman Trejador, figuring he'd hear all about what she'd been able to wring from him when he got back. Well, that wasn't going to happen, so he took his time driving.

Damn. Still so many unanswered questions.

Tabernacle lay ninety or so miles from the city, but the trip involved only two roads: the New Jersey Turnpike to exit 7, and route 206 straight to Tabernacle. Not having to concentrate on twists and turns and intersections left his mind free to ponder other things.

Like Tony . . . or Roman Trejador. He'd always be Tony to Jack. What bothered him was that he'd really liked the guy. Trusted him. And all the time he'd been playing a role. Even playing dead since 1990. Why, Jack would never know. He had mourned his supposed death, even partly blamed himself for it. Now he wished to hell he *had* been killed. Cristin would still be alive.

What bothered him even more was the look on Trejador's face when Jack had tossed him the ama-gi key fob. The shock and revulsion had been real.

Okay, so maybe he'd simply ordered Cristin's death, not her torture and disfigurement. But he'd still ordered her death.

And yet his protestations of innocence on that count had sounded sincere . . .

Jack shook it off. Tony/Trejador had been a superb actor. But his acting days were over. Now he was just dead meat, cooling in his luxury suite until a member of the hotel staff found him. Still, one hell of a more dignified end than he'd allowed Cristin.

Enough. Tabernacle was on the horizon.

The town was little more than a cluster of buildings at a crossroads on a plain at the edge of the Pine Barrens, but it had a town hall, a church, and a cemetery—more than Jack's hometown of Johnson, just a few miles farther down 206.

He drove past the eye-catching cemetery entrance—two square little peak-roofed buildings joined roof to roof by a graceful arch—but behind that was little more than a headstone-studded pancake of winter-brown grass surrounded by a split-rail fence. Jack saw a group of maybe three dozen people clustered left of center. He'd called the United Methodist Church to learn when the service was scheduled, so those had to be Cristin's people.

He made a left on Chatsworth Road, drove along the cemetery's south flank, then found a spot with a view of the funeral party. He'd never met Cristin's folks, and doubted he would have recognized them if he had, what with the way everyone was bundled up against the freezing wind.

He got out and leaned against Ralph to watch. He didn't join the group because he might run into someone he knew. He'd vanished from this life and wanted to stay vanished. But if they were braving the cold, he would too.

11

"Now I'm pissed!" Tommy shouted as he burst into the office.

Just fifteen minutes ago Kadir Allawi's boss had given him what he'd said was the little fucker's address. He looked surprised to see Tommy back.

"What is wrong?" said the Egyptian, leaping to his feet behind his desk.

Tommy had learned his name was Diab.

"That address you gave me is bullshit! He ain't there!"

"Maybe he is out!"

"I mean, bullshit in that he don't live there no more. You gave me a bogus address!"

"These young men, they move all the time. That was the last address he give me!"

"Izzat so?"

Maybe he was covering for him, maybe not. One way to find out for sure. He reached across the desk and grabbed Diab's wrist.

"He has not been in all week! For almost two weeks! I do not know where he is!"

"We'll see about that."

He pulled the cuffs from his pocket. Diab's eyes bulged and he began yammering in Arabese as Tommy snapped one cuff around the Egyptian's wrist, and the other around his own.

"Guess what? Guess who ain't goin' nowhere till I find the little shit who owes me twelve C's in interest."

"I do not know!" Diab wailed as he jittered around and tried to pull his hand free of the cuff. "I have told you all I know!"

In their old routine, Vinny would be standing by with a Taser to quiet him down, but the fat fuck was sitting out in the car. So Tommy hauled off and punched Diab in the face. The guy would have fallen on his ass if Tommy hadn't yanked him back over the desk.

"Where is he?"

Diab's nose dripped blood and he seemed half stunned.

"I do not know!"

"Yeah? Well, maybe one of the other camel jockeys you got workin' for you does."

He dragged Diab through the door into the garage where half a dozen skullcapped bastards worked at their stamping machines. Tommy drew his .38 and fired a shot into the rear wall.

"Now that I got your attention, I'm looking for Kadir Allawi. Any of you know where he is?"

Four shook their heads, two looked like deer in headlights.

"They don't all speak English," Diab said.

"Well, translate then."

Diab babbled something and now all six were shaking their heads. Trouble was, the Egyptian could have told them all to shake their heads like they didn't know nothing and Tommy wouldn't know any different.

Tommy got in Diab's face. "Okay, this is how it's gonna go down. You're gonna ask them again, and if they all say they don't know nothin' again, I'm gonna shoot up one of your stamping machines. And if they still don't know nothin', I'm gonna shoot up another. And then another and another till you're outta business. Got it?"

"But they do not even know Kadir! He keeps to himself. He has no friends here. All his friends are down at the Al-Salam Mosque!"

"Well, I ain't goin' to no mosque, so you tell 'em what I just said. I get Kadir's address or they're outta jobs."

Tommy was hoping one of them would come across because the last thing he wanted to do was bust up those machines. With his detailing business kaput, this looked like a good substitute. An excellent substitute, in fact. Two ways it could go: Take over here, or get a couple of boys, come in some night, and help himself to the stampers. Take them back to Brooklyn, where he'd set himself up in the ciggie biz.

Diab yammered again and once more his workers shook their ragheads.

"Awright," he said, raising the pistol. "You asked for it."

He looked for a place on the nearest stamper he could hit without damaging nothing. He—

The back of his head exploded in pain. He dropped the gun but not before it went off, missing the machine completely. He was halfway into a turn to see what hit him when something crunched into his shoulder. He whirled to see a little camel humper holding a two-by-four. As Tommy reached for him someone jumped on his back and began punching the side of his face. Then another. He dropped to his knees, dragging Diab with him as the workers started kicking him.

Shit!

"Vinny! Yo, Vin*naaay!*"

Suddenly the little brown bastards were losing their grip on him and flying through the air. One slammed against a wall, another landed on a stamping machine, knocking it over. Tommy looked up and saw a human mountain tossing the Arabs around like they was stuffed animals.

Vinny.

Tommy didn't know how he got in here so fast, but he was glad to see a white face, even if it belonged to Vinny Donato.

"What the fuck, Tommy!" he was saying, red-faced as he pulled Tommy to his feet. "What the fuck!"

"Good to see you too!"

"Unlock those cuffs. We're outta here!"

No, he had to find that little shit, Kadir.

"But—"

"Now. Cops coming."

Tommy found the key in his coat pocket and unlocked Diab's cuff. Then the big guy was propelling him through the office and back outside to the car.

"Are you crazy?" Vinny said as they slammed their respective doors. "Are you outta your fucking mind?"

Tommy began unlocking the cuff from around his own wrist but he was so pissed he couldn't get the key into its hole. This was the last straw—the last fucking straw. This fat fuck messes up his business, then he embarrasses him in front of a bunch of ragheads.

"You're asking me if *I'm* crazy? You're really asking me that when you just made me look bad in there."

"I *what*?" Vinny said as he shoved the car in gear and roared down the street. "I made *you* look bad? As I recall you were down on your knees getting the shit kicked outta you when I arrived."

"I coulda handled it—I woulda handled it if you hadn't barged in."

"Really? Who was calling my name? The Egyptian guy you were cuffed to? Funny, it sounded like you."

"Listen—"

"No, *you* listen. No way I woulda heard you from outside."

What was he saying?

"Then how—?"

"I'm sitting in the car and I hear something that sounds like a shot but I can't be sure. I look around and see a couple of people on the street looking toward the garage. So I roll my window down and listen. Then I hear something I *know* is a shot, and it's coming from inside. So I head for the garage, and as I step into the office I hear you calling my name. You know the rest."

Tommy looked ahead and behind. No sign of flashing lights.

"What was that bullshit about cops coming?"

"If I heard the shots, and the people on the street heard the shots, then so did the people living around the garage. You don't think one of them's gonna call nine-one-one? If I hadn't come in you'd be out cold by now. Maybe dead."

Yeah. They'd had him. He'd been on his knees and going down. Next stop for his face: the floor. Tough little fuckers. But no way was Tommy gonna admit that. Not to this son of a bitch.

"Never woulda happened back in the city."

"That's because back in the city people know you're a Gambino and a shitload of hurt's gonna come down on them if they mess with you. These ragheads don't know a Gambino from a bambino."

"I need to find those two fucks."

Vinny seemed to be thinking about something. Finally he said, "Look, I wasn't gonna say this but now I gotta: I told you those two mooks was bad news but you wouldn't listen."

"You never said—"

"I ain't gonna argue with you, Tommy. I said what I said and I said it because these ragheads got their own family. They're like us: Someone comes asking about one of us, what do we say? We don't know nothin', right? They're the same way, plus they got this funky Ali Baba religion that keeps them even tighter. Plus one of the guys you loaned lives here in Jersey—fuckin' Jersey, for Christ sake. What were you thinking?"

Good question, Tommy thought. The same question Tony C would be asking before the day was over. Shit.

"The tall one drives a cab—"

"*Did* drive a cab. He may have decided it's cheaper to find another line of work since he sure as shit ain't pullin' down twelve hundred a week in tips. I think you better face it—you ain't gonna find these guys unless it's by accident or they decide they *want* to be found."

Tommy knew he was right, and if Vinny said anything like that to Tony C, Tommy was up shit's creek.

Maybe tonight would be the night he put Tony and Vinny away.

The idea had hit him in Tony's office last night, and it came with a plan on how to get away with it. He'd actually been reaching for his gun when he realized there was still people on the sales floor of the appliance store. They'd ruin everything. So he'd put it off.

"I'll find 'em," he said, sounding all sorts of confident. "Don't you worry your empty head, Vinny. Leave it to me. I'll find 'em. Now let's get back to the city. We got more vig to collect."

But no matter how much he collected, he was still gonna catch shit from Tony about the ragheads.

That meant tonight had to be the night: Vinny and Tony, dead. He just had to make sure he put off the meeting until after the store was closed, so only the three of them was there.

So simple, really. And he knew just what he'd tell everybody after it went down.

Yeah. Tonight sounded good.

12

It started to snow just as the last of the mourners left. Jack couldn't help but think of Rico and how he'd been praying for snow. Life totally sucked at times.

He hopped the fence and wove among the flakes and the headstones toward the flower-decked coffin. The grounds men would be along soon to lower it into the grave, so he needed to make this quick. But he was determined to have a last moment alone with her.

"Hey, Cristin," he said when he reached her grave, the words rushing through his tightening throat before it shut completely. "Just stopped by to let you know that it's okay that you didn't tell me. No, really. Let's face it, I probably wouldn't have handled it very well and it would have come between us because no matter how often I said I didn't want strings and wanted them even less than you did that wasn't quite true because I was so damn attached to you and I spent every freaking week looking forward to Sunday with you and you know it was more than the sex for me, it was you, you-you-you-you-you. I never met anyone like you and I know for sure I'll never meet anyone like you again and I swear I can hear you laughing in there and saying 'Damn straight!' and aw jeez, aw jeez . . ."

His voice gave out then and his words drowned in a choking sob as he dropped to his knees beside the coffin. He pounded his fist on the lid.

Why-why-why?

He'd found the answer but it was so devoid of sense and logic and meaning that it had become a non-answer. And so the *why* remained.

"You should have this back."

He pulled her ama-gi from his pocket and kissed it. Then he tried to slip it through the seam along the bottom of the coffin lid but it had been screwed down tight. He worked his hand between the coffin and the edge of the dirt and dropped it into the grave. If it couldn't be buried with her, at least she could rest atop it.

And no one would see that obscenity again.

He pushed himself back to his feet and found his voice again.

"Also wanted to let you know we got them. All of them. I had help . . . someone you knew. One of your . . . guys. Edward Burkes. Seems other people had strings to you too. The scales are evened in a way. Well, not really. Nothing makes up for losing you. You wouldn't let me say it to your face, but I'm saying it now. I loved you. I didn't know that until I realized I'd never see you again. But I did. I loved you. I love you still. I—"

He heard a door slam and saw a groundskeeper walking his way from the front gate.

He touched the coffin. "As long as you're alive in somebody's head, you'll never be truly dead. And I'm never gonna forget you. Count on that."

As he walked away he wiped at the tears that were threatening to freeze. He didn't look up until he was hopping back over the fence. A young woman stood by Ralph. She looked different but he knew her immediately.

"Karina?"

Jack's high school girlfriend and Cristin's best friend from those days.

She smiled. "It *is* you. I saw you over here from the grave and thought, I know him." Her smile crumbled as her words broke into a sob. "Oh, Jack, isn't it the worst thing. Isn't it the worst thing ever?"

He couldn't answer. Instead he found himself in her arms, and her in his, clinging to each other like sailors to flotsam as they cried together.

13

Heart pounding, Ernst Drexler snapped off the television and snatched up the phone. He had Trejador's mobile number preprogrammed to the 3 button. It rang but no answer.

Odd. Very odd. The only constants in Trejador's life were the Order and his mobile phone. Everything else changed at whim. Ernst tried again. Still no answer.

That, coupled with what he had just heard on TV, gave the air an ominous tinge.

CNN had reported that another "brutally mutilated" man had been found on another park bench. This man had been discovered in Manhattan but his mutilations appeared identical to the victim found last night in Forest Hills. The only difference was that this man appeared to be of Middle Eastern descent.

That had been enough to set off alarm bells in Ernst. He wanted Trejador's take on the matter.

A third try and still no answer. Maybe he was moving again. One way to find out . . .

He looked up the Lexington Hotel and was connected to the front desk.

"Mister Trejador's suite, please."

"*I'm sorry,*" said a woman's voice. "*Can you give me that name again, please?*"

"Roman Trejador. He's on the twenty-sixth floor."

"*Oh. Oh, just a minute.*" It sounded then like she put her hand over the mouthpiece but her voice still came through. "*Someone's calling about the man in twenty-six-twelve. What do I tell him?*" A male voice said, "*Ask the police.*"

That was all Ernst had to hear. He hung up and stood statue still as a crawling sensation worked its slow way across his stomach.

. . . *the man in twenty-six-twelve . . . Ask the police . . .*

Ernst could see only one way to interpret that. Something had happened to Trejador, something serious enough to get the police involved. Had he become the third "brutally mutilated" victim?

Who could be doing this? It was sheer madness to think this young nobody named Lonnie could have eliminated Reggie, Klarić, al-Thani, and now Trejador. Unthinkable that anyone could work that sort of violent magic.

And yet . . .

He should call the High Council. Of course he had no proof that al-Thani was the mutilated Middle Easterner, nor that anything of real consequence had befallen Trejador, but he should at least convey his suspicions.

The repercussions would be severe. They would not care about Reggie—they barely knew of his existence—but Klarić and al-Thani missing . . . and some as yet undetermined disaster befalling Roman Trejador . . . that was catastrophic. And it all would be laid at his doorstep. He'd ordered al-Thani to send Reggie and Klarić after that damnable Lonnie, and now . . .

Wait. If Trejador was out of the picture—and Ernst was becoming increasingly sure of that with every passing moment—all the blame could fall on the Spaniard. Against Ernst's advice, *Trejador* had ordered al-Thani to bring in Lonnie. All Roman's idea, all Roman's fault.

Yes, this would all work out . . . *if* Ernst could survive whoever was scything through the actuator ranks.

He called information for Lufthansa's reservations number. He'd book the next flight out to Vienna. Austria was his home and he was long overdue for a vacation.

He would call the High Council from overseas.

14

"I wasn't sure it'd still be open," Karina said as they slid into a booth.

The snow wasn't sticking much, so they'd decided, for old times' sake, to go to Olga's Diner in Marlton. Since Jack would be heading straight to the city from there and Karina back to Tabernacle, they'd driven the fifteen miles separately.

The place hadn't changed much. The red neon sign on the roof was still almost as big as the diner itself. Though somewhat worse for wear, the Naugahyde or vinyl or whatever-they-were seats on the booths looked pretty much the same as when they'd frequented the place in the eighties. So did the red Formica tables. Back when they were dating they'd sit side by side, joined at the hip; today the table divided them.

"There's a law somewhere: Olga's can't close. It's an institution."

She opened the menu. "Everything changes," she said, "but not this place. Look. They still serve turkey croquettes with mashed potatoes and gravy. Ugh."

"How can you say 'ugh'? You never tried them. Ever."

She'd been South Burlington County Regional High School's only vegetarian—at least the only one as far as he knew. He could still hear her saying, *If it had a face or a mother, I don't want it on my plate.*

"Well, they just *sound* awful. But not as awful as creamed chipped beef—which they also still have." She gave an exaggerated shudder. "Remember how you used to order that just to gross me out?"

"On toast. Mmmm."

One time she refused to kiss him after he'd eaten it.

"And remember how you tried to convince me that chipped beef never had a face or a mother?"

"Since the scientific community has yet to present convincing evidence to the contrary, I persist in my contention."

She shook her head. "You haven't changed a bit, have you." She put her menu down and stared at him. "Then again, I think you have. We've both changed, haven't we."

He leaned back and looked at her. Karina Haddon hadn't changed much, at least on the outside. Same sparkling brown eyes, same dark blond hair, but wearing it shorter now than when they were dating. Maybe she'd added a few pounds, but they were good pounds.

She used to wear a striped engineer's cap and listen to early Bob Dylan when everyone else was listening to *Thriller* and Def Leppard. She'd been out of step with her peers, just like Jack, but in a different way. Their self-marginalization had brought them together. His first love. Hers too. They'd lost their respective virginities to each other.

College split them—she went off to Berkeley, he to Rutgers. They got together over Christmas break freshman year but after that he never saw her again. He'd been crushed. But now wasn't the time to get into that. He'd carried a torch for her for a while, but it sputtered out years ago.

"Pardon the cliché, but that's part of growing up. Or so I'm told."

"Cristin changed the most, I guess—if what I read in the papers is true."

He saw no reason to deny it. "It's true."

"Cristin . . . a call girl." She shook her head and frowned. "She wrote me she'd run into you in the city. Did you know?"

"About her profession? Not until after she was gone."

"Cristin." She shook her head again. "I knew she was into sex back in high school. I mean, you don't earn the name 'Hot-to-Trot Ott' by being a shrinking violet. But who would have thought she'd hire out as a plaything for horny old men."

Jack felt a flash of anger. "Spare her your feminist ire."

"Feminist?"

"Aren't you the one who sent Cristin a card for Emma Goldman's birthday?"

Her lips twisted . . . not quite a smile. "Oh, that. I got radicalized in freshman year. But I'm kind of shocked you'd defend sexual exploita—"

"Trust me. Cristin was anything but a sexually exploited woman. She knew exactly what she was doing. Had a five-year plan and all."

"You learned all this since she was killed?"

"No. She told me she was a party planner. I never guessed the party was her. But she was still going to FIT with plans to open her own shop once she built up some capital."

"*If* she was saving. Most prostitutes have a drug problem."

He remembered Cristin's bankbook and the surprising balance.

"She'd socked away a considerable amount. Her biggest drug was Cuervo Gold, and only a couple of shooters now and then."

"Still . . ."

"There's no 'still,' Karina—not from you, not from me. It was *her* life, *her* body. We don't get to say what she does with either."

Karina leaned back. "Listen to you. You sound like some of my more radical friends out in Berkeley. Is that why you disappeared?"

Uh-oh.

"What's that mean?"

"A few years ago my folks mentioned that people were buzzing about my old boyfriend dropping out of college and disappearing. Was it what happened to your mother?"

No, he wanted to say, it was what *I* did after. But he didn't want to get into that either.

"It was a lot of things. And please keep it to yourself that you saw me."

"You're not in any legal trouble, are you?"

"Not that I know of. I simply dropped off the map and would like to stay that way." He wanted to get off the subject of Jack. "Back to Cristin . . ."

Karina's lower lip trembled. "Yeah, Cristin. Say what you want about her 'profession,' it's what killed her, isn't it."

"No, a person or persons unknown killed her."

"Who met her through her 'profession,' right?"

"I suppose so."

A tortuous path, but when he boiled it all down to its essence, if Roman Trejador hadn't been one of her regulars, she wouldn't have been in the wrong place at the wrong time.

He felt he had to add, "But you could say the same about a stewardess who dies in a plane crash."

Her eyes narrowed. "Were you two . . . ?"

"Close? Yeah. A little."

"How close?"

None of your business, he decided.

"We talked. We had the high school connection."

She folded her arms. "I'm not even going to ask if you had sex. I knew Cristin."

Jack let that slide. "How about you? Seeing anyone?"

She nodded. "Yeah. Sort of."

"Male or female?"

He hadn't meant to say that. But he remembered Cristin mentioning a brief affair between the two of them and it slipped out.

She reddened. "What?"

"Never mind."

"No, really. Why would you—?"

"Cristin told me about you two that first summer—the summer you said you were staying out west."

Her blush deepened. "My God, you two must have been more than just a 'little' close. Is there anything she *didn't* tell you?"

He shrugged, wishing he hadn't mentioned it. "She said you weren't really into it."

She let out a long, shaky sigh. "We were just trying it out. You know, experimenting. Cristin was more into it—but she just liked sex, plain and simple. If she could get off on it, she was cool with it. I learned that it wasn't for me." Her features bunched up and she sobbed. "I really loved her, Jack. Not that way, it turned out, but every other way. She was a good person, not a mean or hateful bone in her body. Why'd it have to be her?"

As tears streamed down her cheeks, he reached across the table and took her hand. She squeezed his like she was trying to break his fingers.

"I've been asking myself that question all week."

The waitress appeared then, pad and pencil held at ready, and Jack realized he wasn't hungry. An unusual state for him.

He looked at Karina's blotchy face. "You hungry?"

Karina could only shake her head.

He apologized to the waitress and they went back outside. The snow had turned to rain and they got wet during a prolonged last hug.

Watching her drive away he felt like he'd just lived through a Dan Fogelberg song.

15

"What's good here?"

Hadya looked up and saw a vaguely familiar face smiling over the top of the display case. She tensed when she recognized the young man who had been watching the mosque.

She glanced around. Only two other customers, Muslim women buying treats for tonight's fast-breaking iftar. Jala was handling them.

"Hello," she said softly. "Where have you been?"

"Unexpected events kept me busy elsewhere."

"Have you learned anything?"

He shook his head. "Just got here. You?"

"Yes. I found an address where my brother and his friends go. Something . . ." What was the word? "Something not normal is happening there."

"You mean strange?"

"Yes. Strange. Very strange."

His mild brown eyes narrowed. "Strange is always interesting, even if it's just . . . strange. Where we talking about?"

She pulled a pencil from her pocket and wrote *Pamrapo Avenue* on a paper napkin.

"It is down Kennedy, almost to Bayonne," she said, pointing as she slid the napkin across the top of the display case. "There is empty land with a path that . . ." Again the word eluded her. She made an arcing movement with her hand.

"Curves?" he said.

"Yes. It curves behind a house. They are in an old . . . place for cars."

"Garage?"

"Yes. It is there but you cannot see it from the street. Kadir and his friends do not live there. Just work there."

He smiled. "Where did you learn your English?"

Was he going to make fun of her?

"I teach myself."

His eyebrows rose. "How long?"

"Two years now. I listen to tapes. I am not very good."

"You kidding?" he said with a smile as he waved the napkin. "And you write it too. Considering we don't even have the same alphabet, you're amazing."

She felt her face flush. When was the last time she had heard a compliment? About anything. She couldn't remember. She blinked back tears.

"Thank you."

"I can only imagine what my Arabic would sound like after two years of self-study." He tucked the napkin away. "I'll give the place a look."

"Be careful."

"Careful is becoming my middle name." He stepped back from the display case and studied the contents. "Now . . . what's good here?"

She smiled. "Everything. What do you like? We have *kanafeh, halawa, baklava* . . ."

"It's not for me. For a friend."

A girlfriend?

"Very well. What does *she* like?"

"It's a he and he's got a sweet tooth the size of Brooklyn."

What?

"I don't under—"

"The sweeter the better."

"Ah, then you want baklava—the one on the second shelf with the pistachios."

"Heard of that." He bent for a closer look at the glistening lumps of flaky dough. "That's the one with all the honey, right?"

"Full of honey."

He straightened and smiled. "Sounds like a winner. Pack me up a pound."

She placed a sheet of wax paper on the scale, weighed out a pound of the bias-cut pieces, then tied them all into a white pie box. She put an extra piece on some paper and handed it to the young man.

"This is for you."

"Really? Thanks."

He followed her to the cash register where he paid for the pound.

"What's your name?" he said.

She felt another flush coming. "Hadya. Yours?"

"Jack. I'll let you know what I find."

"Don't let them see you."

"If there's anyone there I'll go back tomorrow."

He waved and walked out.

What a nice man. He wasn't for her, but still . . . she hoped he came back.

16

"Pamrapo . . . Pamrapo . . ." Jack muttered as he steered Ralph along Kennedy Boulevard, studying the street signs.

Weird name. Probably Indian—or Native American, as the PC police wanted them called. Jack wasn't much for political correctness, but "Native American" made sense and simplified the confusion: Indians were native to India and Native Americans were native to, well, America. Made sense.

Anyway, New Jerseyans loved to give their places Native American names. Like Hackensack, Hoboken, and Ho-Ho-Kus, and even Mahwah, where Burkes had his safe house. Pamrapo sounded like an anagram of Ramapo, another aboriginal name.

His stomach rumbled. He should have eaten when he had the chance at Olga's, even if he wasn't hungry at the time. But that hadn't been in the cards. He'd had time on the drive back from Jersey to think about his tête-à-tête with Karina. If nothing else, it had made it clear that whatever they'd once had as a couple was gone. He would always have a warm spot in his heart for his first love, but they were two different people now. Too much had happened to him. He was over her just as she was over him. No going back. No reason to.

He bit into the piece of baklava Hadya had given him. *Sweet.* Too sweet by half for him, but hunger demanded he gobble the rest. Oh, man. Abe was gonna *plotz* when he tasted this.

He stopped at a light and there it was: Pamrapo Avenue. But left or right? She hadn't said. He swung right and eased down the short block. Dark had fallen and the streetlights hadn't come on yet, but he drove all the way to its end without seeing any "empty land," as Hadya had put it.

Cute girl. Cute face, at least, because that was all she left visible. Could be bald for all he could tell. Couldn't tell much about the rest of her either because she was swathed like a nun.

She was right to suspect her brother, but no way she could know about the Rabin visit and where and when they planned to set off their bomb unless he told her. Jack hadn't seen any reason to tell her that tomorrow was her brother's big day.

He crossed back over Kennedy. On the other side he found a vacant lot—he guessed that qualified as "empty land"—with a rutted path curving into the bushes, just as she'd described. He stayed on the street and rolled by for about a hundred yards, then killed the headlights as he turned around. He parked across the street and walked to the lot. He followed the ruts for a couple of dozen feet before he spotted the converted garage. Lights glowed from within and he recognized the Chevy Nova parked out front. Too risky to approach much closer.

He returned to Ralph and headed back toward Kennedy.

If they were building a bomb, that would be the place. But Burkes had said they'd need a truckload of explosive to do any real damage from outside the UN. No van in sight at the moment.

But if they planned to hit the UN tomorrow before noon, they'd load up the truck in the morning. Jack didn't know a damn thing about bombs, but if he saw anything like that going down, he'd call Burkes immediately and let him handle it from there.

He'd return early tomorrow—*real* early—for a look inside.

17

Hadya composed herself as she waited for Kadir to answer her knock. She still had her key from when she lived here—before he'd shaved her head—and could have used it to open his apartment door, but that would only provoke him, which was the last thing she wanted tonight.

Jack's visit to the bakery had given her an idea. He'd bought sweets for a friend and it occurred to her that she might use halawah and baklava as a fake peace offering to Kadir—fake because she could not find it within herself to forgive what he'd done to her. The Qur'an said that the best deed before Allah was to pardon a person who has wronged you. Perhaps someday she would be able to forgive Kadir, but the humiliation still burned. And if he planned to hurt innocent people, she had to stop him.

The door opened just wide enough to expose a brown eye. It widened in surprise and then the door opened enough to reveal Kadir's scraggly bearded face.

"Hadya?"

The air wafting from within the apartment carried a milder form of the acrid stench she'd smelled at the converted garage. It must have permeated Kadir's clothes.

She held up the bag of sweets. "I brought you halawah and baklava for your iftar."

And now he frowned, his expression puzzled. "Why?"

"Because it is Ramadan and good deeds are twice blessed."

He looked her up and down, his gaze lingering on her hijab.

"I am glad to see that you are dressed like a righteous Muslim woman. You learned your lesson well."

Hadya went cold inside. She wanted to rake her nails across his smug face. Instead she pushed the bag toward him.

"Here. For you."

"This is unexpected," he said, taking it.

"May I come in?"

He shook his head. "I have guests. We are discussing important matters."

She craned her neck to see around him and spotted three tense faces watching the door. She had no names for them but had seen them all with Kadir at one time or another.

"Oh . . . sorry."

"Yes. Good night."

He closed the door in her face.

Anger blazed, urging her to kick the door again and again until he opened it. She had braved this not-so-safe neighborhood on Kensington Avenue to bring him a gift of sweets, and now she faced a walk home of over a mile in the cold and dark. And what had he done? Taken it and snubbed her without so much as a thank-you.

But the flare died quickly. Venting her anger would accomplish nothing. Sadness and dismay took hold instead.

How terribly you've changed, my brother.

Kadir was a different person. All gentleness had fled. Had an evil spirit taken over his body? No, not a spirit, an influence. The influence of Sheikh Omar.

In her pocket she carried a short steel bar she'd taken from the oven area of the bakery. Early tomorrow morning, while Kadir and his friends were having their pre-fast meal, she would be at the garage, prying the front door open. And if she found what she didn't want to find, what she prayed she would not find, she would have to act. To save others and to save Kadir from himself, she would not hesitate to report her own brother to the police.

18

Tony was in a spitting rage. Like real spit, tiny drops, all over the blotter on his desk.

No surprise there.

"These fuckers are into me for ten G's and you can't find them?" he screamed.

Tommy said nothing. He'd decided that was the way he'd play it tonight. Just stare at Tony and wait for him to give himself a heart attack. Or cough up a lung. Whichever came first.

The lack of response pushed Tony closer to the edge.

"Ain't you got nothin' to say?"

Tommy shrugged. "It is what it is."

Tony's voice rose in pitch and volume. "Are you fucking stoned?"

Even Vinny was looking at him.

Stoned? Tommy thought. Why yes, I believe I am. Very.

He'd been tooting all afternoon and night. Had a little Valpolicella mixed in there too. Make that a lot of Valpolicella. Liquid and powdered courage for what he was about to do.

So simple: Pull his gun and shoot Vinny three times in the chest. Grab Vinny's gun as he goes down and shoot Tony before he can pull the Dirty Harry .44 Magnum that got him his nickname. Wipe off Vinny's gun and put it in his hand.

Story: Vinny got into an argument with his capo and shot him. Tommy, fearing he was next—hey, everybody knew there was bad blood between the two of them—shot Vinny in self-defense.

Trouble was, they was both looking at him now. Had to get their eyes pointed elsewhere, just for a second, just long enough for him to pull his gun.

He pointed at the door to the alley behind Tony. "Hey, who's that?"

Like total jerks they looked and Tommy reached for his pistol—

Shit! His fucking holster was empty. What the—?

His gun—he'd lost it in the scuffle with the ragheads over in Jersey. He'd been so fucking stoned all day he hadn't realized it was gone.

Shit-shit-SHIT!

Tony turned back to him. "Now you're seeing things! Get outta here! You and Vinny are bringing Aldo along tomorrow. And I don't want to see your face again unless you're bringing me my vig!'"

With nothing else to say, and nothing else he could do, Tommy slunk away.

FRIDAY

FEBRUARY 26, 1993

1

Sunrise was still two hours away as Hadya stepped off the bus near Pamrapo Avenue. She had been afraid to walk the two and a half miles from her apartment at four thirty in the morning. A woman out alone at this hour in the cold and dark . . . not only unwise, but dangerously foolish. But traveling at this hour was necessary if she was to have the garage to herself. Kadir and his fellow conspirators—for she had no doubt they were involved in a conspiracy of some sort—would not have even started their suhoor yet, so that would give her plenty of time.

As she hurried down Pamrapo, it began to snow. Light, swirling flakes floating from heaven. It snowed in Jordan, but rarely, and she had neither time nor temperament to appreciate it now. Perhaps later, after she'd seen what was in that garage.

She found the vacant lot and started a careful walk along one of the ruts. She didn't own a flashlight but was sure if she moved slowly enough—

She stopped. Voices echoed from up ahead around the bend.

Kadir? At this hour? Could it be?

She edged forward and saw four vehicles. Two of them were vans backed up to the door of the converted garage. Four men were carrying cardboard boxes from inside and loading them into the vans. Box after box after box. They looked harmless enough. What could be in them?

As she crouched and moved forward for a better look, her foot caught on something and she fell forward.

2

"What was that?" Yousef said, freezing and looking around as Kadir carried another box of the urea nitrate from inside.

"What?"

"I thought I heard someone on the driveway."

Kadir hadn't heard anything, but then he hadn't been out here. Probably nothing—he'd seen a raccoon or two in the yard over the past week. Still, at this point they couldn't take anything for granted.

They'd arrived extra early so they could load the vans in the dark. The boxes of urea nitrate paste looked innocent, but the long fuses and canisters of compressed hydrogen might raise alarms should anyone accidentally get a peek.

He quickly stacked the box in the van and picked up the flashlight from the truck bed. He trained its beam on the rank grass running along the ruts that passed for a driveway and—

Movement in the grass.

"Someone's here!"

He kept his beam trained on the prone figure as he and Yousef ran forward together. A woman? She looked up and his heart sank as he recognized his sister.

"Hadya?"

"Your sister?" Yousef cried in a voice hoarse with shock. "Your *sister*?"

Kadir couldn't believe this was happening. "What are you doing here, Hadya?"

"I am asking you the same question, brother," she replied in Arabic, brushing off her clothes as she rose. "What are *you* doing here?"

"None of your concern. Now you just turn around and—"

Yousef gripped his arm. "No! We cannot let her go!"

Kadir knew he was right. Fuming with anger that she would betray him and jeopardize all his plans like this, he grabbed Hadya's arm and dragged her toward the apartment.

"No!" she said, struggling against him and trying to pull away. She raised her voice. "Let me go!"

His anger exploded. In a burst of rage he slammed the flashlight against the side of her head.

"Silence! Do as you're told!"

The blow staggered her. As her knees wobbled and she began to sink toward the ground, he and Yousef each took an arm and dragged her inside.

Ayyad and Salameh, each with a box of nitrate in their arms, stared in frozen shock.

"What . . . ?" Ayyad said, wide-eyed.

Yousef spoke through his teeth. "Kadir's nosy sister."

"How did she know?"

"Obviously she'd been spying on us."

They dropped her in a corner against the wall where she stared up at him with dazed eyes, rubbing the side of her face.

"Kadir . . ."

"Silence!"

What was he going to do with her?

"Who have you told about this?" he said, keeping his voice low. "Have you told the police?"

"No . . ."

"The FBI?"

"No. Please, Kadir. I don't know what you're doing but you mustn't—"

She cringed as he raised the flashlight for another blow. He looked around and spotted a roll of silver duct tape. He traded the flashlight for that and nodded to Yousef.

"Hold her."

Hadya began kicking and screaming as Yousef pinned her arms. Kadir quickly silenced her by wrapping a length of tape across her mouth and then winding it around her head, hijab and all—once, twice, three times. Her struggles increased as he began to wind it around her body, trapping her arms.

"Stop it!" Yousef said, pinching her nose. "Lie still or I shall squeeze this until you stop moving—forever!"

She couldn't breathe through her mouth and now her nose was cut off. Her face reddened and her eyes widened with panic as she began to suffocate.

Death was the best solution to her meddling, but she was his sister. He was about to tell Yousef to cease when she stopped her struggles.

He released her nose and air whistled through her nostrils as she struggled to regain her breath.

"There," Yousef said. "Now cooperate or next time I will not let go."

Hadya lay still as Kadir finished binding her arms and legs. By the time he ran out of tape she was virtually mummified. She half sat, half lay against the wall, mute and immobile. All she could do was glare up at him.

"You are a very foolish girl, Hadya. You should have minded your own business and not tried to interfere with Allah's will."

She shook her head and mumbled something incomprehensible behind the tape.

"Today we strike a blow for jihad that will shake the world to its roots. All Islam shall praise us and the world will stand in awe of what we have done in the name of Allah. The world will recognize the greatness that is Allah."

She closed her eyes and shook her head again as tears spilled down her cheeks.

"You worry now. You have doubts. That is because you lack true faith in Allah. But consider: Why do you think you fell as you were sneaking around out there? It was Allah. He foiled your treachery. He guides us, and later today all your doubts will vanish when you learn what we have done."

"She is in the way here," Yousef said. "We need to move her."

"What about the kitchen?"

Ayyad waved his hands. "No-no! The nitroglycerin is in there. Use the bathroom."

Perfect. It had no window and they could close the door on her. He and Salameh dragged her in and left her on the floor. Once the door was closed, Kadir turned to the others.

"Let's finish loading so we can find something to eat before sunrise."

The four of them bent to the task of moving the boxes. The urea nitrate in many of them was still a stinky paste, but it didn't need to be dry to explode. The loading was hard work, considering that the weight of the nitrate alone totaled a ton and a half. Since the Econoline vans were each designed to transport a ton of cargo, this was no problem. With the nitrate divided evenly between them, they were burdened with fifteen hundred pounds each.

Next came the nitroglycerin. The handling of that was left to Yousef. He carried the eight bottles one at a time from the refrigerator to the front room.

"I still don't know why we need so many," Salameh said.

Kadir noticed Yousef roll his eyes and understood: How many times had he explained this?

"In theory, we need only one. When one bottle of nitroglycerin detonates, it will explode the other three. And they in turn will set off the urea compound and the hydrogen. All within the blink of an eye."

Salameh frowned. "So, by your own admission we need but one—"

"Things can go wrong, even with Allah's guidance. We will set four fuses in each truck, each leading to a different bottle. All we need is for one to reach its detonator. We can be sure that, with four fuses, no matter how bad our luck, one of them will succeed. Think of it as a race. The fuse that wins has a glorious victory because it renders the existence of the other three unnecessary."

Yousef had fashioned lead-nitrate detonators which he was now attaching to the nitroglycerin bottles. When he was finished he carried the bottles— again, one at a time—to the trucks, where he securely positioned them among the nitrate boxes, four to a truck.

"Now the fuses," Yousef said when he was done. "Make sure they are the right length."

3

As soon as Kadir closed the bathroom door, leaving her in the musty dark, Hadya began working at the tape that bound her. He'd tied her wrists in front of her and, although her arms were bound to her sides, by flexing her spine to the limit she was able to force her hands to her lips. She hooked two fingers onto the edge of the tape binding her head and wriggled them beneath. When she had enough purchase, she worked the edge of the tape down over her upper lip.

She gulped air, greedy for oxygen. Her nose had clogged from walking through the cold and she'd barely been able to breathe through it. Once she had her wind again, she worked the tape down to her chin. Straining against the bonds encircling her torso, she forced her wrists to her teeth and began gnawing at the tape. Soon she'd chewed a small tear.

She clenched the edge of the tear between her front teeth and pulled. Slowly, millimeter by millimeter, the tape began to part. Her neck muscles were cramping but she kept at it until she'd torn through that strip. She flopped back, prone, letting her muscles recoup, but only for a moment. Then she was hunched up again, using her teeth to unravel the tape from her wrists. Slow work because she could raise her wrists only so far.

Finally her wrists came free and she flopped back again, momentarily exhausted. Her muscles weren't used to such prolonged straining contractions.

Her wrists might be free but were of little value with her arms still pinned to her sides. She forced her right arm up until her fingers found the nearest loop of tape. She began picking and pulling at it. She kept her nails short for her work in the bakery; if only they were just a little bit longer . . .

As she worked she could hear them talking. She had approached the garage in a state of fear. Now, after listening to them talk of their plans, she became terrified.

She had to get away . . . had to stop them.

4

"I wish we had remote detonators," Kadir said as he remeasured a length of fuse.

"I have used garage-door openers for bombs in Israel," Yousef said. "But those were smaller. With bombs this size, the blast radius is wider than the range of the remote—especially with all the interference in a crowded city like New York. If you are close enough to set it off, you will die. You might as well stay behind the wheel and press the button. I am willing to be a martyr for jihad, but not yet. Is anyone here anxious for martyrdom?"

Kadir shook his head and noticed Salameh and Ayyad doing the same.

"Good," Yousef said. "We shall all survive to dance on the rubble of the United Nations, on the smoking graves of Rabin and D'Amato and Boutros-Ghali."

The fuses were housed in clear plastic surgical tubing to reduce the smoke of their burning. Kadir and Ayyad had measured them and were remeasuring them to make sure that each was twenty feet long. They burned at a rate of an inch every two and a half seconds. A twenty-foot fuse gave them ten minutes to put themselves far enough away to escape the blast. Kadir had been raised in the metric system and, despite years in the U.S., he still had trouble thinking in terms of inches and feet.

"You will have the hardest part, Kadir," said Ayyad.

Kadir nodded but did not look up.

He needed no reminder. He felt his palms grow sweaty at the thought of what lay ahead at eleven thirty . . . stopping the van in the underpass . . . lighting the fuses . . . running as he'd never run before to put himself out of harm's way . . .

He could do it. He *would* do it.

As he refocused on the present, Kadir realized that the fuse he held was short. He measured again.

"This one is only nineteen feet," he said. "Someone has been careless."

"Cut another," Yousef said. "We have plenty."

Kadir tied the short fuse in knots and uncoiled a fresh length from the roll. He used the yardstick to measure out twenty feet exactly.

"Where is the knife?"

Salameh looked around, then handed him the large carving knife they had been using. As Kadir began cutting the fuse, the bathroom door burst open. Screaming at the top of her lungs, with her blue cloth coat flapping like wings, Hadya charged out on a direct path for the front door. Kadir leaped up to block her way.

"Stop!"

Still clutching the knife he thrust his hands out and she ran into the blade. Both he and Hadya gasped in shock. Kadir released the knife and backed away a step. Hadya stood frozen, her stunned eyes staring at him, then down at the handle protruding from the left side of her chest. She turned, staggered in a small circle, then dropped to her knees. For a second or two she looked as if she might be praying, then she collapsed backward to face the ceiling.

After a few heartbeats of stunned silence, the room broke into a bedlam of alarmed cries around Kadir, but he found himself without voice as he stared at his sister's semi-supine form. He watched the wet red stain spreading from the blade as her blood soaked through the fabric of the abaya she wore under her coat.

What have I done? The question echoed through his numb brain. *What have I done?*

He dropped to Hadya's side and shook her shoulder. "Hadya? Hadya?"

But she made no response. Her eyes remained closed, her chest still.

"She's dead!" he cried. "Allah forgive me, I've killed her."

"It was an accident," Yousef said. "We all saw that."

"But—"

"This was God's will," Yousef said, pulling him to his feet. "You must not let this turn you from our holy course. Come outside with me. You need air."

Kadir stumbled out the door and the two of them stood in the frigid, snow-laced air—Kadir leaning against the wall, Yousef pacing back and forth before him. Neither said anything. All Kadir could think of was Hadya's shocked expression after the knife plunged into her chest.

"It is a terrible thing that has just happened to you," Yousef said after a minute or so of pacing. "But it is a good thing for jihad."

The meaning filtered through slowly. "What?"

"Your sister was a threat to jihad. She allowed herself to become tainted by America and its infidel ways."

Kadir could not argue with that. Hadn't he seen her baring her head in public, putting herself on display as an object of lust for any man who passed?

"She had treachery in her heart," Yousef added. "Else why would she creep up on us like a thief in the night? Had she supported our cause she would have come forward like a proud woman of Islam and offered to help. Instead she plied you with sweets last night to gain your trust and then followed you."

"Followed?"

"How else could she know you were here? Unless you told her."

Kadir shook his head. "No. Last night was the first I have spoken to her in . . . in years."

Had it been that long?

He could not deny the truth in what Yousef was saying. Hadya's behavior was proof that she had only treachery in her heart. And her treachery was like a dagger in his own heart. He supposed he should be glad it had ended in hers.

Still . . . his sister . . .

He saw the appalled faces of his parents, his brothers and other sisters, heard their silent question: *What have you done, Kadir? What have you DONE?*

They must never know—

Yousef startled him by gripping his shoulder. "Come. We must finish loading and take the vans to a safe place where we wait until it is time to move."

He allowed Yousef to lead him back inside. Kadir knew that, despite his superficial sympathy, Yousef was relieved, even glad that Hadya was dead. Knowing what she knew, she jeopardized the entire plan. Had Allah propelled her onto that carving knife? Kadir prayed so.

Inside, Hadya's body was gone, but a red smear led from the front room to the dark kitchen. He averted his gaze and went to help Yousef attach the fuses to the detonators. When that was done they moved the hydrogen canisters to the vans. In each vehicle they placed one on the left side and one on the right, midway along the bay, and secured a third before the rear doors.

Once the doors were closed and locked, Yousef nodded and said, "Now we are done. Now we are ready to make history."

Kadir stepped back into the apartment to look at the blood smear on the floor. He did not know what to do about Hadya. He could not report her death to the police. The ensuing murder investigation would surely lead to him. And yet how could he leave her here to rot or be found by strangers—which would again involve the police and an investigation? He would have to return after his mission was completed and find a way to see to it that she had a proper Muslim burial.

He turned out the lights and went back outside. Ayyad embraced him as he stepped out the door.

"I will be praying for Allah to guide you all."

Then Ayyad got in his car and drove off. The plan was for him to go to his job at Allied Signal like any other day and stand ready should any of the three of them need assistance after the explosion.

"It is time to go," Yousef said. "If we get separated, you both know where to gather?"

Kadir nodded. They had picked out a spot under an old train trestle in Brooklyn, not far from the Al-Farooq Mosque where they had spent so much time over the years.

Salameh got in the minivan, Kadir in the Ryder van, and Yousef in the Hertz van. They started their engines and let Yousef lead the way.

Kadir watched the garage recede in his rearview mirror. He had hoped never to see that building again. Now he was going to have to return and attend to his sister's remains.

Hadya . . . why didn't you mind your business? You would be alive now.

Shaking his head, he followed the others toward the city.

5

Jack checked his watch as he parked Ralph on Pamrapo, downstream from the vacant lot. Five thirty. He yawned. By all rights he should have the place to himself. He zipped up his jacket and grabbed the flashlight, then headed out through the snow.

He took his time following one of the ruts because he didn't want to use his flashlight until the last minute. Falling snow diffused the wan glow from the streetlights and allowed him to make out the garage as he rounded the bend. No lights on inside, which he took to be a good sign.

Kadir and his friends do not live there. Just work there, Hadya had said.

Let's hope she's right, Jack thought as he approached the front door. No storm door, just a door in the wall. He'd brought his lock-picking kit but tried the knob just in case they'd left it unlocked. No such luck.

Well, he didn't need light to pick a lock—everything went by feel. He slipped a tension bar into the keyhole, found a rake that fit on the second try, then went to work. Thirty seconds later he twisted the tension bar to retract the bolt and the door swung open.

He stepped inside and said, "Hello? Anybody home?"

Then the smell hit him. Someone had been mixing chemicals here. He'd taken basic chemistry as a required freshman science course in Rutgers but didn't know an amine from an aldehyde, especially not by smell. All he knew was this didn't smell good.

No answer came, so he stepped farther inside and repeated his call. Still no answer. He turned on his flashlight and swept the beam around. The front room was empty but for a ratty couch, some empty cardboard boxes, and three oil drums.

He checked the drums. Empty, but their inner surfaces were coated with some pasty stuff and the acrid reek rising from within burned his nostrils and made his eyes water.

What the hell had they been brewing here?

As he made a slow circuit of the room, his foot struck something: bunched-up clear plastic tubing with some sort of string inside. No idea what that was. But that reddish brown stain on the floor to his left . . .

"Uh-oh."

He squatted and trained his beam on it. Damn, if that didn't look like blood. And fairly fresh. It led off to the next room.

A little falling-out between the jihadists?

Jack stayed where he was and raised the beam until he spotted a supine figure on the floor at the end of the smear. Something protruded from its chest . . . and it seemed to be wearing a dress.

A woman?

Skirting the smear, Jack hurried forward in a crouch. Yeah, that was a knife handle protruding from between her ribs. For an instant his vision blurred and he saw Bonita on her back with the arrow jutting from her little chest. Then it cleared and recognized the woman's face—

"Aw, shit! *Shit!*"

The girl from the bakery, Kadir's sister . . . Hadya. Who did this? Not her own broth—

She moaned. Barely audible. Had there been any other sound louder than falling snow he might have missed it.

Alive? How could she still be alive with what looked like a carving knife buried damn near to the hilt in her chest? Maybe because it was still there, the pressure of its presence reducing the bleeding?

"Hadya? Hadya, are you—?" He caught himself. He'd been about to ask her if she was all right. "What happened?"

Her eyelids parted maybe a quarter of an inch and she said, "Buh." A tiny sound.

He knelt beside her and lowered his head until his ear was an inch from her lips.

"What?"

"Bum."

"Bomb?"

The tiniest nod.

Yeah, he could believe that, what with the chemical stink and all.

"Tuh . . . tuh bum."

"Two bombs?"

Another nod.

Jeez.

"How big?"

"Trks."

"Trucks? Two trucks?"

Christ. Two trucks of explosive headed for the UN. He flashed the beam onto his watch face. At least he had six hours or so before the eleven thirty Rabin meeting. Time to find help for this gal and then get the word to Burkes.

"I'm going to go find a phone and call for help," he told her.

He didn't know the address but he'd find one, or tell the EMTs how to get here. But no way could he be here when they arrived.

He gave her shoulder what he hoped was a reassuring squeeze. "You're gonna be all right. Just hang on until—"

She coughed a spray of blood, splattering Jack's face, then stiffened, then went limp. Her eyes lay open, glazing as they fixed on the ceiling.

"Hadya!"

He jammed two fingers against the side of her throat, searching for a pulse and finding none.

"Shit."

Gone. Another one gone. Abe had been kidding but maybe he was right: Cristin, Bonita, Rico, Bertel . . . now Hadya. Knowing Jack seemed like a death sentence.

With no other recourse, he used the hem of the coat she wore to wipe her blood off his face, then rose and looked down at her.

Poor kid. She didn't look more than twenty—twenty-two, tops. Had Kadir done this? Yeah, probably.

He could see how it might have gone down: Hadya sneaking up for a look, getting caught, one of the jihadists—most likely her own brother—silencing her for good. It made sense on their part. They were on the precipice of committing a mind-boggling act of terror: killing a head of state, a U.S. senator, and heavily damaging, maybe destroying the headquarters of the world's major international organization.

They couldn't let all that be jeopardized by a single young woman, even if she was the sister of one of their own. They couldn't risk the possibility that she would raise the alarm before they'd done the deed.

"Why didn't you stay out of it?" he said. "I told you I was going to look into it. If you'd just . . ."

What was the use? She was gone. None of this could be undone.

And he'd have to leave her here. But first . . .

He flashed his light around until he found a ratty rag that looked moth-eaten but was most likely chemical eaten. He used that to pull the blade from her chest without touching the handle. He wanted to leave any prints there intact for the police. If Kadir was smart he'd be planning to skip the country should his scheme play out. But maybe he wasn't so smart. If he stayed, this would lead the police to him.

Unless Jack found him first.

Jack would find him first.

He'd start looking, right now. A call to Burkes, a call to 911 about this poor girl, and then over to Manhattan . . . to midtown east . . . to the UN Plaza . . . looking for . . . what?

Two trucks. But what kind?

Hadya's English vocabulary was limited. She'd seen them, but "trucks" from her could mean an enclosed pickup, a panel truck, a van, a goddamn dump truck, for Christ sake. He didn't even know what color.

This wasn't going to be easy. Which meant he'd better get rolling.

6

"Do you know how many bloody trucks there are in this city?" Burkes said, his eyes studying the uptown-bound traffic on First Avenue. "Even an SUV is officially designated a 'light truck.'"

They were seated in the front seats of Burkes's van, idling by a fire hydrant across from the UN complex. They'd move if prompted by NYPD but the diplomatic plates, especially on this block, cut them a lot of slack. Burkes had the wheel, Jack sat shotgun. Rob and Gerald were out wandering around.

"She wouldn't have called an SUV a truck," Jack said.

"You're sure?"

"Absolutely not."

Burkes shifted in his seat. "All right, I've put NYPD on notice that I've had reliable word about a couple of big bombs wheeling around the city and that they're most likely headed here."

Jack looked around at all the traffic flowing by. "Then why isn't the area shut down?"

"Because they're not buying it."

"Why the hell not?"

"They asked me for corroboration and when I couldn't give them any, they looked at me like I was some sort of bampot."

Jack couldn't believe this. "They think you're lying?"

"No, but they can't go disrupting the city on what might well be faulty information. So they want to hear it from the source. What do I do? Give them al-Thani? Bloody lot of good that'll do. And then they'll want to know who turned him into a turnip."

They couldn't give the cops Hadya either.

"Sheesh."

"I can't say as I blame them. Say they believe me and they clamp down.

Word can't help getting out that they're looking for two trucks filled with explosives. You know what happens then."

Jack nodded. "Panic."

"Right. So they checked with their own sources and none of them know a thing about it. They called the FBI and the Bureau has no idea what I'm talking about. Without corroboration they're leery of risking a panic, so they're playing it cagey."

"Why don't I phone in a bomb threat?"

"They get those all the time. UN Security screens everything that comes through the gates, so they're not easily bamboozled."

"Swell. So we just sit here and wait for the bombs to explode?"

"No, we try to look at this as if we were terrorists. That's what I always did when dealing with INLA and Provisionals. Although, to tell you the truth, I can't recall ever having the luxury of a time and a place and the means of delivery." He glanced at Jack. "The Rabin trip is a hoax, by the bye. It was never in the cards. As for Senator D'Amato, he's still in Washington and won't be heading home for the weekend until this afternoon."

"Then who started it?"

A shrug. "We don't know. And no one can imagine why. Whose purpose is served by creating that little fiction?"

Jack thought about that a moment. "Well, al-Thani and Trejador were funding them. If they wanted them gung-ho to wreck the UN, that would be a surefire way to get them on board."

"That it would." He smiled. "But it's not like we can ask al-Thani now, is it?"

"No, it's not."

Jack wondered what was going through al-Thani's mind now—what was left of it.

"Nor Trejador," Burkes added.

"Okay, okay."

He felt bad enough about that already without anyone rubbing it in. If all three of them had burst in and subdued him immediately, Trejador wouldn't have had a chance to poison himself.

"There's two possible MOs," Burkes said. "Suicide, or set the fuse and run. The most effective suicide approach would be to charge down Forty-fourth, right up there"—he pointed ahead—"careen across the avenue, and try to jump the fence. You won't make it, but it'll put you as close as you can get to the General Assembly and your bomb will probably explode upon impact. I recognized the smell of that sample you gave me: urea nitrate. Depending on the balance of urea and nitric acid, its velocity of detonation can get near five thousand meters per second."

"What's that mean?"

"It's an indicator of how powerful it is. TNT runs close to seven thousand m-p-s. Plastiques like Semtex or C-four run a little higher."

"So this isn't exactly top-of-the-line stuff."

"Oh, if we're talking about enough urea nitrate that they need two trucks to transport it, it's bloody plenty. Blow up two payloads, each weighing a thousand or so pounds after you've made that run across First Avenue, and you'll not only demolish the General Assembly, but collapse the front of the Secretariat as well. Increase the payload to fifteen hundred pounds each and you won't leave anything at all standing in the whole plaza. You'll probably break windows across the East River as well."

"And what about us?"

Burkes laughed. "Sitting where we are? We'll be little more than red smears somewhere in the rubble."

"Swell. Anyway, that Forty-fourth thing sounds like a plan."

"Indeed it does, that's why I managed to convince NYPD to put a couple of extra coppers on the last block before First Avenue to pull over and check any vans or trucks that look suspicious, or look like they're traveling together."

"What about Forty-second?"

"It doesn't T-bone the General Assembly like Forty-fourth does."

"Why can't they just blow the trucks as they're passing by on First?"

"That's another possibility, but the center of the blast would be that much farther away from the target, diminishing the impact. With all the buses dropping off and picking up tourists, you're not going to get on the inside lane, so the buses will absorb a lot of the blast. They'll become missiles in the process, but they'll further diffuse the impact. So what's *your* solution?"

He pictured the layout of the complex: It ran between East Forty-second and East Forty-eighth, sitting between First Avenue and the East River.

The river . . .

"What about approaching by boat?"

Burkes shrugged. "You couldn't get close enough to do any real damage to the Secretariat, and the General Assembly would be shielded. Mostly you'd mess up the FDR and—"

Jack straightened in his seat. "Holy shit! The FDR runs under the back end of the UN! If I had two trucks, I'd set off one in front and one in back."

Burkes sat frozen a moment, then grabbed his phone and punched a button.

Jack said, "You calling NYPD?"

"Nah." His Scottish accent thickened. "They'll nae listen." He spoke into the phone. "'Lo, Rob. Take Gerald and a couple of the other lads. Get in uniform and head down to the uptown side of the FDR underpass by the UN. No rush. We've got time. Get there between eleven and eleven thirty and make sure no truck's broken down inside. Then start stopping anything bigger than an SUV. If the driver looks like he's from anywhere in the Mideast, inspect that truck." After a short listen. "Yes, I know they will, but before they do we'll either catch the mingers or scare them off. Right. Snap to it."

"'Before they do' what?" Jack said as Burkes ended the call.

"Rob says the NYPD isn't going to like that, and he's right. But it'll take the coppers a bit to catch on."

"And you put the checkpoint on the uptown side because the downtown-bound lanes put you deeper under the UN."

"You catch on fast."

"I'm a regular Whiz Kid. What do we do now?"

"We stay here and watch the traffic and hope nothing happens. But if something does, stand ready to stop anything before it's too late."

Jack was restless and sick of sitting in the car. He didn't feature standing out there in the snowy cold either, but they might have to.

"Maybe as it gets near eleven thirty we should go out and walk around— feet on the ground, as they say."

Burkes nodded. "Good idea." He laughed. "We'll make a field operative of you yet."

Be still my heart.

7

"Lying son of a bitch!" Tommy said as he dropped onto the backseat and slammed the door.

Vinny had watched him stalk across the street from the taxi depot office. The look on his face had said he hadn't heard what he'd expected to hear.

These were the first words he'd spoken since they'd met up in Ozone Park. He looked horrendously hungover and seemed more surly than usual.

Christ, he'd been loaded last night. What a cavone.

"Who?" said Aldo from the front passenger seat. He'd come along because Tony told him to, but he'd have come anyway in the hope of getting a chance to use his fists on a deadbeat or two. "The dispatcher? Want me to take a coupla pokes at him?"

"Not him. The fucking dune monkeys. The tall redheaded one, Mahmoud with the long last name, whatever it is, yesterday he told the dispatcher he wasn't coming in today, but he shows up this morning all rarin' to go."

"So he's here?"

"No, he ain't here. He's out on the streets looking for riders. Guy didn't want to give me his taxi number."

"What's that? The number on the roof light?"

"Yeah. Said he 'wasn't comfortable' giving it to me."

"No shit? I repeat my offer: Want me to take a poke or two at him?"

"Already did."

"And?"

Tommy held up a slip of paper. "Got the number right here."

"How's the dispatcher?"

"Resting comfortably." Tommy slapped the back of the front seat. "Let's go."

"Where?"

"Hunting."

Shit.

"What?" Vinny said. "Hunting a yellow cab in New York City. Y'gotta be kidding."

"You got anything better to do?"

Vinny looked at the snow, then at Aldo. Aldo shrugged.

He put the Crown Vic in gear and got rolling. Its rear-wheel drive didn't handle too good in snow. He'd have to take it slow.

Double shit.

If and when they ran into this Mahmoud guy, Vinny could tell, just *tell* he'd be in one foul mood.

And maybe that wasn't such a bad thing.

8

11:02 A.M.

After a long, tense wait in Brooklyn, Kadir's Ryder van led the others across the Queensboro Bridge. They had decided to enter Manhattan uptown from the UN. This allowed for the extra time it would take Kadir to follow the roundabout route to the downtown FDR on-ramp on East 63rd Street, the same he'd used on his test runs.

As they came off the Queensboro onto 59th Street, Kadir followed the FDR signs to the right while Salameh and Yousef turned left, taking Second Avenue downtown. Kadir took the ramp to East 62nd where he pulled over and idled. He checked his watch. At twenty after eleven he would drive the three blocks to the FDR and head downtown.

11:10 A.M.

Mohammed Salameh followed Yousef's Hertz van downtown on Second Avenue until they reached 44th Street. There he turned left while Yousef continued on.

He was driving slowly, looking for a place to pull over and idle, when a policeman in a yellow-orange vest stepped out from between two cars and motioned for him to stop.

Salameh's heart began to pound. What was this? Had someone talked? Had there been a leak? He pulled over and waited for the officer to approach his window. He glanced at the paper bag with the smoke bombs sitting on the seat next to him. Should he hide it? His heart picked up a wild tempo. He was in a stolen car with four smoke bombs. Surely his next stop was jail.

He resisted the urge to hide the bag but considered flooring the gas pedal and racing away. He looked ahead at the cars stopped at the light on First Avenue. He had nowhere to go.

He calmed himself. Trust in Allah.

He rolled his window down as the officer approached.

"Good morning, sir," the policeman said. "Where're you headed?"

Quick. Where? Back the way he had come.

"To Queens. Is something wrong?"

The policeman ignored the question. Instead he walked back and peered through the rear windows. After a careful inspection, he slapped the roof of the car.

"Okay. You can go. Have a nice day."

As Salameh eased the minivan into motion, he realized he was bathed in sweat. He passed another policeman watching the street. They were looking for something. What? Maybe it had nothing to do with the UN or a bomb. An escaped criminal? In his rearview mirror he saw the first policeman stopping a panel truck.

Well, whatever they were looking for, it wasn't Mohammed Salameh. He took a few deep breaths, then found a place where he could idle for fifteen minutes.

11:18 A.M.

Ramzi Yousef turned left onto 40th Street and pulled his van over to the curb before he reached First Avenue. Ten minutes here, then he would head for the UN, just two blocks away. He rubbed his hands together and ignored the urgings of his nervous bladder. The moment was at hand.

––––––––––

11:20 A.M.

Kadir pulled the Ryder van away from the curb. He followed East 62nd across First Avenue, then made a left on York. He followed that one block, passing the high-rise apartment buildings of rich New Yorkers, then a right onto 63rd. The downtown on-ramp to the FDR lay just ahead.

Traffic was moving well as he passed under the Queensboro Bridge and Sutton Place. Once again the nearly edge-on domino of the Secretariat Building loomed ahead. The falling snow softened its edges. Kadir smiled. If all went as planned, he and Yousef would erase those edges.

But as he approached the UN underpass, the tunnel where he would stop and light the fuses, he noticed a line of trucks and vans backed up. Men in uniforms he didn't recognize were pulling them over. It looked like they were inspecting them.

No!

Why?

He spotted an off-ramp and jerked the steering wheel right. He followed it onto East 49th Street and looked at his watch: less than six minutes until 11:30. He tried to control his frantic, jittering thoughts. What to do now? Could he arrive at the UN in time to make the frontal assault a double blast?

He clenched his teeth and hit the gas.

He could try.

11:28 A.M.

Ramzi eased into the East 40th Street traffic. The light was green so he made a wide left turn onto First Avenue. He avoided the center lane tunnel for cars wishing to avoid the congestion in front of the UN Plaza. The bus-only lane on the right was packed with buses disgorging tourists—elderly couples, young families, swirling mobs of school children on class trips.

He smiled. What convenient fodder. Their deaths would add to the carnage, the outrage, the terror.

Despite the vested policemen waving the traffic ahead, the cars crawled along. Ramzi slowed his as much as possible between 42nd and 43rd.

This was Salameh's moment. Where was he?

11:29 A.M.

Salameh had crawled along, positioning himself at the stop line as the First Avenue light turned amber. He stopped, but as soon as it turned red, he gunned the minivan straight ahead just as the First Avenue traffic began to move. One car hit his rear fender, then another rammed his front. As horns began to sound, he pulled the pins on all four smoke grenades and leaped from the car. Horns were blaring wildly as he ran back to the sidewalk and up 44th Street.

He had left all the windows open an inch—just enough to let the smoke pour out.

11:30 A.M.

Ramzi saw smoke billowing a block ahead. The policemen directing the traffic began to run toward it. Just then a bus began pulling away from the curb. Ramzi darted in behind it. He had a clear view of the General Assembly and Secretariat.

Perfect.

He set the brake and grabbed the butane lighter waiting in the cup holder. He lit all four fuses at once, then jumped from the van and locked it.

Traffic on First Avenue had ground to a complete halt, so he had no trouble weaving between the stopped cars.

Ten minutes . . . ten minutes to detonation. By that time he would be safely away, waiting for the thunder that would put him in the history books.

11:30 A.M.

"What kind of rounds y'packin'?" Burkes said.

Jack wasn't sure what he meant. "Nines."

"Hardball or hollow-point?"

"Hardball."

Burkes grimaced. "Listen, if you get close enough to one of them, use this."

He handed Jack some leather thing about a foot long. Jack took it. Heavy. "What—?"

"It's a lead sap. A hardball round can go through your target and hit an innocent. The place is crawling with kids. I mean, if it's you or him, then shoot. But if he's in reach, knock the shit out of him with that."

Jack lifted it by the handle and winced as he slapped it gently against his knee.

"Man, that'll crack a skull like an egg."

"Indeed it will. And don't hold back when you swing. You want him to go down and stay down. If—"

He stopped and gaped through the windshield at a plume of smoke rising from the vicinity of the 44th Street intersection.

Both Jack and Burkes were out in seconds. Looking across the hood, Jack figured the MI6 man's puzzled expression mirrored his own.

"That can't be the bomb."

Burkes shook his head. "No explosion. Got to be—"

"A diversion!" Jack said as he saw the patrolmen hoofing toward the smoke. "No, wait! It's jammed the traffic. That means—"

"They're here! But where?"

Jack searched the half dozen lanes of honking traffic for—what? What were the fuckers driving? Movement upstream caught his eye. A dark-skinned guy with an untrimmed beard wove through the paralyzed vehicles. He glanced around and Jack saw his face, his eyes . . .

Manson eyes.

Jack pointed. "That guy there! I've seen him before. He's one of them. Shit, he's on foot! That means—"

"—he's parked the truck somewhere! Has to be by the curb over there! Go!"

Jack pointed toward Manson Eyes as he retreated. "What about—?"

"Forget him. We've got to find that truck!"

As they wove across the street Jack spotted a Ford Econoline van parked against the curb between two buses unloading hordes of kids. *HERTZ* ran along the side.

"There!"

With Burkes close behind he raced to it and grabbed the handle.

"Locked!"

Burkes pulled his Sig and gripped it by the barrel. "Look away!"

The driver's window spiderwebbed with the first blow and shattered with the second. When a familiar chemical reek stung Jack's nostrils, he knew they had the right truck.

Burkes reached through and popped the lock. Jack yanked open the door and crawled inside. It took him a few seconds to get his bearings: the cargo bay was stacked floor to ceiling with reeking cardboard boxes. He saw the tops of three metal cylinders like acetylene tanks. Then he spotted the plastic tubing—four strands of it—similar to what he'd found in the garage this morning, except this was all scorched inside. Smoke leaked from the ends.

Fuses! He'd never guessed it came in plastic tubing.

Christ, how much time did he have? And why four? Why not just one? He glanced out the passenger window and saw nothing but kids—wall-to-wall kids.

Suddenly the kids were blocked by Burkes opening the door. His eyes did a Tex Avery bulge when he saw the boxes.

"Jesus cunting Christ!"

"Tell those kids to run!"

Burkes shook his head. "Won't be any use, lad," he said, his gaze fixed on the load of boxes. "You can't run from this."

"Then we've got to stop it."

Jack began pulling on the fuses—all four at once.

"Do you ken what you're doing?" Burkes said, his accent thickening. "Do you have the slightest idea?"

"Only what I know from movies. A fuse goes to a detonator. Disconnect the two and no explosion."

"Unless the disconnecting triggers one."

Jack glared at him. "Just what I need to hear." He paused, sweating. "So, if I do the wrong thing, we're history. But if I do nothing, we're also history."

"That about sums it up."

"Not much of a choice. Let's chance the wrong thing."

"Do *something*."

Ideally he could crawl onto the boxes, trace each fuse to its detonator, and disconnect it. But he didn't know how long the fuses were and how much time he had—*not much* was probably a pretty good guess.

He'd always admired the way Alexander had handled the Gordian knot, so . . .

He twisted all four fuses around his hand and got a tight grip. With an inarticulate cry that he knew might be the last sound he'd ever make, he closed his eyes and yanked, putting as much of his body into it as he could manage in the confines of the front seat. Some resistance, and then a sudden release—and he was still in one piece.

He began reeling in the fuses. They were long, but eventually he came to the burning portions. Three had pulled free from their detonators, one had not. A black tube with remnants of duct tape tagged along like a hooked fish. Jack pulled it from the fuse, then slumped, swallowing a sob of relief.

"I'm too young to die," Burkes said, sagging against the door frame.

Jack had to laugh. "*You* are? What about me?" And then he realized— "Hey, there's supposed to be two bombs. Where's the second?"

Burkes had his phone in hand. "Haven't heard anything from the lads. I'll give them a call."

While he was talking, Jack ran up and down the outside of the bus lane. No other van or panel truck by the curb, and every one he did see had a driver.

Burkes was just ending his call when Jack returned.

"Rob said they've found nothing, but a fair number of trucks and vans made a quick turn-off before their checkpoint. Could be that was the way they were headed in the first place, could be they had bales of contraband in the back, could be one was the second bomber." He raised his phone again. "I'm going to have NYPD send its bomb squad here."

"Serve them a steaming platter of crow while you're at it."

Burkes grinned. "You can count on that. It's lunchtime, after all. It'll be my treat."

Traffic remained at a standstill in front of the UN. The other truck might be stuck farther upstream.

Jack pointed downtown. "I'm going to have a look that way."

Burkes nodded and began talking into his phone.

Jack wove through the cars, looking for anything with an empty driver's seat.

11:37 A.M.

Kadir had come downtown on Second Avenue. As he passed 44th Street he saw traffic backed up and fire trucks heading toward the UN. Too early still for Yousef's bomb to have exploded, so this must be Salameh's doing.

At least something had gone right.

He continued downtown and noticed that eastbound traffic was backed up on 42nd Street as well. Up ahead he saw a similar backup of cars trying to turn east onto 40th. But 41st Street was empty, and its arrow pointed east. Most odd-numbered streets in the city ran west, but this appeared to be an exception. He turned into it.

He soon understood why traffic wasn't backed up on 41st—it didn't run
through. It dead-ended at a wall overlooking First Avenue near the downtown
end of the UN complex. He'd wound up in the middle of a collection of apartment buildings called Tudor City. Detonating the bomb here would leave the
UN unscathed. He looked at his watch: 11:40. Yousef's bomb should be going
off any second. Kadir had to get away from here.

He raced uptown, crossing an overpass above 42nd Street—still jammed
eastbound and nearly empty westbound. He turned onto 43rd, which took him
west, away from the UN. What to do? He couldn't get near the target.

And then he remembered their first target. Let Yousef do what damage
he could to the UN. Kadir would attack on a second front. Surely the Great
Satan would feel itself under siege from all sides.

11:45 A.M.

Jack found nothing. Every truck and van he passed had an angry or frus-
trated driver behind the wheel. So where was the second truck? If it wasn't
already here, he couldn't see any way it could get here. And then he remembered something al-Thani had said on the recording of Dr. Moreau's interrogation.

Towers off-limits.

What towers? The Trade Towers?

Towering towers.

Why are they off-limits?

*. . . Wouldn't tell me. Nobody would tell me. Just that they mustn't be
damaged. So we diverted them.*

Christ. What if one of the bombers had just become undiverted?

Jack ran for his car.

Noon.

Kadir was so relieved to find Broadway.

He had taken Second Avenue as far downtown as he could, then
worked his way west. When he and Ayyad had come into the city via the
Holland Tunnel they never had to deal with any of this. But he remembered
seeing Broadway on their trip to the towers. Soon after he turned downtown

he saw the towers dark against the sky, their tops lost in the swirling snow clouds.

He wanted Tower One, the north tower. That was the one he and Ayyad had inspected, the one Ayyad said would fall into the second tower and bring both down. Kadir remembered where to place the van. He simply had to find the ramp to the parking garage.

Noon.

They were on Chambers, heading west across Broadway, when Tommy began pounding on the back of Vinny's seat.

"That's him!" he shouted. "I just saw the fucker!"

"Where?" Aldo said. "I was watching every cab and—"

"He wasn't in no cab! He was in that yellow Ryder van heading down Broadway. And it wasn't the redhead, it was the little weasel. Turn around! We got him! Do you fuckin' believe it? We got him!"

"I can't turn around," Vinny said. "It's a one-way street."

"Fuck it! Turn around!"

"Fuck that."

Vinny made a left on West Broadway—sure as hell got confusing down here—and raced along Warren back to Broadway. But no yellow van, Ryder or otherwise, was in sight.

"We lost him!" Tommy shouted, pounding again.

"Ease up on the upholstery. We'll catch him."

Vinny found himself believing that. The goose they were chasing had suddenly become less wild.

Noon.

Jack surged out of the Battery Park underpass and was rewarded with the sight of the snow-dimmed twin towers half a mile straight ahead, both upright and healthy looking.

Instead of weaving down through the city, he'd steered Ralph onto the FDR and hooked around the southern tip of Manhattan. Longer in miles but much shorter in time when traffic was moving. He hoped he'd made up for the other bomber's head start.

The towers weren't on the Cool Buildings list he was slowly compiling. In fact, he considered them a blot on the city's skyline. But he wasn't about to let any goddamn foreign terrorist bring them down. New York had adopted him—this was *his* city now—and no outsider was going to mess with it.

Damned if he wasn't going to enter his house justified.

But first . . . what?

He didn't know what kind of truck he was looking for. The bombers had used an Econoline from Hertz for the front of the UN. Was the second a Hertz too? That would help, but he couldn't count on it.

And which tower—north or south?

This was looking bad.

12:02 P.M.

Kadir breathed a sigh of relief as he spotted the parking ramp for the north tower. Although he had been here only once before, it felt like coming home.

He entered and maneuvered to the B-2 level, where he found an empty space against the wall, just as Ayyad had planned.

12:03 P.M.

"There!" Aldo said, pointing ahead. "Ryder van turning onto that ramp."

"The garage?" Vinny said.

He'd just turned onto West Street and hadn't been looking.

"Yeah-yeah," Aldo said. "I'm sure of it."

"Follow him in!" Tommy said. "We got him now."

Vinny didn't know about that. "These towers are pretty fucking big. If he's headed upstairs, we'll never find him."

"Then we'll find the van and wait for him to come back. Simple, huh?"

"Yeah, as long as that's the same van."

"It is," Tommy said. "I feel it in my bones."

12:07 P.M.

Kadir set the brake, grabbed the lighter, and applied the flame to the ends of the fuses. When he was sure all four were burning, he locked the doors and dashed for the stairs up to street level. Once outside he would hurry uptown. He had plenty of time to put buildings between himself and the blast, but he wanted to be as far away as possible when the tower fell.

He came out of the stairwell and spotted the ramp to West Street on his right. He trotted for that and had just reached the snowy fresh air when he heard a voice behind him.

"Hey, asshole!"

As he turned, a fist slammed into his face—once, twice.

Blinded by pain, he staggered back and would have fallen if someone hadn't grabbed him by the back of his jacket. A big black car pulled up, the rear door opened, and he was pushed inside. The man sitting there grabbed his throat and yanked his head up.

"Hello, raghead."

Oh, no. The thug who had lent him the money. Kadir had thought he'd never see him again.

"I . . . I . . ." What could he say?

"I don't suppose you have my money."

The bomb!

"Please, we must be away from here!"

He smiled. "I'll take that as a 'no.' Which means I get to beat the shit outta you."

"No way, Tommy," said the big driver. "Not in my car, you don't. Mess up your own ride."

The fuse . . . the ten-minute fuse. How long ago had he lit it?

"We must go!" Kadir screamed.

"You ain't goin' nowhere," the one called Tommy said as he pulled a pair of handcuffs from his pocket. "'Cause y'see, you and me we got this . . . this connection, y'know. It's a very complex thing. It's cosmic, it's karmic, it's . . . money."

Kadir turned, opened the door, and leaped. His foot caught on something and he fell, landing hard on the ramp. As he tried to get up, he was grabbed from behind and hurled against the sidewall. His head slammed against the concrete. Through the ringing in his ears he heard a third voice call from the car.

"Vinny says throw him in the trunk and we'll take him somewhere."

"Uh-uh," Tommy said. "We got important stuff to discuss."

"Play your games somewhere else," the driver said.

"You don't want it in your ride, we'll do it right here."

"Fine. Have it your way. But I'm getting off the ramp. Meet us down on the street. We'll pop the trunk when we see you comin'."

"Gotcha," Tommy said.

The feel of the cuff ratcheting closed around his wrist wrenched Kadir from his daze. The bomb! They had to be away from here! Yousef had said the blast wave from the explosion would move at five thousand kilometers per second, and this ramp was the only escape valve for all that force. It would blow debris along here like a giant shotgun. He had to tell this man, this Tommy.

"A bomb!" he screamed. "A bomb will explode."

Tommy sneered as he closed the other cuff over his own wrist. "You got that right. It's about to explode in your gut."

Kadir tried to pull him down the ramp by the cuffs.

"Please!"

The hoodlum yanked him back. Pain exploded in Kadir's gut as a fist rammed into his belly. He doubled over in agony.

"Now, as I was saying before you so rudely tried to get away . . . you and me, we got this connection and it's a very complex thing. It's cosmic, it's karmic, it's—"

The world exploded.

12:17 P.M.

Jack had already made one pass by the north tower and then one by the south without seeing a suspicious van. He'd just turned onto West Street for a second look at north when the ground shook and the sky roared. Ralph bucked and reared like a stallion as flames, smoke, and concrete chunks of all shapes and sizes blew across the street fifty yards ahead of him, carrying two pinwheeling human bodies with them. Jack slammed on the brakes.

Shit! The bomb.

Too late.

He stepped out of his car to see if he could help those two flying humans, and through the smoke he saw a pair who seemed to have the same idea. He continued forward a few steps but stopped when he recognized one of the others: big fat Vinny Donuts. What was he doing here? Then he recognized the other as his pal, Aldo.

They both rushed to the bodies, checked them, then lifted them. Jack couldn't identify the dead men—too much blood. Their bodies flopped limp as rag dolls, like every bone had been broken. Vinny and Aldo carried them toward a black Crown Vic. The strangest part of the bizarre sight was how the two bodies appeared joined at the wrist. Handcuffs?

The trunk was already open and both bodies were dumped into it like sacks of potatoes.

Why were a couple of Gambinos down here? Who were the dead guys? And why were they cuffed together? Jack wasn't going to attempt to explain what he was watching.

When Vinny slammed the lid shut, Jack saw that the Vic's rear window was shattered. Blown out by the explosion?

As the two hoods climbed in and roared away, Jack could only watch them go. The street before him was strewn with broken concrete waiting to tear out the undercarriage of any car trying to drive through.

He looked up at the north tower. He didn't know what carnage the bomb had wreaked inside—had to be considerable—but the tower appeared unfazed. Probably take a helluva lot more than a truck bomb to topple that baby.

He turned at the sound of sirens. Half a dozen cars had backed up behind him. Looked like he was going to be stuck here awhile.

9

"Jesus Christ!" Tony said as he stared into the trunk. "I know you two wasn't exactly buddies, but what the fuck you do to him?"

Vinny had wheeled the Vic around to the back of Tony's appliance store and brought him out to see Tommy. He would've left him on West Street but figured he'd catch the blame when Tommy showed up dead. That was why he'd brought him here.

"Didn't do nothin'," Vinny said.

"Well, somebody did somethin'! Looks like he's been through a meat grinder!"

"Well, you ain't gonna believe this, but here goes."

He gave Tony a rundown of the events leading to the explosion. He was glad Aldo had been along so he could back up his story.

When Vinny finished, Tony was scratching his jaw. "You mean that bomb in the Trade Tower that's all over the news, it killed Tommy?"

"Wrong place at the wrong time," Vinny said, though he was thinking just the opposite.

Good thing he'd moved his car off the ramp when he did. If he'd waited for Tommy to finish his games with the Arab, he and Aldo would've been heading for the morgue along with the other two.

Tony pointed to Kadir's mangled body. "Word is the bomb was an Arab deal. You think this cocksucker . . . ?"

Aldo was nodding. "Yeah. I hadn't thought about it before, but yeah. I like him for it."

Vinny said, "We saw him drive a van into the garage and then come trotting out, heading for the street, like he was haulin' his ass outta there."

"That wasn't no pipe bomb," Aldo added. "You shoulda seen the size of the chunks it blew down the ramp."

"Question is," Vinny said, "what do we do with Tommy?"

"First thing you do is unhook him from this raghead son of a bitch. Then you take him to his place over in Howard Beach—keys gotta be in his pockets somewhere—and you lay him on a couch or his bed. Call me when you're done and I'll put out the word to some of his family so they can 'find' him."

"Why don't we just take him straight to Garibaldi's?" Aldo said.

Tony flashed him a *you-asshole* look. "'Cause a funeral home can't just bury a guy. They need a death certificate and all that."

"Oh."

"And the raghead?" Vinny said.

"Deep-six him so he'll never be found. You're good at that."

Vinny nodded. Easy enough.

10

Just as he had earlier this month, Mohammed Salameh stood on the dock of the Central Railroad Terminal and stared at the twin Trade Towers across the water. The last time he did this he had been with Abouhalima, Yousef, Kasi, and Kadir. Today he was alone.

He'd hurried away from the UN along 44th Street as fast as he could without running, waiting for the sound of the blast. It hadn't come by the time he reached Second Avenue, so he stopped at the corner and waited. The street ran downhill toward the UN complex from there. The Secretariat was obscured to the right, but he could glimpse the General Assembly building down at the end.

He waited and waited for the boom, for the cloud of dust and smoke and debris, but it never came. He was tempted to go back and see what had gone wrong, but was afraid he'd be recognized as the man who abandoned a stolen car in the middle of First Avenue.

He was also afraid that if Yousef had been delayed, the bomb would go off as soon as he peeked around the corner, obliterating him along with everyone else.

After standing around for more than half an hour, he'd walked to West 33rd Street to catch a PATH train to Jersey City. At the station he heard that no trains were running to the World Trade Center because a section of track leading to the center had been damaged by an explosion. Exalted, he got off at the Grove Street stop and raced toward the waterfront. Long before he reached it he spotted the towers, both standing with no sign of damage. He continued all the way to the river, only to be greeted by the dismaying sight of two apparently healthy towers. Not even smoke!

What had happened? No bomb had gone off by the targeted UN, but one had gone off somewhere in the old target, the World Trade Center. *Whose* bomb—Yousef's or Kadir's?

He sighed and turned away. What was he to do now? Wait to be contacted, he guessed. Would they want to make more bombs? Only time would tell.

Meanwhile he would return to the Ryder rental place and see if he could get back his deposit on the truck he had reported stolen.

11

Safe!

Ramzi Yousef relaxed in his first-class seat as the Royal Jordanian jet lifted off the JFK runway. No one could bring him back now. Tomorrow morning he would land in Amman. Sadly, he would have no good news to tell.

The day had been a disappointment all around. His own bomb had either failed to ignite or had been defused. He suspected it might be the latter. He had seen too many police around the UN Plaza. Somehow they had been on higher alert than usual.

At least Kadir had come through, although that too was a disappointment. He had chosen Khalid Sheikh Mohammed's favored target but the bomb failed to topple it.

Ramzi was composing what he would tell his mother's brother. For some reason the news media were making no mention of the UN bomb. Perhaps because it embarrassed them. And perhaps, because it hadn't exploded, they felt they could sweep it under the rug? They certainly could not hide the Trade Tower bomb.

Ramzi too would keep silent about the UN bomb—that hadn't been in his instructions.

The only bright spot in this dour day, the only upbeat news he could offer his uncle, was that America was vulnerable. He and the others had bought the explosive ingredients and mixed them right under the noses of the police and the vaunted FBI. The only reason the towers remained standing now was because they were so well built. That didn't mean they couldn't be brought down. It meant only that their bomb hadn't been big enough. If only they had parked both bombs in the basement . . . the Manhattan skyline would look very different right now.

He knew Khalid Sheikh Mohammed would keep looking for ways to bring down those towers, and Ramzi would be close by his side, helping him.

He looked out at the sparkling lights of the city below.

We'll be back.

12

Good thing Julio had walked him home—if a propped-up stumbling stagger qualified as walking.

Long day.

After the tower blast it had taken Jack an hour and a half to move off West Street. He was an eyewitness, after all, and the cops wanted to know what he'd seen. He told them about flames and smoke and flying debris, but left out mention of Vinny and Aldo and the pinwheeling bodies. The cops would want to know who they were and where they were and Jack didn't want to get into that.

When the opportunity presented itself, he'd tried to call Burkes but the phones weren't working. The cops told him NYNEX had installed a major switching center in the basement of Tower One, so forget calling from anywhere downtown unless he had a mobile. He didn't, so he took their advice and forgot about it.

When they finally let him go, he knew he needed to be with a friend. That left him two choices. He chose the friend with beer. And if he'd stuck with beer, he would have been fine. But he'd started thinking of Cristin, and that prompted a shot of Cuervo Gold in her honor. Which led to another. And another. And . . .

The hard stuff wasn't his thing. He'd thought he was doing fine until he went to stand up from his table.

Jack might—just *might* have made it home without Julio, but he never would have made it up the stairs.

"Got there too late," he mumbled as he reeled across his front room. "News says six people dead, hundreds hurt."

"That's bad for them, meng, but it coulda been lots worse. Least the building's okay. The bomb didn't bring her down. That's important, right?"

"Who gives a rat's ass about the building."

"Oh, I dunno. Maybe the couple thousand people in it."

"Oh, yeah. Them."

Jack hadn't seen anything about the UN bomb on the news, so he hadn't mentioned it to Julio. Maybe he'd saved some lives there, but some special lives were over.

"I don't care about any of them," he said falling face-first onto his bed. "I want Cristin back. And Bonita and Rico."

"I know," he heard Julio say from the doorway.

"It's not fair. I mean, they die and all those strangers live. That's bullshit!"

A voice somewhere in his head was telling him he sounded like a jerk, and he probably did, but he was six sheets to the wind so he was allowed.

Goddamn, this hurt.

SATURDAY

1

Jack awoke to the smell of coffee and a barrage of noise that sounded like a demolition derby.

The room spun as he sat up. He waited for it to settle into place, then pushed himself to his feet. Another rush of vertigo had him swaying but he kept his balance and took very small stutter-steps into the front room. His head was throbbing from the inside but the noise around him intensified the discomfort to an almost unbearable degree.

It seemed to be coming from the kitchen. He turned the corner and found Julio with the pot from the Mr. Coffee machine in his hand.

He looked at Jack and grimaced. "You look all *Dawn of the Dead*, meng."

"Please don't shout."

"I ain't shouting."

Jack cringed as Julio rattled a plate.

"And that other noise . . . must you?"

"Just making some toast. Want some?"

Julio was still shouting but the stomach lurch triggered by the thought of food was worse.

"Coffee. Just coffee. You stayed?"

"Never seen you like that. Worried you coulda died."

"Really? Were I feeling even remotely human right now I might be touched, but—"

"You were gone, man. High-fiving everyone and—"

"Who? Me? I do *not* high-five *anyone*. No way."

"Yeah, you were. And you had your arms around Lou and Barney and got all weepy telling them how much you loved them."

"Oh, Christ. Do not serve me tequila ever again."

Julio laughed. "Just pullin' your chain."

"Really? I didn't get all I-love-you-man?"

"Nah. You just got quiet. Really quiet."

"Better than high-fives."

"Don't know about that. Booze brings out the inner person. Take it from a guy who seen too many drunks. You can pretend you're someone you ain't until you down too many, then the real you comes out. People all ugly inside become ugly drunks. Nice folks become all lovey-dovey. You . . ." He shook his head. "You just got quiet. And you had this look."

"What look?"

He shrugged. "I dunno. I couldn't read it. But something about it told me I better get you out in the air and home."

"Well, thanks for that, but—" He jammed his palms over his ears. "What the hell is that *noise*? They pile driving outside or something?"

"Hey, no. It's quiet. It's Saturday and it's snowing."

Jack looked at the window and heard a pile-driver bang every time a drop of sleet hit the pane.

"Can you make it stop?"

Julio blinked. "What?"

"Forget the coffee. I'm going back to bed."

2

"Lookit this, will ya?" Aldo said as he thumbed through Tommy's black book.

They were sitting in Vinny's office, sipping a little Sambuca to take off the chill of their recent boat trip. They'd sneaked Tommy's broken body into his house and left it there—but not before removing whatever might point to anything illegal. That included his black book and his wallet. Then they'd crimped the raghead into an old Dodge. This morning they'd dumped the package offshore and returned through a snow squall.

Vinny poured himself a little more Sambuca. "Whatcha got?"

"Looks like our boy Tommy was holding out on Tony."

"Yeah? How so?"

Not that Vinny was surprised.

"Loans on his own. Buncha loans right under Tony's nose in Brooklyn and Queens and even a few in Nassau." He flipped pages. "*Whole* lotta gook names from Chinkytown and Little Saigon. He was one busy fuckhead."

That got Vinny to thinking. "How many those loans still alive?"

"Most of them, looks like." Aldo glanced up. "You thinkin' what I'm thinkin'?"

"I'm thinking those loans shouldn't get neglected just because Tommy's dead."

"Yeah, I'm thinking that too. Somebody really should, whatchacall, service them. Know what I mean?"

"I know exactly what you mean. I'm just thinking about Tony."

"Yeah. Me too."

"Sick man."

"Yeah. Not long for this world, like they say. You think it would be right to, whatchacall, burden him with this?"

"Not right at all. Downright cruel, if you ask me. I mean, imagine the hurt of learning that the senior member of your crew had been doin' you dirty for years. *Years.*"

Aldo shook his head. "Break the poor old guy's heart—and him with hardly any time left."

"I'm getting this feeling that it's kinda like our duty to shield him from this."

"I am in total agreement, Vinny. Let him live out his final days in, whatchacall, ignorant bliss. We owe him that."

"We do."

"I'll take the gooks. You can have the rest."

That seemed fair.

"Deal."

They shook hands.

"A little more Sambuca, Mister D'Amico?"

"I do believe I will, Mister Donato."

They clinked glasses.

"*Salute!*" said Aldo.

"*Cent'anni!*" said Vinny.

3

By four o'clock Jack was ready to face the world. Julio was long gone by then. He swallowed four Advil and took a long shower. He couldn't remember being that loaded since a certain keg party at college. He liked to drink but he hated being drunk. Drunk meant physically and mentally out of control and unable to do anything about it.

Julio had mentioned drink bringing out the real you. But according to him all it brought out in Jack was "quiet" and a "look," whatever that meant. As much as he was glad he hadn't turned into the high-fiving, I-love-you-man dork Julio had joked about, that guy would have been better than the other Jack he knew lurked inside—the dark part of him that wrecked knees and busted skulls and threw people off bridges and drove arrows into brains via eyeballs. Good thing the tequila hadn't set that guy free in Julio's last night.

Some people craved the oblivion of a rip-roaring bender, but Jack suspected it was not a good place for him.

The snow had stopped and mostly melted by the time he stepped outside. He caught a cab down to Murray Hill, to the Celebrations brownstone on East 39th. With Saturday night looming, he figured Rebecca would be working.

He was right. When he pressed the call button at the front door she answered.

"It's your uninvited guest from last Saturday night."

Without another word or a second's hesitation, she buzzed him through. She waited for him in the doorway to her office at the end of the hall. She was wearing a tweedy business jacket and skirt, but looked like she hadn't slept since he'd last seen her.

"It's been a whole week," she said when he was halfway down the hall. "Any word?"

He nodded as he approached. "I'll tell you inside."

"We have the building to ourselves."

"Still . . ."

She stepped back and waved him into a paneled reception area, nicely furnished, indirect lighting.

"Not what I expected," he said. "You do real business here?"

"This is where I interview the new girls," she said quickly. "What about Cristin?"

He started the story he'd constructed on the way down—half fact, half bull.

"You know about the Trade Center bomb, of course. People connected to the bombers thought she might have overheard something."

"Oh, God! Is that why you were asking about Arab clients?"

"Yeah."

"Roman Trejador was involved, wasn't he." It didn't sound like a question.

"How do you figure that?"

"I heard on the news. Cristin dead, then her client from the night before she disappeared found dead of cyanide poisoning . . . how can they not be connected?"

"They are. Trejador ordered it—at least that's what one of his people told us."

Her hand flew to her mouth. "Dear God! He was one of her regulars. The cyanide—was it you?"

He shook his head. "He took it before we had a chance to question him. That pretty much says it all."

Trejador . . . Tony . . . whoever he was, total son of a bitch.

"Too quick," she said through her teeth. "Too *quick*, damn it! After all those dates with her, how could he—?"

"He didn't do the actual deed. He had some of his people handle that." He felt his throat constrict. "Turned out she was tortured and killed for something she knew nothing about."

Rebecca's lips thinned to a thread. "Where are they?"

"One's dead."

She leaned forward. "How?"

"Not pretty."

"Good. How many others?"

"Two. If you've been listening to the news you've heard about a couple of 'horrendously mutilated' guys they found in Queens and the city?"

She swallowed. "Those were . . ."

"*Are* . . . they're still alive. How many details on the news? I've been . . . out of touch."

"Not much. But a deputy mayor is one of my clients, and he told one of the girls . . ." She swallowed again. "He went into great detail about what had been done to them."

"It's called Infernum Viventes and—"

"Living hell?"

"You know Latin?"

"Four years of it at Catholic high school—another sort of living hell."

"Yeah, well, with proper care and feeding, they'll probably live in that hell quite a while longer, and every second of it will be pure torture."

She stared at him, shaking her head.

"What?"

"You seem so normal. What kind of mind thinks up something like that?"

"Oh, I can't take credit. A consummate professional came up with it."

"Professional what?"

"Torturer."

She continued to stare. "You're so young, yet the people you know . . ." She heaved a long, sad sigh. "I can't help thinking what Cristin would say about that. If she's up there watching, would she be proud of you?"

Jack suddenly felt as if the building had collapsed on him.

"No, I don't think she would."

He had set out simply to track down the scumbags and settle the books. Somewhere along the line he'd slipped off track and allowed things to get out of hand.

Rebecca squeezed his arm. "I think Cristin would understand the feelings behind what you did. She might not applaud you for it, but I know she'd appreciate the why of it."

Jack realized with a pang that it hadn't been at all about what Cristin would have wanted. It had been all him . . . what he wanted: blood.

"And for what it's worth," she added, "I think they deserve everything that's happened to them."

"But it's still not enough, is it."

Rebecca's bitter smile held an ocean of hurt. "No, it's not. Not even close."

Jack knew exactly how she felt.

SUNDAY

1

Jack watched Burkes step through the door of Julio's and look around. He caught his eye with a wave and the Scot strolled over to Jack's table.

"So this is your office?"

"The rent's reasonable." Jack pointed to a chair. "Have a seat at my desk."

"It's been days," Burkes said as he settled in. "What took you so long to get in touch? Back at the UN you took off to have a look down the avenue and that was the last I saw of you."

Julio came by. "Drinking?"

"Thought you'd never ask. I'm desperate for a bevvy." Burkes pointed to Jack's glass. "What's that?"

"Rolling Rock." He hadn't been able to look at a brew yesterday. But that had been yesterday.

Burkes made a face. "An American lager? Not likely. Got anything *good* to drink? Something with some body to it?"

"You mean like Guinness?"

Burkes slapped the table. "Now you're talking, lad!"

"We ain't got none."

Jack pushed back a laugh. He'd seen that coming.

"But you said—"

"Got a couple Brit regulars who talked me into stocking something called John Courage."

"Bitter!" Burkes said, raising a fist. "Bring us a pint of Courage."

"Make that two," Jack said.

He'd never tried it. He guessed now was as good a time as any.

As Julio sauntered away, Burkes turned back to Jack. "So where'd you go?"

Jack explained racing down to the World Trade Center but arriving too late to catch the bomber. He told them about the dead phones, being detained by the cops . . .

"And then I came here and tied one on."

"Don't blame you. Would've done the same myself had I been free to."

Julio arrived then carrying two pints of amber liquid with a beige head.

Burkes lifted his glass. "Here's tae us. Wha's like us? Gey few, and they're a' deid."

The best Jack could do at the moment was, "Cheers."

Burkes added, "*Slàinte mhòr agad.*"

They clinked glasses and quaffed. He liked it.

"Not bad," Jack said. "Not bad at all."

Burkes smacked his lips. "This place keeps a keg of Courage on tap for just a couple of Brits?"

"You should see them drink. Two hollow legs each." Jack wanted to get to something that was bothering him. "I lost much of Friday night and most of Saturday, but I've been watching TV for a whole day now and it's all about the Trade Tower bomb. Not a word about the UN. What gives?"

Burkes leaned forward and lowered his voice. "A cover-up is what gives. NYPD cleared the area and sent the bomb squad into the van. They found nitroglycerin inside, which they took away in their special truck. Found compressed hydrogen too. That was one *hell* of a bomb those Arabs built. The devastation would have been incredible had it gone off. After removing the nitro, they towed that van away without a by-your-leave. I don't think anyone outside NYPD will ever see it again."

"What?" Then he got it. "Oh. Big black eye if it ever came out how they blew you off."

"Exactly. All sorts of heads would roll and you can be damn well sure you'd be looking at a new police commissioner come the morning."

"They're damn lucky it didn't go off."

Burkes took a big gulp. "*Thousands* are lucky it didn't go off. Thanks to you. Too bad you won't get any recognition for defusing that monstrosity."

"Hell, don't want any. Saved my own skin as well."

"Still, you deserve a medal."

Jack waved his hands. "No, thanks. Noooooo, thanks. You didn't say anything about me, did you? Please tell me you didn't say anything."

"Not a word." Burkes stared at him. "You're a strange sort, you are."

"Just a very private person. A recluse. A hermit even."

"A hermit without a damn nerve in his body. I almost shat myself when
you yanked on those wires. Bravest thing I've ever seen. Or the stupidest."

"Wasn't brave at all, so that leaves stupid, I guess. I saw one option and
took it. Nothing brave about that."

Burkes tapped his temple. "You kept your wits. I'm impressed."

Jack didn't like him making a big deal like this. He tried to change the
subject.

"How about the bombers themselves? What about that Kadir character?
Killed his own sister."

"Not a clue about them. Nobody knows a damn thing. NYPD, FBI—
they've got nothing—*nothing*. A bunch of dobbers, the lot of them."

"And Manson Eyes, the guy who lit the UN bomb?"

"Vanished."

"And what was all that smoke down the street?"

"A minivan with smoke bombs. A diversion, just like we thought. The cops
used that as an excuse to clear the plaza so they could cart off the van with
the bomb." He shook his head. "I'm still impressed as all hell how you dis-
armed it."

"Look, I didn't know how much time we had. I mean, it came down to
three outcomes: Don't pull the fuses and die. Pull the fuses and die. Or pull
the fuses and live until you die from something else."

"Die-die-die!" he said, laughing. "You must have been a Scot in another
life."

"I had an uncle in the Black Watch."

His eyes lit. "The Ladies from Hell! Then you *are* a Scot—at least partly.
Tell me about this uncle."

"Some other time."

He was already kicking himself for saying that much. It had slipped out.

"Right, then. And there *will* be other times."

"What do you mean?"

"I like the way you handled yourself through this whole shambles. The
way you tracked al-Thani. How you took care of business in your friend's

garage. You found out about the bombs—and that there were two of them. If you hadn't been on board, who knows how many would have died? We'd be sifting through a pile of rubble on the East River for days looking for bodies."

"That's kind of an exaggeration—"

"Not at all. You even figured where the second bomber might be headed."

"But I didn't stop him."

"With the proper resources you could have. Anyway, I could use some-one like you now and again."

Jack didn't know what to think of that.

"What's someone like me? And 'use' how?"

"An American who's off the radar and thinks on his feet and isn't too wor-ried about legal niceties. Can I call on you if I find myself in need of someone like that? You'd get paid, of course."

Jack thought about that. Flirting with officialdom. Probably not wise. They'd want tax forms filled out and all that crap.

"I don't know. It would have to be unofficial—I mean strictly under the table."

"Of course. Anything above the table I can get the local coppers to han-dle. No, this would be strictly sub rosa."

Well, then . . .

"Okay. Yeah. Sure. Why not?"

He could use the money. He hadn't earned a cent this week.

"Excellent!" Burkes finished his pint and slammed it down. "Barkeep! Another round. On me!"

2

What a long strange trip, Jack thought as he sat in his front room and stared at the TV.

Well, not so long. Not yet three years in the city, but it seemed like a dozen or so. He'd gained friends and allies in Abe and Julio and the Mikulskis.

Even Burkes . . . Burkes who kept telling him that he'd helped save thousands of lives today. Yeah, well, maybe. But he wished he could have saved four more: Rico, Bonita, Bertel, and dear, dear Cristin. His throat tightened at the memory of Bonita's innocent smile, Cristin's throaty laugh . . . both taken from the world by the same hand.

Their deaths hadn't gone unanswered—the blood on his hands attested to that—but they were gone just the same. Evening the scales hadn't brought them back.

He'd learned lessons in these years, some the hard way. If he had taken the Mikulskis' advice back in that marsh on Staten Island, Cristin and Bonita and Rico would still be alive. He would never make that mistake again.

But what about the next three years? And the three after that? He'd learned that he could look at a situation from a perspective other people didn't have. He could put that ability to use if given the chance. But there lay the crux of the matter: How to get that chance? If he could build up a backlog of successes as a problem solver, word of mouth would keep things going. That was the catch-22: How to build a rep for solving problems if no one was looking to you for solutions?

His gaze strayed back to the TV with its ongoing wall-to-wall coverage of the Trade Tower bombing. For days now the New York stations had wanted to talk of nothing else. Which was fine, because Jack wasn't interested in much else going on in the world right now. He continued to be amazed at how clueless the police were about the identity of the bombers.

The phone rang. Who . . . ?

He turned down the TV volume and let the answering machine pick up.

"Hello?" said a tentative voice he didn't recognize. *"This is Evan calling Repairman Jack."*

Repairman Jack? What the—?

"I saw your ad in the Village Voice *and—I hope I'm reading you right . . . if I am, I think I have a problem that could use your attention. Please call me back at . . ."*

Jack rose and stumbled over to the machine.

Repairman Jack . . . the *Village Voice* . . .

"Oh, no. Abe, you didn't. You *didn't.*"

The message counter read 5. That meant four other calls. He ran through them. Two were about appliances but the other two might involve the kind of work he was interested in. Two mentioned *Newsday*, all the rest mentioned the *Village Voice*.

Jack had developed a nodding relationship with his neighbor Neil. He'd noticed copies of the *Voice* in the foyer by the mailboxes with his apartment number on them. He took the stairs down to the floor below and knocked on his door.

"Hey, Neil? It's Jack from upstairs."

Light was coming through the peephole. It went dark, then a voice filtered through the door. "What do you want?"

"Can I borrow the latest *Village Voice*?"

"Why?"

"Need to check something."

Two deadbolts turned, then the door opened—but only as far as the chain would allow. A folded newspaper poked through.

"Here y'go. Bring it back tomorrow. As in 'not tonight.'"

"Gotcha. Thanks."

Jack hurried back to his own place and paged through to the personals. And there, in the *Personal Services* column, four lines . . .

> *When all else fails . . .*
> *When nothing else works . . .*
> **REPAIRMAN JACK**

The fourth line was his phone number.

This was crazy. He couldn't advertise . . .

Then again, why not? As Abe had said, how was anyone going to know he even existed, let alone the service he was offering? And three out of the first five calls were not about appliances.

Maybe . . . just maybe he could make a living as . . . what? A fixer?

The only downside would be the name. Kind of hokey. He wasn't crazy about the idea of being known on the grapevine as Repairman Jack.

Behind him, the phone began to ring again . . .

www.repairmanjack.com

AFTERWORD

The Facts:

On February 26, 1993, a Ryder van crammed with nitroglycerin, three cylinders of compressed hydrogen, and three quarters of a ton of urea nitrate exploded at 12:17 P.M. in the parking basement of Tower One of the World Trade Center in Manhattan. It killed six people, injured a thousand more, and ripped through six floors of reinforced concrete.

That is the real-life event that anchors the fiction of *Fear City*.

Mahmoud Abouhalima, Mohammed Salameh, Nidal Ayyad, Ramzi Yousef, and Sheikh Omar Abdel-Rahman were all real-life participants. Aimal Kasi killed CIA employees waiting to turn into the Langley HQ.

The Fiction:

Kadir Allawi is a composite of the fanatical followers of Sheikh Omar. Dane Bertel is a composite of all the knowledgeable people shouting warnings that Islamic terror was on its way to the U.S. but who were ignored at every level.

The events transpiring over eleven days in the novel took eight weeks to unfold in real life. Time compression was necessary to maintain a tight narrative.

There was no second bomb in our world (at least as far as we know). But there was in Jack's, because the Septimus Order runs much of Jack's world and had a reason for not wanting the towers brought down. If you've read *Ground Zero*, you know the reason.

Mark Twain said, "It's no wonder that truth is stranger than fiction. Fiction has to make sense."

I've had to leave out a lot of real-life details about the bomb builders because *fiction has to make sense*. If I included them you'd think I was writing a screwball comedy with the FBI playing the Keystone Kops. Or you'd think I was trying to fob off a Swiss-cheese plot on you.

As a for-instance, let's look at the real-life Mohammed Salameh. He manages to get a five-year visa to the U.S. so he can avoid the draft in Jordan. He has terrible vision and flunks his driver test four times in Jersey. Abouhalima finally wrangles him one from Brooklyn. Over the course of the bomb-making weeks he wrecks two cars, the latter accident putting chief bomb maker Ramzi Yousef in the hospital for four days. So, when nearly a ton of explosive is finally ready and packed in the van, who gets tapped to pilot it from Jersey City to the World Trade Center? Right—Salameh.

Miraculously, he completes the drive to Tower One, where the bomb is detonated. But after that, instead of disappearing, he returns to the rental place saying the van was stolen and he wants his four-hundred-dollar deposit back. This leads to his arrest and the unraveling of the conspiracy.

It's not that you can't make this stuff up—you don't dare. Carl Hiaasen can get away with it in his surreal crime novels, but admit it: If I put that in *Fear City*, you'd be saying, *You can't be serious, Wilson. No one would let him drive the bomb van.*

I won't even start on how many opportunities the FBI had to prevent this but dropped the ball every time. You can find all the head-scratching details in my main source on the bombers and the bomb, *Two Seconds Under the World* by Jim Dwyer, David Kocieniewski, Deidre Murphy, and Peg Tyre.

In case you're wondering: Sheikh Omar Abdel-Rahman, Nidal Ayyad, and Mohammed Salameh were arrested in the weeks after the bombing. Mahmoud Abouhalima and Ramzi Yousef fled the country but were arrested overseas and brought back for trial. All are serving life sentences in maximum security prisons. Aimal Kasi was executed for the murders outside CIA HQ in Langley.

THE SECRET HISTORY OF THE WORLD

The preponderance of my work deals with a history of the world that remains undiscovered, unexplored, and unknown to most of humanity. Some of this secret history has been revealed in the Adversary Cycle, some in the Repairman Jack novels, and bits and pieces in other, seemingly unconnected works. Taken together, even these millions of words barely scratch the surface of what has been going on behind the scenes, hidden from the workaday world. I've listed them below in chronological order.

Note: "Year Zero" is the end of civilization as we know it; "Year Zero Minus One" is the year preceding it, etc.

THE PAST
"Demonsong" (prehistory)
"The Compendium of Srem" (1498)
"Aryans and Absinthe"** (1923–1924)
Black Wind (1926–1945)
The Keep (1941)
Reborn (February–March 1968)
"Dat Tay Vao"*** (March 1968)
Jack: Secret Histories (1983)
Jack: Secret Circles (1983)
Jack: Secret Vengeance (1983)
"Faces"* (1988)
Cold City (1990)
Dark City (1991)
Fear City (1993)

YEAR ZERO MINUS THREE
Sibs (February)
The Tomb (summer)
"The Barrens"* (ends in September)
"A Day in the Life"* (October)

"The Long Way Home"[†]
Legacies (December)

YEAR ZERO MINUS TWO

"Interlude at Duane's"[**] (April)
Conspiracies (April) (includes "Home Repairs"[†])
All the Rage (May) (includes "The Last Rakosh"[†])
Hosts (June)
The Haunted Air (August)
Gateways (September)
Crisscross (November)
Infernal (December)

YEAR ZERO MINUS ONE

Harbingers (January)
"Infernal Night"[††] (with Heather Graham)
Bloodline (April)
By the Sword (May)
Ground Zero (July)
The Touch (ends in August)
The Peabody-Ozymandias Traveling Circus & Oddity Emporium (ends in September)
"Tenants"[*]

YEAR ZERO

"Pelts"[*]
Reprisal (ends in February)
Fatal Error (February) (includes "The Wringer"[†])
The Dark at the End (March)
Nightworld (May)

[*] available in *The Barrens and Others*
[**] available in *Aftershock & Others*
[***] available in the 2009 reissue of *The Touch*
[†] available in *Quick Fixes—Tales of Repairman Jack*
[††] available in *FaceOff*